The BOSS

Also by Aya de León

Uptown Thief

The BOSS

WITHDRAWN

AYA DE LEÓN

KENSINGTON PUBLISHING CORP.
www.kensingtonbooks.com

DAFINA BOOKS are published by

Kensington Publishing Corp.
119 West 40th Street
New York, NY 10018

All Kensington titles, imprints, and distributed lines are available at special quantity discounts for bulk purchases for sales promotion, premiums, fund-raising, and educational or institutional use.

Special book excerpts or customized printings can also be created to fit specific needs. For details, write or phone the office of the Kensington Sales Manager: Kensington Publishing Corp., 119 West 40th Street, New York, NY 10018. Attn. Sales Department. Phone: 1-800-221-2647.

ISBN-13: 978-1-4967-0474-0
ISBN-10: 1-4967-0474-6
First Kensington Trade Paperback Printing: June 2017

eISBN-13: 978-1-4967-0475-7
eISBN-10: 1-4967-0475-4
First Kensington Electronic Edition: June 2017

10 9 8 7 6 5 4 3 2 1

Printed in the United States of America

To Shannon Williams, 1966–2015
an OG Justice Hustler
without whom these women would
never have fully come to life

Acknowledgments

The second book in a series is a little easier, because you can follow the path you hacked through the jungle to write the first book. But still I could never have done it alone. Thanks to my agent, Jenni Ferrari-Adler; my Kensington team: Esi Sogah and Lulu Martinez. Special thanks to my consultants: Antonia Crane, Rachel Aimee, Gina Gold, and Jasmine Sanders; my family: Stuart, Anna, Dee, Coco, Alicia, Tobe, Paci, Larry, Nina, and Sasha; my Deb crew: Louise, Heather, Jennifer, and Abby; my extended writers' community: Carolina, Pam, Aurora, Glad, Susie, Toni, Shailja, Adrienne, Peech, and NaNoWriMo. Other black women from Chicago who have inspired me: Juanita Capri Brown, Alysia Tate, and Patricia Smith. And my own union, UC-AFT Local 1474.

Book 1

Chapter 1

The industrial street was quiet and dark, except for the brightly lit corporate headquarters, which had been built from an old warehouse. The company was celebrating its one-year anniversary, and they had a quartet of searchlights rotating in front of the party, shining huge, blinding beams of light into the never-dark Manhattan sky.

Tyesha and Kim waited outside in the idling taxi, checking the time. Marisol had been inside the building too long. She was usually quick in opening a safe and she should have been in and out once she picked the lock of the CEO's office.

The driver glanced through the rearview mirror at the two girls in the back of the cab. Would he remember them? Two young women in catering uniforms, one black, one Asian. They both had their hair pulled back tight into long ponytails made of dark, fake hair. Kim's was straight. Tyesha's ended in a perfect ringlet.

In the distance, Tyesha heard shouting. Men's voices—agitated and furious. There wasn't supposed to be any noise, just Marisol slipping quietly out of the building and climbing into the cab with them.

She and Kim exchanged looks. Shouting changed everything.

"Are we leaving or waiting?" the cab driver asked, glancing at the running meter.

"You know what?" Tyesha said to the driver. "Our friend just texted that she's not ready. Let me pay you now."

Tyesha began to push Kim out of the cab, scooting behind her.

"What the fuck are you doing?" Kim hissed in her ear.

"Trust me," Tyesha whispered back as she pulled several bills from her wallet and gave them to the driver.

He drove off, leaving them alone on the empty street.

"We didn't need any witnesses," Tyesha said.

"But how are we gonna get out of here?" Kim asked.

"You can hot-wire a car, right?" Tyesha asked.

"I used to do it as a teenager," Kim said. "But only old cars. The new ones aren't that easy."

Suddenly, both their phones buzzed. The text from Marisol was empty. Meaning she was on her way out, and from the sound of things, Tyesha expected she was coming quickly.

"Can you hot-wire that one?" Tyesha asked. She pointed to a beat-up eighties-model van.

"Does that shit even run?" Kim asked as they hustled over to the vehicle.

Tyesha wrapped her arm in a newspaper and busted the window. The shouting got louder as Kim climbed in and pulled the wires.

Tyesha looked toward the building to see Marisol running across the long expanse of the parking lot. She was dressed in a catering uniform identical to theirs, but under her arm she held a large black purse, which she gripped with both hands.

Her long, wavy ponytail flew behind her as she ran, followed by several men, including two in security uniforms.

"Hurry!" Tyesha said.

Tyesha saw a spark and then heard the blessed churn of the engine starting up.

"Get over here!" Kim said, climbing into the backseat.

"What the fuck?" Tyesha asked. "Put the damn thing in gear!"

"I can't drive a stick," Kim said.

Marisol was bearing down on them, headed for the pedestrian opening in the chain-link fence, with a half dozen men closing in behind her. Tyesha left the front passenger door open and clambered over the stick shift to the driver's seat.

She put the car in gear and engaged the clutch. Marisol flew into the vehicle, and Tyesha took off, the passenger door swinging wildly. A handful of cash bricks tumbled onto the floor of the front seat.

In the rearview mirror, she could see a dark SUV pull up. The men piled into it.

"This is the last—" Marisol panted. "The last time I rob one of these motherfuckers at their offices. Too much damn security. I'm gonna start"—she wheezed—"start hitting their apartments."

"Hold on!" Tyesha yelled, as she screeched around a corner.

As all three of them lurched to the left, Marisol and Kim reached for their seat belts.

The SUV tore around the corner in pursuit.

"Can we outrun them?" Marisol asked.

"In this piece of shit? I doubt it," Kim said.

"I can probably outmaneuver them," Tyesha said. "As long as they don't call the cops."

"I think they had some underage girls in there tonight," Marisol said. "Definitely a lot of cocaine. I doubt they want cops around."

They continued to barrel forward, wind blowing in through the broken window.

The SUV was gaining on them, as the light ahead of them turned red.

"Slow it down," Marisol demanded.

Tyesha tried to slam on the brakes, but a brick of cash had wedged beneath the pedal.

"Tyesha!" Kim screamed.

Tyesha's eyes widened as the cross-traffic began to move forward on the green, and their own car flew into the intersection.

Marisol threw her arms over her head. Kim gripped the back of the seat in front of her. Tyesha squeezed her eyes tight, her right leg jamming down on the pedal, in vain.

The car whizzed into the traffic, clipping a cab and barely missing several other vehicles.

Tyesha opened her eyes when she heard the crash behind them. The SUV hadn't been so lucky. It had sideswiped a delivery truck and spun off onto the sidewalk.

Her heart was in her throat, but the three of them in the stolen van were okay.

They headed for another red light.

"What the fuck?" Marisol asked.

"It's stuck!" Tyesha shouted. She glanced down to see the wedged brick of cash.

"Take the wheel while I get this damn money," Tyesha said to Marisol.

Her mentor reached over to steer as Tyesha dislodged the cash.

"Brake now," Marisol yelled.

Head still under the steering wheel, Tyesha jammed the heel of her hand down on the brake. The car stopped abruptly, crashing the rest of her body against the pedals. And because she hadn't pressed the clutch, the van abruptly died.

"Kim!" Tyesha said. "You gotta hot-wire it again!"

Tyesha climbed up to the seat, and Kim climbed down below the steering column. As she began to work, the light turned green and motorists behind them honked and cursed.

Tyesha kept her eyes on the mirror. In the distance, she saw a security guard running toward them, hand on his gun.

"One of the guards is coming, but he's on foot!" she said.

Kim restarted the car and scrambled up into the front seat with Marisol. Tyesha grabbed the wheel and made a sudden left turn, barely missing a limo.

As they swerved, Kim clung to Marisol to keep from being thrown against the windshield.

"We gotta ditch this van," Marisol said.

Up ahead, Tyesha saw an alley and pulled in.

"Quick," Marisol said to the two of them. "I'll hail a cab. Wipe down the van."

Tyesha grabbed a rag from the floor of the van and tore it in two. She gave half to Kim, and they proceeded to wipe off all the door handles, the wheel, the seat belts, the wires, and any places they might have grabbed while the van swerved. Fortunately, the vinyl surfaces of the seats were textured and wouldn't hold prints well.

Both their phones lit up with texts.

Tyesha saw it was from Marisol: "Kim, we gotta go."

"I can't fuck around," Kim said. "NYPD definitely has my prints on file."

Thirty seconds and some thorough scrubbing later, Tyesha and Kim sauntered out of the alley.

It was a perfectly normal Manhattan evening. A cluster of teens was crossing the street. An older couple holding hands strolled behind them.

Tyesha and Kim joined Marisol in the back of a cab. Just three women headed home from some restaurant service job. They looked a bit like a diversity ad for a hiring brochure: one African-American and brown-skinned, one Latina, one Asian. All three with curvy figures, long hair, and full makeup.

The driver paid them no attention. He talked on his cell phone in what sounded like Arabic, although he had a large American flag on display.

"Lower East Side, please," Marisol said, and gave him an address. The driver pulled away from the curb, still talking into his headset.

Keeping her hands low, Tyesha handed the brick of cash to Marisol.

"This fucking money nearly killed us," Tyesha murmured.

"Or helped us escape," Marisol said quietly. "Depends how you look at it."

"Good thing I didn't piss myself and leave a puddle of DNA in that damn van," Kim said.

"Let's start checking different city news outlets," Marisol said. "I wanna make sure those guys in the SUV are okay."

Tyesha pulled out her phone.

"Why do you even care?" Kim asked.

"We only steal from these corrupt assholes," Marisol said. "We're just wealth redistributors, not executioners."

Chapter 2

Two years later

For days after her sister interrupted the party, Tyesha would be unable to recall how happy she had been about her big promotion. They were eating her favorite cake—red velvet— and celebrating Tyesha's rise to executive director of the Maria de la Vega Community Health Clinic.

As a child she'd certainly spent lots of time in health clinics—as a client. In fact, she was twelve years old before she realized that some people had a particular doctor that they saw in an office. Someone who knew their name and had their health history in a little chart that they could pull out and read. But the anonymity of clinics had a plus side. At seventeen, the bored nurse practitioner couldn't say, *Hmmm, Tyesha, this is your fifth case of chlamydia.* Instead, they fell for her wide-eyed, surprised look and gave her the antibiotic prescription with a handful of condoms.

But now she was the director of a women's health clinic, where they kept files for everyone, even if they just came once, and the clinic workers could talk to you about how hard it was to get a guy to put on a condom sometimes. They even taught girls how to put it on with their mouths so the guy didn't realize what they were doing. *Executive Director*. From the vantage point of the girl she'd been, it might as well be *Queen of England*. The directors of those health centers had been people she only saw in smiling photographs on the wall.

Now she was in charge of this storefront clinic on Manhattan's Lower East Side. Now it would be her photo on the wall. Her chocolate-brown face, large, wide-set eyes, broad nose, and full lips smiling down from the wall of the bustling lobby. Even this cramped, windowless little conference room, with gum under the seats and the occasional bit of graffiti carved into the fake wood of the round table—she was in charge of this, too.

She sat around the table with Marisol Rivera, her mentor, and the outgoing executive director, as well as Eva Feldman, the clinical director. Rounding out the crew were her best friends Kim and Jody—girlfriends—who were also involved in the clinic. More specifically, they were all part of the team that had fund-raised creatively to keep the clinic open.

Marisol had raised a champagne glass: "To Tyesha!" And they all toasted and drank. Then Marisol reached down under the table, her dark hair falling across her brown face. She lifted a large box onto the conference table and sat back, her plum lips in a grin of anticipation.

Tyesha had almost cried when she opened the box and found the briefcase. She almost wept at the soft but sturdy leather—a brown so dark, it was nearly black. Marisol hadn't bought this out of the back of any trunk on West 27th. The large, rectangular briefcase was embossed with the logo of an expensive uptown Spanish leather designer.

Tyesha was speechless.

"I got one for Marisol when she started as executive director," Eva said. Eva was somewhere in her sixties, thickly built and gray-haired.

"You mean you've had your briefcase for ten years?" Tyesha asked. Marisol's case didn't look brand-new, but it didn't look a decade old.

"They're guaranteed for life," Marisol said.

And just as Tyesha went to lift the briefcase out of the box, the door to the conference room had opened. Her older sister had swept in. Jenisse. Sixteen years older, but hot as a cougar in her tan leather coat, skintight cream-colored dress, and stiletto boots.

"Sorry to interrupt. This a birthday party or something?" Jenisse asked, the contempt barely disguised beneath a curling smile. "Apparently I gotta bust into Tyesha's job cause she can't call nobody. You ain't heard I was in New York? How you gonna let forty-eight hours go by and not come see about your own sister?"

Tyesha got over her shock and stood up. "No, I didn't know," she offered in a twin sarcastic tone, but without the fake smile. "Seeing you didn't bother to call. And I know you have my number or could get it. Besides, as I recall, your last words to me were: 'Bitch, I don't need your help, so get outta my house.'"

Her sister tilted her head to the side, scrutinizing Tyesha. "New York ain't been feeding you right," she said. "You need to let me make you a few dinners. Get the rest of your ass back. Plus your hair looks raggedy." Jenisse tossed her head. She was lighter skinned, and the permed and pressed auburn hair that fell down her back was all her own.

Tyesha's hand reached involuntarily for the roots of her own perm, which, admittedly, had grown out a bit.

"Deza's here," her sister said. "She can do your hair right."

Tyesha snapped to attention at the name of her niece. "You brought Deza?"

"And Amaru." Her sister's youngest daughter. "Zeus paid for all of us to come."

"How long are you staying?" Tyesha asked.

"Long as his business takes, I guess," Jenisse said, inspecting her nails.

Marisol stood up. "So you're Jenisse," she said. "Tyesha always said you were beautiful, but I still wasn't prepared. And I like the way you pay attention to detail. Beauty is sometimes about the little things, right? I've been wanting to do a top ten list of things girls get wrong in the beauty department. Maybe you could give me some tips while I give you a tour of the place?"

Jenisse was startled, but she let Marisol take her arm and guide her out the door.

After the door closed, Jody asked, "Are you fucking kidding me?" Her sandy brows furrowed under spiky short blond hair. "Your sister comes into your party talking shit?"

"Why today?" Tyesha asked, slumping down into the chair. "Why she gotta show up and burn down my life again *today*?"

"So, that's your fucked-up big sister?" Kim asked. She cut her heavily lined eyes in the direction Jenisse had gone.

"I gotta open up the door and air out the passive-aggressiveness," Eva said, wearing the frown of concentration that went with her therapist face. "Was that really the last thing she said to you? 'Bitch, get out of my house?'"

"I was home for the holidays a few years ago," Tyesha said. "I had confronted her about going off with Zeus for days at a time and leaving my nieces to fend for themselves. Deza was maybe fifteen at the time. Amaru was ten."

"Who the fuck is Zeus?" Jody asked.

"Jenisse's man," Tyesha said. She noticed she'd been unconsciously running her hand back and forth along the soft leather of the briefcase. "They been together twenty-five years."

"So he's the girls' father?" Eva asked.

"I don't know for sure," Tyesha said. "They're not married, but he supports all of them. He's a big drug dealer in Chicago. My two nephews, Jenisse's oldest, both ended up in jail trying to go into the family business."

"Damn," Kim said. "And this family drama show has set up shop in New York?"

"Indefinitely," Tyesha said, shaking her head.

"How she gon' just walk up on yuh job like dat?" Lily asked, sucking her teeth. Tyesha's first real friend from New York always broke into West Indian patois in expressing outrage or disgust.

When Lily had come up from the subway, her phone was ringing with a call from Tyesha and the tale about Jenisse's visit.

"Older sisters," Lily scoffed. "So much attitude, so little time. You gonna be up later?"

"Yeah," Tyesha's voice came through the phone. "I got a date with some guy from Tinder. I'll probably have fucked him, kicked him out, and be ready to talk by eleven thirty."

It was nearly seven thirty in the evening and still light, although dim with the summer storm cloud cover. Lily strode purposefully down the busy avenue near Wall Street, a dark brown Amazon towering over both men and women in her stilettos. She and Tyesha had diverged in their careers, but their friendship stayed strong.

"I'll call you," Lily said. "My shift ends at midnight. Now let me go clock in before these barbarians try to take it out my hide."

Lily put away her phone and walked up to the brightly lit sign of the One-Eyed King. The strip club had the image of the same winking cartoon monarch from a playing card, but he was surrounded by nearly naked women of various races.

Lily looked like the dark brown girl in the picture, tall, hourglass-shaped, and chocolate-skinned.

She was back to the One-Eyed King after a three-year run on Broadway. The production of *Lap Dance* had promised "real strippers" and had put out a call for women who had worked in strip clubs to audition. Lily had been selected from among hundreds of dancers and had gotten her Actors' Equity membership. Those three Broadway years were a time of consistent income, paid breaks, and health insurance. She finally got blood work, cavity fillings, and contact lenses.

Unfortunately, the touring company dropped the "real strippers" commitment, as the show's brand had already earned its street cred. So in Cleveland and Dallas and Denver, classically trained ballerinas and modern dancers did the choreography that Lily and others had helped develop, while the "real strippers" went back to stripping.

After the show closed in New York, Lily had gone to some other auditions, courtesy of her Actors' Equity card, but she didn't have what most of the shows were looking for. As a six-foot, dark-skinned woman, she didn't fit in with most chorus lines, and dancing in carnival back home and stripping in the U.S. didn't prepare her for the chorus of most Broadway shows.

She would have taken the work if she could have gotten it. Working in a union show got her a consistent living wage. The Broadway dancers had been a mix: some friendly, some snobby, some with a lurid curiosity about what it was like to actually strip. The director even had the exotic dancers share some of their experiences with one of the principals so she could get "into character." She took copious notes on a yellow pad.

The One-Eyed King had some dancers with classical training, but it was completely lacking in pretense. The working conditions, however, were decidedly less worker-friendly.

As Lily hustled in the door, the bodyguard blocked her way with a grin. "What?" he asked. "No hug hello?"

"Get out of my way. I can't be late to check in." She shoved him aside with her shoulder and looked for the assistant manager with the clipboard who should have been sitting on the tall stool by the dressing room.

The clock said 7:24. The stool was empty.

She turned to the security guard. "Where's the clipboard? I need to sign in."

He shrugged. "I just watch the door."

"But you can vouch for me that I'm here on time," Lily insisted.

"Sorry, I don't have a watch," he said with a shrug.

"Bastard," Lily muttered. Management didn't like her because she was mouthy. Sometimes they pulled this kind of thing, hoping she'd check in late. They had recently changed their policy. Previously, they had just charged a late fee. But now, one tardy could mean probation. Two could mean demotion. Three could mean fired.

Behind her she could hear the clacking footsteps of other girls coming in.

"Who's on tonight?" a girl named Giselle asked. She was a brown-skinned Latina. "Where's the clipboard?"

"Ah can't find it," Lily said. Her Trinidadian lilt was strongest when she was upset.

"Girls, the assistant manager is AWOL. Let's make our own sign-in sheet," Giselle called to the other dancers. Suddenly five sets of hands were searching for a piece of paper. Everyone except another Trinidadian girl named Hibiscus. She and Lily didn't get along. "I signed in already," she said, and hurried past the pandemonium muttering at Lily under her breath. "Yuh look fuh dat."

A long-legged Asian girl ripped a flyer from the Maria de la Vega health center off the bulletin board. "Let's use this," she said.

They flipped it over to the back, which was blank. Lily and the other girls wrote their names and signed.

"But how do we prove that we were here on time?" Giselle asked. Not only was the assistant manager still missing, but the security guard had disappeared, as well.

"Our word against his?" the Asian girl suggested.

"I know," Lily said. "Giselle, gimme your phone."

Lily took Giselle's smart phone and laid it on the stool beside the sign-in sheet. She lit up the display and took a picture of it. Giselle's phone said 7:30. A few seconds after she snapped the photo, the dial said 7:31.

"What did that other West Indian girl say to you?" Giselle asked Lily.

"Just that this is my own fault for making trouble," Lily muttered.

"Bullshit," Giselle said, but she closed her mouth as the assistant manager strolled in with the clipboard.

He was in his thirties with pale skin and a scruffy beard. "You girls are late," he said. "I was here at seven thirty."

"Your watch must be off," Giselle said. "All of us were here at seven thirty. We made our own sign-in sheet."

She showed him the photo.

"I emailed that to your boss," Lily said.

"Oh, shit! Oh. shit!" A young blonde woman rushed in, and the manager handed her the clipboard.

"I dunno what she worried for," Lily muttered to Giselle. "Blonde, double D, and barely legal looking. She not gon' get no demotion up in here."

"White girl rules," Giselle muttered back.

"She not white," Lily said. "She moved here from Guadeloupe when she was little."

"But she looks white," Giselle said. "They might dock her just to make her work harder. Lotta appetite for that type in the private rooms. So far, she only been dancing."

Tyesha felt restless. Ever since she could remember, she had been waiting for her life to settle down into a stable adult

THE BOSS / 17

groove. And yet now that it had, she felt flat somehow, under-whelmed. No more heists with Marisol and the crew. No more
escort dates. She was nine-to-fiving it every day. The hours of
her day were full, and there was a never-ending set of crises
at the clinic, yet she still felt understimulated.

Her family was a jolt of the wrong kind of stimulation. All
the anxiety and none of the excitement. Maybe dating could
fill the void a little?

The guy had looked cute enough on Tinder. Tyesha swiped
right, and they had good, flirty banter, but something was
missing. He had lovely broad shoulders and his ass held up his
jeans nicely, but his conversation was doing nothing for her.
Some stupid stockbroker chat.

The last few guys she'd dated were too street. Hot dudes
in hoodies who'd gotten her number on the subway. They
could fuck but wanted to play stupid games with her by not
texting her back for days. What? Like she was gonna get too
attached? The dick wasn't that good. She thought maybe a
more professional type would be to her liking, but no. This
guy acted like the black wannabe-wolf of Wall Street.

". . . to make your money make money," he said. "But of
course if you—"

"It's not true," Tyesha said.

"Excuse me?" he asked.

"That money makes money," she said. "It doesn't."

"That's the whole principle of investment," he said.

"No," Tyesha said. "Money doesn't make money. Labor
makes money. People put money in a bank, and the bank in-
vests it. Usually in industries in other countries where the
workers get paid shit. That's how the profits are so high, and
the returns are big. Which is why the greatest accumulation
of capital happened during slavery in the U.S. The profit
margin of the labor was so extreme."

He blinked. "Okay, so maybe you're right. But then what
do we do? Go live off the grid in a cave? Everything about

the current economy is connected to something shady. I'm not taking a vow of poverty for political correctness."

"Me neither," Tyesha said. "But at least acknowledge it, you know? Don't go around acting like money is just fucking and making little money babies without anyone getting fucked over."

He grinned. "That's what I like about you, Tyesha. You can use 'fuck' in two different ways in an analogy about socially responsible investing. You're so hood but you're also such a brainiac. Where did you go to school?"

"Columbia," she said.

"Business?"

"Public health."

"And what do you do again?"

"I run a women's health clinic."

"Like I said,"—he smiled—"socially responsible. So you make sure women get taken care of. Who takes care of you?"

It was the first insightful thing he'd said all night. "Are you offering to take care of me some kind of way?" Tyesha asked.

"Maybe," he said.

Tyesha smiled. "What did you have in mind?" she asked.

When Lily went to the dressing room in the One-Eyed King, it was locked.

"What bullshit is this?" she asked.

"They're converting it to a champagne room," said one of the security guards.

Lily groaned, along with several of the other women, and they piled into the second dressing room. It was maybe eight by ten feet, with a small coat rack just inside the door. There was a large mirror on one wall, with lighting above and below, and a shelf that had black plastic buckets of cosmetics. On the adjacent wall was a bank of battered gray lockers.

They were twelve-inch cubes, just large enough for a pair of shoes, a small purse, and a costume—assuming the costume had as much fabric as a bathing suit. In the other dressing room, they'd had a proper coat rack, and much larger lockers.

As the dozen or so girls tried to change in the cramped quarters, the low murmur of complaint was punctuated by exclamations when they accidentally elbowed and bumped each other.

One of the managers walked in without knocking. "Quiet down, girls," he said. "As you can see, we've consolidated dressing rooms, but that's not the only change. House fees are gonna go up by twenty-five percent, because dance time is increasing. Everyone does two songs per set on stage."

"How we gonna make any money?" Lily asked. While media myths imagined that strippers made money from the singles placed in their G-strings, the more lucrative part was lap dancing in the champagne rooms.

"That's what champagne is for," he said. "Think of your time on stage as an extended commercial."

"So we have two champagne rooms now?" Giselle asked.

The manager shook his head. "We're turning the old champagne room into a VIP lounge for special guests of the owner. It's a new social space within the club."

"Social space?" Lily said, her voice thick with sarcasm. "I don't come here for my social life, I come here to make money. But if our dance sets are twice as long, and our champagne room is only half as big, we'll make half as much."

"Less than half," Giselle said. "House fees are going up."

It was one of the few industries where the labor force had to pay in order to work.

One girl stood up. "Oh, hell no. I'm going back to the club I used to work at in Queens."

"It'll be the same there," the manager said. "This policy is going into effect in all the clubs in the chain."

"Which girls get to work in the VIP lounge?" the young blonde asked.

"The girls don't work in there," the manager said. "Participation is optional. It's just a social environment where you can get to know friends of the owner. You know, network."

"You're pimps now?" Lily said, her voice rising. "Pimping us out to friends of the owner? Who I fuck or if I fuck them for money is my business. Ya tryna make it your business. With this new setup, no girl can make money unless she goes in your new VIP room and 'socializes' by sucking a few guys off."

The manager shrugged. "New York state law prohibits sex for money exchanges. It's just a social environment."

A dancer named Tara strolled to the dressing room area from inside the club. She was a curly-haired white girl with a tattoo on her chest. "How come there's a bed in that new room?"

"A bed?" Lily asked.

"A king-size bed," Tara said.

"What are we gonna do in there in that social environment with a bed?" Lily asked, eyes blazing. "Huh? Are we supposed to take a nap with friends of the owner?"

"If you and a friend want to take a nap, that's your private decision between consenting adults. Now hurry up and get dressed. You all go on stage for a preview in fifteen minutes."

As he ducked back out of the dressing room, Lily slammed the door behind him.

She fumed and paced as Giselle got Tara caught up on the changes.

"This is out of the fucking question," Lily said. "We need to go on strike is what we need to do."

Tara agreed.

Giselle stood with her jaw clenched. "You're right, Lily, but my rent is already late. You know I got two kids."

The young blonde from Guadeloupe shrugged. "I can't walk out tonight. Tuition is due."

Several of the girls didn't say anything either way. But everybody who spoke up agreed that the situation was fucked up, but it was too close to the end of the month, and everybody had bills to pay.

Hibiscus spoke up: "Some of us don't want any trouble. We just wanna dance and get our money."

"I don't want trouble either," Lily said. "I hope we can make it work, but I have a bad feeling that they're gonna make it impossible before long."

Tyesha could feel the last strains of the orgasm fading away in her body. The stockbroker was a good fuck, even though he was corny.

She rolled to the edge of the bed and put her underwear back on.

"What's next?" he asked. "We never did get to that bubble bath."

Corny, she thought. She looked at him, sprawled on her four-poster bed, the rich brown of his skin against the burnt orange of her sheets.

"I've gotta get up early for work," she said.

"Okay, Executive Director," he said. "Can I call you?"

"Sure," she said, and wrote her number across the cover of his *Forbes* with a Sharpie marker, right across billionaire Jeremy Van Dyke's face.

"You got something against Jeremy Van Dyke?" he asked.

"Nope," Tyesha said, smiling. "I even met him once. He was a donor to the clinic where I work."

After he went home she texted Lily: **I'd rate him a 6.5. Got the job done. But nothing special.**

Lily was her best friend—her only friend in New York

from before she started working at the clinic. None of her student friends from pre–sex work had made the cut. She'd carefully brought up sex work issues with them, and they would start out by saying things like they thought "sex workers deserved support," but eventually they all ended up offering pity or scorn, and sometimes both. After she graduated, she stopped calling or returning calls.

Lily was actually the one who got her started in the world of sex work. They'd met as waitresses at a dive bar near Columbia when Tyesha was an undergraduate. Lily wasn't a student and had been in New York longer. When Lily quit to waitress downtown at a "gentlemen's club"—with bigger tips and chances to meet men who weren't broke students—Tyesha had followed her. Lily had also gotten Tyesha her first date for money.

But a couple of years ago, Marisol, Tyesha, Kim, and Jody had stumbled into the CEO heists: the unwitting benefactors who provided her job and her condo. So even though she could tell Lily anything about her years in sex work, her life as a thief was still a secret between them.

Lily was in the champagne room, giving lap dances. In the dim light, she could see men sitting in all of the chairs against the walls, each with a dancer gliding above and over him. Their club didn't allow touching, but it was so cramped that it was harder to work.

She was with Pierre, one of her regular customers. He was in his fifties, and she could never tell if he was white or just light-skinned. He was obsessed with her ass, which didn't particularly settle the question, but she was currently shaking it in his face, a slow, winding motion. She gently brushed a thigh against the front of his pants as she turned around, feeling his erection. She leaned forward, shimmying down over him, then gazing into his eyes.

"You like that when I put my ta-tas in your face, don't you?" she asked, teasingly.

"You're so beautiful, Cleopatra," he murmured.

"You didn't come see me last week," she whispered in his ear, a pout in her voice. "I was devastated."

"I had to travel for business," he said. "One of these days, maybe you'll come with me."

Lily giggled, a high, tinkling sound that otherwise seemed out of her register. "Pierre, you know that's against the rules. Just don't make me wait two weeks again." She finished the dance with a soft brush of her ass against the fly of his pants and a gasp, as if she were on the verge of an orgasm. Over the years, there had been a few customers who actually did it for her like that, but Pierre certainly wasn't one of them.

Just before eleven p.m., Lily strutted onstage. The young blonde from Guadeloupe had just stepped into the audience and was giving a lap dance to one of the customers.

He was drunk. "Come on, baby, let's go into the VIP room to socialize." He tried to grab her, but she slid deftly out of his grasp.

"No thanks," she said with a big grin. "I just love dancing for you."

One of his boys stood up and pushed her into the drunk guy's lap. He grabbed her, and Lily could see her struggling to get away, her smile at half-mast, her eyes wide and brow furrowed. The customer stood up, attempting to march her into the VIP room.

"Security!" the girl yelled, but it was hard to hear her over the music. She twisted away, but this time without the grin. Two of the man's friends stepped behind her so she couldn't escape. The customer grabbed her wrist and pulled her close, then slapped her.

Lily yelled to the security guard, "Do something!" He shrugged and stayed posted up against the column.

Lily stepped off the stage in the middle of her number. She grabbed the manager.

"Why isn't security doing anything? That guy just slapped one of the dancers."

"He's a friend of the owner," the manager said. "Get back on stage."

Lily turned back to the drunk guy. He was still pulling on the blonde. She looked around. Another girl had stepped up to dance in Lily's spot, and most of the guys in the club weren't paying attention. She could see the girls on all six stages were keeping up their game faces, but their eyes kept flitting to where the drunk guy was still manhandling the blonde.

One of the security guys stood up from the column he was leaning against. He began walking briskly toward the altercation. Before he could arrive to restrain the guy, the manager intercepted him and sent him back to his post. Lily could see his face was tight with anger. The club explained to the dancers that their house fees paid for security. But here they had four security guys, and none of them was going to help.

Lily was furious. She strode over to the customer and punched him in the face. He went down hard as Lily put a protective arm around the blonde from Guadeloupe and dared the drunk guy's friends to do anything. There were three of them, and they began to square off against the two women.

Lily looked again at the manager and the security guards, all of them standing around doing nothing.

Suddenly the music stopped. Giselle stood by the sound booth, and Tara turned on the work lights. Both were stony faced and looking from Lily to the manager.

"That's it," Lily said. "We're shutting this place down."

Giselle stepped up next to Lily with the power cord to the sound system in her hand. "I'd rather blow my landlord for a free month's rent than put up with this bullshit," she hissed to Lily.

The patrons all began to stand up, squinting and grumbling.

"Hey," the manager said, switching the lights back off. "Get back to work. Where's that fucking power cord?"

Giselle passed it behind her back to Lily, who wound it around her hips a few times under her extremely skimpy Catholic schoolgirl skirt and hid both ends in her cleavage.

Once the cord was hidden, she stepped forward to the manager.

"It's bad enough that your new policies practically force us into your VIP room, but you're gonna let a guy drag her in?" Lily said. "That's crossing the line. We're walking out. Come on, girls. Let's get our shit and all go out together."

A handful of the girls remained on the stage. Their eyes darted from Lily to the manager. One was Hibiscus, the other girl from Trinidad; she stood on the stage in a squat. Another was a young Latina with blue hair and no papers. She had both arms and one of her legs wrapped around the pole. But all the sensuality and languor had left her body. Instead, her limbs were all tense angles as she clung to the pole like a tree in a storm.

The patrons looked uncomfortable and disoriented. They blinked against the unaccustomed light, which showed the grime on the walls, dust in the corners, and cobwebs on the ceiling.

The dozen girls in the walkout all crossed to the tiny dressing room. On the way through the club, a young black man in thick-rimmed glasses came up to Lily.

"I got the whole thing on video," he said. "Where the drunk guy slapped her and everything. Gimme your info and I'll send it to you."

"Meet me in the alley out back," she said and slipped into the dressing room.

As quickly as they could, the dancers retrieved their purses and cash from the lockers.

When they headed out through the club, the manager yelled threats. "This is your last chance to get back to work or all of you are getting fired. And who stole the DJ's power cord?"

The alarm sounded as the girls went out the back exit and hit the alley with summer-weight jackets barely covering their lingerie. Most of them had on extra-high dancing heels, but had street shoes and clothes dangling from their hands.

Several of them changed shoes or stepped into jeans and skirts right on the street. They held onto each other to avoid letting their bare feet touch the wet ground.

The security guard who had tried to help came out, as well.

"I dunno what the fuck was going on in there," he said. "But I can't work somewhere that I'm supposed to turn a blind eye to some shit like that."

As he strode off down toward the street, the nerdy black guy walked up the alley and approached Lily again. He was around thirty and handsome behind the glasses. He walked alongside the group of women as they headed down the alley to the avenue block, repeating his request for her information.

"Seriously," he said. "I'm not trying to hit on you, I'm an investigative journalist. I can't post it myself, because it's illegal to film, but you want this to get out there, right?"

"Yeah," Lily said. "Send it to a friend of mine. Tyesha at vegaclinic dot org."

He typed the address into his phone and headed off down the street.

"Are you okay?" Lily asked the young blonde from Guadeloupe.

"I'm fine," she said through clenched teeth. "Can I get a copy of that video? In case I want to sue the club?"

"Of course," Lily said. "Could I have your permission to post a clip on the Internet? I'd make sure no one could recognize your face."

The young blonde agreed as they reached the end of the alley.

"What do we do now?" Giselle asked Lily as they stepped out onto the street, which was still lively at nearly midnight.

"I gotta call my girl Tyesha," Lily said, as they walked past the club's front entrance. "She'll know."

Suddenly, a big group of white thugs came thundering down the street. "You bitches need to either get back up on a pole or get off this street if you don't want to get your asses kicked."

Several girls ran down toward the opposite end of the street, but some others got cut off and had to run into the building. Lily ran into the dressing room as several girls ran out the rear door and back out into the alley. The emergency alarm sounded again.

Through a crack in the door, she could see the owner, Teddy Hughes, come into the club, a white man in his fifties, with a craggy face and unnaturally black hair.

"Are the girls all gone?" Teddy asked the manager, the one who had refused to do anything.

"Yeah," the manager said. "Why'd Viktor have to send his goon squad? He's supposed to be the silent partner."

"Those weren't Viktor's goons," Teddy said. "They belonged to the nephew, Ivan. Fucking Ukrainian mob. Those assholes are nothing but trouble."

Lily slid her cell phone out of her purse and pulled up the recording app.

She hit record just as the manager said, "What's done is done."

Lily nearly dropped the phone when there was a sudden loud banging on the club's front door.

She heard the street door open and close.

"What the hell happened?" a loud voice with a Slavic accent asked.

"Your nephew went too far with one of the girls. He slapped her," Teddy said.

"That's not what Ivan says," the Slavic voice insisted. "He says she was a tease. She said yes at first, then no."

"A hundred guys were in here and saw it," Teddy, the owner, said.

"Did you see it?"

"No, but my manager here did."

"You need to keep your girls in line," Viktor, the Ukrainian guy, said. "We're your biggest investors, remember?"

"And your nephew just cost you a lot of money," Teddy said. "This is a strip club, not a brothel. Girls have the right to choose to spend time with customers in private rooms. What they do in there is not my business."

"But the money this club makes is both of our business. Which is why I insisted that we convert that second dressing room to a deluxe VIP room," Viktor said. "Two or three girls for the man who can afford it. Get some bigger spenders in here. Why do the girls need a second dressing room anyway? It's not like they have a lot to put on." He laughed.

"It's really cramped in there," Teddy was saying. "We have a dozen girls, and they're squeezed in like sardines. I'll show you."

Lily heard footsteps heading toward her. She looked around the dressing room. There was little cover, but she managed to wedge herself between the two coat racks and pulled a forgotten trench coat over herself like a curtain. It covered most of her body, but she was still easily visible.

"First let me see the new VIP room," the Ukrainian man asked.

Lily heard the door open to the former dressing room. This was her chance to sneak out. She crept from her hiding place in the dressing room and peeked out toward the front door. Two thickset men lounged in the lobby.

Lily snapped her body back into the dressing room. She glanced around and saw a rolling stool. The room was illuminated by a bare bulb overhead, and there were also lights around the one large mirror. Lily rolled the stool underneath the light bulb and unscrewed it a quarter turn. The overhead light went out.

With the illumination coming only from the makeup mirror, the room was shadowy enough. She ducked back under the raincoat and called Tyesha.

"Girl," Tyesha began. "Mr. Wall Street's stocks could definitely perform—"

Lily hit several of the numbers on the phone to get Tyesha's attention.

"What the fuck?" Tyesha asked.

"You gotta help me, Ty," Lily hissed into the phone. "A girl got grabbed at the club. We all walked out, but then some Ukrainian thugs came for us. I'm hiding in the dressing room. I think they'll kill me if they find me."

"I'm on my way," Tyesha said. "Silence your phone. I'll text when I get close and pull up in the alley."

A moment after Lily hung up the phone, the door to the dressing room opened.

"Damn light is burned out again," the owner complained.

The Ukrainian shrugged. "All these dressing rooms look the same. There's plenty of room. Fire all those bitches who walked out tonight. If the new girls complain, fire them, too."

Then the owner snapped off the mirror lights and walked out, leaving the door open a crack. Lily crept from her hiding place and saw that both men had headed into the office. The two thugs were still at the front door. She stepped back into the shadows and waited.

Chapter 3

Thirty minutes later, Tyesha texted that she was close. Lily looked out; none of the men had changed position.

Lily looked around the room. She spotted a blue bobbed wig that had been abandoned on the counter and snatched it up. On the coat rack, she saw a long pink raincoat that one of the dancers had left behind. She pulled it down slowly so that the hangers wouldn't bang together like a warning chime. She rummaged around in a locker of lost and found clothes, and found a pair of thigh-high white stockings and a garter belt.

As she put on all the clothes, her heart sank. She realized she would need to leave her best pair of stilettos. If she wore them, they would only slow her down. And she couldn't carry them because she needed both hands free. She jammed them under a pile of towels and stood at the door, her heart hammering.

A burst of laughter and the clink of glasses could be heard from the office. One of the thugs at the door got a phone call. Lily could faintly hear a siren from the street.

Finally, her phone lit up. From Tyesha: **in the alley**

Lily slung her purse across her chest and zipped her cell inside. She waited for the thug on the phone to speak: "You tell that dick-brain—"

She took off, swinging open the dressing room door and sprinting down the back hallway, turning off the light as she ran.

The thugs saw her and snapped into action, rushing after her.

The sound of running boots got the attention of the two men in the office, who stepped out into the hallway, carrying shot glasses. The owner also had a bottle of vodka in his hand.

The thugs ran past them. All they could see was a flash of blue wig, and long, pale legs running beneath the pink raincoat.

Lily's stockinged feet slapped against the cement floor, followed by the thudding of the thugs' boots.

"Catch that bitch," the owner yelled, but Lily had made it to the end of the hall.

She hit the back exit at full speed, jamming the bar with the heels of her hands. The door opened, and the emergency alarm sounded.

Four pairs of men's shoes could barely be heard above the wail of the alarm.

Lily exploded out of the building, a Technicolor streak of hot pink, electric blue, and white.

Tyesha's silver compact two-door was waiting in the alley, passenger door open and dirt smudged across the license plate. Tyesha started moving the car at the sight of Lily, who ran alongside the vehicle for a few strides before leaping in.

Just as she closed the door, the four men spilled out of the building. The two thugs had guns drawn.

Tyesha watched the road as Lily peeked over her shoulder to see the men fire off two shots. She screamed as a bullet whizzed past. One of the thugs began to run after the car, but the Ukrainian shouted something, and he stopped.

Tyesha took the corner, tires screeching.

"Did we lose 'em?" Tyesha asked.

Lily was panting. "I think so." She waited to see if anyone

would come running around the corner. "And it's too far to get their cars out of valet."

"We did it!" Tyesha crowed, grinning and yanking off the dark wool cap she had pulled low over her face. "And your little disguise was a genius move."

"Are you kidding me?" Lily said. "I'm the darkest girl in the place. One look at my legs and they'd know it was me."

After they'd driven for a block, Lily added, "Damn, I shoulda taken my shoes."

Tyesha rolled down the windows and let the night's cooling humid air whirl through the car. Both women's hair flew around them in the hurricane breeze.

This was it, Tyesha thought to herself, her heart beating from the close call, but her body filled with elation. The feeling she had been missing lately. The excitement, but also the sense of purpose. Something she couldn't find in dating or day-to-day work. The hard grit of the fight, and the soaring taste of the win.

As they drove, Lily played the recording of the owner and mobster talking.

"Nothing you caught is particularly incriminating," Tyesha said.

Lily sucked her teeth. "I couldn't get it when he said 'Ukrainian mob.' Where are you going? This is the long way to my apartment."

"We're not going to your apartment," Tyesha said. "If the mob is involved and you're a known troublemaker, you need to stay away for a few days. We're going to my apartment."

Tyesha turned down the block of her brownstone to see a figure sitting on the first of the three steps that led down to her basement apartment. She drove quickly past, but she could see that the figure was female. The girl's head was down, so she couldn't see her face. Her hair, however, was fabulous, with pink tips that swooped from high up near her temple on one side, down to below her ear on the other. The bob was asymmetrical, but the dye job was diagonal.

"Who's that?" Lily asked.

"No idea," Tyesha said. "And I never give the clients at work my home address."

They circled the block, and this time the girl's head was up. As they drew closer, Tyesha recognized her niece, Deza. She had a similar heart-shaped face to Tyesha's, with the same full lips and large brown eyes. As always, the girl was a walking advertisement for her hair business.

"Deza!" Tyesha shrieked, double-parking and running out of the car. As the two women embraced on the street, an SUV nearby was pulling out.

Lily got behind the wheel and took the parking space.

"I missed you so much, Auntie," Deza said into Tyesha's shoulder.

"How are you? How's everything?" Tyesha asked.

As Deza gave a noncommittal murmur, Lily walked down to the apartment door, and Tyesha introduced the two of them.

They exchanged pleasantries while Tyesha opened the door. Her apartment had a compact living room decorated with Tyesha's framed diplomas, blown-up posters of Serena Williams in a sultry evening dress on the cover of *New York* magazine, and the cast of *Orange Is the New Black* on the cover of *Essence*. In front of the turquoise couch, a half-empty bottle of wine sat on the coffee table. Beside it was a pair of wine glasses—one with Tyesha's shade of lipstick.

"Uh-oh," Deza said. "I was hoping to sleep over. Unless you've got a boyfriend here."

"Just a friend," Tyesha said. "And he left hours ago."

"Tyesha needs a boyfriend," Lily muttered. "But nobody's been good enough since she stopped seeing Thug Woofer."

Deza did a double take. "What?! Auntie, you were messing with Thug Woofer. As in *the rap star*?"

"We just went out a couple of times," Tyesha said.

"A couple of times?" Deza's mouth was wide open. "And you didn't tell me?"

"Once to the Oscars," Lily put in.

"You what?" Deza nearly shrieked.

"Stay out of this, Lily," Tyesha said.

"Sure," Lily said. "As soon as you tell your niece why you broke up with him."

"We didn't break up," Tyesha said. "He wasn't my boyfriend. We just went on two dates."

"Wait," Deza said. "You *dumped* Thug Woofer?"

"He was rude," Tyesha said.

"He's the mad dog of rap," Deza said. "You didn't expect a Boy Scout, did you?"

"It's complicated," Tyesha said.

"How complicated could it get in two dates?" Deza asked. "Did he hit you? Pull a weapon?"

"He pressured her for sex," Lily supplied.

"He what?" Deza asked. "He went out with you twice and you didn't give him none?"

"And it's not like she wasn't feeling him," Lily said.

"He acted like I owed him sex," Tyesha said. "Like I told you. Rude."

"So in all that time when you were dating him and not having sex, it didn't occur to you to tell him you had a niece that was a rap artist?" Deza asked.

"I was just getting to know him," Tyesha said. "And I didn't like what I found out. If he couldn't make the cut for me to have sex with him, he certainly didn't make the cut for me to trust him with anything connected to your career."

Lily opened her mouth to speak, but Tyesha cut her off. "Lily, we need to stay focused and look at this video."

"What video could be more important than my auntie dating Thug Woofer?" Deza asked.

"It's a video of a girl getting grabbed in a strip club," Lily said. "He tries to drag her into a room until the other strippers rescue her and walk out, but then the Ukrainian mob comes to break it up."

"What show is this?" Deza asked. "Something new by Shonda Rhimes?"

"Not a show, baby," Lily said. "It's my life from three hours ago."

"Damn," Deza said.

"I just have one more thing to say about Thug Woofer," Lily added with a grin and turned to Deza. "You remember how he surprised everybody when he did that soft boy album, 'Melvyn'? Remember how he dedicated it to T? Guess who T is?"

"Are you kidding me?" Deza asked. "Are you fucking kidding me? He dedicated his heartbreak album to you?"

"You don't know that for a fact," Tyesha said. "It could be some girl named Tiffany. Tanya. Tremaine."

"Bullshit," Lily said. "He knew he fucked up, but you wouldn't give him a second chance."

"A third chance," Tyesha said.

"Please!" Deza said. "Please give him a third chance. And you can give him my demo CD. Please, Auntie. This could be my big break in hip-hop. I'm begging you."

"No, baby. I'm sorry," Tyesha said. "When I'm done, I'm done. Don't ask me again."

"I can't believe you," Deza said. "You always told me that it was okay to date a guy who could move your life forward in some way. But now you're up here in New York, with your big job and your nice apartment, and your big baller life without us. So I guess it was okay to date guys who moved *your* life forward, but the rest of us are on our own. Mama was right about you."

Deza stood up and grabbed her purse.

"Deza, wait!" Tyesha said.

But Deza had stormed out the door.

Tyesha rushed to get her own purse, but Lily pulled her back.

"Leave that girl," Lily said. "We have our own drama to deal with."

"How you gonna just tell her all my business with Thug Woofer?" Tyesha asked.

"Cause I'm fucking jealous," Lily said. "If I had the number one rapper in the U.S. dedicating albums to me, I would be fucking him and living the good life, not dealing with this bullshit at the One-Eyed King, now would I?"

"It's not that simple," Tyesha said.

"Those are some high-class American problems," Lily said. "You gotta go read *Oprah* magazine or some shit cause I can't help you with that. Right now, I got some stripper problems that you need to help me with."

Tyesha nodded. "Stripper problems take priority," she said. "Hoes before bros." They tapped fists, and the two of them sat down at the computer.

Tyesha opened up the email. The reporter hadn't lied. He'd managed to get a shaky but clear recording of everything that had happened inside the club. It was perfect. You couldn't see the girl's face, but you could see the guy's.

"So do we send this to the *New York Times* or some shit?" Lily asked.

"Nope," Tyesha said. "We're just gonna post it on the clinic's website."

She put on the headline "New York Strippers Walk Out After Security Stands Silently By During Violent Assault." She left all the dancers anonymous, but named the club.

After she posted the video, she put it on social media.

Five minutes later, she checked her Twitter account, and there were already a hundred retweets. An hour later, Lily was snoring gently in the bed beside her, but Tyesha was wide awake. Every few minutes, she would check her phone to see hundreds, then thousands of retweets. But the image that nagged at her, kept her awake, was the memory of the first time she heard Thug Woofer's soft boy album.

Thug Woofer's album had dropped several months before. At the time, she hadn't seen him in weeks. She was with her girls in Cuba and was thrilled to be in a country that wasn't particularly bothered with the number one rapper in the U.S.

They were at the Hotel Palacio in Havana. Tyesha, Marisol, Kim, and Jody were in the living room of the suite finishing a large breakfast.

"I'm going out on the balcony to study," Tyesha said, picking up a plate of bacon and setting it on top of a pile of books. As she slid open the balcony door, Tyesha heard shouts and traffic noise. Inside the suite, the TV was turned to a low murmur in the background.

Marisol poured herself a cup of coffee and buttered her toast.

"Hey, it's *Ellen*," Kim said, and pulled Jody over to the couch to watch. Kim turned up the volume.

Marisol joined them on the couch, as Ellen DeGeneres came dancing out into the audience at the top of her show to "Macho Man" by the Village People. Midwestern white audience members danced along with awkward, poorly timed moves.

Marisol ate her toast in the recliner while Kim lay with her head in Jody's lap on the hotel couch.

"Ellen is still totally hot to me," Kim said. "I'd do her in a minute."

"Better not," Jody said.

The music faded. "Speaking of macho men," Ellen said, "one of our guests today is rap sensation Thug Woofer!" The audience applauded.

As the show cut to a commercial, they showed a photo of the rapper in front of a platinum tractor.

"Should we tell her?" Kim said.

Jody shook her head.

When they came back from the commercial break, Thug Woofer came out in a button-down shirt and a sweater. His jeans, while low slung, didn't seem to be threatening to fall off his ass.

He hugged Ellen and sat down.

"So, we were backstage getting to know each other, and I feel like we're really friends now," Ellen said. "So what should I call you? Thug? Thugsie?" The audience laughed.

The rapper laughed, too. "Usually, I just go by Woof to my friends."

"Okay, Woof," she said. "So you've been dubbed 'the bad dog of rap' and 'a canine hurricane of destruction,' but lately you've decided to change your image a little bit. Can you tell us about this new project?"

"Sure, Ellen," he said. "This is my new album, and it's a different side of Woof. It's called *Melvyn: The Real Me*."

"As in?" Ellen asked.

"It's what my mama named me," he said. "Melvyn."

"Tyesha!" Kim yelled. "You have to come see this!"

"What?" Tyesha asked, stepping in from the balcony, blinking to let her eyes adjust to the comparatively dim indoors.

"Is your publicist angry?" Ellen asked Woof. "I can see how 'the bad Melvyn of rap' or 'hurricane Melvyn of destruction' don't have quite the same hook."

"What?" Tyesha asked. "You interrupted me studying so I could see Woof on TV? You know tomorrow is my last day before I go back to New York."

"Wait," Kim said, grabbing Tyesha's wrist. "Listen."

"For this album concept, I wanted to take it back to the old school," Woof said. "I remember one of the first rappers I heard was in my auntie's collection, some old LL Cool J, called 'I Need Love.' That was the first time I ever heard a rapper say 'I love you' in a song."

"I thought LL Cool J was hard as hell," Ellen said, and the audience laughed.

"Underneath every hard-shell rapper is a guy who needs love, Ellen," Woof said.

"Aww," Ellen said and turned to her audience. "Isn't that sweet?"

"Awwwwww!" the audience agreed.

"So this is the first single we'll be releasing off the album. It's called 'Third Chance,'" Woof said. "And I want to dedicate it to a special someone. She knows who she is. And I may have realized too late, but T, if you're out there, I'm sorry. I was lucky to get a second chance with you. I probably won't get a third chance, but this song is my hope and prayer that maybe I could."

"Okay," Ellen said. "T? If you're listening, this is for you. And everyone else, here's a clip of the real Thug Woofer, off the album *Melvyn: The Real Me.*"

On the screen, Woof mostly walked along the river, rapping and looking mopey, with flashbacks of the silhouettes of two people walking along the river together.

"He's not bad." Jody shrugged. "Nice alliteration."

"I don't have time for this shit," Tyesha said and walked back out to her books.

The next afternoon, the multipurpose room of the Maria de la Vega clinic was packed with reporters. Tyesha had consulted with Marisol, who had called a press conference to discuss the viral video from the strip club and the subsequent walkout.

The large space was standing room only, with members of the press sitting in a motley assortment of metal and plastic folding chairs.

On the walls around them were posters for the clinic's newly published *Sexy Girl's Guide to Staying Safe and Healthy in NYC* and schedules for the clinic's mobile health van, which served Lower Manhattan. These were interspersed with images of attractive, confident young women from the clinic's demographics that encouraged them to:

Use condoms . . . every time.
Watch your drink.
Recognize the signs of an abusive relationship.

"This is our moment," Marisol said. Now that we've drawn attention to the situation, we need to shame the strip club into doing the right thing."

Tyesha stood off to the side with Lily, Marisol, and Kim. Lily was touching up Tyesha's makeup.

"I only care that my face isn't shiny. I don't need to look like a runway model," Tyesha said.

"My older sister works with one of the top makeup artists in New York," Lily said. "She didn't teach me how to do basic makeup. Only gorgeous."

"Looking good can't hurt," Marisol said.

"I still don't know why I need to be the face of the clinic," Tyesha said. "You're always so good at this."

"I wasn't at first," Marisol said. "I learned to be good at it. Like you will, too. Part of growing into being executive director."

Lily stood Tyesha up and twirled her around. She had on

her best navy blue suit, a pink silk blouse, and high-heeled pumps.

"You look amazing," Kim said.

Tyesha looked in the mirror. Her large eyes were extra smoky, and her full lips looked like a fifties starlet's with the matte plum lipstick. Lily had sculpted her cheekbones with several dimensions of blush.

"Don't overthink it," Marisol said, handing Tyesha a piece of paper. "We spent all day preparing this speech. Just read it off the paper. When it comes time to take questions, I'll be up there next to you. If you don't have an answer, just look at me, and I'll step in, okay? Or Eva will, since she's the shrink and attorney."

Tyesha nodded, but her hand shook as she took the paper. *Just read it. Just read.*

She felt that same low-grade panic she had when it was time to speak in front of her classes at school. She was sweating and slightly nauseated. But in class she was talking in front of academic white people. She was on her own in those classes. This was different. She was speaking for her folks. Her girls had her back. The audience of reporters was at least half people of color.

In the front of the room, they had a screen, which was showing Nashonna's video. The twenty-something African American former stripper turned rapper who had the current number one hip-hop album. Woof had done a verse on one of the tracks, but the favorite at the clinic was the hit single "What the Stripper Had to Say."

On the screen, Nashonna strutted around in a thong and bra while surrounded by rappers dancing in go-go cages suspended above, throwing money at her.

You didn't care what the stripper had to say
You let the pole get in the way

You had some kind of jones
to see me dance to some weak hip-hop with
fake-ass moans.

At this point, the rappers all moaned on cue and made parody faces of female sexiness.

No-talent rappers in the club throwing money
around
I'm in the dressing room writing rhymes to take
you down
You paid to see me make it clap
Well, motherfucker, now you gonna hear me
rap . . .

As Tyesha walked across the room, she let Nashonna pump her up. This was their chance to have their say. All she had to do was read the speech.

As she was on her way to the podium, a black man in his early thirties approached her. He was handsome behind a pair of thick-rimmed glasses, but bourgie like the stockbroker from Tinder. Maybe Lily was right. She did sort of compare all the men she met to Thug Woofer, and none of them quite measured up.

"I'm the reporter from the *Village Voice* who sent you the video," he said. "I was doing a piece on strip clubs in the city, but I didn't expect to get that kind of footage."

"Thank you so much," Tyesha said.

He put out his hand. "I'm Drew Thomas," he said.

"Tyesha Couvillier," she replied.

"I know," he said. "I looked you up online. You're from Chicago, right? Are you related to the Couvillier family who ran the Urban Peace Accord Center?"

Tyesha hadn't heard that name in nearly a decade. Hadn't

set foot in the center for just as long. She had a sudden flash-back of the center opening. She hadn't been more than ten. But she had sat in the front row with her family. She looked up at her auntie standing at the microphone, her voice ring-ing through the center like a preacher:

> Street violence is a public health epidemic in our com-munity. It's not on the public health agenda, because white middle class people don't have to deal with it, but many of our children don't live long enough to die of AIDS, cancer, heart disease, even diabetes.

Tyesha recalled how her aunt had had the respect of all the gangs. How the murder rate was dropping in the neigh-borhood, due to her work.

But when Drew brought it up, she didn't flash back to the jubilation of the center's opening or the accolades from the City Council. Instead, her mind was invaded by the sensory recall of a burning smell. The night the Urban Peace Accord Center was torched to the ground.

"Here," Drew said. "Let me give you my info."

Tyesha felt dazed as the reporter handed her his card. She slid it into the pocket of her suit jacket, over her hammering heart. Her fingers felt numb.

Without recalling the walk across the room, she found herself at the podium, in front of all the expectant faces. She was flanked by the clinic staff on one side and the strippers on the other.

She pulled out the piece of paper she hadn't realized she had been clutching in her pocket, tightly enough to crush it. She smoothed it on the podium with moist palms.

She attempted to speak, but her voice was hoarse. She cleared her throat.

"Good afternoon," she began.

And then she smelled it. Smoke. Some motherfucker was smoking just inside the door. Jody, the tall spiky-haired blonde, strode up to him and grabbed the cigarette. She stomped it into the linoleum floor and tossed the guy out.

But Tyesha could only smell smoke. Her heart continued to hammer under Drew Thomas's card. The words on the crumpled paper swam before her eyes. She couldn't seem to get enough air. She could barely inhale for fear of pulling the remains of a burning building into her lungs. The charred shell of everything her aunt had worked for.

She knew she was supposed to say something, but she couldn't focus, could barely breathe.

Suddenly, she heard a voice whispering in her ear. "I'd like to introduce Marisol Rivera, former executive director of the Maria de la Vega clinic."

Miraculously, without enough clean air or lung capacity, she managed to utter those whispered words into the microphone. And then Kim pulled her back to join the ring of women standing behind the podium. Tyesha stood rigid, barely hearing Marisol read the speech on the page, deftly translating the words, "I stand here before you as an African American woman" to "I stand here before you as a Puerto Rican woman, saying that labor issues are health issues."

When the fire alarm began to ring, Tyesha barely registered the sound. It blended with the sound track of the charred Chicago memory in her head.

"Those motherfuckers," Kim hissed, as she took Tyesha's arm and they evacuated the building.

"Why are we even going out?" Lily asked. "We know it's a false fucking alarm. They just wanted to sabotage the press conference. There's no fire. It's raining, for fuck's sake."

"We've been firebombed before," Marisol said. "I'm sure you're right, but we can't take the chance."

Tyesha found herself standing out on the street in lower Manhattan in the rain, staring at the clinic, perfectly intact. But in her mind, all she could see was the smoldering peace center, from the vantage point of her young teenage self.

Chapter 4

When Tyesha had first moved to New York, she'd lived in student housing near Columbia. She had been excited to visit nearby Harlem; had even hoped to live in that Chocolate City within a city. But by then the gentrification in West Harlem meant that tenants fit into two categories: long-term residents—a significant portion of whom were in public housing—or the more affluent types who were pushing them out. Tyesha didn't fit in either category. And East Harlem had her totally priced out.

After she no longer qualified for student housing, she lived in Brooklyn. Again, she had hoped for a black neighborhood, but instead she had found a surprisingly affordable studio in Sunset Park. Her apartment was right next door to a Mexican restaurant, although the neighborhood was largely Puerto Rican and Dominican at that point. And those Dominican hairdressers down the block had her hair looking freshly done every day. Jenisse and Deza would have approved.

She was still living there when she received a windfall of cash earlier in the year. Her immediate plan was to buy a place in Brooklyn. It hadn't been easy. Her windfall wasn't enough to afford to buy a whole building outright, and she didn't want to be a landlady with a big mortgage. Her dream was to buy on a chocolate block, but she needed a building that had been converted to co-ops or condominiums.

A lot of places were for sale in up-and-coming hipster neighborhoods. She could visualize them in ten years, filled with professionals who worked in Manhattan. Tyesha fit that description, but she wanted to live where she heard loud voices ringing from front stoops on summer evenings. She wanted shouting kids on the days she was home from work. She wanted to see young women wearing tight clothes and wheeling strollers.

She had been looking for several months when she found a rarity: a brownstone that had been converted to condos in Crown Heights. The basement flat, a cozy one bedroom, was in her price range.

So she got her chocolate neighborhood. She saw plenty of brown skin and tight, brightly colored clothes, and she heard loud voices. But the cadences held sounds of the islands instead of the South. There was one soul food joint nearby, but it wasn't that great. Most of the eateries sold roti or jerk. So her takeout napkins were as likely to be stained with green-gold curry or brown stew chicken as rust-colored barbecue sauce.

She was more likely to fend off the advances of Horace and Linton as she waited for her order, as opposed to Tyrell and Shawn. She might even take Norris's phone number, although she was unlikely to call.

Her Chicago neighborhood had been 95 percent black, and that demographic stretched far beyond the edges of her daily life. School, church, her aunt's house, even Jenisse's nearby, more upscale neighborhood had been overwhelmingly African American with roots in the South.

Brooklyn was different. They even had some low-rise public housing that slowed the tide of gentrification. But when she walked to the subway—six blocks—she stood between white guys in business suits and hipster chicks with blonde dreadlocks as she waited on the platform for the Manhattan train.

She felt at home with her West Indian neighbors in the same way she felt deeply at home with her friend Lily. Yet there was an intonation she missed. Once, a punk-looking black guy drove by on a bike, with a boom box bungee corded to the rear rack blasting Al Green. The wailing tenor called to her like a long-lost relative.

Still, on evenings when she walked home leisurely from the subway, she took in the sounds of soca or dancehall music blasting from apartment windows. She saw front stoops with clusters of shirtless young men drinking beer with labels she didn't recognize. She couldn't always understand their patois, but she recognized something about them beyond words: the way their plum lips curved into smiles revealing crooked white teeth, and the way their low-slung jeans hung from their hipbones, showing off taut abdominal muscles. She recognized the mix of tight fades, dreadlocks, and nappy curls on their heads. She recognized the razor designs carved into the dark of their hair, only a shade or two darker than their skin. She recognized the gold in their mouths and on their necks, although the gold bangles on their wrists were less familiar.

Likewise, the women's hips and asses in tight jeans and short skirts was familiar, as were their long, synthetic braids in bright colors and midnight blue-blacks that were equally unnatural. She recognized their dark lipsticks, their long, sparkling fingernails, their oversized earrings, and the sharp retorts they shot back at the comments that chased their curving hips down the street.

But on the night of the press conference, Tyesha didn't notice anything on the way home from the train station. The rain had stopped, and she walked with her head down, lost in thought. When she looked over at her building, she saw Deza sitting out in front of her apartment again.

"You can't call?" Tyesha asked her niece. "You know I have a phone."

"Clearly not one you know how to use in an emergency," Deza said. "How you gonna go out with your hair looking like World War Three?"

Tyesha put a hand up to her head. Her press had been thoroughly rained on, causing it to turn back to waves where she'd relaxed it, and to kink up wildly at the roots where the perm had grown out.

"Some motherfucker pulled a fire alarm at work and I was out on the street without my umbrella," Tyesha said.

"Auntie," Deza said. "Lemme fix that up for you. You need help."

"I can't argue with you on that count," Tyesha said, and opened the door.

Half an hour later, Tyesha was sitting at the kitchen table while Deza expertly sectioned and flatironed her hair.

"So what was this press conference about, anyway?"

"You see that viral video where the strippers walk out of that club?" Tyesha asked.

"The one where that guy grabs and slaps the girl giving him a lap dance and tries to drag her into that room?" Deza said. "Hell, yeah. Everybody seen that."

"That's where Lily works," Tyesha said.

"The West Indian girl I met here?"

"Yeah, and my clinic is advocating for the strippers."

"Damn," Deza said. "That's cool, Auntie Ty. It's like you take after Aunt Lu."

The name stung. The memory stung. She could still feel the singe of smoke in her nostrils. Lucille was Deza's great aunt and had died when Deza was in kindergarten. Jenisse never brought her kids around the center. So Deza had never heard her preach peace to an audience of young gangbangers.

Had never heard her demand street violence and cop violence be put on the Cook County public health agenda.

"But I'm not like her," Tyesha said. "I was supposed to give a speech, but I choked out there today. I just lost it. Couldn't even speak. My ex-boss had to take over."

"Of course you're like her," Deza said. "I did a report on her in high school for a local heroes assignment. She was all about public health, just like you. All about black and brown folks, just like you. If she was still alive, you'd be working at the Urban Peace Accord Center in Chicago. I bet you never woulda moved to New York."

"You're probably right," Tyesha said. "Auntie Lu kept my mama and your mama in check. If either of them got too crazy, I could call her and she'd run interference."

"Keeping it real, if she was still alive, she probably woulda raised me and Amaru," Deza said.

Tyesha hadn't thought of that. "Probably would have. Your older brothers used to stay with her a lot of the time." Tyesha said it quietly.

The flatiron hissed as Deza smoothed down a section of hair.

"So why are you all in New York, anyway?" Tyesha asked.

"Zeus," Deza said.

Tyesha wondered why Deza and Amaru referred to him by his first name instead of "dad" or "my dad." Still, Tyesha had grown up without a dad, so who knew what you called them? Or maybe it was a Chicago drug kingpin thing. Maybe he was just Zeus to everyone.

"He wants to expand his business into New York," Deza said.

"Dear lord," Tyesha said. "That's all I need. Your mama coming around and Zeus getting into some kind of turf war with the thugs in this town."

"The way I look at it," Deza said, "it's an opportunity for all of us. Especially me. Now I know you don't want to hear this, but I gotta say it. When we heard we were coming to New York, Amaru was all upset because she has a girlfriend in Chicago. But I was excited because I thought, finally, I'll be in the city where something can really happen for me as a hip-hop artist. And then I hear that my favorite auntie—"

"Your only auntie," Tyesha said.

"—knows Thug Woofer," Deza said, setting down the flat-iron. "Now I came at you a little sideways before because I was in shock. But I've had time, and I've worked on my pitch. So just hear me out, and if you say no, I'll let it go."

"Okay," Tyesha said. "Fine."

"Don't do it for me," Deza said. "Do it for yourself. You had this rapper who is fine as fuck, rich as fuck, successful as fuck, dedicating albums to you. Yeah, maybe it's some bull-shit. But you owe it to yourself to find out."

"He's not as rich as he seems in those videos," Tyesha said.

"He's rich enough," Deza said. "Twenty years from now, you don't want to be reading about how he settled down with some nice executive named Talisha, who looks just like you."

Tyesha laughed at that thought.

Deza went on. "Then Thug Woofer and Talisha gonna be living the dream with three kids and a big-ass house and you're like goddamn, that was supposed to be my life. I've listened to the Melvyn album. It's some real shit. Some Drake type of sensitive shit."

"That's the thing about Woof," Tyesha said.

"You calls his ass Woof?" Deza said. "You're on a single syllable basis?"

"He's like Dr. Jekyll and Mr. Hyde," she said. "One minute, he's wooing me at a nice restaurant, and the next, he's like some rude motherfucker on the bus."

"Listen to the album, Auntie," Deza said. "Just give him a chance to explain." Deza pulled a CD out of her purse and set it on the table. It was burned on a computer and said "Melvyn" in Sharpie marker. "When you like what you hear, call him," Deza said.

"*If* I like what I hear," Tyesha said. "I'll call him. And *if* he's not acting like Mr. Hyde, I'll ask him to lunch. And *if* he says yes, I'll bring up your demo at lunch. That's it. If he says no, don't ask again."

Tyesha thought about the last time she'd seen Woof. It was their third date. Prior to that he'd taken her to the Oscars. Flown her to L.A., put her up in a stellar hotel, and not even pushed for sex. She had let her guard down.

Shortly after the L.A. trip, Tyesha and Woof were drinking at an uptown bar that looked over the river. She had come from the clinic's board meeting and he had been at an industry function.

"Look at us," Tyesha said. "With your artist gear and my suit, we're like some kind of romantic comedy."

"Or a porno." He laughed. "The executive and the bad boy."

Tyesha chuckled and drank. "When I graduate and work at the clinic full-time, this is gonna be my everyday look."

"Will you miss your current job?" he asked.

"Hell, no." She ate a handful of almonds from a bowl on the bar. "Public health is my real job."

He had pressed for details of her entry into sex work.

"Do you really wanna hear this?" she had asked.

Woof shrugged. "I'm definitely curious."

She had recalled her first bad client who broke her jaw.

Woof traced a finger along her jawline. "I'm glad you're okay," he said.

They left the bar and started strolled along the river, arm in arm. The night was warmer than usual for March, but they could see their breath. Streetlamps reflected off the water, as well as distant moving lights of ferries and party boats.

Woof put his arms around her. "So," he said, "I was wondering if maybe we could go home together tonight."

Tyesha blinked and stepped back. "Whoa. Can you wait a minute before you make a move?" She shook her head. "I'm still trying to get the taste of broken jaw out of my mouth."

"I can make it better," he said, leaning in to kiss her jaw.

"Seriously," Tyesha said. "Back up, please. Give me a minute."

He stepped back. She folded her arms and stared out at the river.

"Woof." She turned to him. "I realize this is our third date."

"Our fourth date, Tyesha."

"Third," she said. "It doesn't count if I got paid."

"You expect me to be up here going on dates with you, and not get none, and sit around and listen about you fucking other dudes for money?"

"You asked—" Tyesha broke off. "You know what? Never mind. This dating thing isn't working."

"Not working?" Woof asked. "I usually don't even date." He began to pace. "I been a gentleman, I brought you flowers and took you out. Isn't it time for me to get my reward?"

"I'm not gonna fuck you as a reward," she said. "I'm certainly not gonna fuck you if you act like an asshole. Not for cash or a fancy dinner. Obviously you can only think of me as a ho."

"It's what you do, isn't it?" Woof said.

"Fuck you, Woof," she said. "That's the only fucking you're gonna get from me, tonight or ever."

"Don't walk away from me!" He caught up to her and grabbed her arm, spinning her around.

"Get the hell off me," Tyesha said. She reached for her panic keychain and pressed both buttons. An alarm split the air.

"What the fuck?" he said.

She twisted free and ran along the river.

That had been Thug Woofer's second chance. They had first met when he was a client. He was an asshole then, too. But he'd showed up at her job, given her flowers, and sweet-talked her. She remembered the track she had seen on the *Ellen* show, "Third Chance." It seemed sort of corny and cliché, like it could be any guy who screwed up with any woman. Men like Woof didn't deserve a third chance, but she had promised her niece. Deza had indicated that she should start with track four, a song called "Double Standard."

> *I be steady fucking*
> *Say I like 'em wild*
> *But somehow I expect my girlfriend to be an*
> *innocent child?*
> *Why am I so scared that I'll be compared*
> *We coulda had something real if I only dared*
> *But when I get out my comfort zone*
> *I put my thug face on*
> *Like I don't give a fuck when I do*
> *Like I wasn't straight stuck on you*
> *Your confidence, I couldn't handle it*
> *I punked out with a double standard*
> *If you let some other dude manhandle*
> *You gotta let me get an angle*
> *My ego got frantic*
> *I defaulted to the double standard*

But the track that stunned her was called "Make it Matter," which he dedicated to a cousin who had been shot by the police.

You were nineteen when I was ten
I idolized you back then
You were the star of the family
Visiting from the university
When they said to work hard in school
It sounded good so I could be like you
So when those ten bullets hit
I couldn't figure out what description you fit
Was it the scholar with straight A's that fall
Or the basketball coach at the local juvenile hall
The cousin who tutored me on the phone in
*   math and was never impatient?*
Or the son who always mowed the lawn when
*   he was home on vacation?*
After you died, it was like the family scattered
Cause they gunned you down like your life
*   never mattered.*

His words transported Tyesha from a roadside in South
Carolina to a sidewalk in Chicago, and the tears began to
fall. Throughout the song, they streamed down her face. Her
aunt's death had the same effect on her own family. When the
song ended, she sat up and wiped her eyes. For the first time
since Drew Thomas had identified her as a Couvillier, niece
of Lucille Couvillier, she could breathe without smoke in her
lungs.

She composed a text to Thug Woofer.

Hey.

~~Hey.~~

She wrote a dozen versions, but finally settled on:

I been listening to Melvyn. Powerful. Let's talk.

She couldn't quite bring herself to send it. Not while she
was feeling so raw. She was exhausted from rescuing Lily the

night before and then the press conference. She couldn't trust her judgment when she was this tired. She left it in draft form on her phone and went to bed.

That evening, Lily walked in early to the One-Eyed King. The humidity was nearly 100 percent, and these were the months that Lily gave up the pressing comb for a weather-proof weave. She was wishing she could cut her hair and wear it natural. Then she could wear wigs on stage and be herself the rest of the time. But the wigs often looked tacky if she threw her head back when doing pole work, not to mention that once her wig had nearly fallen off. And natural hair was out of the question on stage. Black strippers already made less in tips. In the place she danced, wearing short, kinky hair was like asking for an 80 percent pay cut. So much bullshit on this job just trying to make a living. She came early that night because she was sure no one would be there to sign her in. She knew management would be beyond pissed. But they wouldn't have had time to replace all the dancers, and they certainly weren't gonna lose any more money by being closed for a night. This was when she needed to be extra careful. They would use any excuse to fire her.

As she was waiting to sign in, Hibiscus strolled up—the Trinidadian girl who refused to leave during the walkout. A security guy came out and handed Hibiscus the sign-in sheet.

Lily tried to sign after Hibiscus was done, but the guard took the list. "You can't sign in," the security guy said to Lily with a smirk.

"At least now you admit you're keeping me from signing in to my job," she said, and sucked her teeth.

"You can't sign in because you're fired," the guy said.

"See?" Hibiscus said. "I told you keep your mouth shut. Not everybody so high and mighty they can afford to lose this job."

"Fired for what?" Lily asked.

"Insubordination," he said. "Walking off the job. Disturbing the peace. You name it."

"I can't fucking believe this," Lily said. "I need to see the manager."

She pushed past the other girl and strode toward the office. The security guard yelled after her: "And don't even bother going to the clubs in the boroughs, because you're banned from the whole chain."

As his voice followed her down the hall, she made a detour into the dressing room and dug under the pile of towels to retrieve her shoes.

"This is bullshit," she said, as she stormed into the office.

But instead of the owner, there was a young man sitting at the desk. The same guy who'd tried to drag the blonde into the VIP room.

"What's bullshit?" he asked with a leer. The security guard filled the doorway behind her.

"Nothing," she said, and backed out of the office, pushing past the guard and striding quickly out onto the street.

She nearly bumped into two other girls coming to work.

"I got fired," Lily said. "For last night."

"Hell no," one of the girls said. "They can't single you out."

But it turned out they hadn't. One by one, the girls who had walked out all found out that they'd been fired. Except the blonde from Guadeloupe, who was invited—at the special request of the young man who had tried to pull her into the VIP room—to keep her job. She declined.

The knot of dancers stood on the sidewalk outside the club.

Early evening traffic went by, and a double-decker bus of tourists gawked at them.

"This is fucking scandalous," the brown-skinned Latina Giselle said. "When we were on Broadway—"

"Give me a goddamn break," said a young woman who was smoking a cigarette. "I'm so sick of hearing about how good you had it on Broadway. Well, you ain't on fucking Broadway now. You ain't even at the fucking One-Eyed King anymore."

"Will you just let me finish my fucking sentence?" Giselle said. "When we were on Broadway, we had a union, and the management couldn't pull any of this kind of shit. Not the dressing rooms, not the harassment, not firing us."

"Then we need to form a union," Lily agreed.

"A union?" one of the younger girls asked. "What strippers do you know that are in a union? That's for the nurses who keep their uniforms on."

"I know some dancers who sued their club," Lily said. "It was a class action suit for wage theft. They all got paid."

"Yeah, but like three years later," the girl with the cigarette said. "My bills are due now. Not in three years."

"Some girls did form a union," said one of the other dancers who had been in the Broadway show. "In San Francisco. I saw a movie about it."

The smoker took a last drag on her cigarette. "This ain't San Francisco. This is dog-eat-dog New York," she said. "People leave their heart in San Francisco. You leave your heart in New York, some motherfucker will snatch it up and sell it. Fuck that." She flicked her cigarette butt into the street and hailed a cab.

"Well, I'd like to be in a union again," the young girl from Broadway said.

"I don't have time for this," one of the other girls said. "I'll see if I can pick up a shift at Vixela's. I gotta pay my babysitter for the week, so I need to make money tonight. I can't get involved in some union drama."

"It doesn't have to be one or the other," Lily said. "Not if we work together."

"Yeah," Giselle agreed. "Do what you gotta do tonight while those of us with free time start work on a union."

"Count me out," one girl said. "I just got my certification to teach pole dancing."

"What?" Lily asked. "Those bitches wanna steal our stripper style, but then be like 'whaaaat?'" She batted her wide eyes and let her mouth fall into a slack circle. "'Strippers? We've never even heard of strippers.'"

"I'm done," the girl said. "In pole dancing, we don't need a fucking union because nobody's trying to assault us on the job or pressure us into giving blow jobs in a VIP room." She stormed off down the street.

"Yeah?" Lily yelled after her. "That's because you all play the good girls and leave the dirty work to us."

"Lily," Giselle pulled her arm. "Let her go. Let's focus on strategizing with the people who support us."

The women agreed. Some knew girls who worked at other clubs in the chain.

"Who's got connections with the club in the Bronx? Who's got Brooklyn? Queens?"

"What about Staten Island?" one girl asked.

"They have a location on Staten Island?"

"Don't talk shit about Staten Island," she said. "That's the club where I started."

"Okay," Giselle said. "All five boroughs. But for now, it's strictly word of mouth. We can't let the management know we're trying to unionize, okay?"

All of them agreed. And then Lily made sure she had everyone's phone numbers to stay in touch.

Three of the girls headed over to Vixela's.

"Is it true you can't make any money there unless you do VIP?" one asked.

"Yeah," said the one with the babysitter. "Don't even waste your time if you just wanna dance."

The next day, Tyesha had a stack of paperwork to handle in her office. It had been Marisol's office originally. Her predecessor had it done up in designer leather furniture, wood paneled walls, and a massive wooden desk. Southern exposure brought warm indirect light into the room and sustained several plants. The office manager had to water them. Tyesha always forgot.

Throughout the day, she kept pulling up the draft of her text to Thug Woofer. Every time she went to send it, her heart beat hard. What if he was already serious with someone else? It had been several months since his album dropped. The most disconcerting part was when her mind wandered off into recalling their one kiss. Maybe because there hadn't been any sex, it had just left her hungry, curious, yearning.

She sat in her office with her finger hovering over the send button. Her mind played tug-of-war with itself. What if she would make a fool of herself by texting him? But she had promised Deza. Yet if this Mr. Nice Guy shit was all an act, then she didn't want to fall for it. But that kiss. Could she really live without knowing what might follow a kiss like that?

Her body buzzed with a yearning curiosity. Just then her phone flashed an incoming call. It was the stockbroker. He'd been calling all week.

"Tyesha," he said. "Hey, where've you been?"

"Busy," she said. "Can you come over tonight?"

"Tonight? Yeah, I—sure—"

"Good," she said. "Wear a kilt with no underwear. And don't bother with any small talk. Just be down to fuck."

"Okay," he said. "But I don't have a kilt."

"I'm sure you can get one by nine tonight," she said.

"This is New York City, not Indiana. Isn't that where you're from?"

"Ohio," he said.

The stockbroker showed up at nine fifteen. His kilt was in shades of blue, green, and black.

Tyesha knew it was petty and probably unfair. Since she stopped doing sex work, she was ready for the guys she dated to be the ones to make an effort. She hadn't waxed since she left the business, and it made her feel overgrown and feral.

"Look," the stockbroker said. "As you can see, I got what you asked. But I need to tell you, as I was walking up here, I asked myself 'what am I doing?' I'm not this desperate. Really, I'm not. You're a sexy woman. But I want more than to be someone's boy toy."

Tyesha tilted her head. She had to repress the *awwwww* that threatened to escape her mouth. He was so cute when he got feisty. She liked a guy who wouldn't let himself be played with, even if she also liked playing.

"I respect that," Tyesha said. "In fact, it's kind of sexy. But I definitely can't offer you more than boy toy status."

"I appreciate your honesty," he said, and turned to leave.

"Don't rush off," she said. "Can't we have some good-bye sex?"

His face brightened. "Definitely," he said, with a laugh. "I'd hate to think I bought a damn kilt and stood on the subway freezing my balls off for nothing."

"Hmmm," Tyesha said, reaching underneath the pleats. "They don't seem cold to me."

Around the same time, Lily was walking up from the subway to the One-Eyed King in the Bronx. It was a two-story brick building, but it looked particularly low-slung, as it was located around the corner from a towering hospital. Lily approached the club's staff entrance, as she had always done when she picked up shifts there.

"ID please," the security guard demanded.

"ID?" Lily asked. "I never been asked for ID before."

"Fine," the guard said. "Tell me your name, and I can find you on the employee list." He lifted a clipboard with names and headshots.

"Never mind," Lily said, and strode around to the front entrance.

"ID please," the woman at the customer entrance asked, barely looking at her.

Lily handed it over and the girl looked up, eyes wide.

"Lily, you can't be here," she whispered.

"Why not?" Lily asked. "I'm not coming in as an employee. Just a member of the public. To a public place."

"They got your picture on the wall here," the girl said. "You're on the no-fly list. I have orders not to let you in."

"Okay," Lily said. "Will you give these to the girls, then?" She handed over a stack of flyers the size of business cards.

"I don't want to lose my job," the girl said.

"Neither did I," Lily said. "Just leave them in the dressing room. No one needs to know it was you."

"Okay," the girl said, taking the flyers. "I saw that video. To hell with these guys."

Two hours later, at the One-Eyed King in Brooklyn, one of the dancers had to pee. Badly. Since the managers had consolidated the dressing rooms to make another VIP lounge, there was only one bathroom for all the girls in the dressing room. Two stalls, and one of the toilets was broken.

It would have been fine if she did something else for a living, but for the next hour, she'd be dropping into wide-legged squats. It wouldn't do to piss herself on stage.

"Hurry up!" she said, banging on the stall door.

"I just started my period," the girl inside said. "I gotta dam up the river before I go on."

And I got my own waterfall to worry about, the full-bladder girl thought.

She stood at the stall door for a moment. It was covered with stickers that represented various music albums, indie bands, political slogans, and sex industry-related websites, both for customers and professionals. One said: "I'm ready for my sex vacation!" It listed sex worker burnout prevention tips. As she leaned forward to see the fine print of the website, she felt a stab in her bladder.

Fuck it. The management didn't like them using the front office restroom, but it was better than pissing on the customers.

She threw on her dress and slipped into the office restroom.

After she relieved herself, she stepped out of the stall to find a tall black woman.

"You work here, right?" the woman asked in a West Indian accent.

"I'm sorry," the girl said. "I know we're not supposed to use this bathroom, but—"

"It's okay," the woman said. "I'm not management. I'm Lily, one of the girls who got fired from the Manhattan club. We're starting a union. Would you be interested?"

"Fuck, yeah," the girl said, taking a few small flyers and giving Lily her phone number.

When Lily walked out of the restroom, a security guard was waiting for her.

"I have orders to escort you out of the building," he said.

"Why?" Lily asked. "I'm just here to watch women dance and jerk off like everyone else."

"Am I escorting you out or throwing you out?" he asked without any humor.

"Fine," she said. "I'm leaving."

As they passed by the girl at the door, he growled. "Please refund this bitch's money. She's not allowed in."

"I didn't pay to get in this place," Lily said. "It's a weeknight. Women get in free."

Book 2

Chapter 5

Tyesha and Kim stepped off the subway and strode down the street to the One-Eyed King in Manhattan.

"Damn!" a young man said as he walked past them. "You got a nice ass on you, girl."

"Thank you, baby," Kim yelled back, and she and Tyesha laughed. Kim's ass wasn't exactly flat, but it was like a dime to Tyesha's silver dollar.

"Wait," the guy said. "I wasn't—"

The two girls kept walking and weren't bothered to hear the rest of it.

Inside the One-Eyed King, they claimed to be looking for work and gave their names as Keisha and Sue. Keisha had a long blond weave, blue false eyelashes, and silver lipstick. Sue wore black lipstick and several face piercings.

It was the day after Lily and the union girls had done the flyer drops at the other strip club locations, but Tyesha was convinced that their best next step was to try to get some dirt on the owners. They both wore body cameras.

"It's a miracle they didn't recognize you from the press conference," Kim said. She wore her camera in a jewel in her belly button.

Tyesha arranged the body cam among the oversized rhinestones in her bustier. "It's the one good thing that came from me being unable to speak," she said. "I wasn't in most of the news clips, so they haven't seen my face."

For the next three hours, they just danced for mediocre tips. Kim gave a couple of lap dances. Both of them turned down VIP invitations, but several of the other girls didn't.

In between dance sets, Tyesha went to talk to the manager. As she walked down the hallway, she turned on her camera and called Kim on her phone. "How does it look?" she asked Kim.

In the bathroom stall, Kim watched Tyesha's video image from her smart phone.

"Tilt your chest up a little," Kim said. "I won't be able to see the manager's face."

"I don't want him to think I'm trying to hit on him," Tyesha said.

"He sees hot girls all day," Kim said. "I doubt he'll be bothered. Tits up."

Tyesha threw her shoulders back and pressed her chest upward.

"Better," Kim said.

Tyesha caught the manager on his way out of the office. "So how does VIP work?" she asked. "If I go in, how much do I get?"

The manager shrugged. "Whatever happens between consenting adults is whatever happens."

Tyesha scoffed. "Fine, what's the room rental fee or whatever? I mean, who do I give a cut to?"

"There's no cut," the manager said. "Like I told you. The VIP room is optional—if you take a liking to a customer, you can like him in private."

In the cab on the way home, Kim and Tyesha counted their money. Mostly singles. Less than two hundred dollars after they paid all of their fees.

"Do you think he was telling the truth?" Kim asked.

"No way," Tyesha said. "They must have some kind of system. But obviously, they're not gonna tell the two new girls from off the street."

"Right," Kim said. "Especially not after a viral video and a press conference."

"So we can't get any evidence that they're pimping," Tyesha said.

Kim nodded. "Maybe if one of us hid in the VIP, we could manage to document that they're running a brothel."

Tyesha shook her head. "The clinic's position is for the decriminalization of sex work between consenting adults. We can't be part of prosecuting someone for it. That'd be too whorephobic."

"So what do we do?" Kim asked.

"Take this to the team and we'll figure out the next steps."

The following day, Tyesha and Lily sat around the conference table with Eva Feldman, the Maria de la Vega clinical director, who was also an attorney.

Eva was the first older white person Tyesha had ever really trusted. She reminded Tyesha of teachers she'd had back home in the Chicago public schools. Her aunt had taught her to be polite to white people and that it was good to have them on your side. But you didn't want to get close to them, and trusting them was certainly not an option. Chicago was profoundly segregated, so she didn't have any white peers until college.

Eva was Jewish, and her parents had survived the holocaust in Germany, so she had a toughness and solidity that Tyesha didn't often find in white people. Like Jody, she was ready to kick some ass for you if you were one of her folks.

"So I called their lawyers," Tyesha said to Eva and Lily. "They're insisting the dancers can't unionize because they're independent contractors, not employees."

"Independent contractors?" Lily said. "I'm a stripper, not an independent contractor."

Eva was busy clicking on her laptop.

"So," Eva said, "when you get up on stage, you can wear what you want, dance how you want, and interact with the clients any way you like, right?"

"Are you kidding me?" Lily asked. "They threatened to fire me for wearing braids instead of a straight weave."

"In other words," Eva said, "you couldn't get up on stage and do an interpretive dance to an Audre Lorde poem?"

Tyesha and Lily burst out laughing.

"Only if I wanted it to be my last night working there," Lily said.

"Then they can't claim you're independent contractors," Eva said. "According to the IRS regulations, one of the main criteria deciding employment status is about whether or not the employer has the right to control what the individual does while working for them."

Lily sucked her teeth. "They've gone as far as insisting we have to have all the hair waxed off our nanny."

"Doesn't sound like a contractor to me," Tyesha said.

The following day, Eva was yelling into the speakerphone during a conference call with the strip club's attorney and the owner.

Even though they weren't there in person, Eva had worn her best navy power suit and a red silk blouse. She had on low-heeled pumps and towered over the phone, a plump fist on her hip.

"So I'm gonna lay out two choices for you," she said. "Option A: You can either officially change their designation to employees right now, giving them the right to unionize. Or option B: I can call the IRS and report that—since you opened in the nineties—you have been illegally classifying your employees as independent contractors. In which case, the One-Eyed King would be liable for twenty years of back taxes. And then I guess the girls won't need a union, because the tax bill will probably bankrupt the business, especially when you figure in contributions to social security, workers' comp . . . shall I go on?"

"The girls have all signed contracts that they understand they're liable for their own taxes," the attorney said. "The IRS won't bite. But file suit. Maybe you can get a settlement in a few years."

"I hate to do this, but we may have to bring criminal charges for pimping and sexual assault. As you're likely aware, we have a video and several women who will testify."

"They're just disgruntled former employees that got fired," the attorney said.

"Don't you mean disgruntled former independent contractors?" Eva asked.

The line went mute for a moment, while the strip club owner and lawyer conferred.

"What do you think?" Tyesha asked, after they muted the phone on their end, as well.

"I think they're in trouble, and they know it," Eva said.

"Hello?" the lawyer's voice came back on the line. Tyesha unmuted it.

"Fine," he said briskly. "We'll designate them all as employees."

"And rehire them," Eva said. "With a written contract."

"Sure," the attorney said. "But the terms will be the same ones they've verbally agreed to. And that's it. No other changes."

"Not good enough," Eva said. "I need to know that all the girls will get their jobs back."

"These girls are at-will employees," the attorney said. "My client doesn't have any obligation to rehire troublemakers."

"Fine," Eva said. "I don't have any obligation to avoid calling the IRS to report what I just learned about your fraudulent employee policy or to avoid pressing criminal charges."

"Hang on," the attorney said, and the line went mute again.

"That's right, motherfuckers," Tyesha said, holding down the mute button.

"I think we got 'em cornered," Eva said.

"I hope so," Lily said. "I need my job back."

"Well, you're about to have two jobs," Eva said. "Dancer plus union rep. Here's the name of the labor activist Marisol got to help."

Eva handed Tyesha and Lily a sticky note with the name and number of a woman from the theatrical union.

"Marisol knows this chick?" Tyesha asked.

"A friend of a friend," Eva said.

They were interrupted by the sound of the One-Eyed King's attorney coming back on the line. "Hello?"

"So are we agreed?" Eva asked.

"We're agreed," the attorney said. "The girls can come in and sign the W2 forms and get the new written policies."

"Perfect," Eva said. "And the dancers will be sending me screen shots of those policies. If there's any shady language that isn't in line with what we've agreed to today, I'll call the IRS and the prosecutor's office first. I won't have you wasting all of our time with some bullshit."

"Trust me, Ms. Feldman," the attorney said. "There won't be any need for you to make those calls."

"Good," she said. "And that's *Doctor* Feldman."

She hung up, and both Tyesha and Lily high-fived her.

"You a lawyer and a medical doctor?" Lily asked.

"A psychiatrist," Eva said.

"Damn," Lily said. "I thought the Jamaicans were supposed to be the ones with all the jobs."

* * *

The next morning, Tyesha went to the Manhattan One-Eyed King, saying she had left her purse.

She had on a blond wig, a long black coat, and gloves.

"Can I go in and look for it?"

The security guard grinned at her. "Sure, baby."

As she walked in, she strategically placed a piece of clear tape to keep the front door from closing. After walking noisily on high heels into the dressing room, she took them off and tiptoed across the hall.

She stood in the silent hallway and pulled the lock picks from her coat pocket. Carefully, she picked the lock on the office door.

Her hands shook a bit. A sudden burst of canned laughter made her start, nearly dropping the lock picks. She scrabbled with jittery fingers and breathed to calm her nerves. They had practiced this on several different doors. She was stunned at how easy it was to pick a lock. So easy, in fact, that she had decided to install a chain on her own apartment door.

Finally, she was in. She closed the door silently behind her and texted Kim.

Kim slipped in through the open street door, dressed identically, except with a purse in her gloved hand. She crept through the quiet club, down the back hallway to the emergency exit. She slid a Metrocard under the lock to prop the back door open, then crept back to the front of the club.

"Found my purse," she called over her shoulder, but without turning her face around. "Thanks, guys."

As the men turned toward the TV, Tyesha began to search the office.

It was a cramped box of a room, with a small desk and two chairs. The management had turned every possible square inch of the real estate into VIP areas. She dug through ledgers and files looking for evidence. She took a few pictures of different documents, but found nothing seriously incriminating. They were late with their quarterly IRS payment, but so was the clinic. She downloaded everything from the computer onto a jump drive.

In the next room, she could hear the guards watching one of the music channels on cable. "Who's the best rapper?" a woman's voice asked. "Thug Woofer versus Big Dane."

Tyesha groaned inwardly with the mention of Woof.

"Naw, man," one of the guards said. "Big Dane way mo ratchet. He got a wife in jail and his girlfriend can't go to his concerts cause she on house arrest. Look at Woof, man. You heard his album from last year? *Melvyn: The Real Me*? He on some punk-ass shit. We shouldn't even call him Woof anymore. Call his ass 'Meow.'"

The other guard laughed.

"This year's Grammys have a lot of competition in rap," another female announcer began. "Thug Woofer's new album, *Melvyn, the Real Me* is likely to be nominated in several categories, including best album, best song, and best male artist. Remember him from last year? The bad boy of rap? Well, he's certainly changed his tune."

"Wait a minute," one of the guards said. "Who was that girl?"

"What girl?" the other guard asked.

"The one with Thug Woofer on the red carpet."

Tyesha strained to hear what they were saying, but it sounded like they were just playing a clip from one of Woof's videos. Damn, no matter where Tyesha went—from her family to a strip club—Woof was always haunting her.

"She looks like that girl we just let in the club," the guard insisted.

"You're tripping!" the other guard said.

"Wind it back," the first guard asked.

"You can't wind it back," the other guard said. "This is broadcast TV."

"I'm serious," the first guard said. "I'm gonna find the clip on YouTube."

Abruptly, the audio from the TV program was turned off, and Tyesha felt nearly sick to her stomach.

As she opened the office door, she could hear strains of the theme music from the Oscars the previous year. How many times had she watched that clip on YouTube? Her breath caught.

"Thug Woofer!" one of the reporters had called. "Who's your date wearing?"

"Dilani Mara," he called back.

"That does seem like the same girl," the second guard said. "He was fucking with one of the strippers who works here?"

"I'm gonna Google her," the first guard said.

"What you putting in for search words?"

"Thug Woofer red carpet Oscars date," the first guard said.

"These are just pictures," the guard said. "None of them say her name. Why do you even care?"

"I feel like I seen her somewhere before," he said.

Tyesha could feel her body tense as she waited for the download of the hard drive to complete.

"Here it is!" the guard said. "Tyesha Couvillier. She's a graduate student at Columbia."

"Stripping here?" the other guard asked.

"Tuition," the first guard said. "Lemme Google her name."

Tyesha's stomach seized up.

"Yep," the guard said. "Tyesha Couvillier. Public health. Graduated. Now she's an executive director at the Maria de la Vega health clinic."

"Those bitches?" the second guard said. "Those are the bitches who been fucking with the club."

"What?" the first guard asked.

"If you saw her before, I bet it was at that press conference," he said. "Find the clip."

Tyesha slid out her phone and texted Kim: **I think they're on to me. Get ready to open the back door.**

As she sent the text, Tyesha heard Marisol's voice in the background: "Sex workers have a right to decent working conditions, to safety from sexual harassment—that's right, sex workers can set limits. If she agrees to a lap dance, she hasn't agreed to . . ."

Kim texted back: **Standing by**

The drive still hadn't finished downloading. Tyesha texted: **On my signal**

"She must be a goddamn spy," the guard said. "What the fuck was she really doing here today?"

"You think she took something?" the other guard said. "Planted a fucking bomb? I don't know."

"You check the dressing room," the guard said. "I'll check the office."

Tyesha crouched under the desk and held her thumb over Kim's number.

She heard keys in the lock, then the guard came into the office.

She pressed her thumb down and the phone began to ring silently. A few seconds later, the back door's shrieking alarm rang throughout the building. As the two guards ran down the back hallway, Tyesha sprang from under the desk, yanked the drive out of the computer, and ran out the front door.

Behind the building, the two guards ran down the alley to see an Asian girl getting up from the sidewalk.

"You see a blond black girl go by?" they asked.

"That bitch knocked me down and ran past me." She gestured with her shoulder toward the busy avenue block to her left.

The two guards ran out to the street. Kim hustled in the other direction to meet Tyesha.

That evening, the two of them sat around the conference room with Marisol, Eva, and Serena, the clinic's office manager. Serena was a pale, petite, transgender young woman with wispy, flyaway hair. Her strong features revealed her Greek immigrant roots.

"I been looking through these files all day," Serena said. "I can't find anything incriminating. Unless you count a few sex tapes."

"I looked at the ledger images, too," Marisol said. "Nothing."

"Could they be using the sex tapes as some kind of leverage over the girls?" Eva asked.

"I doubt it," Tyesha said. "They were raw footage of multiple takes. These girls looked more like amateur porn actresses than girls having sex with a hidden camera."

"Damn," Marisol said. "So where does that leave us?"

"Ready for the long haul of organizing a union," Eva said.

Later that night, Tyesha stood on the elevated subway platform headed home with a bag of groceries. A train came that was headed in the opposite direction. She stepped toward the tracks and craned her neck to see if her train was coming. No sign of it.

She pulled up her text to Thug Woofer again. She had asked God for a sign. And today she had been recognized and then chased because of Woof. Was it a sign that he was dangerous? That he was inevitable? But she thought of the guards' reaction to the rapper's new album. Woof had risked the scorn and ridicule of guys like that, in order to show something more vulnerable. She had heard the lyrics. She closed her eyes and pressed the button.

I been listening to Melvyn. Powerful. Let's talk.

Tyesha's stomach seized up. She immediately regretted sending it. Who was she kidding? It had been months. He was a famous rap star. Of course he had moved on by now. Probably wouldn't even remember her number.

It was getting dark and still no sign of her train. Passengers kept coming up the stairs and cramming into the platform. Another train came in the other direction and helped relieve the congestion.

Suddenly, she had an awful thought: She hadn't even put her name in the text. How arrogant was that? She might as well have opened with: *of course you still have my number in your phone* . . . Should she send a *PS: it's Tyesha*? Ugh. She composed the PS then deleted it, then was halfway through composing it again when she got a text.

Tyesha! Is this my third chance?

Tyesha laughed out loud.

I think so . . .

Hell yeah we can talk. Call me!

She felt the knot return to her stomach.

Busy tonight . . . lunch tomorrow?

Whenever you say . . . how bout that steakhouse we went to?

Sounds good

They set it for noon.

Tyesha pressed the phone against her chest and wanted to scream. On the crowded train platform, she held it in, so it came out more like a squeak. She felt excited and mortified.

In the distance, she could finally see the lights of her train coming.

She called Deza. "A certain rapper said yes to lunch," Tyesha blurted. "We're meeting tomorrow at noon."

Deza provided the full-throated scream that Tyesha had been feeling. As the train pulled up with a screech, Tyesha let out her own shriek at half volume, and it bubbled into a laugh.

Tyesha boarded the train listening to Deza howling with delight in her ear. By the time she got a seat on the train and the doors closed, she had only a few minutes to talk before the train dipped into a tunnel.

In the background, Tyesha could hear her sister, Jenisse.

"Girl, have you lost your mind? What you screaming about?"

"So get me that demo CD tomorrow morning," Tyesha said.

"Yaaassss!" Deza crowed. "I love you, Auntie, you're the best! The best! The best! I'll burn the demo at your house when I come over to do your hair."

"I'm not doing my hair for this date," Tyesha said.

"Oh, yes you are," Deza said. "I'm not having Thug Woofer pass on my album because you look raggedy."

Tyesha's train was approaching the tunnel.

"Deza, I—"

Her niece cut her off. "Are you coming to Amaru's game Tuesday?"

"What game?" Tyesha said. "Nobody invited me."

"I'm inviting you now," Deza said.

"Okay fine," Tyesha said. "But I'm not—"

Her phone dropped the call.

She began to text Deza that she really wasn't going to get her hair done.

As the train pulled into the tunnel, she could see her reflection in the window glass. She didn't look raggedy, just not freshly pressed. It might not hurt to make a little bit of an effort. She could always dress down.

The next day was Saturday, and when Deza came over, she brought Amaru.

The younger sister was lanky and muscular, with short natural hair, an athletic bra, and basketball shorts.

When Tyesha hugged her niece, the top of her head came to the fourteen-year-old's nose.

"How tall are you now?" she asked.

"Six feet," Amaru said with an *aww shucks* in her voice.

"I'm looking forward to your game Tuesday," Tyesha said.

"It's just an exhibition thing," Amaru said. "One of the coaches from Syracuse is in town and she wanted to see me play."

"That's fabulous, girl!" Tyesha said. "Don't sell yourself short."

"So enough about that," Deza said. "Let's get my demo going."

"I been telling her to put the best stuff first," Amaru said. "But she don't want to listen to me."

"Your sister's right," Tyesha told Deza. "You want to start off strong."

Deza shook her head. "I don't want it to go downhill," she said. "It's gotta build momentum."

"But what if they don't listen to the whole thing?" Amaru said. "It's not like a basketball game where they stay to see who wins."

"Yeah, well, this isn't basketball," Deza said. "This is him taking my auntie out and trying to get in good with her. He gonna listen."

Deza set up her laptop to burn the CD and turned to Tyesha. "So what are we doing with your hair?"

That day, Deza's own hair was a combination of weave, flatiron, natural texture, several bright colors, and the original dark reddish brown that the three of them shared.

"Something much simpler than what you got going," Tyesha said. "Just press it straight with a little bump of a curl on the bottom."

"One of these days you gotta let me do something interesting," Deza said.

Tyesha rolled her eyes. "So, Amaru, sounds like basketball is really your thing, huh?"

"I'm serious about it," Amaru said. "But certain people can't seem to see it."

"Zeus wouldn't pay for Amaru to go to an athletic boarding school," Deza said. "Mama been on Zeus." Deza began a shrill impression of her mother. "As much money as you got with yo cheap ass. You need to spend some real cash on yo kids. Not just cute outfits."

Tyesha knew it was more complicated. Their dad, Zeus, was an OG, almost old enough to be Jenisse's father. Tyesha knew that the girls were born before Jenisse was exclusive with Zeus. They were probably his kids, but not definitely. Maybe, without the certainty of paternity, he was willing to pay for them to look cute but not the bigger investment of boarding school.

"I think it's also connected to this trip to New York," Amaru said. "I think he's fucking with some crazy Ukrainian mob guys here. He doesn't know what his income is gonna look like for the next four years."

"Well, if he wanna save money," Deza said, "he need to fire that motherfucker Reagan."

Tyesha recalled the man in question, Zeus's bodyguard and right-hand man.

"Ever since my titties started to grow, he been sniffing around," Deza said.

"Me, too," Amaru said, looking down at her chest, which was mostly pectoral muscles. "Even without much titties."

Tyesha recalled him from her own teenage years. She didn't see him much, but he always had a leer for her, sort of secretly, outside of Zeus's view.

"Did you tell your dad?" Tyesha asked.

The girls rolled their eyes.

" 'He don't mean nothing by it,' " Deza mimicked her father. "Besides, Reagan is always a perfect gentleman in front of Zeus."

"He says he's like a son to him," Amaru said, bitterness in her voice. Tyesha waited for her to say more. She wondered if Amaru was upset because she, the butch daughter, had been passed over for such consideration. Or maybe it was because Zeus's actual sons—Deza and Amaru's older brothers—had tried to be part of their dad's business, but it landed them in jail.

"Do you think we could kill Reagan and blame it on the Ukrainian mob?" Deza asked. "If Zeus wasn't paying that motherfucker's bills, he'd have money for Amaru's school."

"Nah," Amaru said. "I don't really want his money for school. I'ma make my own way. Like Auntie Ty did."

"God bless the child that's got her own," Tyesha said.

Chapter 6

Later that morning, Tyesha rode the subway to the steakhouse where she and Thug Woofer had had their first date. Actually, their very first meeting had been a different kind of date. Marisol had sent her, Kim, and Jody to do an unofficial engagement party for Woof's brother. They had done a surprise strip show, and Tyesha was supposed to have sex with Thug Woofer. But he had been too drunk.

Tyesha had definitely gotten paid up front. She was ready to leave, but Thug Woofer was vomiting, and she couldn't seem to lay him on the bed in a position where he wasn't at risk of choking. A consultation call with Marisol had led to her getting paid overtime to study there all night instead of at her own apartment. It wouldn't do to have a dead rap star and three escorts wanted for questioning by the police. When Thug Woofer woke up in the morning, Tyesha was ready to go take her test. The rapper, however, had a hangover and the mistaken impression that she'd stayed to get the sex he'd been too drunk to offer the night before. He went from smug to belligerent when Tyesha wasn't interested. Initially, he had offered cash and refused to make an appointment with the madam. But when his attitude escalated, she had cussed him out and made a dramatic exit.

She assumed that was the end of it. A bad client. But then he had wooed her, showed up at her office with roses and good manners. He took her on a real first date and didn't press for sex at all. Then he had taken her to the Oscars. She was just starting to like him when he acted like an ass again. His words on the *Melvyn* album seemed persuasive, but was this just more Jekyll and Hyde?

As she strode from the subway to the steakhouse, she took a deep breath of summer air. Fortunately, it wasn't so humid to undo all of Deza's work. It had rained the night before, and she had an umbrella just in case. Why was she even making such a fuss? This lunch was for Deza. It didn't matter whether Woof had changed or not. All she had to do was get the demo into his hands. A good meal was just a bonus.

As she approached the restaurant, she could see him waiting out front. He held a bouquet of flowers—no, as she got closer, she could see it was an orchid.

He looked up and down the street, brightening when he saw her. He set down the orchid and pulled her into a hug.

"Tyesha Couvillier," he said.

As she pressed against him in the hug, she realized she had forgotten how cut he was. His chest and arm muscles were thick and taut—she could feel them even through his light rain jacket.

"Can I still call you Woof?" she asked.

"Call me whatever you want," he said, as they walked into the restaurant.

The waitress swept them immediately to the same table they'd had before. Woof ordered a whiskey, and Tyesha got a rum and Coke.

"This is for you," Woof said, after the waitress left. He slid the orchid across to her.

"Thank you. It's gorgeous," Tyesha said. "And I brought you a little something."

He raised his eyebrows. "Really?"

She slid the CD out of her purse and onto her lap. "See, it's really my niece you should be thanking. She's the one who got me to listen to your new work."

"Please pass on my appreciation," he said. "Would she like an autograph?"

"Not exactly," Tyesha said. "She's a rapper, and she made me promise that if I liked your album, I'd ask you to listen to her demo CD."

Tyesha handed him the disk.

As he took it, his hand lingered on hers. It was cool to the touch, the skin smooth and the palm firmly muscled.

"Okay," he said. "I promise to give it the usual demo treatment. I'll listen to thirty seconds. Then it either goes into the 'listen further' pile or the recycle pile."

"She'll be thrilled," Tyesha said.

The waitress brought their drinks and took their food order. Woof ordered steak with greens and mashed potatoes. Tyesha got the same thing she'd gotten the last time: fried chicken with yams and cornbread.

"So what about you?" he asked. "You graduated from Columbia?"

She nodded. "I'm the director of the clinic now."

"Does that mean you're also the new madam?"

Tyesha nearly choked on her drink. "Hell, no," she wheezed and sputtered. "We shut down the escort service after . . . after we got a big donation. I just run the clinic."

She continued to cough, and he stepped around the table to pat her on the back. She took a sip of water.

"You okay?" he asked.

"I'll be fine," she said, her voice still a bit hoarse.

"So I gotta ask," he said, sitting back down. "How did you get into the escort business in the first place?"

"It's not really that much of a stretch," Tyesha said. "I grew up on the South Side of Chicago, in South Shore. You grow up a broke hot girl in my neighborhood? Everybody trying to holla so you have your pick. You look around at the generation before you to see how their choices turned out. You could date young Mr. Broke But Sincere. End up with three or four kids—because when you get pregnant, you wanna keep it since you so in love—and you end up being broke along with him. Meanwhile, you don't get to go to college, so you work at some dead-end job all your life and raise your kids. Maybe you save up to go on a cruise once a year. Or you do like my older sister. You hook up with a drug dealer, and you have money, but he's always the boss. None of those roads was for me. I learned you could date brothers with money, but not get all wifed up. Just hook up and let them do something for you. Your hair, your nails, your clothes. Get you a job interview, a scholarship. Something. That's how you get out the hood and end up in New York getting your master's. Only a short step from that to cash."

"You started as an escort?"

"I guess the Sugar Daddy was the gateway drug," she said, laughing.

Woof laughed, too. "You mentioned something about that last time we were here."

Tyesha shook her head. "He started out as a boyfriend, til he said he was married. So I told him straight up, I didn't have time to be some married man's plaything for free. I had to keep up my grades, plus I was working four nights a week at some stupid-ass waitressing job to pay rent. I couldn't be wasting my precious time fucking with a relationship that wasn't going anywhere. If he wanted to date me, he needed to pay my bills so I could quit my job. I only got in the escort biz when his wife found out and he quit me."

"You thought he was gonna leave his wife?" Woof asked.

"I was never that naïve," she said. "That's why he needed to pay my bills."

"I wish I was as smart as you when I first got into the music business," he said.

"You got taken for a ride?" she asked.

"I was the naïve one," he said. "I was like, yeah! Money, girls, spotlight, and shit," he said. "I bought my mama a house. But soon I realized I hadn't looked out for my own interests. The fame gets tired fast, and then you're just running around twenty-four-seven making money for someone else. Now I know why Prince had 'slave' written on his forehead—may he rest in peace. When you and I first met, I was in a bad place with my career. It's no excuse for acting like a dick, but I've since renegotiated my contract, and I feel more like a human being. So I can act more like one."

"So who's the real Thug Woofer?" Tyesha asked. "The guy across from me or the guy on Wikipedia?"

He laughed. "Oh, Lordy. My manager pays people to make dangerous allegations on there, like I killed somebody or I have three baby mamas."

"Any of it true?"

"No," he said. "Just part of the image. No murders. No kids."

"No murders is good," Tyesha said. "But other than your condom anthem 'Roll It On' I'm surprised about the no kids part. Seems like it goes with the territory."

"I got some good financial advice when I was starting out," he said. "The biggest financial drain on a male artist is child support."

"Or marriage," Tyesha said.

"Yeah, but nobody gets married by accident," Woof said. "No matter how drunk you are . . . unless you're in Vegas"

"Speaking of marriage," Tyesha began. "How are things going with your brother's engagement?"

"Crazy." Woof shook his head. "None of the women in my family—my mama, my aunties—got married, never even really shacked up much, so they trying to live out they dreams in this wedding. They probably trying to get the girl all up in some white disco dress from the seventies."

Tyesha laughed. "If I ever get married—and I doubt I will—I'll just go to city hall."

"You don't want a big wedding?"

Tyesha shook her head. "If there's one thing you learn in my business, it's how many men cheat. The man has five lovely children and still wants to get laid every Friday night like clockwork. Gotta outsource. Half the households in America oughta have a sex worker on the goddamn holiday card. Just Photoshop the girl on the stripper pole into the family vacation shot from Disneyland."

"That's so cynical," Woof said.

"No it's not," Tyesha said. "I just wish people would be honest. In most marriages, if it's not strippers or escorts, it's porn for sure. I'm just saying, if marriage in America is supposed to be a sacred covenant between one man and one woman, then how come it's really between mister, misses, and a chesty redhead named Bambi?"

"You don't think I shoulda hired y'all for my brother's party?" Woof asked.

"I think his fiancée can make a choice to see reality or live in denial. She knows her man is on the road with you, and she knows how you get down," Tyesha said. "Speaking of the road, you traveled anyplace interesting lately? I heard you were in Dubai . . ."

Suddenly, he came around the table and knelt beside her.

"Tyesha, I can't small talk with you. I got your niece's demo, but I'm not gonna make it through this meal if I don't know whether you're just here to give me that CD. I swear I'll listen to it either way, but you gotta let me know. Do I still have a chance after fucking up twice?"

Tyesha wasn't expecting so much so fast. She cleared her throat. "I think that depends on you," she said. "You're gonna need to show me that you can be the same person for more than one date. This here,"—she put up her hand and swirled her wrist around to indicate him—"this guy, this nice guy needs to be the guy I deal with. I don't need flowers every time I see you, but I need some basic standards. Like no pressuring me for sex. Ever."

"I gotta ask," he said. "Are you still—I mean, is your job just in the office or do you sometimes—?"

"No," she said. "But it shouldn't matter whether I'm still doing sex work or not. No pressure ever."

"No pressure," he said.

"I need to know . . ." Tyesha searched for the words. ". . . that you're not just being nice because you want to get something. That you really respect me. That you have respect for women in general. I can't really fuck with you if you're still making music like your early stuff."

"I know," he said. "I mean, I didn't always have respect. Obviously. But I took the Rapper Respect Pledge. And I been learning some lessons about changing how I see women."

"Well, that's what I learned," Tyesha said. "From dating you. I thought you could treat other women like shit in public but still be good to me. Because I was special or something. But it didn't work that way."

"If you give me a chance," he said, "I can show you that I've changed. Not only the lyrics that I rap, but how I treat my woman."

The waitress came over with their plates, and he walked back over to his seat.

The moment the plate of fried chicken landed in front of Tyesha, she dug in. She realized she hadn't eaten all day.

"So I was seeing this therapist," he said between bites.

Tyesha froze, a bite of food nearly entering her mouth.

"Boy, you really tryna make me choke to death today." She laughed.

"It wasn't like I went in search of therapy," he said. "But that last date we went on, and I was acting like—"

"Like it was my duty to have sex with you because I was a sex worker," she added.

He cringed. "Yep, that night. So after you walked away from me, I got mad. I got drunk and threw a chair through a plate-glass window at my recording label's office."

"Wow," Tyesha said.

"They sent me to this lady for anger management," he said.

"She gave you tips on how to calm yourself?" Tyesha asked.

"Actually the opposite," he said. "She was always trying to provoke me. Get the anger going. She called me a coward."

"Really?"

"'Punk-ass bitch' was how she put it," Woof said. "I was so mad that I picked up my chair and threw it through her window."

"Oh, shit," Tyesha said. "Did she call the cops?"

"Nah," Woof said. "It was special glass. The chair bounced off and fell on the floor of the office. Then she just sat there behind her desk and looked at me. 'Well, that didn't work, did it?' she said."

"Damn," Tyesha said. "She's a badass. I might need her info to refer a few clients to her."

"Probably out of your price range," Woof said. "She mostly works with famous people. They call her 'The Narcissist Whisperer.'"

"I'm surprised she hasn't moved her practice to DC," Tyesha said. "But in this city, I bet her calendar is full."

"So, I was standing there in her office," Woof said, "my whole body shaking with rage. And she just had this really matter-of-fact voice. 'So this is where you break the window, and I call for help and your anger gets to be the problem. But your anger isn't the problem. It's your shame and fear about showing yourself to the real world. And you cover them up with the anger. That's what you need to deal with.'"

"Shit, Woof."

"She handed me the tissue before I even realized I was crying," he said. "I started working on *Melvyn* that night. I wrote the whole thing in forty-eight hours."

"Therapy," Tyesha said. "Not what I expected."

"I didn't mean to lay this all on you, but I know you have counselors and stuff at your job, so I didn't think you would judge. And I wanted you to know that the change you see in me is real. Not some bullshit good behavior."

Tyesha smiled. "Duly noted." She reached out and squeezed his hand.

He smiled back, and for the next fifteen minutes, they ate in a friendly silence. She sopped up the last of the gravy with a biscuit.

"I won't judge if you lick the plate," he said.

She laughed. "I didn't realize I was so hungry."

"You want dessert?"

"Definitely," she said.

They got a chocolate bourbon layer cake and a pecan pie à la mode.

The cake arrived, and Tyesha picked up her spoon.

"Wait," Woof said. "Allow me."

He dipped the spoon in the tip of the chocolate frosting and placed it on her tongue.

Tyesha pressed the morsel slowly against the roof of her mouth and let the bitter chocolate, rich butter, and sugar unfold in her taste buds.

"Oh my god, that's so good," she said.

He took the other spoon, but she caught his hand.

"My turn," she said. "Close your eyes."

He did so, and she took a spoonful of the cake and dipped it silently in his whiskey.

"Open your mouth," she said.

As his full lips parted, she could barely resist the urge to lean over the table and kiss him, but instead, she drizzled the whiskey off the chocolate onto his tongue. Then, as his tongue reached out for the bite, she slid it into his mouth.

His eyes flew open in delighted surprise.

"Damn," he said, his eyes closing again. "That's so good with the whiskey."

They smiled at each other and finished the cake.

"I think I'm getting a little buzzed from the bourbon," Tyesha said.

"Can I drive you home?" he asked.

"Nope," she said. "Taking it slow, remember?"

"Okay, then when can I see you again?"

"I'm swamped at work," she said. "And my one free night, I gotta go to my niece's basketball game."

"Your niece is a rapper and a ballplayer?"

"My other niece," Tyesha said.

"Take me with you," he said.

Tyesha shook her head. "You're the number one rapper in the U.S. I can't just take you to a high school auditorium. Besides, it's her big game. I can't let her get upstaged."

"I'll go in disguise."

"That's crazy," she said.

"For real, Tyesha," he said, a begging note in his voice. "I wanna spend more time with you. I wanna meet your family. I'll use an alias."

"Melvyn?"

"I think I blew my cover on that one already."

"I saw you talk about it on the *Ellen* show, by the way."

"Why didn't you call then?"

"I . . . wasn't ready," she said.

"You ready now?"

"I'm ready to see if you can fool an auditorium full of teenagers. What's your new alias?"

"Clarence."

"And how are you gonna be disguised?"

"Will you disguise me? We can meet up ahead of time, and I'll wear whatever you say."

"Anything?"

"Anything," he said. "With just one rule. It's got to be something you find sexy. So if you like dudes in tiaras and sequined ball gowns with a train behind them, count me in. But if not . . ."

"Okay," she said. "Deal."

The following night, all the dancers onstage at the One-Eyed King had on thongs that said:

I

♥

U

This was written on the triangle at the top of the back, with "nion" in smaller letters disappearing down the crack of their ass.

I

♥

U

n

i

o

n

The girls strutted around with their secret and were particularly enjoying the night, shaking their asses in the clients' faces extra vigorously. They were jubilant. The next day was the press conference where they would officially announce that they were forming a union.

After the place closed, Lily and three of her girls were on their way out to get a cab. The street was deserted that late, but they were always careful to leave in packs. The four of them had purses and backpacks filled with high heels and sweaty clothes that needed washing.

They began walking toward the relative light and bustle of the avenue a block down the street when a pair of Ukrainian mob thugs stepped out of the shadows.

"You think you won because you got your job back?" one of them asked, pushing aside his jacket so they could see his gun. "You never win, understand? Nigger and spic bitches like you never win. You shake your big ass for us and stop making trouble. Take what we give you. You're lucky to have that. Lucky to be alive. So get the fuck out of here, and count your blessings."

Lily and her girls turned and ran. Lily's heart was in her throat. Would he shoot them in the back? They rounded the corner onto the bright, busy avenue, and they didn't hear any running footsteps behind them. Still, they hustled into a pair of cabs. Guys like that, big guys with guns, they didn't have to run. They knew where she worked, and they had her personnel file, so they knew where she lived.

At nine the next morning, Lily, Marisol, and Tyesha were in Tyesha's office.

"Those motherfuckers," Marisol said. "I hope you're not gonna let them intimidate you."

Lily sucked her teeth. "Those badjohns been trying to

scare the shit out of me from day one because I've been speaking my mind and because I'm black. Fuck them."

"Good," Marisol said. "So I'll do the main speech today, but I'm gonna call on you to read the remarks we prepared, okay?"

"No problem," Lily said.

A sharp knock on the door, and then Serena walked in.

"Marisol," Serena said, "I have a long distance call from Cuba for you. It's Cristina. She says she's been trying your cell."

"Take it at my desk," Tyesha said. It seemed strange to see Marisol back at the desk of what had originally been Marisol's office. "Do you want privacy?" Tyesha asked.

Marisol shook her head and picked up the phone, while reaching for Tyesha's hand.

Their fingers gripped tightly as Marisol listened for a moment.

"Who's Cristina?" Lily whispered to Tyesha.

"Marisol's little sister," Tyesha said. "Their mother died, and Marisol practically raised her. She lives in Cuba now, and she's pregnant."

Lily nodded.

Marisol's face hardened as she said something in rapid Spanish and hung up.

"Is everything okay?" Tyesha asked.

"There's a complication with Cristina's pregnancy," Marisol said. "It's probably fine, but . . ."

"But you need to be there," Tyesha said. "That's your baby sister. Having her first baby. You need to go."

"Are you sure?" Marisol said.

"That girl is your heart," Tyesha said. "We got plenty of hands on deck. And the speech is already written, right?"

"Oh, thank you," Marisol said. She gave Tyesha a quick, tight hug before grabbing her purse. "I'll keep you updated about Cristina. And you need to keep me posted about the press conference."

"Don't think about it for one more second," Tyesha said. "We got this."

Marisol ran out of the door.

"You seem so calm," Lily said. "Considering you're gonna have to give the speech. And you panicked last time."

"Oh, there's no way I'm giving the speech," Tyesha said. "That union organizer chick can do it."

"The domestic workers' union organizer who's been mentoring me?" Lily asked. "She's fabulous."

"Unfortunately, no," Tyesha said. "We got another organizer from a theatrical union. Y'all are dancers, too. No worries."

Four hours later, Tyesha stood in the community room with a familiar knot in her stomach. Once again, the room was set up with a podium for a press conference. This time, the seats were all filled. They had also taken the precaution of adjusting the settings on the fire and smoke alarms. They would alert security, but not ring with a piercing sound unless security had checked it out and identified a real threat.

Drew, the *Village Voice* reporter, approached Tyesha.

"Is it true the girls are going to announce the union today?"

"You'll need to wait til the press conference like everyone else," she said.

"Oh, come on," he said. "I gave you the viral video that even made this whole media campaign possible. Can't you give me the scoop? Even if I can just tweet it out before anyone else? Just a five-minute head start?"

He lifted his phone to take her picture. She caught his arm to lower the phone.

"Okay, but no photo," she said. His skin felt warm to her touch; she could feel the pulse in his wrist.

THE BOSS / 99

He switched the phone into recorder mode and put it in front of her mouth.

"Sex work is work," Tyesha said. "And workers deserve justice. But like most workers, they don't get it unless they fight for it. That's what unions are for. Exotic dancers are no different."

"Nice!" he said. "Can I tweet that?"

"Wait three minutes," Tyesha said.

"So, when can I do a full-on interview with you and ask all about your connection to the Couvillier legacy in Chicago? I've already got the historical image for the article."

He flipped through his phone and pulled up a photograph of her aunt standing in front of the Urban Peace Accord Center in Chicago.

Suddenly, Tyesha felt foggy, slightly disembodied.

Kim grabbed her arm and pulled her away to the side of the room.

"I'll email you to set up the interview," Drew called after her.

But Tyesha couldn't hear him from the ringing in her ears. A few minutes later, she heard Kim's voice.

"Tyesha, are you listening to a damn thing I'm saying?" Kim asked.

"Yeah, sure." Tyesha blinked and turned to focus on her friend's words. Kim stood beside Jody, off to the side of the podium.

"There's been a mix-up," Kim said. "The woman from the theatrical union is stuck in Denver. Her plane had mechanical problems."

"Then who did I just meet?" Tyesha asked. She had a vague recollection of shaking a woman's hand and confirming that she was ready to make the speech. She was a white woman in her fifties. She had an asymmetrical gray haircut, a dress made of Van Gogh's night sky fabric, and character shoes.

"That's what I'm trying to tell you," Kim said. "This is not the union organizer. This is a friend of hers who's a former theatrical union member."

"Okay," Tyesha said. "Close enough."

"Absolutely not," Kim said.

"What's wrong with her?" Tyesha asked.

"First of all, she's like a hundred years old," Kim said.

"It's not about age," Jody insisted. "Eva might be even older than her, but Eva gets it."

"She referred to Lily as a striptease dancer," Kim said. "She talked about friends of hers who used to do burlesque in the seventies."

"Okay, so she's a little out of date," Tyesha said. "But the connection came through Marisol."

"No," Jody said. "If Marisol was here, she'd have figured out right away that she's not the one. Did she agree to do the speech Marisol wrote? I have an extra copy if she needs it."

Tyesha waved off their concerns. "She took it, and she said she said she would use it as a guide."

"You need to take control of this," Kim said. "Marisol worked on that speech all last night. She knows just what to say."

"Well, Marisol isn't here, is she?" Tyesha said. "And I'm not good at giving speeches, so we're stuck with this old school chick, and I don't want to hear any more about it."

Tyesha stalked across the room to Eva. She felt her phone buzz in her blazer pocket. She pulled it out and there was an alert from Drew: **BREAKING: 1-Eyed King strippers unionize. "Sex work is work. Workers deserve justice. Exotic dancers no diff." @TyeshaCouvillier @Vega_Clinic**

She turned off her phone and approached Eva. "It's time to start," she said. "Give the welcome and introduce the woman from the union."

"Are you sure—?"

"Eva, will you please just get this fucking press conference started?"

Eva pursed her lips. "I do so under protest," she murmured to Tyesha, then turned to the crowd.

"Welcome, everyone, to the Maria de la Vega health clinic. My name is Dr. Eva Feldman, and I'm the clinical director here. As you all know, some unfair labor practices have been affecting the workers of the One-Eyed King franchise." She introduced the woman from the union.

The woman smiled at the crowd and ignored the paper on the podium.

"Young girls come to New York every day," she began. "With a dream in their heart and a few dollars in their pocket. They dream of Broadway stages and end up on poles. And there are men who prey on these girls' dreams."

"Thank you," Eva said, and swooped the union woman away from the podium before she even knew what was happening.

Jody pressed the speech into Tyesha's hand and stepped up to the mic. "I'm one of the young women who came to New York with other dreams and then ended up stripping. But it's a job like any other, and it's fine as long as the working conditions are reasonable. But sometimes management takes advantage of the fact that this labor force doesn't always know our rights. Here to tell us more about it . . ." Jody turned to Tyesha.

Tyesha pressed the speech to Kim's chest and pushed her forward.

Jody's eyebrows went up. "Here to tell us more about it is Kim Chŏng," Jody said.

Kim stepped up to the podium, and Jody had to lower the mic nearly a foot.

Kim smoothed out the crumpled paper and blinked at it. "I grew up in this neighborhood. Or one a lot like it. In Queens. And I lived with my immigrant single mom. Until she got deported. Anyway in my time as the . . . as . . . someone who volunteers in this clinic, I've seen girls come through who have been mistreated in every conceivable way. Sometimes by fathers, stepfathers, and uncles. Sometimes by boyfriends and husbands. Other times by pimps and clients. And a lot of times by police and other authorities. But the one thing that never changes: women and men who work in the sex industries have a right to health, safety, and livable working conditions. This should be true for these women and men, regardless of the work they choose to do in these industries. Let me be very clear, anyone who is being forced to sell sex for someone else's benefit isn't a sex worker, she or he is a victim of sexual trafficking. That is a crime, and those exploiters should be punished. Some work in these industries includes exchanging sex between consenting adults, and we believe that should be decriminalized. But I am particularly outraged that this most recent outrageous mistreatment of sex workers comes not from a shadowy pimp or an abusive partner, but a fully legal, licensed business in the state of New York. And these workers have a right to organize themselves to fight this mistreatment, and so it is my great honor to announce that the Five Borough Exotic Dancer's Alliance has been formed, and has begun its union drive."

The supporters in the room burst into applause.

Eva stepped up to the podium. "We won't be taking questions, but there are press releases on the table, which include this statement and some background information. Thank you for coming today."

Half an hour later, the five of them were in Eva's office: Tyesha, Kim, Jody, Eva, and Lily.

"What the fuck?" Kim fumed at Jody. "Why'd you pull me up front? You could have given the speech yourself."

"Three white women talking?" Jody said. "I don't think so. This is a movement being led by women of color. I never even danced at the One-Eyed King."

"What made you think that woman would understand sex work issues just because she happened to be in a theatrical union thirty years ago?" Kim asked Tyesha.

"What the fuck," Jody said. "It was some cliché sob story like Gypsy Rose Lee meets Annie. I was ready for a bunch of tweens to come out and start a 'Hard Knock Life' dance number any minute."

Lily sucked her teeth. "You needed to just read the damn speech, Tyesha. Or next time let me do it."

"You're hired," Tyesha said, her jaw tight. "And now that the press has finally left, I need to get back to running this clinic. Which is my actual job, not giving speeches."

She glared at the rest of the women, daring them to say anything more.

None of them spoke as she stalked out of the room.

Later that afternoon, Tyesha had Woof meet her at a costume store in the Village.

It was a bright but cloudy day, not too warm and not too humid, so she walked from the clinic on the Lower East Side. It felt good to let her legs stretch out for the dozens of blocks, not just the usual rush-sit-rush of her days in the office.

Along the way, she ran into a man with an ice cream cart, and she bought a mango Popsicle. "*Gracias, bella,*" he said, handing her the change.

She strode up to the Village, feeling the warm air on her skin and the cool mango juice melting in her mouth. She could feel the stress of the conference melting away, as well.

As she came around the corner to where she was meeting Thug Woofer, she saw him standing outside the store. He had on a hoodie and dark glasses. In spite of his particularly camouflaged appearance, she could tell it was him from the silhouette of his body. The upright posture, broad shoulders, and long legs. He had headphones on. She couldn't see them, but the slight bounce of his head indicated music.

Sure enough, as she got closer, she saw a silver cord snaking from either side of his head to the back pocket of his jeans. His hands were in the front pocket of his hoodie. As she got closer, she could see his toe tapping in a staccato beat that didn't blend with the music.

She realized it was more of a tic than a movement with the beat.

He's nervous, she realized. Nervous to meet me. Looking at her watch, she realized she was three minutes late. The stop for the Popsicle had delayed her.

"Woof!" she called, waving.

He turned, and his cool face split into a grin.

"Hey," she said, and let him pull her into a hug.

"You smell good," he said. "Sweet. Like fruit punch or something."

"I had a mango Popsicle," she said. Impulsively, she leaned forward and kissed his cheek, leaving the cool print of her lips.

"You seem to have had the aforementioned Popsicle very recently," he said. "Either that, or you're part of the undead."

She laughed. "Very much alive," she said. "Now let's go shopping."

First she took him to a shoe store.

"Cowboy boots?" he asked as the salesclerk brought several tall boxes. "Seriously? You know I'm from the Southeast, right?"

"The whole point is that you don't get recognized," she said.

"But it's supposed to be stuff you find sexy," he said. "You like cowboy boots?" He lifted a black-and-turquoise snakeskin pair and held them aloft.

She looked him up and down. "I like them on the right brother."

"Okay, then," he said, trying them on. "Yee haw."

Tyesha shook her head. "This isn't the look."

They compromised on a pair of black work boots.

"Unlike the cowboy boots, I might actually wear these again," he said as Tyesha led him into a wig store.

He picked one in curly auburn with bangs. "Uh-oh," he said. "You're not gonna dress me up as Rick James, are you?"

"No way," she said, picking up a shorter black curly wig. "Ice Cube, circa 1991?"

He laughed so suddenly that he almost snorted. "Excuse me while I beg the lord to forgive me for whatever I've done and make sure you don't have me going out in a Jheri curl."

"No curl," she said.

"An Al Sharpton press?" he asked, picking up a salt-and-pepper shoulder-length wig.

"Nope," she said, walking down an aisle that had novelty wigs.

He passed a row of Technicolor bobs. "Blue might bring out my eyes," he suggested.

"Your eyes are brown," she said, laughing.

"So are yours," he said.

"Here it is!" Tyesha reached for a dark brown wig.

"Dreadlocks?" Woof asked. "Isn't it a bit classic Lil Wayne?"

"Don't worry," Tyesha said. "Nobody would ever mistake you for him."

"I hope not," Woof said, trying the wig on over his sleek low fade.

"Damn," he said. "I really do look like someone else."

"And not Lil Wayne," Tyesha said.

"You find long hair sexy?" he asked. "I might have to grow mine."

Tyesha shrugged. "The hair thing is mostly for disguise. Especially the facial hair."

She walked him to the front counter, where he tried on a full beard and mustache.

"Damn," he said. "If it was white hair, I'd be Santa Claus."

"But take off the shades," Tyesha said.

For the first time since they'd met that day, he took off his sunglasses.

"How does he look?" Tyesha asked the young woman at the counter. She was black or maybe Afro-Latina, with a straight press.

"Looks good," the girl said. "You wanna get both?"

"Absolutely," Tyesha said.

Woof handed the girl his card.

"Melvyn Johnson!" she shrieked. "Oh my god, it's Thug Woofer! Can we get a picture with you?"

"I think the disguise is gonna work," Tyesha murmured dryly.

Next, she took him to a trendy teen store and had him try on a Count Chocula T-shirt.

"Is this a girls' store?" he asked.

"Definitely," Tyesha said. "But the XL should fit you. It'll be a little bit Incredible Hulk in the shoulders, but in a good way."

He stepped out of the dressing room. "So, what do you think?"

"I like," Tyesha said. "It's perfect how your nipple is right under the Count's eye."

He put his hand over his chest. "I'm not used to the peek-a-boo nipple action. Basically, I'm used to my clothes being either on or off."

"Well, Clarence feels differently, and so do I," Tyesha said.

"You're saying you think I look hot?" Woof asked.

"Not yet," she said. "But you will as soon as we get you in some different pants."

At a trendy unisex store nearby, she found what she was looking for.

"Magenta?" he asked. "You want me in magenta pants?"

"And these are still a little loose," she said. "Can you try them on in a size smaller?"

When he came out of the dressing room, he smiled ruefully at her. "I don't think any fabric has touched this part of my ass since I was in diapers."

"As I recall, you're definitely a saggy boxer kind of guy."

"How you gonna just refer to information you learned in a professional capacity?"

"The tragic vision of that fine ass going to waste in saggy boxers is an abomination I can't unsee," she said, laughing.

"Well, this is certainly making up for it. I might need to buy some briefs to go with these jeans. If not a thong."

"Thong sounds good," Tyesha said.

"I'm not buying a thong until we're on much closer terms," he said. "And I don't mean that as pressure, just incentive."

He bought the jeans, and they stepped out onto the street. "Okay, so I've got pants, shoes, and a shirt. Is my disguise complete?"

Tyesha shook her head. "The jeans aren't right."

"Thank god you've come to your senses, woman," he said.

She took him by the hand and led him down the street to a small tailor shop.

"You want me to wear a plaid blazer?" he asked.

"No," Tyesha said, picking up another garment. "Try this."

"A skirt? Seriously?" Thug Woofer asked, incredulous.

"First of all, it's a kilt," Tyesha said. "Second of all, it's sexy just the same way a skirt is on a woman. Easy access.

Third of all, it'll keep people from recognizing you because it draws attention downward. And you have nice legs."

"Thanks," he said. "I never thought I'd say this, but I miss the tight magenta jeans."

"Oh, no," Tyesha said. "This is the one."

Chapter 7

The next evening, Tyesha brought her date to Amaru's basketball game. "Clarence," in the dreadlock wig, the beard, the Count Chocula T-shirt, the work boots and the kilt. She also put her fake glasses on him.

The game was in a high school auditorium in Queens. It reminded Tyesha of her own high school, with frosted windows, fold-down bleachers, and the uncontainable energy of hundreds of teenagers.

Tyesha got a text from Deza that they would be on the far wall on the right-hand side. She and Woof made their way through the crowd of loud, brown faces.

Deza saw Tyesha and waved, then her face fell when she saw her date.

Tyesha introduced them.

"Pleased to meet you," Deza said, and pulled Tyesha aside. "Who is this clown? I thought you were seeing Thug Woofer again."

"I told you," Tyesha said. "We went out and I gave him your CD."

"But you're gonna see him again, right?"

"Relax," Tyesha said. "It's only been a few days. It's not like we locked anything down."

"I can't believe you're out with some fool in a skirt when

you could be out with Thug Woofer," Deza said. "Auntie, you crazy."

Tyesha smiled. "I'm gonna get back to Clarence, okay? Try not to be rude."

"So, that's Deza?" Woof said, when Tyesha returned.

"You passed the litmus test," Tyesha said. "She's your biggest fan, and even she didn't recognize you."

"It's the skirt," Woof said.

"It's a kilt," Tyesha said.

"She called it a skirt, didn't she?"

"She might have," Tyesha said.

"Unfortunately," Woof said, "skirt or no skirt, you'll have to tell my biggest fan that her album didn't make the cut. Maybe in the future she'll be ready."

Tyesha sighed. "I told that girl—" She took Woof's hand. "Listen, 'Clarence,' I knew the first thirty seconds weren't gonna blow you away. I told her to put her strongest stuff first, but she's hardheaded. Just listen to track four. Please. Whenever you get a chance. Just that one track. At least hear what she can do at her best."

"I got a rule," Woof said. "One listen only. I been drilling that into aspiring emcees for over a decade. Do you know how many mad mediocre rappers would be knocking on my door if it ever got out that I gave someone a do-over?"

"First of all, it won't get out," Tyesha promised. "I won't even tell her you made a first pass. And second of all, somebody here broke her rules—not once but twice—for you."

"Okay, fine," Woof said. "I'll put it in the bottom of my listen pile. You got fast-tracked before, but the second chance goes to the back of the line. I should get to it by this time next year."

"Think of it this way," Tyesha said. "As long as Deza stands a chance, she'll push me to keep dating you. It's like an insurance policy."

"That's fucked up," Woof said. "You'd keep dating me just so I'd listen to her demo?"

"No," Tyesha said. "I'd keep dating you because I like you. I'm just saying she's on Team Woof. She even got mad at me for going out with Clarence instead of you."

Woof laughed out loud. "I always said that when you're the best, you're your own biggest competition." He stretched out an arm and put it around her.

"Whatever, Clarence," Tyesha said, but she leaned back against his arm, even as Deza walked back to her seat and glared at them.

Then they just watched the game.

Amaru was great. She scored forty points, including several three-pointers. She didn't dunk, but had a vicious lay-up. She was the don't-give-a-fuck kind of player, who hurled herself after the ball as an offensive player and into the way of it on defense.

Halfway through the game, Jenisse finally made it.

"Mama, where you been?" Deza asked.

"Your daddy was supposed to bring me, but we got into a fight," Jenisse said. "I was waiting for a taxi, then traffic was bad."

"He's not coming at all?"

"I'm here," Jenisse snapped. "What? That ain't good enough. His fucking majesty needs to come or it don't count."

"That's not what I meant," Deza said, and sat back, folding her arms.

As Deza no longer blocked Tyesha's view of her sister, Tyesha leaned forward. "Hey Jenisse. This is my friend Clarence."

Jenisse looked "Clarence" up and down.

"Of course it is," she said. Jenisse folded her arms across her chest and leaned back in her seat.

"And now you know why I moved to New York," Tyesha murmured.

* * *

Fortunately, Amaru never lost focus. Toward the end of the game, she was fouled while shooting a basket and got a pair of penalty shots.

She stood at the free throw line, dribbling with her eyes closed. Tyesha could see her chest rise as she breathed in and then shot the ball effortlessly into the hoop. Swoosh. Both times.

It had been ages since Tyesha had been on a date like this. Comfortable with the guy and around her family? Maybe not since high school. Maybe never.

After the game, Amaru came running up, flushed and sweaty.

"Auntie Ty, you came!"

"Of course," she said, and introduced Clarence.

Amaru shook his hand absently. "I want y'all to meet my mentor, Sheena Davenport."

"From the WNBA?" Tyesha said. "Damn."

Sheena walked up to them, over six feet and powerfully built. She grinned at Tyesha with a gorgeous, full-lipped grin. Even though she was tall and strong, she wasn't exactly butch. She had on eye makeup and a slick gloss on her lips. Her hair was swept back from her face in long, tiny dreadlocks.

"So you're the auntie that Amaru's always talking about," Sheena said, taking Tyesha's hand and hanging on to it. "I didn't expect somebody so young and hot. Although I should have known, sexy as they mama is. How you doing, Jenisse?"

"Fine, thank you," Jenisse said. "You got my daughter a scholarship yet?"

Sheena laughed. "Almost," she said. "I'm about to introduce Amaru to some coaches from Syracuse and Boston College."

"So," Sheena said, turning back to Tyesha, "Amaru tells me you're in New York now. But if you're ever back home to Chicago, look me up."

She handed Tyesha her card, and walked off with Amaru.

"Damn, baby," Woof murmured. "You so fine, even the women trying to holla."

"Sorry I didn't introduce you," Tyesha said. "I didn't expect to meet Amaru's mentor tonight."

"I don't know," Woof said with a chuckle. "You sure you ain't gay at all? You seemed pretty mesmerized. That sister had serious game."

"I thought you were your only competition," Tyesha said.

Woof laughed. "If I call you next week and they tell me you took an unexpected trip to Chicago, I'll know what happened."

Tyesha laughed. "I don't think so," she said. "Come on, Clarence. Let's get out of here."

An hour later, they were sitting on Tyesha's turquoise couch. The orchid sat on the coffee table, between two glasses of wine.

"Your niece can really play some ball," he said.

"I'm so proud of her," Tyesha said.

"And your sister can really throw some shade."

"Tell me about it."

"Y'all don't really favor each other at all."

"That's because we have different fathers," Tyesha said. "I met her dad once. He's really light-skinned and slim. I never met mine."

"But your two nieces look so much alike," Woof said. "They gotta have the same dad."

"That's the official story," Tyesha said, "but you never know in my family. For years, my mama told me I had the same dad as Jenisse. Then she acted like she'd never said it. And because she got saved by Jesus, she said all that was behind her and not to talk about it."

Woof shook his head. "Sounds like some of my aunties," he said. "That's what I like about you, Tyesha. You're up here in this big city, doing your badass thing, but underneath it all, you're just a country girl from Chicago."

"Country?" Tyesha said. "I'm a city girl."

"But where was your mama born?" he asked.

"Chicago," Tyesha said.

"And your grandmamma?"

Tyesha rolled her eyes. "Mississippi, but she spent her whole adult life in Chicago. Not that it matters."

"It does matter," he said. "You got the South on you like only folks from Chicago can," he said. "Like a little piece of it was sealed up in a time capsule from 1952 or something. And now you wear it like perfume."

"What does it smell like?" Tyesha asked. "Mules and burlap?"

"No," Woof said. "Like red dirt and honey. I never been able to resist it on you."

He leaned in to kiss her. This time she could smell the lotion on his skin, feel the tickle of stubble on his lip. He wrapped his arms around her and she felt the strength of his hands, the tightness of the embrace.

She could feel herself getting heated. She pressed against him all the more insistently.

"Tyesha," he said, "I want you to know I really care about you."

"I know," she said, running her hands up and down the ridges of his back and arms.

"I really am sorry I was such a dick back when we were dating before," he added.

"Apology accepted," she said. "Moving on." She began to unbutton her blouse.

"Hold up," he said, and closed his eyes. He was breathing hard, but slowly.

"What the hell?" she asked.

"I just needed a minute to meditate," he said.

"Now?" she asked.

"Yeah," he said. "I mean, do I want to have sex right now? Yes, definitely. But I need a minute." He straightened up on the couch and put both feet on the floor. He rested his hands in his lap and took a few deep breaths.

Tyesha couldn't believe it.

Eyes still closed, he said, "I don't want to fuck this up. There's too many conversations we haven't had yet."

"Like what?" she asked. "Birth control? Condoms? I got it covered."

"No," he said, opening his eyes. "Like are we exclusive? Other than Clarence, I mean. Because I don't want you to be with anyone else, once we're together."

She was taken aback. "Woof, we just started—"

He put a finger to her lips. "I don't expect that from you right now," he said. "Which is why we can't do this yet." He buttoned each of the buttons back on her blouse.

As his fingers grazed her breasts, she could barely breathe.

"So we're just dating," he said. "Til you really trust me. And if it takes a hundred dates, I'm in. For real."

"A hundred dates?" she asked.

"Speaking of dates," he said. "Do you wanna be my date to Nashonna's album release party?"

"Are you kidding me?" she asked. "Nashonna? Yes!"

"Good," he said. "One date down, ninety-nine to go. And now, if you'll excuse me, I need to get out of here and try to meditate some tranquility and non-attachment into my dick."

That night, Tyesha dreamed she was back at a basketball game at her high school, holding hands with Thug Woofer. At least, at the beginning of the dream, it was Woof. Later, she looked up from the game and found herself holding hands with Kyle, the first boy she'd ever kissed.

Tyesha woke up disoriented, feeling a slight trace of the excitement and anxiety that marked her last year of middle school.

At age fourteen, Tyesha had never had a boy's tongue in her mouth before. It was like eating caramel, but you didn't chew or swallow, and it was a different kind of sweet. Kyle. She couldn't remember his last name—or if she'd ever known it—but she recalled his hands, his tongue. Warm. All of him was warm, and a hard spot pressed against her panties through his jeans and his underwear and her jeans and her underwear. She could feel the outline of him, and it made her a little nervous but also curious and excited.

Her aunt Lucille worked at her middle school, so she had a chaperone who drove her to and from school, and the boys didn't want to get on the wrong side of Ms. Couvillier. Also, Tyesha knew there were dangers. She had seen her friend Shanique get in big trouble earlier that year, but that was with an older guy. Kyle was different. He was a high school sophomore, so he was only two grades older. He lived in her building, and flirted with her in the hallway. He passed notes to her with cheesy lines.

Girl, I can't hardly look straight at you. Your beauty is like staring at the sun—blinding.

That day, her mama was still at work, and Aunt Lu had been called to handle a crisis at school. The moment her aunt walked out of the building, there was a knock on the apartment door. Kyle.

"Tyesha," he said. "Jewel of South Shore. Has God smiled on me to give me a moment alone with you?" Fifteen minutes of sweet talk and handholding. Another quarter hour of kissing. He began to run his hands over her breasts, sliding down the fabric of her T-shirt. Then under the shirt, then unhooking her bra, then sliding off her jeans, but promising to keep her panties on. Then an insistent stroking of the soft cotton against her crotch. He had just begun to slide them down. Tyesha had her eyes closed, rolled back in her head with the ecstasy of it, when the apartment door opened.

She opened her eyes to see his underwear and jeans down

around his ankles, his erect penis standing at attention for a moment, before her aunt strode in, and he pulled one of her mother's embroidered couch pillows over himself. Tyesha blinked, wide-eyed, first at the size of his penis, then at the unexpected "Jesus Is Lord" message that quickly supplanted it.

"Don't be shy *now*, Kyle," Lucille Couvillier said plainly. "You ain't got nothing I ain't seen before. Tyesha, pull yourself together. We have an errand to run."

As the blood began to rush to her face, Kyle pulled his pants up and left without a good-bye. Tyesha was too dark for her aunt to really see her blush, but she wasn't looking at her niece. She was halfway to the door, hitching her purse up onto her shoulder and pulling out her car keys.

Shamefaced, Tyesha followed her aunt down the three flights of stairs. When they walked out of the building, she saw Jenisse. Her sister was sitting on a broken bench with her best friend from high school. Amaru was still in Jenisse's belly. Aunt Lucille walked over and scooped a four-year-old Deza up into a hug, and the girl wriggled out of her arms and went back to playing tag with the best friend's son. The two kids chased each other back and forth on the treeless concrete around the bench.

"So was it true, Aunt Lu?" Jenisse asked. "Did Tyesha have some company over to the apartment?" She sucked her teeth. "Folks wanna act like I'm the only Couvillier who's fast."

"Jenisse," Aunt Lucille said. "I'm glad you called me. But it leaves a bad taste in my mouth that you seem more interested in getting your sister in trouble with me than keeping her out of trouble with that boy."

Jenisse didn't have a retort for that. Tyesha kept her head down and let Aunt Lu take her by the arm and lead her to the car. Several young people greeted them on the way down the block.

Lucille Couvillier drove a Pontiac. It was from the 1980s,

and was so dirty that someone had written "niggas betta wash me" in the film of dirt. With a swipe of her hand, Aunt Lucille had wiped off the "niggas betta" and left the rest. Once inside, she leaned over and unlocked Tyesha's door.

Once she had pulled away from the curb, Aunt Lucille said without preamble. "I'm taking you to Planned Parenthood."

"I'm sorry, Aunt Lu," Tyesha began.

"Nothing to be sorry for," came her aunt's unexpected reply. "Boys have sweet talk. Warm hands. Tasty kisses. You think I haven't seen Kyle passing you little notes?"

Tyesha was mortified. She thought she had been so discreet.

"What kind of birth control were you planning on using?" her aunt asked.

Tyesha shook her head. "I didn't—I wasn't expecting—"

"Are you already sexually active, or was this going to be the first time?" Aunt Lucille asked.

With that, Tyesha burst out crying. Maybe it was going to be, or would have been. In the moment, it had felt so good, exciting, a delicious secret. But was he gonna stick it in her? He seemed so ready, and he hadn't said a word about it. She sobbed, filled with a jumble of feelings: disappointment in Kyle, shame, and the queasy, half-terrified, half-grateful feeling that she'd avoided something awful.

By the time they parked near Planned Parenthood, the tears had subsided, and her aunt handed her a tissue.

"I know you think me and your mama are the same," Aunt Lucille said. "Both of us watching you like a hawk, making sure these knucklehead boys don't get you alone. But the difference between us is that your mama wants you to save it for marriage, and I want you to take charge of this part of your life."

"By getting birth control?" Tyesha asked, glancing up at the clinic building.

"By doing all kinds of things," Aunt Lucille said. "Birth control. Condoms. Masturbation."

"Aunt Lu!" Tyesha was scandalized.

"I told you, I'm not your mama," she said. "Even though I'm the one who took her to get birth control, back in the eighties."

"My mama?" Tyesha asked. She had only ever known the devout Christian version of her mother. All traces of the fast teen and young woman she'd been had washed away with the blood of Jesus.

Aunt Lucille put a gentle hand on Tyesha's face. "It's not a moral issue, baby. It's about you having a good life. I don't want you going along with these boys for the ride. I want you to know where you're going. What do you want from these boys? What do you want to give them? What do you want to keep for yourself?"

"I don't know," Tyesha said.

"Well, until you're sure, I think you should get the birth control shot," Aunt Lucille said. "I know your mama wouldn't approve, but I think the one thing we can agree on is that we don't want you to end up like your sister, Jenisse."

Tyesha did get the shot that day. But it was over a year later before she had sex for the first time. She was in tenth grade. And she never so much as spoke to Kyle again.

Chapter 8

The next day, Tyesha and Lily were sitting with Eva in Tyesha's office.

"This is great," Tyesha was saying to Lily. "You got almost all the girls to sign the union cards."

"Definitely," Eva said. "You only need over fifty percent, but you have more like eighty percent of our original list."

"But the club pulled a fast one," Lily said. "They hired twenty new part-time girls who only work once a month. They told them verbally that they would only be hired if they agreed not to join the union."

"That's totally illegal," Eva said.

"Tell me about it," Tyesha said. "That's why the girls representing the clubs in the boroughs are on the way over here now. They're bringing one of the new girls who's willing to talk on the record."

"Everything's set up for a legal deposition to get her testimony today," Eva said.

As Serena, the clinic office manager, walked in with a video camera, Lily got a text.

"Bad news," Lily said. "The girls are on their way from the subway, but they said some guys in a car started following them."

"Oh, hell, no," Tyesha said, and pulled out her own phone to call clinic security.

"Meet me at the front door," she said into the phone.

"They just turned onto Avenue D," Lily called out.

Tyesha and Lily met two security guards in the lobby, one female, one male.

"We'll go meet them and escort them in," Tyesha said.

The four of them stepped out of the clinic and headed south. The summer storms had finally cleared, and it was a bright, muggy day.

When they turned the corner onto Avenue D, the street was crowded. But once a pair of women with a toddler got into a cab, they could see a trio of fashionable young women headed their way. Tyesha recognized Giselle, the brown-skinned Latina, and then Tara, the white girl with the tattoos, as the two other union organizers who worked with Lily. Between them was a younger, shorter girl, arms crossed anxiously across her chest as she walked.

Sure enough, a dark sedan moved slowly along behind them, holding up traffic. Several other motorists beeped at the sedan and went around.

"I don't like this," Tyesha said. "Call them and give me your phone, Lily."

Lily handed Tyesha the phone.

"Giselle, it's Tyesha. Do you see us walking toward you?"

"Yeah," Giselle said. "You brought cops?"

"Just security guards," Tyesha said. "They work for the clinic."

A pair of young men jogged toward them. Tyesha overheard them talking as they sped past: "I know those girls looked good, but how you gonna block traffic just to ogle some ass?"

Tyesha kept her eye on the girls and the sedan. She spoke

into the phone again: "When the light turns red, I want you all to start running toward us, okay? Tell your girls."

In the distance, they could see her turn to the other women. Several motorists honked and drove around the slow-moving sedan.

"Tell us when," Giselle said.

Tyesha looked up. The light turned yellow, and a dry-cleaning delivery car plus two cabs cut into the intersection as the light was turning red.

"Now!" Tyesha yelled.

The girls took off toward them. It was a glorious moment, the trio of them in bright summer clothes, with hair flying and brown skin glistening in the city sunshine.

Then, a moment later, a man leaned out of the passenger window of the sedan.

Tyesha's first thought was that he was too late. Nothing he could say would turn those girls around. They wouldn't even hear him.

But then he slid his arm out of the window, and Tyesha saw the handgun.

The first shot cracked loud through the air.

"Ohhhhhh, fuuuuuuuck!" Tyesha yelled and ducked down behind a garbage can.

Lily flattened herself against a building. The security guards ducked, too.

As the thug emptied his gun, Tyesha heard screams from the girls and some of the bystanders.

Before the light could change, the sedan did a three-point turn out into traffic in the opposite direction, nearly side-swiping a pizza delivery car.

A moment later, the three girls clattered up on high heels, cursing and terrified.

"Oh my fucking god!"

"Is everybody okay?" Tyesha asked.

"Do I call the police or no?" the woman security guard asked, her cell phone out.

The young Latina shook her head.

"No cops," Tyesha said. "But I'm sure somebody else called. Come on. Let's get back to the clinic before they show up."

They ran the block and a half to the clinic, and Tyesha hustled them in through the back.

"Somebody trying to kill us now?" the young Latina asked.

Tyesha shook her head. "They just want to scare you. If he had really wanted to hit you at that range, I'm sure he could have."

"If he wanted to scare us, he did," Tara said.

"Not me," said Giselle. "He just pissed me off."

They trekked up the stairs to Tyesha's office.

Eva opened the door for them.

"Is everything okay?"

"Some guy took a few shots to scare them," Tyesha murmured to her. "Nobody's hurt."

"Thank god," Eva said. "Well, I got the deposition set up. Who's the new employee?"

The young Latina shook her head. "I don't want to do it anymore. I wanna do the right thing, but not if it gets me shot." She was short and thickset, a rhinestone piercing just below her lip.

"I understand," Eva said, turning off her lawyer voice and putting on her shrink voice. "Something like this is terrifying. Do you want to tell me about it?"

"No," the girl said. Her arms were still folded across her ample chest, but now her hands were clenching and un-clenching as they gripped her upper arms. "I just want to get out of here."

"Okay," Eva said. "Why don't you give yourself a couple days to recover. Then let's see how you feel."

The girl was adamant. "Nah. I'ma feel the same. I quit. I don't want no part of it."

"You can't let them intimidate you," Lily said.

"*Espérate, nena,*" Giselle began, but Tyesha put up a hand.

"You gotta do what's right for you," Tyesha said. "But can you do us one favor? Can you tell all the new girls what happened?"

"I'll tell all the ones I know," the girl said.

"Thank you," Tyesha said. "And if you change your mind—about testifying or about wanting your job back—we'll be here."

The girl shook her head again. "One shift a month to have motherfuckers shooting at me? I don't think so."

Later that night, Tyesha was getting ready for bed when she got a call from her eldest niece.

"Deza, I haven't heard back from Thug Woofer on your—"

But she broke off when she realized Deza was crying. "Auntie Ty, you need to come get us."

"Your mama and Zeus fighting again?" Tyesha asked.

"Come now," Deza said. "Please."

"I'm on my way."

Tyesha stepped into her yoga pants and grabbed her keys on the way out the door.

Twenty minutes later, Tyesha was stepping out of the elevator on the seventh floor of the Brooklyn Gardens Hotel, and she texted Deza as much. The nondescript hallway was beige with forgettable muted watercolors on the wall, but halfway down the hall stood a tall black man in a long gray coat. Zeus's bodyguard, Reagan.

The Chinese food she'd had for dinner lurched in her stomach.

"Tyesha," he drawled from his post. "Is that you? Girl, I used to think you was hot when you was jailbait, but I do be-

lieve you just heated up over the years. I heard you been running a hospital or something. A shame you ain't come in you
work clothes. I'd love to see that fine ass in a skirt."

"Reagan," she said. "You know you really do live up to
your name. Both crack and AIDS flourishing on your watch.
A liar and a fake but somehow you keep duping the good
people—or Zeus in this case—into re-electing you."

He gave a grunt of disapproval and grabbed her arm. "One
of these days you gonna realize it pays to be nice to me."

She went to shake him off, but he tightened his grip. She
was just wondering if she would have to punch him, when
the door swung open.

Deza burst into the hallway with an overnight bag.

From inside the hotel room, Tyesha could hear a vaguely familiar nineties rap song and raised voices. She heard the deep
bass of Zeus's voice in an incomprehensible rant, into which
Jenisse interjected sharply, "Well, I don't give a fuck—"

"Amaru, come on!" Deza shouted into the suite, adding
another layer of noise.

"I can't find my gym bag," Amaru said. Through the door,
Tyesha could see her youngest niece looking around wildly,
brows knit, nearly in tears. "I'll be in trouble if I miss my workout tomorrow."

"We can get you new stuff," Tyesha offered.

Deza walked in and stood in the middle of the room. Then
she picked up a pair of basketball sneakers from beside an
armchair and led her sister out into the hallway.

Tyesha pulled both girls into her arms. "Let's just get out
of here, okay?"

Zeus's baritone voice sounded from inside the suite, "No,
bitch, just shut your ass up, okay?" His words gained in clar-
ity and volume as he came closer to the door.

Tyesha pulled both girls to the other side of the hall and
out of the way.

"That's right, nigga," Jenisse's voice came, shrill and contemptuous. "Run off like you always do. Can't stand up to your own woman, no wonder some pussy white boy mobsters kicking yo faggot ass. You betta get back in here!"

Zeus tore out of the hotel room with his fists clenched. "Either I'm leaving or I'ma kill yo ass. Right in front of yo kids. You put one hand on me and you made your choice."

Tyesha pulled the girls tighter and marched them toward the elevator. She clenched her body against the sound of a scream or a shot.

Instead, she felt the whoosh and smooth feel of fabric against her arm as Zeus strode past, towering and regal in a black cashmere trench coat. Reagan was right on his heels, like a pale shadow.

Tyesha stopped and let the two men take the elevator car down.

Just before the door closed, an empty liquor bottle flew out of the suite and hit the hallway's opposite wall.

"That nigga ain't shit!" Jenisse slurred from inside the room. "Ain't even dog shit."

Tyesha couldn't tell if she was crying or drunk or both.

Deza started pulling Tyesha toward the elevators.

"Is she gonna be okay?" Tyesha asked.

"I think so," Amaru said. "As long as he's gone."

"I don't give a fuck about her one way or the other," Deza said.

As they waited for the elevator, Jenisse began a loping walk toward them. She had an empty brandy glass in her hand.

"I don't fucking believe it," Deza muttered.

"What the hell you think you doing, Tycsha?" Jenisse asked. "You taking my kids out of my house?"

"It's not your house," Tyesha said. "It's a hotel. That Zeus paid for."

"And nobody invited you, bitch," Jenisse said.

"Here we go," Deza said through clenched teeth.

"Deza called me," Tyesha said. "So I guess that was my invitation."

"She an ungrateful little bitch, too," Jenisse said. "Just like you. See? Bitches always trying to take you down. Take yo man. Take yo kids."

"And I shoulda taken them that time in Chicago," Tyesha said. "But I was too young to know what to do. But now I know. I'm letting them decide. Girls, you wanna come with me?"

"Hell, yeah," Deza said. Amaru didn't answer, but she held tight to Tyesha.

"You know where to find your kids," Tyesha said. "When you're sober and not ready to brawl with their father right in front of them."

"That nigga deserve it."

"Maybe," Tyesha said. "But they don't deserve to have to watch it."

"What you gonna do, Amaru?" Jenisse asked. "You gonna be a little traitor bitch like yo sister, or you gonna stay with yo mama?"

Amaru said nothing, but tears started to fall down her cheeks.

The elevator arrived.

"Actions speak louder than words, baby," Jenisse said. "You get on that elevator, and it's just like you spat in my face."

Tyesha moved toward the elevator, and Amaru stood frozen, her arms cradling the pair of lilac-and-turquoise basketball shoes.

"You ain't the one here who's fucked up," Tyesha murmured in her ear. "Jenisse always been a mean drunk. You ain't gotta put up with her shit."

Tyesha felt Amaru's arm squeeze tighter around her. Tyesha backed into the elevator with her arms around both girls.

"Fine!" Jenisse spat. "Ungrateful spoilt motherfuckers."

She threw the brandy glass at them, but it swung wide and broke against the wall as the doors closed.

Tyesha and her nieces rode the elevator down to the basement parking garage in silence. Amaru cried noiselessly.

In the parking garage, the three of them climbed into Tyesha's silver compact two-door. She fished a tissue out of the glove compartment and handed it to Amaru, who wiped her eyes and blew her nose.

When Tyesha turned on the car, the sound system began automatically playing the last music Tyesha had listened to: Deza's CD.

"Do you want me to turn it off?" Tyesha asked.

"I don't care," Deza said.

Tyesha let it play.

> *Young black women barely got a chance these*
>   *days*
> *Brothers act like they the only target but plenty*
>   *bullets shooting my way*
> *On the other hand, we got Sandra Bland*
> *I don't understand why folks act like just the*
>   *black man is being destroyed*
> *Say Rekia Boyd*
> *Yeah, say her name*
> *Cause the reaper came*
> *We gonna have a roll call*
> *for Mya Hall because you can't deny*
> *the fact of Spring Valley High*

As they drove across Brooklyn, Deza burst out, "Why couldn't she stay in Chicago? Why she gotta chase a man all over the fucking country? She afraid he gonna fuck somebody else? He already does that in Chicago. He stayed with

her psycho ass for twenty-five years. Why she gotta stick to him like some kinda crazy bitch Velcro? I'll tell you why. Because he's her job. Looking cute for him. Fucking him. Nagging him. Fighting with him. That's all she does. That's all she's ever done. She has his babies then can't be bothered with us except how we become new subjects for her to bitch at him about. I hate her. I fucking hate her."

It was surreal, Deza's recorded voice and the beat rapping a litany of violence against black women and the live rant against her mother.

Tyesha turned the music off.

"I'm sorry, baby," she said.

"But she's never sorry," Deza said. "Never. Not once. I fucking hate her."

Brooklyn sped by, the long-standing mom-and-pop stores and restaurants, interspersed with hipster galleries and boutiques.

When they arrived at Tyesha's building, they had to circle the block looking for a parking space. A trendy bar had moved in around the corner and it was harder than ever to park now.

Amaru spoke for the first time since they had left the hotel. "Is that Thug Woofer out in front of your place?"

Tyesha looked over, and it was.

"Oh my god," Deza said. "I look totally fucking crazy." She pulled down the passenger vanity mirror and wiped under her eyes. She smoothed her hair.

"I need lipstick!" she yelled.

"Don't look at me," Amaru said.

"Auntie Ty, you got some for me?"

Tyesha shook her head. "I ran out with just my phone and keys to come get you."

Tyesha found a tiny parking space and deftly maneuvered the car into it.

"Thug Woofer," Deza said. "I'm meeting Thug mother-fucking Woofer. I need to look like I'm ready to be a star."

"Deza," Amaru said, "you're a rapper, not a model."

"You so damn butch, you don't understand," Deza said.

"Lipstick or not," Tyesha said, "here he comes. Put your head up and believe in yourself."

Tyesha stepped out of the car. "Hey, Woof," she said. "What are you doing here?"

"I was worried about you," he said. "I heard there was a shooting on the Lower East Side that maybe had something to do with your clinic. So I called, but then you didn't answer."

Tyesha fished her phone out of her sweatshirt pocket. Sure enough. Five missed calls and several texts from him.

"As you can see, I'm fine," she said.

He pulled her into a tight embrace. She could feel the warmth of his body, even through the thick tracksuit. He smelled like sweat and some kind of soap.

When Tyesha let go from the embrace, her two nieces were standing against the car smiling.

She took Woof by the hand and introduced him to both of them.

"I'm looking forward to hearing your CD," Woof said.

Deza was uncharacteristically tongue-tied. She just nodded and smiled.

"And Amaru," Woof said. "Nice game the other day."

"You were there?" she asked, her mouth falling open.

"I just told him all about it," Tyesha said. "Let's get inside."

She led them down the stairs and opened the door of the brownstone.

"The girls were just coming to sleep over," she told Woof.

"I'm sorry to interrupt," Woof said.

"Interrupt my auntie all you want," Deza said. "In fact,

we don't need a babysitter or anything, Auntie Ty. Like if you and your company wanted to go out or something. We can make ourselves at home."

"Are you sure?" Tyesha asked. "Amaru, you're okay?"

"I got six-thirty practice," she said. "I'm going to sleep in the next fifteen minutes." She was pulling off her loose jeans to reveal a long pair of cotton hoop shorts that hung to her knees.

"And I'm gonna stay up and binge-watch the latest season of *Badass Femcee Battle*."

Deza draped a jacket over Tyesha's shoulders. "And you shouldn't be out without your coat. Here. Have fun."

"Deza, this doesn't feel right," Tyesha said. "You've just been through a very traumatic—" But she broke off mid-sentence because her niece had closed the door in her face.

Woof shook his head. "You told me she was on team Thug Woofer, but damn."

"Did I just get put out of my own house?" Tyesha said. "That's pathetic."

"Should you go back in?" he asked.

Tyesha fidgeted with the house key in her hand.

"No," she said. "The way their parents are acting, they might be here for a while. I need to get ready for the long haul. I can't be watching over them every minute."

Thug Woofer nodded.

"So, where should we go?" Tyesha asked.

"My place?" he suggested. "I wanna be comfortable and I don't mind driving you home later."

"You still in that midtown penthouse?" Tyesha asked.

Woof laughed. "No, girl. I'm right here in Brooklyn."

It was only a fifteen-minute ride to his place, a gorgeous loft in Williamsburg that looked out on the river.

It was so different from his previous apartment. The last place was like something out of an old episode of *Cribs*. It was a caricature of how a rap artist was supposed to live. A sunken living room, platinum records, and album cover posters on the walls. An entourage of guys sitting around watching television and talking shit.

But this place was open with unadorned walls, a few plants, and a small waterfall in the corner.

"It's beautiful here," she said. "I realize I haven't really seen that much of Brooklyn. Mostly I've just been in Manhattan between the clinic and Columbia. And with my apartment, I just walk to the subway or get takeout down the street."

"Your nieces weren't really just having a sleepover, were they?" he asked. "Something seemed like it wasn't quite right, especially when I first saw you."

Tyesha sighed. "Nope. Their parents got ugly. I love those girls. But my sister?"

"I know her type," Woof said. "Hard on the outside, soft on the inside."

"Soft?" Tyesha asked. "Ain't nothing soft about my sister."

"I know that type because I'm that type," he said. "I never let anybody see anything soft about me. Mad all the time. Rude. Disrespectful. Oh, I know all about it."

"It's one thing for her to be like that with me," Tyesha said. "But with her girls, her daughters? I see how she treats them and I wonder if I should've stayed in Chicago. They've only been in New York a few days, and they're already calling me to rescue them. Their mama's drunk and abusive. Their daddy has Chester the molester as his fucking bodyguard. I know what it's like. I know what it's like to have that mama not checking for you and creepy motherfuckers everywhere and nobody to turn to. Who takes care of those girls?"

"From what I can see," Woof said, "they take care of each other."

"It's not good enough," Tyesha said.

"Looks like they turned out okay," Woof said. "They're

almost grown now. A short step away from being out the house. So the real question is, who takes care of you?"

"I been taking care of myself," Tyesha said. "For years."

"What about that sugar daddy you had back in the day?" Woof asked.

Tyesha chuckled. "Nope," she said. "He took care of my bills, but I was the one taking care of him, emotionally, sexually."

"What if I wanted to take care of you?" Woof said. "I mean, you got your job and everything, but what if these walls were a safe zone where all the troubles of the world couldn't get to you. Where it wasn't your job to fix it. Where you could just have some peace . . . and pleasure?"

He leaned forward, his lips slightly parted. His fingers slid softly along the side of her neck. Not pulling her toward him, but brushing, suggesting. When his lips touched hers, she felt a mix of emotions. A yearning for the peace and pleasure he offered, but the opposing tug of wariness. As his body moved closer, she could feel a sense of desire rising. The strength of it scared her, and she pulled back from the kiss.

"Peace and pleasure sure do sound good," she said, but with the slightest shrug.

"But there's one catch," he said. "You gotta be my girl-friend. It's not just a drop-in spa."

"Is Thug Woofer trying to lock it down?" Tyesha asked. "Is that what's happening here?"

"I think that's what's happening here," he said.

"What happened to a hundred dates?" she asked.

"I blame your family," he said.

"How you figure?" she asked.

"I wanted to wait to give you the really good stuff," he said. "But you came over here all upset, and I just couldn't have you up here in all this distress without using my most powerful medicine."

"And what is that?" Tyesha asked.

"Well, you know I'm from the South," he said.

"I do know that," she said.

"From the backwoods," he said.

"I know," she said. "Cackalacky."

"Well, where I'm from, they got root doctors," he said.

"Oh, really?" she said.

"Definitely," he said.

"You gonna try to work a root on me?" she asked.

"I got something for you that's directly from Africa," he murmured. "And it'll cure whatever ails you."

Tyesha laughed. "I hate to tell you," she said. "But there are a lot of brothers out there making the same promises. And I do believe using some of the same—ah—natural remedies."

"Oh, but mine is organic," he said.

"Really?"

"And no preservatives," he said.

"I hope it's not vegetarian," she said.

"No, baby," he said. "Definitely not. Feel."

Gently, he took her hand, and guided it to his erection. He let go, but she took a moment to press her hand down the length of it through his track pants.

"That's definitely not a plant," she said. "A tree maybe, but not a plant."

He laughed. "That's how much I want you to be my woman," he said. "That much."

"Maybe it's time to plant that tree," she said.

As they kissed again, she could feel her body release the knot, the clench she'd been feeling since she'd gotten the call from Amaru. Finally, she uncoiled toward him. Let herself sink into all the desire she'd been feeling. All the hunger she'd been holding herself back from. It was delicious, intoxicating.

She sank into the place where there was only a pair of bodies and fire. His lips pressing hers, her tongue in his mouth, his hands undoing buttons, sliding under her blouse, lifting her breasts out of her bra, the hiss of pleasure as his hands grazed her nipples. Her body arching, kicking off her shoes to straddle him on the couch. She wrapped her legs around him and pressed. The moistening spot between her legs against the hardness between his, pulsing beneath the slippery fabric of his track pants.

She unzipped his jacket and slid it off, feeling the sloping ropes of his muscles beneath. Then pulled off his T-shirt, running her hands up his chest, his neck, his face. She smoothed his hair back from his face. Feeling the tiny coils of the short fade in the front, the way they bounced beneath her fingers. She looked him in his eyes. Wide and brown and open.

Slowly, eyes locked, he removed her blouse. He slid the fabric of it gently against her skin, providing the contrast between the silk and the slightly rougher texture of his palm. Like a striptease, but he was undressing her instead of himself. He pulled her shoulders out of the bra and began to rotate it around, tugging the straps up, so they pulled against each of her erect nipples until, one by one, they snapped free. He rotated the hooks to the front and undid the catch.

They pressed against each other, both naked from the waist up. He ran his hands down the sides of her torso, and then down over her ass, wide and full with the straddle, her skirt hiked up to the tops of her thighs. Putting both hands beneath her ass, he stood up, lifting both of them off the couch. She wrapped her arms around his neck and held tighter. He strode across the apartment holding her up, and pushed the bedroom door open with his elbow. The room was dark, the only illumination coming in through the window, with lights from the city.

He lay her down on the bed—it was firm, but with soft linens—and began to unzip and slide off her skirt. He buried his face in her navel and moved down, pulling aside the thong and parting her lips to slide his tongue inside.

Tyesha cried out with the sweetness of it. He began to move his tongue right against her clitoris. Rhythmic. Insistent. She moaned and twisted. Could barely breathe. She gripped the string of her thong and when he thrust his tongue inside her, she gasped and pulled so hard that it snapped.

She reached to tangle her hands in his hair, but it was too short. Nothing to catch hold of. And she found herself unable to hang on, spiraling, falling into pleasure. The undulating waves of her orgasm rocking her from the inside out.

When she was finally back to herself, she saw him, grinning, kneeling above her, rolling on a condom. She blinked at the fullness of him. Then he was pressing gently into her. She was so wet that he slid easily, but the pressure of his girth opened her further. The sensation of pleasure, pushing toward an edge of pain.

He straightened her leg and turned them over. Then he drew up her legs and thrust up into her. She felt him throughout the core of her, thrusting deep into her, pressing, stretching against her opening, and then the shaft of him, stroking insistently against her clitoris. She moaned, barely able to hold herself up. He gripped her ass, leaned up and took one of her breasts in his mouth, licked, then ran his tongue back and forth across both nipples.

She was moaning more insistently now, as if he was pressing the sounds out of her. But he was totally silent, eyes locked on hers, whenever she managed to open them. And then she could feel herself on the verge of climax.

"Are you close?" he asked in a hoarse whisper.

She couldn't speak, only nod her head mutely.

He straightened her leg again and turned her over, crashing their hips together, thrusting hard inside her. With a deep moan, her eyes flew open. His face was a mix of softness and tension, as if the pleasure was more than he could stand. And as she looked at his face and felt the fullness of him inside her, she could feel herself crack open, deeper this time. And they both came, howling and trembling, together.

Chapter 9

Tyesha stumbled in to work late and in her sweats from the night before.

Serena took one look at her and walked out. She came back a few minutes later with a cup of coffee. "Tyesha, can you confirm the press conference for today?"

"What press conference?"

"About the shooting yesterday," Serena said. "One of the girls tweeted that they got shot at, and the tweet went viral. Lily said she assumed we were having a press conference."

Tyesha took a sip of the coffee and shook her head to clear it. The shooting seemed like a month ago. She'd lost sight of work, between the distress call to pick up her nieces, the drama with Zeus and Jenisse, and her night with Thug Woofer. Just recalling him, she felt a throb between her legs. A press conference? Strippers getting shot at? Viral tweets? She could barely process it.

"Yes," she said. "Tell them we'll have a press conference."

Her phone rang again and it was a Chicago prefix.

Tyesha picked it up.

"Hello?"

"Hey, baby," her mother's voice said. The tone was familiar, but it was particularly jarring today.

"Is everything okay?" Tyesha asked. She was afraid that maybe Zeus had come back and killed Jenisse. Or vice versa.

"I just know that God is good all the time," her mother said. "But I been praying about you and your sister all night long. Ever since Jenisse called last evening, I been worried about the both of you and my grandbabies."

"Mama," Tyesha said, "Jenisse musta drunk dialed you after I left the hotel. The girls called me to get them outta there cause their parents were fighting."

"Jenisse is just worried about those girls," her mother said.

"Worried?" Tyesha said. "She was throwing brandy glasses at them. Cursing them out. Mama, things with Zeus almost got physical, and Jenisse was plenty abusive with the girls. Then she got vicious again when they tried to leave."

"I know Jenisse has her faults, but what this family needs is a little more forgiveness," her mother said.

"Forgive Jenisse?" Tyesha said. "Why? She hasn't even apologized. Jenisse doesn't need my forgiveness. It's those girls that she's hurt and those girls who are gonna hate her."

"Jenisse was fifteen when that man came sniffing around," her mother said. "I know what it's like to be a young mother. You do your best, but you make mistakes so big because you just don't know any better. Jesus died on the cross so all our sins could be forgiven."

"Mama, I'm at the office," Tyesha said. "I can't really stay on the phone."

"I'm just saying," her mother continued. "Your sister ain't bad, she just lost. Everybody can't have two college degrees like you."

"How do you know I even have those degrees?" Tyesha asked. "It's not like you came out for the ceremonies. Even after I sent you the tickets."

"You know I don't like to fly," her mother said.

"The second time it was a train ticket." Tyesha was surprised to feel the prick of tears in her eyes.

"Baby, you're preparing your crown in the world," her mother said. "I'm praying to God to prepare your crown in heaven. Your sister, too. I just want both of you to get right while you're in this world. Get right with God and get right with each other."

"I gotta go, Mama," Tyesha said.

"Remember what I told you," her mother said. "You don't know the whole story. Jenisse ain't bad, she's just lost. Only God can judge."

"Okay, Mama," Tyesha said. "I'll talk to you soon."

Three hours later, Tyesha was in the multipurpose room wearing a suit and facing the press. She stood behind one side of the podium with Eva, Kim, and Jody. On the other side stood the union organizers, Giselle and Tara. Lily was at the podium, reading a prepared statement.

"Yesterday afternoon, at approximately two p.m., I was walking down Avenue D to meet the organizers from the other One-Eyed King franchises in the boroughs, and a dark SUV was following them. Then the man in the passenger seat leaned out and shot at them. No one was injured, and the gunman fled. But this illustrates the kind of intimidation that sex workers are up against. Everyone expects to profit from our sexual labor but won't let us earn a decent living. And our attempts to unionize are not only met with unfair labor practices, but also violent criminal activity. All we want is a safe and fair working environment. But apparently that's something we'll have to risk our lives to get. Thank you."

They hadn't taken questions at any of the press conferences, but a man from the *Daily Clarion* raised a hand. "Excuse me," he said loudly.

"We said no questions," Eva explained.

"But how do you know?" the *Daily Clarion* guy asked loudly.

"Come on, man." Drew stood up, the geeky black guy from the *Village Voice*. "They said no questions. Show some respect."

"How do you know this was a retaliation for union efforts?" the *Daily Clarion* guy insisted. "I mean, couldn't it have been one of their boyfriends or something."

Lily slowly turned around. "Eh-eh? What nastiness is dis? You wouldn't be asking dat same question to someone from the teachers' union. But if somebody shoots at some sex workers, they must be to blame? You pissin tail!"

"Lily!" Tyesha said, grabbing her friend's arm. But not before half of the reporters in the room had tweeted out the video of Lily cursing the reporter.

The crew managed to get Lily quieted down before she could mouth off any more.

"Tyesha, when is enough gonna be enough?" Jody said. "You need to talk to Eva about your stage fright or something. You gotta get on that microphone. This was a disaster."

An hour later, Tyesha walked back into the multipurpose room. Most of the reporters had left. The only people who remained were the union reps, as well as Kim and Jody, who were talking to Drew from the *Village Voice*. However, as Tyesha folded up some of the chairs, she noticed one lone woman sitting on the far end of the room.

"Can I help you?" she asked. The woman was maybe fifty, with a tight but busty figure, obviously the result of hours in a gym. She had brightly lipsticked pouty lips, and was Latina or maybe African American and light-skinned.

"Are you Tyesha Couvillier?" the woman asked. "The executive director?"

Tyesha nodded. "And you are?"

"Etta Hughes," she said. "My husband owns the One-Eyed King."

Tyesha blinked. "I'm not sure you should be here. We're communicating through our attorneys at this point."

"It doesn't matter what the lawyers say," Etta Hughes said. "There's no way Teddy's gonna let that union go forward."

"Excuse me?" Tyesha said. "That could land him in jail."

"It's not Teddy's fault," the wife said. "It's the Ukrainian mob."

"Well, then I guess he shouldn't have gotten into business with them," Tyesha said, preparing to walk away.

"Wait," Etta Hughes said, grabbing her arm. "They've got something on him. They're using it as leverage, and they won't let him agree to the union terms."

"Hold on a minute," Tyesha glanced across at her team, talking to the reporter. "We need to go into my office."

Ten minutes later, the two of them were sitting at the coffee table in Tyesha's office with Jody and Kim.

"What do they have on your husband?" Tyesha asked.

"A gun," Etta Hughes began.

"They're threatening to kill him?" Jody asked.

"No," the wife said. "It's a gun that killed somebody. They say it's got his DNA or something. If there was any way you girls could get that gun back, I know he'd give your union the green light."

"You want us to help him get out of a murder charge?" Tyesha asked.

"It wasn't murder; it was self-defense," the wife insisted. "The One-Eyed King used to have two owners, and the other guy got in bed with the mob. All of a sudden these Ukrainian thugs were coming around the club. And they've been making changes—really awful changes. I used to work there, so I know what it's like."

Jody rolled her eyes.

"My husband didn't agree with the changes, and he and his partner got into a fight about it. They'd both been drinking. He pulled a gun on my husband, but Teddy wrestled it away from him and the gun went off. Shot the partner in the head. Then Teddy panicked. The mob said they'd take care of it. They had my husband tell the cops a story about a robbery. But then they kept the gun and used it as leverage. So now if they ever turn the gun over to the cops, Teddy will look guilty."

"We're not going to cover for a murderer," Tyesha said.

"I was there. I saw it," Etta Hughes said. "But nobody will believe my testimony. I'm his wife. They'll just say I'm lying for him."

"What makes you think we could get this gun?" Kim asked. "Even assuming we wanted to."

"Because you're Marisol's girls," the wife said. "She always knew her way around a good hustle."

"And let's say we give him this gun," Jody said. "What assurance do we have that he'll keep up his end of the bargain and greenlight the union?"

"I'll make sure he does," Etta said.

"So basically, this all hangs on you," Kim said. "We gotta believe you that he's not a murderer and trust you that you can make him do the right thing."

"That's right," the wife said. "Ask Marisol. We go way back. She'll vouch for me."

"Marisol is out of town," Tyesha said.

"Well, when she gets back, tell her what I said," the woman insisted. "Tell her Etta Lang gave her word."

Later that night, Tyesha woke up in Thug Woofer's bed. As she blinked awake, she saw him propped up on his elbow, looking at her.

"What are you staring at?" she murmured, wiping her eyes. The clock said 2:16.

"You," he said.

"Damn," she said. "You could really make a sister feel self-conscious."

"I just want to know all about you," he said, putting his arm around her and pulling her into a kiss.

"You're not the only one who's curious," she said, settling in next to him. "I got things I wanna know, too."

"Like what?" he asked. "Ask me anything."

"Are we really doing this?" Tyesha asked. "At two seventeen in the morning?"

"Is there a better time?" he asked.

"Okay," she said. "I wanna know if you've paid for sex a lot."

"No." He laughed. "I always said only losers paid for sex. But I was secretly just curious as a motherfucker. And you were supposed to be my loophole."

"Your what?"

"Yeah," Woof said. "I wasn't paying, my manager was paying. It wasn't really for me, it was for my brother's engagement."

"But then you got too drunk to do it."

"I know, and I was pissed off, because you were like, call the office. And I was like, I can't call the damn office cause then I'd be a fucking loser."

"But you called anyway."

"I couldn't stop thinking about you," he said. "Who is this fine-ass chick who's gonna take my money, not fuck me, and then cuss me out."

Tyesha guffawed.

"Served me right," he went on. "I got so damn drunk cause I was jealous of my brother." He lay his head back on the pillow and looked up at the ceiling. "I've never admitted that to anyone before."

"Boy, you admitted it that night," she scoffed.

"I what?"

"You went on and on about how he had a woman who loved him, but you only had bitches who wanted your money."

Woof turned over and buried his face in her neck. "I'm never gonna drink again."

"It was actually kind of sweet," Tyesha said.

"No, it wasn't," he said.

"Maybe not sweet but cute . . . in a kind of pitiful way," she said.

"Changing the subject," Woof said. "Can I ask you a question?"

"No, I've never paid for sex," Tyesha said.

"Ha ha," Woof said. "I wanna know how you ended up with a madam?" he asked. "Did you answer an ad on Craigslist or what?"

Tyesha shook her head. "Nothing like that. I met Marisol when she was on a panel at Columbia about sex work."

"And she was there as a madam?"

"No way," Tyesha said. "She was there representing the clinic. I asked to interview her for my senior thesis, and during those interviews we got to know each other."

Tyesha recalled that day, sitting in Marisol's office and deciding to confide that some of her information about sex work came from books, and some came from direct experience selling sex.

"You know," Marisol had said, "sex work wouldn't have to be as bad as it is if the women and men in the industries could just have a little more choice and protection."

Tyesha had gotten the idea that Marisol might know about some of it from her own experience, but she never said anything outright. After Tyesha finished with her thesis, they stayed in touch from time to time.

Tyesha graduated, and things went smoothly until the first semester of her public health master's program, when her sugar daddy's wife had found out. There was a ton of drama,

146 / *Aya de León*

and the sugar daddy had dumped her. Tyesha didn't know who else to talk to about it, so she came by Marisol's office to vent.

"I really liked him, you know?" Tyesha said. "But I can't even get to any feelings about the breakup, because I'm so busy tripping about the money."

"This is one of the problems with the single-patron arrangement," Marisol said. "One guy has a lot of economic power in your life."

"I wouldn't even mind having more than one patron," Tyesha said. "I mean, as long as they were clean and, you know, a guy I would consider fucking without the cash."

Marisol nodded.

"But I'm a graduate student. I don't have time to coordinate some complicated situation for myself."

Marisol opened her mouth and took a breath as if to speak, but then stopped.

"What?" Tyesha asked.

"Nothing," Marisol said.

"What were you gonna say, Marisol?"

"You walk in more than one world, Tyesha," Marisol said. "So do I. I'm a public health administrator, but I also hear a lot about what's going on out there from women who know— what's going on out there, and what's more and less safe at any given time. And I'm not always sure when it's appropriate to color outside the lines and when it's best to keep everything inside the safe little boundaries. Whatever you've shared with me about your personal life, I still think of you as a student I'm sort of mentoring in my capacity as a public health administrator."

"What would you say to me if I came to you as a sex worker looking for a quality hookup?" Tyesha asked. "If I wasn't a student?"

Marisol studied Tyesha for a minute. "If a young woman as smart and sophisticated as you came and asked me about a hookup, I would tell her that I do know of a possible opportunity in the escort business."

"Like a call girl?" Tyesha asked.

"The preferred industry term these days is 'escort,'" Marisol said. "A situation with management."

"Who's the manager?" Tyesha asked. "Is he cool?"

"It's a woman," Marisol said. "But she keeps a very low profile."

"It's you," Tyesha broke into a smile. "Isn't it?"

"Let's talk," Marisol said, and cancelled her next appointment.

When she told Thug Woofer about it, he laughed. "I told you, that woman is a straight-up pimp. I could feel it when I went to her office."

"She is not a pimp," Tyesha said, smacking him playfully. "Pimps hate women and exploit the workers. Marisol donated all her profits to the clinic."

"Okay, fine," Woof said. "Then not a pimp, but straight up ruthless in doing business. She's like a ghetto Puerto Rican Olivia Pope—'it's handled.'"

"What you know about getting something handled?" Tyesha asked.

"I think I might be about to handle something serious right now," he said, reaching for her hip. "At two thirty-three in the morning, no less."

Tyesha laughed and rolled on top of him.

Marisol Rivera walked the three blocks from her boyfriend's house to the Maria de la Vega clinic building. She had a studio apartment on the top floor. She'd been back in town since noon, but had spent the afternoon making love with Raul.

She had returned from Cuba relieved. Her sister Cristina would be fine, just needed to be on bed rest. Which would be hard, because the Rivera women liked to keep it moving.

Cristina had insisted that Marisol come back to New York. After all, weren't Cristina and her boyfriend, Juan, both doctors?

But when Marisol had first gotten the summons, she had imagined months without her boyfriend, Raul. Just the thought of being apart fueled a ravenous hunger inside of her. And so when she came back, she made love to him as if she'd been gone months instead of days. She could have stayed another few days in his bed, but duty called.

She'd gotten several cryptic messages from Tyesha, her successor as clinic executive director. Tyesha said she had an urgent matter, something she refused to discuss on the phone.

Marisol walked up to the health center and was glad to see everything in order. No fires, no bomb threats. The clinic waiting room was full of young women in tight clothes with brightly colored weaves and dye jobs.

A few floors up, she entered her old office—now Tyesha's. Tyesha sat on the couch next to Eva and looked up as Marisol came in.

"Thank goodness Cristina's okay," Eva said, hugging Marisol.

"Things seemed to go well on this end, too," Marisol said. She hugged Tyesha. "I didn't think Lily cussing out that reporter was such a disaster," Marisol said, as she sat down on the couch. "He deserved it. But what's this thing you can't ask me on the phone?"

Tyesha leaned forward in her chair. "Etta Lang," Tyesha said. "Can we trust her?"

"I think so," Marisol said. "I haven't seen her in years, but she was always good folks. Why?"

"She's Etta Hughes now," Tyesha said. "She's married to Teddy Hughes."

"The owner of the One-Eyed King?" Marisol said. "How did I miss that?"

Tyesha explained Etta's offer, the gun in exchange for Teddy backing the union.

"But can we trust her?" Tyesha asked. "To keep him to his word."

"Definitely," Marisol said. "Etta was always very persuasive with men."

"You're not really gonna do this, are you?" Eva said.

"I think we have to at least try," Marisol said. "We can't have girls getting shot at by these mobsters. The only way to get them to leave the girls alone is if they don't have a stake in the business."

"Okay," said Tyesha. "I guess we're robbing the mob."

Book 3

Chapter 10

Several days after Marisol came back from Cuba, Tyesha walked into her own apartment, heavy-lidded and still slightly sex-drunk.

She had come home after that first night with Woof to check on the girls. They had bounced back from their parents' fight. Staying at their auntie's house lifted their spirits—Jenisse and Zeus could act crazy, but they didn't have to stay and witness it. Tyesha had given them spare keys and told them to make themselves at home.

Now she was back a few days later, and creeping into her own house at five a.m. Deza and Amaru were asleep side-by-side on the fold-out couch. Deza lay on her stomach, her hand flung out over the edge and hovering in space. Amaru's elbow was bent next to her head and her forearm pressed down her short hair. She snored slightly.

Tyesha recalled babysitting them when she was young. How relieved she was when they finally fell asleep. She wasn't that much older than them. Just twenty-nine to Deza's nineteen and Amaru's fourteen. But it was this nostalgic memory—along with the sex—that made her feel generous and forgiving toward them.

The place was a mess, but she couldn't quite get mad about it. Several pizza boxes littered the coffee table. In the kitchen, Tyesha learned that pizza delivery seemed to be the plan B, as every scrap of edible food in the fridge had been eaten, along with all the ramen, canned tuna, and crackers.

The sink was full of dishes. The kitchen table was cluttered with pressing irons, fake hair, and debris from a home perm.

The tubes from the perm just reminded Tyesha of lube and had her smiling to herself. She couldn't seem to get mad. Even when a glance at her closet showed that the girls had raided it. Likely Deza for the femme clothes, although a sniff of her overcoat revealed that Amaru had worn that particular garment. She always smelled of peppermint soap, whereas Deza wore a trendy department store perfume.

Tyesha saw the orchid from Woof, nearly hidden on the coffee table among the girls' mess. She swooped it up and took it into her bedroom. The light wasn't as good, but she didn't want it to get knocked over. Or worse yet, crushed under a sodden basketball jersey.

The bathroom was a wreck, with blue hair dye pooling in standing water at the bottom of the sink. Tyesha's hairbrush was a tangle of hair, various colors and lengths, as if both girls had used it.

But she lost it when she saw the curling iron still plugged in, still hot. Only an inch away from a crumpled tissue and a ball of fake hair.

She tore into the living room and woke the girls up.

"No, no, no, and hell no," she said. "Wake the fuck up, Deza, I need you to see this." She waved the curling iron in front of the two girls. "You really need to clean this place up, but I coulda waited til daylight to tell you that. On the other hand, this curling iron? Hot? Left on for hours next to tissue and fake hair? Hell, no. Hell motherfucking no. You wanna stay here? I need to NEVER see any shit like this again. I bought this co-op apartment, and I'll be damned if it I let you burn it down."

"I didn't do nothing, Auntie Ty," Amaru said. "You know that was Deza." She groaned and rolled over.

"I know you get up to pee at least once every night, which means you walked right by that curling iron with its little red light on."

"Sorry, Auntie," Amaru said, and buried her head under the covers.

Deza, however, was more awake.

"You been at Thug Woofer's this whole time?" she asked hopefully.

"No," Tyesha said, the heat from the curling iron in her hand inspiring malice. "I spent the last few nights with Clarence."

The next day, Marisol and Tyesha walked down to the waterfront to meet the strip club owner and his wife.

"Even though she knows me, I want you to take charge of the meeting," Marisol said. "You're the executive director now."

The day was hot and humid, but a cooler breeze came up off the river. It brought the briny smell of polluted water. A ferry glided by in the distance.

After a gaggle of tourists set off on a walking tour, Tyesha could see Teddy and Etta Hughes headed toward them. He had that distinctive Grecian Formula black hair, and she had her sandy brown hair piled up on top of her head. As the couple approached, the wife's face broke into a big smile, and she stepped forward to hug Marisol.

"Let's get right to it," Tyesha said. "What does the mob have on you?"

"I'm just supposed to tell all here?" he asked, his craggy face pinched into a frown. "Like these two girls are supposed to help me get out from under the entire Ukrainian mafia?"

"Don't waste our fucking time," Tyesha said. "You wanna be squeezed between the mob and a well-organized group of sex workers who have the *New York Times* on speed dial, be my guest."

"Teddy, she's right," his wife said. "I called them because I know they can help. You gotta trust somebody."

"Your wife told us that they had evidence to connect you to a homicide," Tyesha said. "Is it true they have the weapon?"

He blew his breath out. "They have the gun. I didn't do it, but it has my prints."

"We don't care if you did it or not. If we get it, will you agree to our unionization demands? Sick leave. Worker's comp, unemployment, and health insurance. Overtime pay for holidays. No fees for dancing. Bring back the second dressing room. Plus a retirement fund."

"You have my word," he said. "If you can really get the mob off my ass."

"Your ass is your own business," Tyesha said. "All we're agreeing to do is get the gun. No guarantees."

"And if you don't get it," he said, "you can kiss your union good-bye."

"Obviously," Tyesha said. "But we won't be refunding any of the expenses."

"What expenses?" he demanded.

"The expenses of setting up the heist," Tyesha said. "You think the head of the Ukrainian mob will give us your gun because we're cute and we ask nicely? Or maybe he just leaves it laying around and we can swap places with the house cleaners?"

"Think about it," Marisol said. "He'll probably have all kinds of security we'll need to get past."

"Fine," he said. "I'll authorize a few hundred."

"Hundred?" Tyesha said. "Try a few thousand. We don't even know his security setup yet."

"I'm not gonna let these chicks hustle me," Teddy said. He turned to walk away.

"No, baby," Etta said, grabbing him around the waist. "This is an investment in our future."

"But I could spend all this money and they still can't get the gun back," he said.

"It's cheaper than hiring a lawyer if that gun ever turns up," she said.

"I don't wanna take that risk," he said.

"You don't wanna take that risk?" Tyesha said. "You? Losing a few thousand dollars? You know what? Fuck this bullshit. We're gonna be the ones risking our lives. Risking jail time for breaking and entering or worse if the mob catches us. And for what? To get you out of a mess you got yourself into. And what's our reward? To get you to follow the fucking law and let these workers unionize, just so they can then fight with you to get you to stop treating them like shit? As far as I can see, this is one big fucking charity mission to clean up your mess, and you want us to do it on our own dime? You're just one entitled motherfucker, aren't you?" She turned from them. "Come on, Marisol."

"Wait!" Etta said, as Marisol turned and fell in step with Tyesha.

"It's not your voice I need to hear, Etta," Tyesha said. "Your man needs to act like he's the one getting rescued, not the one doing something for us."

Etta ran up and grabbed Tyesha's arm to stop her. She turned back to her husband. "Say something!" Etta yelled.

He stood silent, arms crossed over his chest, jaw tight.

"I can't do it," Etta said, her voice cracking. "I can't watch you sabotage our only chance to get out from under this. What about me? What about our kids? Maybe she's right. Maybe you are a selfish, entitled son of a bitch. Maybe I should be the one walking out."

She linked her arm through Marisol's, and the three women turned to leave.

"Etta, get back here!" he yelled.

"Why?" she demanded, tears streaming down her face. "So you can sabotage our family with your stubbornness? No, Teddy. You need to make a choice."

She turned and followed Tyesha and Marisol.

"Okay," he said.

When Tyesha turned around, his mouth was contracted into a tight circle and his eyes were focused far in the distance past the river.

Etta ran back to him. "Oh, thank you, baby. You won't regret this, I promise. These girls are gonna make it right. I know it."

Tyesha and Marisol walked slowly back. "Fine," he said, his voice tight. "I'll agree to your demands."

Marisol looked at Etta. "But how do we know we can trust him to keep his word?"

"We been together almost two decades," Etta said. "All he's been talking about these last few years is getting his club back."

"Well, I don't trust him," Marisol said. "But I trust you."

Etta nodded.

"And I don't trust either of you," Tyesha said. "But I trust Marisol, so we're gonna figure out how to get this gun back. But don't cross us, or you'll see that a bunch of pissed and well-organized strippers is a hell of its own."

They shook on it, and Tyesha and Marisol headed back to the office.

"You did great," Marisol said in the back of the cab. "You were tough, direct. Good threats, too."

"Sure," Tyesha said. "I'm fine when it's just a few people. But that press conference . . . That's the biggest group I've ever stood in front of. I used to get nervous at school, but never quite like this."

"Do you wanna maybe talk to Eva about it?" Marisol asked. "It's not an everyday thing, but part of the job is talking to the public."

"Maybe before the next press conference," Tyesha said. "But right now, we got our hands full running the clinic and trying to rob the mob."

That night, Tyesha, Marisol, Kim, and Jody met to plan the mob heist.

"Just like old times," Kim said. "Except our mark is the mob and not one of those Ivy Alpha guys."

"And we don't have Kim on the inside," Jody added. "What's our point of entry?"

"Probably our best shot is for somebody here to seduce one of the mob guys," Marisol said.

"But it can't be any of us, because we've all been seen in the press conferences," Kim said.

"Wait a minute," Tyesha said. "Jody's only been seen as herself: short, spiky, sandy blond hair, no makeup, butch clothes. If we do her up as Heidi Honeywell, they'll never recognize her."

Heidi was Jody's escort persona, a femme fatale.

"Brilliant," Kim said.

"And if we do her up as a blonde, that should give us access via the mobster's nephew—Ivan, the one who grabbed the girl at the club," Tyesha said. "She'll be just his type."

"Be careful, baby," Kim said. "He's a predator."

Jody laughed. "I got something for him. I'm gonna dust off my dominatrix personality. And my Taser."

Chapter 11

The following night, Tyesha and her nieces were playing spades in the apartment when there was a knock at the door.

"Are you expecting Thug Woofer?" Deza asked, jumping up off the couch and putting on a fresh coat of lipstick.

"No," Tyesha said.

Deza opened the door to find Jenisse.

"Okay, girls," her sister said. "Babysitting time with Auntie Ty-Ty is over. So pack up your shit, because we're going back to Chicago."

"What?" Amaru said. "School doesn't start for another month. I'm just getting into a workout rhythm here."

Tyesha came over and put her arm around Amaru.

"Yeah, Mama," Deza said. "Auntie Ty's gonna get me the hookup in my music career."

"I know y'all think your Auntie can work miracles, but I'm sure she's tired of your little slumber party. Especially when she can't just send you back. Like I said, we're going back to Chicago. I got your plane tickets. Now go get yo shit and come on."

"Mama," Deza said, "this is some bullshit. We came to New York with no notice, nothing. You were just like, 'pack yo shit, Zeus is going to New York.' So we get something going here, and now you're like 'let's go.'"

"Don't you cuss at me, little girl," Jenisse said. "And when you pay the bills, you can make the rules."

"It's not like you pay the bills," Deza muttered.

Under her arm, Tyesha could feel Amaru tense.

Jenisse turned her head sharply. "Excuse me?" Jenisse asked pointedly. "What did you say?"

"Nothing," Deza said.

Jenisse put her hands on her hips, and any pretense at politeness fell away. "Now you listen here, you little ungrateful bitches," Jenisse said. "That motherfucker doesn't just pay for shit out of the goodness of his heart. Just because he got money don't mean we got money, and it certainly don't mean you got money. I been fucking that nigga and stroking his overblown ego for thirty years to make sure his ass is in a good mood when it's time to throw down money for his kids. So yes, I do pay the bills. Now get yo asses ready and let's go."

"We're not going," Deza said. "You and Zeus have a fucked-up relationship, but that's not our fault. Auntie Ty said we could stay, and we wanna stay."

Amaru swallowed hard and nodded.

"You think Auntie Ty is ready to take on a pair of no-job heifers like you all?" Jenisse said with a laugh. "Think again."

Tyesha looked directly at her sister. "They can stay if they want." Her voice was gentle, but not apologetic. "It's up to them."

"Oh, so *now* you want them," Jenisse said. She turned to her daughters. "You about fifteen years too late. Just so you know, it was your precious auntie who told me to get an abortion when I was pregnant with Amaru. And when I told her I wouldn't, she said she was sorry I had Deza. That's right. I gave you life. Life, you ungrateful little bitches. And she thinks you both a mistake. So I'll be at the hotel, and our flight leaves Saturday. But if you don't come tonight, you're on your own to get back to Chicago."

Jenisse turned on her heel and slammed the door behind her.

Tyesha was stunned. Jenisse's revelations left her as mute as when she had stood at the podium.

Amaru was crying, her eyes on the floor with tears dropping down onto the lacquered hardwood.

Deza's eyes were focused out the window, staring out as a police car came shrieking up the street, lights flashing, engine roaring, wheels splashing down the slick pavement.

"Is it true?" Deza asked quietly.

Tyesha struggled to form words. "I—it's—it's not how it sounded," Tyesha said, curling her arm tighter around Amaru. "I love you both. It's—I was just worried about the kind of mom Jenisse was. And I thought . . . she was having kids for the wrong reasons. To keep your father. I mean, when she got pregnant with you, Amaru, your brothers were running the streets and getting into trouble and—"

She broke off and looked at Deza sitting on the floor against the front of the couch, her arms wrapped around her knees. "Deza, you were barely in kindergarten and Jenisse seemed to think she could just keep having kids and give them to Mama and it was all good, but I knew Mama's health wasn't great, and it was only a matter of time before Jenisse was gonna have to actually take care of you, and that looked like a bad plan. The only people Jenisse seemed to be able to think about were herself and Zeus."

"You're right, I guess," Amaru said. "When we lived with Grandma, it was cool. But since we been living with Ma, it's been all bad."

"But now you got me," Tyesha said, a tear sliding down her own face. "And getting to know you these past days, I'm so glad you were born. I can't believe how much I love you both."

"But if I got pregnant today, you'd tell me to have an abortion, wouldn't you?" Deza asked. "Don't lie."

Tyesha blew out her breath. "I—it's a paradox." She searched for the words. "It's like the *idea* of a child isn't the same as an actual child. Jenisse having more kids was a bad *idea*. But then you were born, and you became real. Beautiful, precious human beings."

Amaru's face was still puckered in a frown. "But how can a good life come from a bad decision?" she asked.

"It's not about good and bad," Tyesha said. "It's about making a commitment to raise a child. Like Deza, if you got pregnant, I'd hope you got an abortion because I know you'd resent the hell out of a kid coming between you and your basketball career. It's like . . . I believe in protecting and supporting the life that's already here. So once you got here, I'm committed to making sure you fulfill your dreams . . ."

"Did you ever get pregnant, Auntie Ty?" Deza asked.

"No," Tyesha said. "But that's probably because Aunt Lucille made me promise to use emergency contraceptives if I ever had unprotected sex."

"If I could get pregnant from sex with a girl, I'd have an abortion," Amaru said. "Nothing's gonna get in the way of basketball."

"So I hope you can understand why I said what I said to your mama," Tyesha said. "I knew how abusive she could be, and I would never want someone so abusive to have power over a child. But now you're old enough that you never need to live with her abuse again. My house is your house."

"For real?" Deza asked. "We could actually live with you? Permanently?"

"For real," Tyesha said. "Amaru, should I be looking at schools for you in the fall?"

Amaru shook her head. "I gotta go back to Chicago," she said. "But one of the girls on my team says I can stay with her when school starts."

"Deza?" Tyesha asked.

"Ain't nothing for me in Chicago but two crazy parents and an ex who broke my heart," Deza said.

"What ex?" Tyesha asked. "Do I need to go to Chicago and kick his ass? Where do I find this motherfucker?"

"He's one of the most famous DJs in Chicago," Deza said. "Everywhere you go, you'll see his picture, hear his mixes on the radio. It's like I couldn't get away from him. I'm so glad to be in New York. I can go three or four days without hearing that motherfucker's name."

"Tell me about it," Tyesha said. "When I stopped seeing Thug Woofer that last time, I had to leave the country to get away from reminders of him."

"But how am I gonna get back to Chicago in the fall?" Amaru asked.

"Mama gonna calm the fuck down before then," Deza said.

"And if she doesn't," Tyesha said, "I got you covered. For plane fare and whatever else you need for the start of the year."

"Thank you, Auntie Ty," Amaru said, and she threw her arms around Tyesha's neck.

"So it's settled," Tyesha said. "Amaru, you're staying for the summer, and Deza, you're here indefinitely."

Deza smiled. "More like temporarily," she said. "I'm just staying til Thug Woofer discovers me and sends me out on tour."

Tyesha just smiled and nodded, figuring she'd need to get Deza a real bed.

Late the next night, Tyesha, Marisol, Kim, and Jody sat around in Tyesha's office with the latest updates on the mob heist.

Kim and Jody sat on the black leather couch, and Marisol and Tyesha had the two matching chairs.

"So Kim and I staked out the Ukrainian mob bar all week," Jody said. "What's the plan? I get all sexied up and hang out in the bar til the nephew comes in?"

"I think that's too risky," Tyesha said. "We want you looking so hot that he can't ignore you. But we don't want you in there looking hot for three hours and fighting off the rest of the mob."

"I can handle myself," Jody said.

"We don't want him walking into a bar brawl," Tyesha said. "You and I can stake it out. We'll wait outside in the car til he comes in."

"That won't work," Kim said. "Some of the mob guys live above the bar, and there's a back stairway. Sometimes he goes up to their place for a little pre-drinking. We need someone actually inside the bar, watching til he comes in."

"So can one of you dress down and sit lookout til he gets there?" Jody asked.

"One of us?" Kim asked. "No, baby, we're all too brown for that place."

"What about Serena?" Jody asked.

"We agreed to keep it just the four of us," Tyesha said.

"Serena was pretty ride-or-die with that last job," Kim said. "She almost took a bullet for the clinic."

Marisol shook her head. "I agree with Tyesha," she said. "We've made it this far by keeping it to the four of us."

"Plus Eva," Tyesha said.

"Eva knows what we're doing, but we've never asked her to be a part of it," Marisol said.

"Then it's time to ask her," Tyesha insisted. "She'd be a perfect lookout. An older woman in a bar. She could watch everyone for hours. It'd be like she was invisible."

"There's gotta be another way," Marisol said. "I'm not asking Eva."

"Don't worry," Tyesha said. "I'll ask."

* * *

The next morning, Tyesha knocked on Eva's door.

"Thanks for fitting me in," Tyesha said, stepping into the cluttered office. She sat on the chair across from Eva's desk, which was covered with tall piles of client files and a stack of self-help books.

"Is everything okay?" Eva asked. "Did the girl agree to testify?"

Tyesha shook her head.

"Did those thugs try something new?" Eva asked.

"About that . . ." Tyesha said. "We have a . . . a plan in place to handle the mob. We just need a little help—"

"Legal help?" Eva asked.

"I hope not," Tyesha said.

Eva's eyes narrowed. "You and Marisol are cooking up another crazy plan, aren't you?" Eva said. "Didn't you two learn anything from your many narrow escapes from disaster earlier this year? Why would you tempt fate after you survived those heists?"

Tyesha swiveled in the chair and observed the narrow office's therapy side. It was open and peaceful, with two chairs, a couch, and a Zen sand garden on the table.

"Just let me explain the situation," Tyesha said.

"No," Eva said. "Don't tell me anything. So when I get a subpoena, I can pass the polygraph when I say I didn't know anything about it. So there can be somebody left to run the clinic when all of you are in jail."

Tyesha took a deep breath. "Okay," she said. "Let me ask you this. You know that guy in the One-Eyed King video who tries to drag the girl into the VIP room?"

"How could I forget?" Eva asked.

"Would you be willing to sit in a bar and look out for him?" Tyesha asked.

"Does this plan include him getting what's coming to him?" Eva asked.

"Definitely," Tyesha said.

"Just sit and have a few drinks?" Eva asked.

"Yeah," Tyesha said. "And when you feel ready to leave, just call one of us and say you're headed home."

"Can I drink the good stuff?"

"Supposedly they have an amazing Inheritance vodka martini," Tyesha said.

"Good," said Eva. "Because I'm too old to drink cheap liquor."

That afternoon around four p.m., Eva went to the Ukrainian mob bar.

It was a narrow space. A few men sat on stools at the long bar, and an empty pair of small tables were squeezed between a men's and women's restroom down at the end.

Behind the bar, one sign boasted that they stocked more than seventy-five brands of vodka. Another sign advertised a food menu: stuffed cabbage, stuffed peppers, *varenyky* (pierogi) in varieties of spinach, potato, and cheese.

A young bartender approached her, wiping the dark wooden bar with a stained cloth. He had bleached blond hair and a ribbed sleeveless shirt. He made Eva a vodka martini, which was indeed as good as Tyesha had promised.

A couple of hours later, the place had filled up. She had to wait a half hour for a plate of cheese pierogis, but the savory dumplings were worth it. She even got a couple with fruit for dessert.

It was after eight p.m. and Eva was sipping her way through her second martini when the nephew finally came in through an interior door across from the bar. He made a loud entrance with several cronies, elbowing his way across the crowded, narrow room. He greeted the bartender by name and ordered a round for his friends, although he was obviously already drunk.

Eva texted a signal to Jody and walked out.

Jody walked in and leaned on the bar next to where the nephew was waiting for his drinks.

He said something in Ukrainian, but Jody shook her head. "I speak English," she said.

"American, huh?" he said. "I like it. Come talk to me."

Jody shook her head. "No thanks," she said. "I'm just looking for the bathroom."

"You obviously don't know who I am," he said. "My uncle owns this bar."

"Then maybe I'd be interested in your uncle," she said. "I don't date from the kiddie table."

He grabbed her wrist, but she elbowed him hard in the chest.

"Don't you fucking walk away from me," he said.

She made her way to the women's bathroom without even turning her head. Inside there were two stalls.

She stood behind the bathroom door and flattened herself against the wall.

A moment later, the nephew loped into the room.

When the door opened, Jody caught the handle, using the door to screen her from view.

The nephew looked into each stall.

As he leaned into the second stall, Jody stepped forward and planted her feet. "What the hell are you doing in here?" she demanded.

When he turned around, he lunged at her. He managed to grab her breast with one hand and her arm with the other, but he was too drunk to be stable.

She put all her weight behind her shoulder and sprang at him, toppling him back. He went down in a slow, wobbling arc, hitting his head first on the stall wall, then on the toilet. He was knocked out before he even hit the ground.

He let out a whimpering groan as she stood over him and called Tyesha.

"You okay?" Tyesha asked.

"It was easier than I thought," Jody said. "I didn't even have to use my Taser."

The next night, they followed the same routine. Eva sat unobtrusively at the end of the bar and drank until the nephew came in.

Jody had barely ordered a drink when the nephew came up to her.

"Please," he said, "let me pay for that."

"Get away from me," she said.

"Listen," he began. "I'm sorry about last night. I was so drunk. I'm not even totally sure what happened. Only that my cousin found me in the ladies' room with a bump on my head. Please, let me buy you a drink to apologize."

"Fine," she said. "You can buy my vodka shot. But I still don't date at the kiddie table."

"I'm Ivan," he said and offered to shake.

"How nice for you," Jody said and ignored his hand. "I drink Inheritance."

He ordered the shot. "Did I mention my uncle owns this place?" he asked. "And there's a party at my uncle's house this Saturday. You might like to come? Meet some guys at the grown-ups' table?" He gave a forced laugh. "Here's the information."

He handed her a card with an address.

"I'll think about it," she said. "But if I show up, you need to understand that I'm not coming as your date, because I'm not interested in you."

"Understood," he said. "It's just a peace offering."

"Maybe I'll give peace a chance and see you Saturday," she said and downed her shot. "Thanks for the drink."

The following day, Jenisse showed up at Tyesha's office.

"I need to talk to you," Jenisse said. She had on tight designer jeans and stiletto sandals. Her short-sleeved blouse was sheer silk, with ample cleavage spilling out of the camisole clearly visible beneath.

"Listen, Jenisse," Tyesha began, "I wasn't trying to undermine you, but—"

"Don't nobody care about that anymore," Jenisse said. "That's old news. Listen, I need you to get saliva samples from Deza and Amaru for a DNA test."

"Why are you coming up here on my job asking me to get something from your own kids?" Tyesha asked. "Get it from them yourself."

"Neither one of those little bitches will pick up the phone when I call," Jenisse said.

Tyesha shrugged. "How is that my problem?"

Jenisse set her jaw. "Listen, I know I ain't no mother of the year, but I get shit handled for my babies. If they don't wanna live with me, then they need another situation. Deza's grown and can live with you or that DJ in Chicago or whatever. But Amaru's too young. Mama was the main one taking care of them, and then Deza took care of Amaru."

"Amaru wants to go back to Chicago," Tyesha said.

"You don't know everything," Jenisse said. "Amaru begged me to send her to this basketball boarding school, but it costs a ton of money. Zeus wouldn't pay last year. Anyway, I think that's where she oughta go. That's really what I been fighting about with him. I finally got him to admit that he don't wanna spend all that, because he ain't sure that he's Amaru's daddy. He been saying that shit about both girls since I got pregnant. So I said, let's do a DNA test. And he said okay to test both girls. If they both his, he gonna send Amaru to that school. He might even send Deza to cosmetology school."

"So I'm supposed to get a sample of their saliva and send it in?"

"Here's the kit," Jenisse said. "Zeus already sent in his sample and paid for the test. Just get the girls to do it, okay?"

"Of course," Tyesha said. "I'll do it as soon as I have them both together."

"Good," Jenisse said. "My plane leaves for Chicago tomorrow. You got my number if those girls need anything. I know we ain't friends, Tyesha, but we family."

And she swept out, leaving a cloud of perfume in her wake.

The following night was Saturday, and a dark limo pulled up outside the security gates of a massive stone house just north of the Bronx.

Tyesha sat in the car wearing a chauffeur's cap. Marisol, Jody, and Kim sat in back. All four had on in-ear walkie-talkie communicators.

"Okay, test the camera," Tyesha said.

She activated the recording device on Jody's necklace. Suddenly, the image of the car's interior and the back of Tyesha's head with the chauffeur's cap came up on the laptop.

"Looks good," Marisol nodded approvingly.

"Let's do this," Tyesha said, and maneuvered the car back onto the road, and up to the security gates.

Jody rolled down the window and gave the nephew's name to the security guard in the booth.

He made a phone call and looked her over as she waited. The limo's windows were blackout-tinted. Marisol and Kim sat in a rear-facing middle seat, completely hidden from the guard's view.

The guard nodded. "He'll meet you at the house," he said.

The heavy, barbed-wire-topped gate slid open, and Tyesha drove the car up the winding driveway.

The four of them could see a wide lawn and silhouettes of hedges and distant outbuildings.

They pulled up to the front of a mini mansion the color of wet sand.

Jody slid out of the car in a clinging navy blue dress, and Ivan came down the front steps to meet her.

The limo slid quietly away to a paved parking area filled with limos and town cars. Several guys in chauffeur's caps were standing around talking and smoking.

Meanwhile, Ivan took Jody by both hands. "You made it," he said, grinning at her.

"You're lucky I was bored tonight," she said.

"So what's your name?" he asked. "You never told me."

"Heidi," she said, as she clacked up the porch steps in stiletto sandals, her long blond ponytail swinging behind her.

He put a palm on her back, as if she needed steering into the house.

"Hands off, junior," she said, pushing his arm away.

He pulled open the large wooden door and they walked into a foyer. Off to the left, she could see a room with several security guards and a bank of monitors. Jody turned so that the camera got a good view.

"They don't hide the security setup, do they?" Kim said in the back of the limo.

"I don't think they're trying to hide it," Tyesha said. "I bet he's advertising for everyone here that he's got loads of security."

As they walked in, Jody pretended to be preoccupied with her phone.

"Is the cell reception bad here?" she asked.

She held up the phone as if to get a signal, but was really snapping still pictures of the security setup and the camera locations.

Ivan grabbed her phone. "I want your attention tonight," he said.

Watching and listening from the video monitor in the limo, Tyesha felt panicked.

"Marisol, get ready to go in after her if need be."

Over the monitor, they heard Jody's voice, a combination of irritation and boredom: "Give it back, junior," she said. "Daddy's company is in the middle of fighting a hostile take-over. I'm a shareholder and have to lobby other shareholders to keep him from getting ousted. The vote is Monday morning."

From the body camera on Jody, they could see Ivan's chest, and the phone gripped in his hand with the security photo clearly showing.

"What?" Jody said with a sneer in her voice. "Did you think I came here to give you my undivided attention? Did I hurt your wittle feewings?"

"I don't usually let girls talk to me like this," Ivan said, an edge in his voice.

"You're lucky I'm talking to you at all," Jody said. "Now give me my phone."

From the body cam, the team could see the blurry image of both her hands, her blue nails in motion as she fidgeted with the panic gizmo. She could hit the alarm if he called her bluff.

He held the phone aloft, out of her reach.

Jody and all of the team saw the screen go dark as the phone auto-locked.

"Fine," she said. "Go ahead and look. It's really an ex that's been texting me. I'll see myself out."

"I'm sorry, Heidi," he said. "I just wanted your atten-tion."

"Men get attention by being interesting," she said. "Boys get it by being annoying."

"Please," he said. "Stay."

"Don't ever do that again," she said brushing past him to walk into the party. She snatched her phone from him and took the panic alarm off alert mode.

Inside, the foyer opened up into a large room with tall win-dows and a marble floor. It was filled with attractive young women and older men. Occasionally, a man would have a woman over forty on his arm, but those men were usually over sixty. Ivan took Jody across to the open bar.

A bartender rushed over to help him.

"She better not drink anything he gives her," Kim said, as she watched from the car.

"A vodka shot for my friend," Ivan ordered.

"I'd rather have a beer," Jody said, and grabbed a closed bottle. She banged it open on the edge of the bar.

"That's not very ladylike," Ivan said.

"But a vodka shot is?" Jody asked.

"Let me show you around," Ivan said.

"What?" Jody said. "You gonna show me the nursery? The playroom?"

"Actually . . ." Ivan began.

"If you say bedroom, I'm calling my chauffeur," she said.

"How about the hot tub?"

She shook her head. "I live in a house twice this size. What can you show me that I haven't seen before?"

"How about I show you my uncle's office?" Ivan asked.

Jody raised her eyebrows. "Really?" she said. "That does sound interesting." She downed half her beer and set the bottle on a side table.

Ivan took her by the hand and led her down a long corridor. At the end of the hall was a large door. Ivan produced a key and unlocked it.

"Do the grown-ups know you're in here?" Jody asked.

"Maybe," he said, and swung the door open.

The room was dark mahogany and leather, a deep burgundy that was almost black. It had an oversized antique wooden desk. On the walls were several oil paintings in large frames. Rural landscapes and nude women.

"Nice," Jody said. "Now where does your uncle keep the good liquor?"

She opened several cabinets and peeked behind a few pic-

tures. Inside the limo, the three team members shared a si-
multaneous intake of breath as they caught sight of a safe's
dial behind one of the landscape paintings.

"I don't see any good booze," Jody said. "Let's go back to
the bar."

"I thought maybe we could look around some more,"
Ivan said.

"Who are you, Dora the Explorer?" she asked. "I told
you I'm not your date. Now let's get back to the party."

"I was thinking maybe we could have our own little private party in here," he said, pulling a bag of white powder
from his pocket.

"Oh, please," she said and walked to the door.

"What'd I do?" he asked, pocketing the bag and scram-
bling after her.

Jody paused in the doorway, with her phone out. "You
don't get it, Junior," she said. "I came in my family's limo.
I'm not one of the party girls out there who's ready to drop
her panties because there's an open bar. If I wanted coke or
heroin or ecstasy or whatever's in your little bag there, I
would call my dealer and get stuff that's ten times better
quality." She turned her back on him and strode down the
hall. Pulling out her phone, she commanded, "Claudette,
bring the car, I'm leaving."

Tyesha climbed into the front seat and started the limo.

Back in the house, Ivan hurried after Jody: "I didn't mean
to offend you," he said.

"Save it." She waved a hand over her shoulder and walked
out the front door, with him trailing after her.

Tyesha stood outside the limo with a blank expression.
She held the back door open. Inside the limo, she had raised
the partition between the middle and rear compartments, so
Marisol and Kim were completely hidden. Sometimes Marisol
had used this kind of limo when a pair of dates wanted privacy to have sex in the car.

"Please," Ivan begged as Jody slid in. "Heidi, give me another chance."

"This was already your second chance," she said.

He handed her his card. "Look, call me and tell me how I can make it up to you."

She took the card. "That's unlikely," she said and slammed the door in his face.

Chapter 12

The next evening, Tyesha sat around the kitchen table with her nieces, finishing up some Vietnamese takeout.

"I like this Sunday dinner thing," Deza said. "It's like something on TV. With Mama and Zeus we never eat together."

"So your mama left for Chicago yesterday," Tyesha began.

"Can we get some news we can use?" Amaru asked.

"Well," Tyesha said, "I mention it because she said she's been calling you both and you haven't picked up."

"I been busy," Amaru said sullenly.

"I haven't," Deza said. "I just don't want to talk to her. Would you pick up her call after that shit she pulled?"

"No comment," Tyesha said. "But she came by my office this week because she had something she thought was important, and for once I agreed with her."

"Papers to make me an emancipated minor?" Amaru asked.

Tyesha shook her head. "A DNA test," she said. "For Zeus."

Amaru leaped up from the table. "Oh, hell no," she said.

"It's just a saliva swab," Tyesha said.

"I ain't got even a drop of spit for that cause," Amaru said.

Deza agreed. "It's just part of some bullshit plan of hers to make herself more valuable to him because she's a legit baby mama. Fuck that."

"Actually," Tyesha said, "Jenisse was thinking it might be a good time to send you to that athletics academy you were interested in, Amaru."

"Now?" Amaru said. "She trying to get me in that boarding school now? I begged her all through middle school. Begged. But she needed us around. Now that we ain't around anyway, she don't mind letting me go? Besides, I heard them talking about it years ago. Zeus refused to get the test back then. Only now that there's money involved is he gonna be bothered. He never really wanted us. He only wanted the boys. Took them everywhere with him. Did everything with them. Look how that turned out. Fuck him. And his test. Fuck them both."

"But Amaru," Tyesha said, "this could be good for you."

"I got my plan already," Amaru said. "I'ma stay with my friend in Chicago. I don't need shit from them. I don't even want to be his kid."

She knocked her chair over, and then ran to the front door, slamming it behind her.

Tyesha rushed after her, "Amaru, wait!"

Deza came up behind her aunt. "Let her go," she said. "She'll walk for twenty minutes to let her food digest, then run a few miles, then her endorphins will kick in, and she'll be fine."

"And then she'll do the test?" Tyesha asked.

"With her stubborn ass?" Deza said. "No chance. In seventh grade Mama said that she might be able to go to that school, and she got her hopes up. She's way too afraid of being disappointed again."

"But we need these DNA results," Tyesha said.

"What if it shows we ain't his?" Deza said. "Fucked up as he is, he's the only daddy I ever had."

"First of all, that's ridiculous," Tyesha said. "You look just like him. Second of all, your mama is crazy in a lot of ways. But we both know that her life plan has been to be Zeus's number one woman. She wouldn't mess that up by having some other man's baby. I'm convinced she would have had that abortion if there was even a chance either of you wasn't his."

Deza nodded. "That sounds like Mama."

"So what do we do?" Tyesha asked. "Can you get some of Amaru's spit in her sleep?"

"Hell, no," Deza said. "Can't they test hair?" Deza picked up the test kit. "Call the lab."

As it turned out, the lab could test hair. Tyesha gave them her office address to send the test kit for hair instead of saliva.

The following afternoon, Tyesha, Marisol, Kim, and Jody sat around in Tyesha's office, looking over the floor plan of the mobster's house that Jody had drawn.

Serena knocked at the door, and Tyesha flipped over the floor plan.

"Come in," she called.

Serena walked in and handed Tyesha the DNA test kit that the lab had sent over.

"Are you testing your ancestry?" Kim asked. "Turns out I'm not just Korean, but also part Chinese, Japanese, and a little bit of French. Thank you, colonization."

"No," Tyesha said. "Some family drama."

The four of them waited until Serena had closed the door behind her.

"Anyway, back to the planning."

Jody drew X's on the floor plan where she had observed cameras. "You shoulda let Serena stay," Jody said. "None of us knows how to do something this sophisticated."

"I'm starting to think that maybe Jody's right," Tyesha said. "We need Serena. We'll just have to trust her."

"And she finally got her papers," Kim said. "So we don't have to worry about immigration anymore."

"It's not only about trusting her," Marisol said. "Even though she finally has her residence status, she's still a trans woman. If we get caught, they'll send her to a men's prison. Have you thought about that?"

"Then we need to make sure not to get caught," Tyesha said. "And we need to make sure that she's only helping us with the tech stuff, not actually out at the job."

"Besides," Kim said, "Serena can decide for herself which risks she wants to take."

"I agree," Jody said.

"So everybody's in favor but you, Marisol," Tyesha said.

Marisol's mouth was tight. "I can see that," she said. "But you only see one side of her. You see the efficient computer whiz and the perfect assistant. None of you were there when Serena came into the clinic as a client. She was running from a homicidal boyfriend and on the verge of suicide. Do you know what the life expectancy is for immigrant trans women? When I took away her razor, I promised her that she could have a good life. A safe and peaceful life. Don't make a liar out of me."

"Serena has that now," Tyesha said. "But she also wants to help keep other sex workers safe. Don't underestimate her."

Marisol didn't like it, but she didn't object when Tyesha went out into the reception area and asked Serena to come in.

Serena sat on the couch between Marisol and Kim. She was so petite that she fit easily between them. Her light fly-away hair had a bright green streak among the auburn.

Tyesha looked at Marisol to start the conversation, but Marisol looked back, eyebrows raised.

Tyesha took a deep breath: "Serena, you know how things have been a little crazy with the strippers' union."

Serena nodded.

"Well, we might need a little . . ." Tyesha searched for the words. "A little technical assistance."

"Sure," Serena said. "How can I help?"

"It's . . . ah . . . sort of more like—" Tyesha began, but Kim cut her off.

"Like hacking," Kim said.

Serena's eyes lit up. "I got a few skills in that department," Serena said.

"But really it's more than that," Tyesha said. "We need technical assistance to gain entry to a physical location."

"Count me in," Serena said. "I—"

Marisol cut her off. "I don't want you to feel pressured," Marisol said. "After all, you just got your green card."

Serena tilted her head to the side. "Seriously, Marisol?" Serena said. "I sent donors up to your escort service for years. I knew there was other stuff going on. But I kept my mouth shut because I'm loyal, and I figured you'd tell me when you were good and ready. Besides, maybe I'm off the streets and have a green card, but plenty of folks around here are ass out. I'm not gonna play it safe when they depend on us. Just tell me what you need."

Marisol opened her mouth to protest, but Tyesha spoke first.

"Can you help us hack a security feed?" Tyesha asked Serena.

"What type of system?" Serena asked.

Tyesha nodded to Jody. She pulled up the photos on her phone of the security system at the mob mansion.

Serena sat looking at the images for a long time. She blew up the photos and peered intently at some of the details.

After a couple of minutes, Tyesha began to get uncomfortable. She looked over at Marisol, who had raised an accusing eyebrow. Maybe this had been a mistake. Maybe she should have taken more time to consider whether or not to involve Serena.

"I need to get my laptop," Serena said.

"Why yours?" Tyesha asked.

"I have better cloaking security for some of the searches I need to do," Serena said.

Marisol's eyebrow went down, but Tyesha still felt uneasy.

Half an hour later, Serena closed her laptop and set down Jody's phone.

"I can't hack it from my computer," Serena said. "It's an old-school system—analog. I'd have to actually splice into the feed through the wires."

She pulled up a picture from Jody's phone that showed the front of the mob mansion. Jody looked almost ghoulish with her pale skin and platinum hair. Serena blew up a section next to the stairs as large as she could make it.

There was a slight L-shaped shadow. Serena snapped a screen shot of the area and blew it up three more times.

"The photo isn't that sharp with the low light," Serena said. "But I would bet that this is the box."

"That makes sense," Jody said. "It's right outside the security guards' room."

"I can't see the detail well enough, but there's probably a lock on it," Serena said. "If one of you can get past that, I can hack the feed and it'll be online. I should be able to monitor if we have a nearby van."

"One of us can definitely get through the lock," Tyesha said, glancing at Kim. "Then what?"

"Someone would need to distract the guards for a moment while the video system resets," Serena said.

"Will the screens go blank?" Jody asked.

"Maybe," Serena said. "Maybe a glitch. Maybe snow. We just need them looking away for a moment."

"Okay," Tyesha said. "So we just need to pick the lock, hack into the system, distract the guards, get a van, and you can monitor and hack it from there. Anything else?"

"My laptop doesn't have the hardware or the software needed to hack a feed," Serena said. "I'll need some pretty sophisticated equipment."

"Our benefactor isn't going to like this," Tyesha said, thinking of Teddy Hughes.

"Nope," Marisol agreed. "But we'll just have to sell him on it."

"Okay," Tyesha said. "Let's flesh the plan out, do up a budget, and set a meeting with our benefactor and his better half."

The five of them worked on brainstorming late into the night, and after several hours, they had a workable plan. They'd just need a medical van, a pile of video hacking equipment, another limo, and a strong, quick-acting sedative that wouldn't completely inhibit sexual performance in a man.

Tyesha showed up at Thug Woofer's house with a bag of takeout and a DNA paternity hair test kit in her briefcase.

"Sorry our dinner turned into a midnight snack," she said. "I had to work late."

"It's all good," Woof said, sitting down on the couch. "But this is definitely a Melvyn type date, not a Woof date." He gestured to the takeout on the coffee table. "None of this could go in a rap video. Where's the yacht?"

"Well, if we had a fireplace instead of a fountain, it could be a nineties R and B video," Tyesha said.

Woof laughed, and leaned back on the couch, pulling her with him. She lay back against his chest.

"I like it," Tyesha said. "This is more everyday and less larger than life. Just two people eating some food in a Brooklyn apartment. Is this a sign that you live here permanently now?"

"I'm here for the foreseeable future," he said. "But I haven't put anything on the walls because I don't know how long I'm staying. Nothing's permanent. I'm learning that in my meditation. Everything changes. And our attachment causes suffering."

"My fucking sister causes suffering," Tyesha said. "And it doesn't seem to matter how unattached to her I get."

"Breathe," Thug Woofer said. "Feel the connection, and then release."

Tyesha laughed. "What kind of meditation is that? Your dating habits? A philosophy of not getting attached?"

"My previous dating habits," Woof said. "With you I've always been serious. At least after that first date, where—it was professional."

"Why me, though?" Tyesha asked. "You meet thousands of girls. There's like five billion women on the planet, and most would say yes to you. Why me?"

"First off, I only really like black women, so that cuts down several billion," he said. "And then it's always something. A lot of those women are just gold-diggers. I could be any guy with money or fame. They just want a piece of the shine."

Tyesha leaned back and gazed at the potted plants. She didn't recall anything like that in his old apartment.

"Then there's the career women. And I'm too hood for a lot of them. I mean, they think I'm sexy, but I don't fit at their dinner parties. I even met this one chick at a meditation retreat. She wasn't bourgie, but, you know, I use the N-word sometimes."

He paused for a moment, and all they could hear was the trickle of the fountain. It had clear stones in it, bright colors, but clear glass and not blingy.

"I mean, I know all the history, but I also grew up using the word, and it's got a history with me personally. Like this one guy Darnell I grew up with. I mean, that's my nigga. Plain and simple. I'll punch any white boy who tries to use it, and I stopped using it in my music. Bitch and ho, too. I get it now that I have a responsibility to young black people. But if it's the weekend and I'm kicking it with my niggas, I'm kicking it with my niggas. I mean my baby uncle used to call me his favorite li'l nigga and he'd hug me. It's a private conversation."

"The meditation chick didn't get it?" Tyesha asked.

"She gave me this lecture," he said. "Seriously talking down to me. Like that same day at the meditation retreat we wasn't talking about how life is a paradox. Nigga is a paradox. It's a part of me, just like it's part of our history. Black people always taking ugly shit and finding ways to put love in it. I choose my words carefully when I make music now, but I'm not gonna censor myself when I'm with my woman."

"My auntie used to tell us not to use it," Tyesha said. "But sometimes I'd hear her talking to my mama late at night, talking bout 'these niggas driving me crazy.' "

Woof laughed. "Yes, just like that. I remember that night, with that girl. I was like, Tyesha would understand this. I wouldn't have to explain. She would already know."

"You saying you tryna be my nigga," Tyesha asked.

"Hell, yeah."

"Well, then, come over here and show me, my nigga," she said.

Woof tilted his head to the side. "You sure you can handle it?"

"Try me," she said.

Woof walked over to the stereo and put something on. He had walked halfway back across the room when Tyesha heard the opening guitar lick from a song that had come out when she was in high school.

It was a female rapper named SoSleek, a one-album wonder. She was as unapologetically plus-sized as she was sexy, and she distinguished herself from the crowd of female emcees by rapping about what she liked in bed and getting men to please her, instead of the other way around. She had recently had a career revival on the reality TV show *Badass Femcee Battle*.

Tyesha threw back her head and laughed. "No, you didn't," she said.

"Oh, yes," Woof said, sliding his hands around her hips. "I definitely did."

SoSleek opened with the song's hook:

That nigga got me sprung
Does magic wit his tongue

Woof pulled Tyesha into a kiss and undid the back of her skirt and licked his finger. Then he slid his hand down into her underwear.

Tyesha moaned and pressed herself against him.

With Woof's other hand, he unbuttoned her blouse. Fortunately, her bra hooked in the front, and he undid it.

He pressed her up against the back of the sofa and began to hungrily lick one of her breasts while caressing the other. His other hand pressed between her lips, his middle finger stroking insistently.

Tyesha squirmed with pleasure, the back of the couch making escape impossible.

Woof pulled up from licking her nipple and devoured her in a kiss.

Tyesha could barely breathe, her knees threatening to buckle.

Woof pulled his face back and surveyed her. Head thrown back, eyes half closed, mouth spilling moans. She gripped his shoulders with her hands to stay up, her nails nearly breaking the skin.

"Are you close?" he asked.

Tyesha couldn't speak—only gave a slight whimper in the affirmative.

A slow grin spread over Woof's face, and he pulled his

hand from her underwear and flipped her over the back of the couch.

Before Tyesha knew what was happening, he had come around and was pulling off her underwear and hiking up her skirt.

While his finger had been insistent, his tongue was merciless. She came right away, but he wouldn't stop. He grabbed her ass with both hands to keep her in place and balanced himself on his elbows, using his tongue, his lips, and even an occasional gentle nip until she came again.

Only then did he take off his jeans and roll on a condom. When he slid inside, she was liquid and felt nearly boneless.

"Damn, girl, you feel soo good."

After holding back, he stroked furiously for a moment.

Tyesha's eyes flew wide.

"Like that?" he asked. "Can I make you come again like that?"

"Yes," she gasped, and she came. Then he did.

A few moments later, she woke up from having dozed off for a moment. Her arm had fallen asleep, pinned under Woof's shoulder.

"I don't think I can move," she said with a laugh.

Woof roused himself. "Lemme get this condom," he said.

As he pulled out and went to dispose of it, Tyesha realized he had left the song on loop. SoSleek continued to declare:

That nigga got me sprung
Does magic with his tongue.

In the morning, she woke up in his bed, not quite recalling if she'd walked there or been half carried.

She leaned over and woke him with a kiss.

"I need to get going," she said. "Is it still a walk of shame if I'm not ashamed?"

"Don't go home," he said. "Stay."

"Some family business I gotta handle," she said.

"Can't you handle it tomorrow?" he asked.

"I guess I could," she said. "But I can't go back to the office wearing the same clothes, with my hair uncombed."

"Just tell me what you need," Woof said. "I'll get it for you."

"I'm not talking about a toothbrush Woof," she said. "I need a business suit."

He leaned over and picked up his smart phone. "What size?"

"Are you kidding me?"

"No," he said, tapping on his phone's screen. "You like Dilani Mara, right? What about this suit?" He indicated a magenta silk suit with a classic rounded collar. It was cut with the designer's signature hourglass proportions.

He ran his hands down the side of her body from her shoulder to her knee. "You probably wouldn't even need to get it tailored. My personal shopper could pick it up for you and drop it here in the morning. Along with a toothbrush. And somebody to do your hair."

Tyesha's eyes widened. "That suit is fucking gorgeous, but I don't—I mean—"

"Maybe this is the part of the date that's a little less Melvyn and a little more rap video," he said. "So what do you say?"

"I say I'm a size twelve," she said. "And this is much better than a yacht." She rolled over to kiss him again.

The next day, Tyesha wore her Dilani Mara suit to the meeting with Teddy and Etta Hughes. It was hot and muggy, so she didn't want to meet on the docks. She'd be sweating in five minutes, even with the lightweight fabric.

Instead, they met in Penn Station. Marisol and Tyesha stood around in the Long Island Railroad terminal. They had waited about twenty minutes when Teddy and Etta came in and stood next to them. Tyesha pulled out her phone and pretended to dial, then began talking.

"So," she said briskly, "we've done the initial assessment and will need an additional seven to ten thousand for equipment. I know this is above what we had originally discussed, but the client has a totally antiquated system, and this is what's needed to get things into the twenty-first century."

"Are you fucking kidding me?" Teddy asked, abandoning the ruse of the phone and glowering at Tyesha.

Tyesha put a finger in her ear and turned her back to him. "This is a professional operation," she said. "I'm not working with a bunch of fucking amateurs. I have no problem walking away. You need this much more than we do." She tapped the screen of her phone and turned back to Marisol.

"There's one client that'll be spending time in jail," Tyesha said pointedly. "No need for that trip upstate now."

Tyesha picked up her briefcase, and the two women began walking out.

Before she hit the door, Marisol's phone rang.

"If those motherfuckers are calling from their cell, it'll be Etta's ass," Marisol murmured, rummaging through her bag. "I told them clearly no cell communication."

But instead, the call was from a 212 number.

Marisol picked up her cell, and Tyesha looked over her shoulder to find Etta standing at a nearby pay phone.

"Why don't the two of you go to the coffee spot behind you," Etta suggested. "I think we'll be able to work something out."

Tyesha and Marisol walked over and stood in line behind a woman ordering several iced frappuccinos. Tyesha and Marisol could see the couple arguing. At first, Teddy was heated, but Etta began to cry and then jabbed him in the chest several times. He moved in close and hissed something at her, then pushed her away and stormed off.

Etta walked over to the coffee franchise and took a couple of napkins to wipe her eyes.

"Ten thousand," she murmured to Tyesha and Marisol. "I can have cash by tomorrow morning."

"Well done," Tyesha said, and she and Marisol headed down to the subway.

The following night, the team sat around in Tyesha's office, preparing for the next phase of the plan.

Jody picked up her burner phone and called Ivan, the mobster's nephew. She put him on speaker.

"I'm bored," Jody said. "Say something interesting or I'm hanging up."

"Heidi?" Ivan asked.

"How is my own name supposed to be interesting to me?"

"First of all, I'm sorry I insulted you with that cocaine," he said. "How about you come over for some limited-edition vodka?"

"I'm busy later," she said. "I was just bored."

"Well, soon my uncle's going out of town for a week," he said. "We could have the place to ourselves. And I got this vodka, just hoping you might call."

"I guess I'll consider it," Jody said. "Assuming I don't get a better offer. I'll text you tomorrow night if I'm coming," she said. "How will I get in?"

"I'll text you the gate code."

The next day after work, Tyesha stopped by her place to pick up a few things before going back to Woof's. Both girls were out of the apartment. Which was good, because she didn't want to have to explain to Deza that Woof was buying her three-thousand-dollar suits.

After changing into sweats, she watered the orchid and set it out in the window box. Then packed an overnight bag with her own business clothes for the next day.

She grabbed her toiletries and stood in the bathroom look-ing at the hairbrush. She still hadn't sent off the sample for the DNA test kit. The hair in the brush was mostly brown with rainbow strands. Clearly both of the girls had been using her brush.

She pulled out a few strands. Amaru had medium-short, natural hair. Tyesha had a press instead of a perm, so some of the kinky hairs could have been hers from the day she came home with her hair soaked and turned back. Deza's hair was permed and pressed with streaks of different colors.

She called Deza's phone. "How do I sort out all this hair?" she asked. "We can't just send all this to the lab."

"Why not?" Deza asked. "Zeus is paying for it. Let the lab sort it out. It's just mine, yours, and Amaru's in there."

"What about all the fake hair?" Tyesha asked. "Isn't it mine, yours, hers, and a hundred different women from India?"

Deza laughed. "Maybe last month, but all my fake hair is plastic right now."

"I'll see what they say," Tyesha said.

When she got through to the lab again, they said that for an additional fee, they could sort through and test all the hair with bulb roots. They could easily test whether or not they were full siblings, and could also test whether or not they were daughters based on Zeus's saliva sample.

Tyesha went back to the bathroom and tugged at the ball of hair. The bristles had balls on the end, so it was tough. Finally, with a hard tug, the ball came free. Her hand swung back from the effort and she burned herself on the flatiron that Deza had left on again.

"Goddammit!" she yelled, running her burned hand under cold water.

She called Deza to read her the riot act, but got voice mail. She couldn't kick them out now that she'd promised they could stay. But would these girls really end up burning her apartment down?

Seething, Tyesha unplugged the pressing iron and left an angry note. She dropped the rainbow-streaked ball of hair into the test kit and took the hairbrush with her to Woof's. They could get their own damn brush.

A couple nights later, Jody and Tyesha rolled up to the mobster's house in the limo. There was no one in the guardhouse. Tyesha punched in the code that Ivan had given Jody.

They drove up to the front door, and Jody stepped out of the car in a slinky purple dress and ankle boots. Inside her ear was a communicator that kept her in touch with all the rest of the team.

The front door opened, and Ivan came out to meet her.

"My uncle's gone for the next three days," he said.

Jody shrugged. "Let's see if this vodka was worth my time."

Again, the team in the car watched as he led her into the large living room.

He walked across the gleaming marble floor to the large liquor cabinet between a pair of bay windows. The bottle was violet-colored and shaped like a stalagmite. He began to unscrew the cap.

"There's no ambience in here," she complained. "Let's go back to that office room I saw last time. This place feels like we're early for ballroom dancing lessons or something. It's more cozy in there. More . . . masculine."

"Sure," Ivan agreed, snatching up the bottle and two shot glasses.

The two of them walked down the corridor to the office. This time Jody let him keep his hand on her back.

He opened the office door, and she walked right in and sat on the desk.

She watched carefully as he poured the shots and made sure he drank first.

"Wow," she said. "That is good vodka. Not to mention that it heated me right up. Can we open a window?"

He scurried over to do as she requested. A lukewarm evening breeze wafted in.

She patted the desk next to her. "Come sit by me," she said. "You're kind of cute when you're obedient. In a sort of puppy dog way."

When he sat down, she grabbed him and gave him an aggressive kiss. He reciprocated and reached for her breast, but she slapped his hand. He reared back, eyebrows up in surprise.

"I call the shots," she said.

"Absolutely," he said.

"Let's go to your bedroom," she said.

He readily agreed, and on the way out of the office, she carefully slid a piece of linoleum in place to keep the door from closing.

In his bedroom, she pulled a flask out of her purse. "My favorite vodka cocktail," she said, taking a long pull. "An original recipe. I call it crazy ice."

"Let me taste it," he asked.

She leaned forward and kissed him hard as she dropped something into the flask. Pulling out of the kiss, she handed it to him. "Swirl this around under your tongue to get the full sensation." He took a drink and swirled it for a moment.

"You like that?" she asked.

He nodded.

"Then take it all," she said with a grin.

He emptied the flask, and she pulled him down onto the bed.

After several minutes of kissing, she started to unbuckle his belt. She pulled down his pants and underwear. He looked down at his raging erection and gave her a lopsided grin. She pulled a packet of lube from where she had tucked it in her bra. His head began to droop. Before he could nod off, she squirted the lube onto him and gave him a quick hand job. Then she texted the team that he was knocked out.

Fifteen minutes later, Kim drove up to the security checkpoint in a concierge medical van and punched in the code.

By the time she knocked on the door, the security was in high alert. But they calmed down when they saw that the visitor was an attractive Asian woman in a cocktail dress.

"He didn't say he was expecting two girls," one of the guards said.

Jody swept into the foyer. "Dr. Chen," she said. "Thank you so much for coming."

"I'm sorry, miss," the guard said. "Your friend isn't authorized to be here."

"Friend?" Kim said, outraged. "I'm not her friend, I'm her doctor."

"And if you must know," Jody said, "the condom broke and she's bringing me emergency birth control."

"I'm sorry, but you'll need to arrange to see your doctor on your own time," the guard said.

"Are you kidding me?" Kim said. "I was on my way to a banquet with the governor."

As Jody and Kim argued with the guards, Serena and Marisol slipped out of the limo.

Both had on black clothes and dark wool caps. Marisol also had on a costume bodysuit that made the silhouette of her upper body look like a man's. The pair of them crept up to the security box on the side of the house.

Marisol pulled out the lock picks and began to tinker with the lock. Serena found the company name on the box and looked up specs on the company's website.

A moment later, Marisol had the box unlocked. Serena

opened her toolkit and Marisol held the flashlight while Serena cut and spliced various wires.

Five minutes later, Marisol closed and relocked the box, then hunkered down in some shrubs beside the house.

Serena climbed into Kim's medical van and opened her laptop. She pressed the code to activate the security hack. A moment later, all twelve cameras came online.

Inside the mansion, Kim handed Jody a package.

"Listen, Heidi," Kim said. "This is the last time I'm doing this. It's not an emergency, it's become a lifestyle. Come see me in my office and we'll give you the birth control shot."

Kim strode back to the van and drove back down the driveway, with Serena in tow. They parked just outside the property.

Inside the fake medical van, they were able to see and record everything on the real security feed. Meanwhile Serena went to work. After a half hour, she had rigged the monitors to show the security guards a loop of nothing happening in the office.

"All clear," Serena said into her communicator.

Jody crept down the stairs and into the mobster's office. She slid the window all the way open and reached down to pull Marisol up into the study.

"We need to move that camera," Serena's voice came through on the communicators. "I can't see the safe."

Marisol couldn't quite reach it, but Jody had the height.

Serena and Kim directed her until they had a clear, albeit off-center, shot of the portrait.

In the ski mask, Marisol couldn't hear well enough to crack the safe, so she pulled it off and cracked it with the stethoscope, then put the mask back on and simply turned it to the combination.

When the safe cracked open, she rummaged through the contents and removed a gun in a Ziploc bag. She pocketed the bag, closed the safe, and climbed back out the window.

Jody closed the window behind her, then left the office, removing the linoleum chip and letting the door close securely.

Serena caught the robbery on tape while showing the guards a video loop of a quiet, empty office.

"So that's it?" Serena asked, once Marisol was back in the van. "Marisol, should I talk you through taking out the hack of the video feed?"

"Not yet," Tyesha said. "We need to come back tomorrow night for the second video shoot."

"The second what?" Serena asked.

"It's a mash-up video," Tyesha said. "We're mixing the video of Marisol in the man-suit with an actual man."

"It might be better if you don't know," Marisol said.

"Are you kidding me?" Serena said. "If you're trying to mix two videos, I'm the only one on this team who has the skills to do a decent job of it. So what's the plan?"

"We come back," Tyesha said. "And Heidi gets Ivan to be . . . basically Marisol's stunt double."

"So it looks like he's the one that robbed the uncle," Serena said. "Oh, shit."

"Oh shit is right," Marisol said.

Half an hour later, Tyesha knocked on the house's front door. When the guards opened it, they saw a nondescript woman in a chauffeur's cap and loose-fitting uniform. She demanded to talk to Heidi Honeywell.

Jody appeared at the foot of the stairs in a men's shirt and yoga pants. "Claudette, stop calling and texting me. Tell Daddy I'm not coming home tonight," she said.

"I have orders to take you home, miss," Tyesha said.

"I don't care what he says," Jody said.

Tyesha walked over and whispered something to Jody.

"Fine!" she said sullenly.

To the guards she said, "When Ivan wakes up, tell him I've been kidnapped by my own family."

* * *

Jody returned to her apartment after the job. She and Kim lived in a cozy one-bedroom in the Village.

The moment Jody unlocked the door, she kicked off the high heels, and stripped off the dress.

"Honey, I'm home," she said, flinging the slinky purple garment onto the couch and padding across the living room in sheer boy shorts and her bra.

"I'm in the bedroom," Kim said. "Everything went okay?"

"Piece of cake," Jody said. "I'm gonna take a quick shower."

She removed the fake pony tail, and washed her short hair, which had been gelled into place against her scalp. She lathered her entire body up three times with unscented soap, trying to get Ivan's noxious cologne off her skin. Finally, she dried herself and opened the bedroom door.

In the center of the bed, Kim wore a cheerleading uniform. She was posed in a half-split, with pompoms in the air.

"Go Jody! Go Jody!" she cheered.

Jody chuckled and blushed a little. "Oh goodie," she said. "We're playing the girl soccer star and the cheerleader."

"You did great out there tonight," Kim said. "I thought you deserved some appreciation on the home field." Kim did a series of high kicks revealing the fact that she wasn't wearing any underwear.

Jody grinned and walked slowly over to the bed, letting her towel drop. She lay down below Kim.

"Gimme a J!" Kim said.

"J," Jody said.

Kim planted her feet on either side of Jody's head and spelled out her name, while shaking her hips from side to side.

Jody grinned from beneath her. "I'm loving this halftime show," she said.

As Kim twisted and rocked, the pink of her labia winked at Jody from within the dark pubic hair.

"What does it spell?" Kim asked. "Jody! Jody! Gooooo Jody!"

Kim slid down so that she was lying on top of her girl-friend.

"You're the best," Jody said, pulling Kim into a deep kiss.

"Mmmm," Kim said. "Lemme get this uniform off." She began to pull off the shoulder strap.

"No," Jody said. "Leave it on."

She turned Kim over and lay on top of her, running her hands down the polyester fabric, onto the smooth flesh of her thighs. Slowly, she peeled down the top just enough to nuzzle Kim's breasts, stroking the nipples until Kim began to moan.

Then she trailed her finger up Kim's inner thigh, moving ever more slowly as she got toward the top. She began to make tiny circles with her fingertips as she began to press her fingers between Kim's legs. Her girlfriend was wet, eager.

Jody slid two fingers inside Kim and slid her tongue down across her clitoris.

Kim gasped and Jody pressed deeper, inserted a third finger, and licked harder.

Kim threw her head back and pushed herself up onto her elbows. But then, unexpectedly, she pulled back, swiveled, and turned Jody over.

Kim lay on top of her in a sixty-nine and buried her face between Jody's legs.

Jody moaned and grabbed two handfuls of the cheerleading skirt, pulling Kim up toward her, pressing her face into Kim's labia, licking, sucking.

Because Jody was taller, they couldn't both lick at the same time, so they took turns. Kim slid her fingers under Joy's ass and gripped her tighter, pressing her tongue inside, then licking back up across the clitoris.

Jody slid two fingers inside Kim and stroked her clitoris with a thumb. "Are—are you close?" Jody gasped.

"Not even," Kim said, and began to lick mercilessly.

"Wait, I—" Jody said, but Kim pressed four fingers inside her, thrusting in rhythm with her tongue.

And then Jody began to howl with the pleasure of it, coming hard, gripping the cheerleading uniform so tightly, she tore one of the seams.

Afterward, Jody began to laugh. "The cheerleading uniform gets me every time," she said. "The old high school fantasy . . . that the girls could be cheering for our team, also. Not just those asshole football players."

"Go Jody, go!" Kim said.

"Now lemme do you," Jody said.

"Wait til I get my pompoms," Kim said. "So I can cheer you on."

Chapter 13

Tyesha took the following day off work. She slept late and hung out with her nieces til evening. She arrived at Woof's apartment around nine at night with a bag of Thai takeout and no underwear.

"I hope you brought a bottle of champagne with that pad Thai, because we got something to celebrate," he said.

"What's that?" Tyesha asked.

"I just got offered a million-dollar deal to collaborate on a blockbuster movie sound track," he said. "And best of all, they wanna record right here in New York City."

"That's great," she said, and kissed him.

"And I'll be collaborating with one of the greats of the industry," he said.

"Beyoncé?" Tyesha asked.

"Not that great," Woof said.

"Black?" Tyesha asked.

"Yep," Woof said. "Older than Beyoncé."

Tyesha guessed several in succession: "Mary J. Blige? Alicia Keys? Jill Scott? Erykah Badu?"

"A little older than them," Woof said.

"Chaka Khan? Sade? Are you recording with Sade?"

"Nope," he said. "And by the way, it's a dude."

"Usher?" Tyesha asked.

"Right era," Woof said.

"Ginuwine?" Tyesha asked.

"Nope, but you've got the sexy factor going," Woof said.

"Maxwell?" Tyesha asked. "Oh my god, are you recording with Maxwell?"

"I can't believe you can't get this one," he said. "A sexy black male R and B singer from the nineties?"

"I'm totally stumped," Tyesha said. "Who the fuck could it be? I named everyone."

She looked up at him, expectant. "Tell me!" she said. "Did they resurrect Prince or something?"

He laughed. "No, it's Car Willis."

Her face didn't fall as much as it pulled back in horror. Car Willis was short for Carter Williston, the aging R and B vocalist from Chicago, who had risen to fame with his sexy bad boy singing in the nineties, and then had risen to infamy for allegations of serial statutory rape of young teen girls. Yet somehow, his record label's attorneys had always gotten him settlements and acquittals, even in the case of paparazzi photos of him having sex with a fourteen-year-old high schooler. There were also allegations that he had urinated on one girl.

"It's okay you didn't guess it," Thug Woofer said.

"Didn't guess it?" she said, nearly spitting each syllable. "You think I'm upset because I didn't guess it?"

"When I got the call, I was worried they were gonna send me to L.A. or Atlanta," he said.

"Or Chicago," Tyesha said. "Where I grew up."

"No, those Chicago labels are a little small-time for me," Woof said.

"Where Car Willis is from," Tyesha said. "Where he used to piss on teen girls."

Woof drew back. "I mean, I know about those photos, but didn't that get sorted out?"

"Sorted out?" Tyesha said, her voice at the edge of a yell. "How do you sort out being fucked and pissed on by a grown man and then the photos shared all over the fucking world?"

"Yeah, it was fucked up," he said. "I mean she was under-age and everything, but—"

"So if it was fucked up, why are you doing a project with him?" Tyesha demanded.

"It's business," Woof said. "I'm not dating him. I'm not giving him a good Samaritan award. I'm not hiring him as a babysitter."

"Are you fucking kidding me?" Tyesha said. "I'm a black girl from Chicago. I have friends whose lives he destroyed."

"Tyesha, what he did was fucked up, but that was a long time ago," he said. "I mean, I've done some fucked-up things, too. Do you think I'm some kind of angel?"

"Have you ever raped anyone?" she asked.

"No," Woof said. "Of course not. But I've promised girls things for sex. I've told them I loved them when I didn't. I've definitely—you know—pressured a few women."

"I remember," Tyesha said.

"Don't be like that," Woof said. "I know it was fucked up. And I've changed. Most guys have done something foul."

"Were all the women adults?" Tyesha asked. "All the ones that you pressured or lied to? Adults as in over eighteen?"

"Of course," Woof said. "Tyesha, it's work. How you gonna let my work come between us? I never let your work come between us, and you were . . ."

"A ho?" Tyesha asked. "Were you gonna say I was a ho? Well, I'd rather be a ho than a rapist. A child rapist. That's what that sick-ass nigga is. I can't believe you're doing an album with a goddamn child rapist."

"I saw those pictures," Woof said. "She wasn't a child. Maybe a teenager."

Tyesha grabbed the bag of Thai food and threw it against the wall.

"What the fuck?" he asked, and advanced toward her.

"Nigga, don't you touch me," she said.

Something about the rage in her eyes stopped him. He looked from the splatter of Thai food back to her face.

She continued in nearly a whisper, "When you figure out the hundred things that are wrong with everything you said in this conversation, don't call me. Don't ever fucking call me again. Ever."

She snatched up her bags and walked out.

She arrived at her empty apartment, still furious, but a tendril of heartbreak had threaded out from beneath the rage. How could he? The tears had just begun to press behind her eyes, when Deza came running into the house.

"Auntie Ty, have you seen my demo CDs?"

Tyesha blinked. "I think I—do you need it right now?"

"Yes!" Deza said, rummaging wildly through a pile of disks. "Joe's waiting for me in the car."

"Joe? Who the fuck is Joe?"

"The DJ for the open mic," Deza said breathlessly. "Joe gave me a ride home and now he wants to hear my CD."

"Oh, hell no," Tyesha said. "These motherfuckers offering young girls rides home, talking 'bout 'I wanna listen to your demo CD'? That's a bunch of bullshit. I'm 'bout to give this trifling-ass Joe a piece of my mind."

"No, Auntie—" But the rest of Deza's words became an incomprehensible muddle, through the haze of Tyesha's fury and memory.

Eighth grade. She and her best friend Shanique had been at the McDonald's after basketball practice one day. Shanique was nearly a head taller and the team's star player. Tyesha mostly sat on the bench, but they were otherwise inseparable. After they ordered the food, they were surprised to find that their Happy Meals had been paid for by an older man they met.

He asked for their numbers. Tyesha hadn't given hers, but

when she went to the bathroom, Shanique must have. They saw him again after practice a few days later, and he was much more familiar with Shanique. He had given her a stuffed teddy bear that said "I ♥ U."

The man turned out to be Car Willis. He had promised Shanique the love of the century. They'd eventually get married and move to Hollywood. But she needed to show him she was ready. That she wasn't too scared or too young for this real, grown-up love. He set up the meeting and picked her up in a limo.

But Tyesha wasn't looking at a limo, she was standing beside a dented station wagon. The present moment returned. She could hear Deza's voice behind her, indistinct and shrill, drowned out by the loud rap music that was blasting from Joe's car. Through the open window, Tyesha could see a head of curly hair under a stingy-brim straw hat.

"The fuck you think you're tryna pull here?" Tyesha demanded. "This girl is nineteen and even though she's from Chicago, she got family. And I will personally kick the ass of any motherfucker who—"

She broke off as the curly head turned up and Tyesha saw the face of a young Latina woman with bright red lipstick and wide, surprised brown eyes, topped with false lashes.

Tyesha blinked and faltered. Her mouth opened, but no sound came out.

Deza advanced on the pair of them, her mouth in a grimace.

"Joe, this is my Auntie Tyesha, who I been telling you so much about," she yelled over the music, arms folded across her chest.

"Auntie Ty, this is Yolanda Gutierrez, the DJ at the open mic who's been encouraging me," Deza said, pronouncing the Yo of Yolanda with a hard Spanish Y like a J.

Yolanda had her perfect eyebrows raised and her lips pursed in an *is-this-broad-crazy?* expression. She turned the volume down, and Tyesha stood in the relative quiet floundering for speech.

Finally she found words. "Yolanda, I'm so sorry. I thought—you maybe—anyway, please forgive me. And thank you—for listening to Deza's demo CD—in advance. I gotta go."

Inside the house, Tyesha sat on the couch. She stared into the middle distance, her eyes not seeing the cluttered room, the athletic clothes hanging off the back of the living room chair, the tracks of fake hair spilling out of a plastic bag onto the coffee table.

Tyesha remembered that day in Chicago. She had just started getting her hair permed. She was thirteen, and instead of the hot comb on Sundays and braids all week, she had a real perm and could press it herself with just a curling iron. Still her mama did it special for church on Sundays. Her first Sunday with her permed and pressed-by-mama hair—hanging almost to her shoulders—made her feel special. Almost a woman.

In another first, Tyesha had gotten her first winter coat that wasn't one of her sister Jenisse's castoffs. For the first time, she got to choose. Her mother let her get a red parka with a big hood. Shanique teased Tyesha, calling her "Li'l Red" from Little Red Riding Hood. They had a secret code where a cute guy was a "woodcutter" and a creepy guy was a "wolf."

None of the girls in their church were allowed to have boyfriends, but some of them managed it. Some snuck and met boys, but they didn't have aunties like Tyesha's Aunt Lu. She seemed to be everywhere and knowing everyone and everybody owed her a favor. Most of them would be glad to report back to her aunt if they ever caught a favorite niece squeezed up in a corner with some boy.

So Tyesha had to settle for living vicariously through friends. Today in church, her eyes kept darting toward the door, where she was expecting her friend Shanique to come in any minute, glowing from a clandestine date she'd had after school on Friday. Shanique had told her mother she had a special basketball practice, but Tyesha knew better. She imagined Shanique's face, both dimples flashing into view, as the girl tried to suppress a grin that the Lord would not approve of, ready to spill stories of first kisses and the way it felt to have a boy's hands on you.

Friday at school, Shanique had been squirming with excitement, barely able to contain herself in fifth period pre-algebra. "Chopping wood after school!" was how she described him in the note she passed to Tyesha. She had been talking to him on the phone every night for a few weeks. He would call after her mother had left for work and Shanique was home with her grandmother. It seemed that there was more than one secret to Shanique's date. Tyesha couldn't wait to find out.

At first, when Shanique came in, Tyesha thought she was a better actress than expected. No dimple. No suppressed smile. She kept her eyes downcast. But it was when the choir sang that Tyesha knew something was really wrong. Her friend moved her mouth in a lackluster pantomime of the words. No sound came out. When it was time for her solo, another girl stepped up to the mic.

Tyesha figured Shanique must have been caught. Or worse yet, her mother had found out and prevented the date. But no secrets were spilled that day. Shanique just sat beside her through the service, a deflated version of herself, and walked out with her mother immediately after church ended.

Tyesha planned to press her friend at school the next day, but Shanique was absent. First a day, then a week, then two. Eventually, Tyesha caught up with Shanique's older cousin. The girl had been trying to avoid her, but Tyesha cornered her in the rec center bathroom.

"Where's Shanique?" Tyesha asked.

"Sorry, Li'l Red," the girl had mumbled. "I don't know."

The cousin couldn't meet her eyes and tried to push past her, out of the bathroom.

"What happened to her?" Tyesha pushed right up against the girl, feeling a dull pain where her own budding breasts pressed against the hard bone of the girl's rib cage. The girl was tall like her cousin, but more flat-chested.

"I don't know nothing," the girl mumbled, and tried half-heartedly to get away. But Tyesha had seen her before on the basketball court. She played on the high school team. Tyesha knew this tall girl could drive past any opponent if she wanted to. But her listless defense here in this bathroom made her look thirsty to confess.

"You know what happened, don't you?" she yelled at the girl, pressing a determined hand to the girl's solar plexus.

The girl burst into tears, and then it all came out.

Deza stormed back into the apartment, as "Joe" drove away. "Auntie Ty, I don't mean no disrespect, but have you lost your black mind? I mean, WTF?"

"Deza, I' so sorry. I thought—I mean—it's just—I thought Joe was a man. You know, an older man trying to take advantage."

"Auntie Ty, are you serious right now?" Deza asked, incredulous. "My own father has a bodyguard that I swear is a serial killer, always tryna creep up on me and Amaru. Plus I'm a nineteen-year-old female emcee and been in the rap game since I was sixteen. Do you know how many motherfuckers I've had to fend off, talking about 'come to the recording studio I got in my house.' Motherfuckers with a microphone in their closet offering me and my girls forties and weed. If I didn't know how to handle myself, I'd have been a casualty of hip-hop long ago."

Tyesha looked at her niece. She remembered pushing her on the baby swings. How had she gotten so grown?

"You're right," Tyesha said. "I just—something happened with my best friend in middle school and Car Willis—"

"What?" Deza asked. "Your best friend in middle school was fucking with Car Willis?"

"Not fucking with," Tyesha said. "It was statutory rape."

Shanique and Car Willis had had sex—because she needed to show him she was woman enough to please a grown man—but first he'd shown her some porn. Just vanilla. A black man and woman having sex.

As an adult looking back, Tyesha had imagined Shanique watching the film, seeing what must have been the delighted expression on the actress's face, hearing her breathless encouragement: *Yes! more! give it all to me!* How could a thirteen-year-old know fact from fantasy? The real sex would have been nothing like that.

Shanique had gagged. Had cried with the penetration. After he finished, he had sent her home on the bus, flecks of blood in the semen pooling in her panties. He was cold and scornful now because she had failed to please him. Failed to be grown enough. There would be no wedding. No Hollywood ending. No more calls. No second date.

Shanique had feigned sick for days, but her mother had found out when she caught Shanique crying on the toilet with a burning in her vulva that turned out to be an infection.

Shanique never came back to school or to church. Her mom moved the family down South to live with a great aunt.

"That's fucked up," Deza said, shaking her head. "My DJ boyfriend was a little older than me—seven years—but I made the move on him. And it's not like I was a virgin."

"Seven years?" Tyesha asked.

Deza's phone buzzed, and she looked at it. "It's Yo. She got a last-minute call to spin a hip-hop set in Bed-Stuy. She said she can swing back and get me."

"You should go," Tyesha said.

Deza grabbed her coat and ran out the door. She had almost closed it behind her, when she turned and stuck her head back in. "I'm sorry about your friend."

Tyesha nodded as the door closed, and she heard the jangle of keys and deadbolts turning.

In the now empty apartment, Tyesha felt stripped and naked after the rage subsided. The fresh and bitter slice of Woof's betrayal blended with the never-healed bruise of losing Shanique. And through it all, the heaviest grief that there was no fairy-tale ending. Just when a black girl thought she had made it through the woods alive, just when she relaxed into maybe loving the woodcutter, she would learn he was on the side of the wolf.

Chapter 14

The next day, Tyesha woke, having shed the initial layer of grief and reached a new wave of fury. How could Woof have agreed to do an album with Car Willis? She had slept poorly. In the morning, she had called up Marisol and vented about it. She had lunch with Jody and Kim and ranted some more.

"You're better off without him," Jody said. "What is this, like his third big fuck-up?"

"I wanna say I thought he'd changed," Tyesha said. "And then it just sounds pathetic. This time I'm done for good."

"So I always thought he was a dick," Jody said. "But I can see some of the appeal. You're high powered, and you need a guy who won't be running around sucking his thumb and worrying that he's not in your league."

"Did you have breakup sex?" Kim asked.

"Are you kidding me?" Tyesha said. "I couldn't even entertain breakup sex when the name Car Willis has been on my lips within the past hour."

"Well, then, no wonder you're still so upset," Kim said. "You need a little something to help you forget him. What about that stockbroker? Wasn't he always trying to see you?"

"I don't know . . ."

"Tinder calls, girl," Kim said. "Swipe now, get some tonight."

"Tinder's too misogynist," Jody said. "Try Bumble—the girl gets to choose."

"I gotta go," Tyesha said. "I have meetings all afternoon."

As it turned out, her last meeting was with Drew, the geeky black reporter from the *Village Voice*.

The two of them sat on the leather couch in the office. He had his notebook in his hand and a digital recorder on the coffee table.

Through his questions, a story emerged. The Maria de la Vega clinic had been founded by Marisol Rivera and Eva Feldman to serve the sex work community of lower Manhattan. They provided a full range of services to support the sexual and emotional health of sex workers. They also provided money management and career planning to help the workforce, primarily young women, think about their futures in an industry that was high paying but also high risk and high burnout. This included entrepreneurial and skills training for long-term professional development within the sex industries, and also planning and support for those who wanted to exit the industries.

Tyesha had taken over as executive director in June, shortly after she had graduated with a master's degree in public health from Columbia.

Tyesha shared a sanitized version of her own background in the industries. She had been a waitress in a strip club. She mentioned that she had done a bit of exotic dancing at private parties but had too much stage fright to strip in the clubs. She didn't mention that she had done her dancing during escort gigs, where the clients were really paying for sex.

Instead, she played it up like waitressing taught her firsthand what it was like for the dancers, and that was why she had put the resources of the clinic behind this union fight.

"And you come from a long line of public health fighters," he said. "Lucille Couvillier, she's your paternal aunt, right?"

"Maternal," Tyesha said. "I have my mother's last name."

"Your father's last name is?"

"Unknown," Tyesha said. She took a breath and just said it out loud. To a reporter. "I don't know who my father is."

He blinked twice and began scribbling on his notepad.

"What?" Tyesha asked. "Weren't expecting that type of ghetto drama?"

"Not just ghetto drama," Drew said. "My little brother. We just learned that his father wasn't my dad. I'd prefer ghetto drama to middle-class drama. At least it's honest."

"How old is your little brother?"

"Twenty-five," he said. "Imagine going a quarter century thinking the man who raised you was your biological father and then learning it was someone else. A friend of the family who was always around. That's some bullshit."

Tyesha shook her head. "As a kid I used to wonder some-times, but then I just let it go. My mama wasn't gonna tell me, and nobody else knew, probably not even the guy. And it's not the only paternity issue going on in my family. My sis-ter—this is all off the record, right?"

"Of course," he said. "The story is just gonna focus on the clinic and the stripper strike. In fact, we can wrap up the interview. Is there anything you'd like to add?"

Tyesha looked at her watch. "Oh my god, has it really been two hours?"

"Time flies when you're participating in award-winning journalism," he said with a grin.

"And it's seven thirty," Tyesha said. "No wonder I'm so hungry."

"Well, do you wanna grab something to eat?" he asked. "I'd love to talk with you more. Off the record, of course."

"Sure," Tyesha said. She hadn't bothered to cancel her

dinner date with Thug Woofer. They had plans to go to their spot, the uptown steakhouse. But her "don't ever call me" should have been cancelation enough.

"What would you like to eat?" he asked.

"Sushi."

It turned out that Drew was from Springfield, Illinois. He grew up in Champaign-Urbana, where his parents taught at the university. But he had spent time in Chicago as a teen and understood her cultural reference points.

"You know," he said, "I was in Chicago when they torched the Urban Peace Accord Center. My grandmother lived in South Shore and we all used to go for Thanksgiving. She lived just down the street from the center. We heard the sirens and ran over to see what was happening." He shook his head. "I'll never forget the sight of the burning building. They estimated that the gang who burned it down had used the equivalent of a full tank of gasoline. My parents lost it. 'This is why we moved out of this hell hole . . .'"

Tyesha remembered. She had also stood outside the center and watched it burn.

Sitting at the sushi restaurant, she felt the same burning in her eyes.

"Oh my god," Drew said. "Tyesha, I'm so sorry. I didn't mean to upset you."

She shook her head, her eyes brimming with tears, but they didn't fall. She opened her mouth to speak, but couldn't.

It was the memory, but also she had only felt rage about the breakup with Woof. Remembering Chicago—that fire, her aunt, losing someone she really loved—put her in touch with the loss of Woof. Whatever else she could say about him, he was a guy who kept getting her hopes up. But this latest Car Willis fiasco was the final straw. She had fallen in love with a mythical creature, like a unicorn. Thug enough to understand her rough upbringing, but successful enough not

214 / Aya de León

to be threatened by her. She was a fool to think that his past, all that *bitch-ho-pussy* line wouldn't raise its ugly head in some kind of way. She thought that just because he was respectful to her that it would be enough. But it wasn't enough. He couldn't treat her well and team up with a guy who preyed on young teen girls. She needed to fuck with guys who understood that.

She was so used to writing off most guys she met because she had worked as an escort. But she was out of that business now. She looked across the table at Drew. His forehead was furrowed and his eyes were concerned. How had she convinced herself that this kind of guy wasn't for her?

"What do you think of Car Willis?" she asked.

"Excuse me?" He blinked at her.

"The singer, Car Willis," she said. "What do you think of him?"

"I think it's a symptom of our society's sickness that he's not rotting in jail," Drew said.

Just then, the waitress arrived with their dinner order.

Tyesha had ordered hers with extra wasabi. She loaded it into the soy sauce until it looked like old guacamole, a greenish brown.

"Why do you wanna know what I think of Car Willis?" he asked.

"Just a Chicago thing," she said, holding a piece of tekka roll aloft.

"Well, you're about the right age," he said. "Did he ever hit on you?"

"Friend of mine," Tyesha said. "It was . . . it was fucked up."

"Damn," he said.

"Enough about him," she said.

She dipped the sushi in the spicy soy sauce and ate it. The burn rose through her nose and throat to her eyes. The tears spilled down her face.

"Are you okay?" Drew asked.

"Wasabi," Tyesha croaked, and took a sip of sake. "I like it hot."

After dinner, they walked back toward the clinic.

"I was wondering," she said, "would you like to maybe get a drink somewhere?"

"I have a confession to make," Drew said. "I didn't invite you to dinner to talk off the record. I invited you because I find you really attractive."

She smiled. "Then I'll take that as a yes to the drink."

They found a cozy bar down the street and ordered a round of drinks.

"Are you married?" she asked after the waitress left.

"Wow," Drew said. "You ask the hard-hitting questions first. Car Willis. Marital status."

"That's not an answer," she said. "Do journalists know all the tricks of evasion?"

"Sorry," he said. "Not trying to be evasive. Not married. No girlfriend. Last date was two weeks ago. No sex. She was a white woman I met at a club. Sex was an option, but I couldn't get it up after she put on Miley Cyrus."

Tyesha burst out laughing. "Are you serious?"

"Not entirely," he said. "I actually could get it up but that was just a physiological response. I wasn't really into her. And the Miley just completely killed it. So there's my deal. How about you?"

"Well," Tyesha said, "when I first moved to New York, I was dating a guy and found out that he was married. So I like to ask that question up front before I get even the least bit invested. And I had recently reconnected with someone I dated a while back. But the problems that pulled us apart before pulled us apart again. I dumped him and am eager to move on."

The waitress appeared and handed them their order.

"Could having a drink with me be construed as part of the moving on process?"

"I'm hoping so," she said. "I guess I don't usually date guys like you."

"What?" he asked. "Left-handed guys? I assure you, everything they say about our sexual prowess is true."

"No," she said. "College-educated types."

"Really?" he asked. "Why not? You have a master's degree."

"I don't know," she said. "Black women just outnumbered black men everywhere in college. And so many of the brothers were dating women who weren't black. And it was too much of a fishbowl. I just found it easier to date guys from the neighborhood. By the time I had graduated from college, I had never even dated a guy who was also in college at the same time as me."

Drew shook his head. "You look like one of those women in *Essence*," he said. "With your briefcase and your fly suit. You should be with, like, some Morehouse man."

Tyesha laughed and nearly spit her drink.

"Not hardly," she said. "The only college educated guy I dated was the married man."

"Well, let me present myself officially," Drew said. "Drew Thomas. I did my undergraduate work at Brown. Then I got my MA in journalism at UC Berkeley. Single. Employed. Childless. And looking for a Chicago-raised black woman with a public health master's degree. Ivy League graduate work preferred. Also, must have strong interest in sex work advocacy, and some labor organizing is a must. I know it's specific, but there are millions of women in New York City. I'm keeping my hopes up and my standards high."

She laughed and raised her glass. "To high standards."

They toasted.

* * *

Drew's apartment was the classic Village closet. It wasn't much bigger than Tyesha's office. On one side was the kitchenette. A half-size refrigerator stood beside a small Formica counter with a toaster oven and a microwave. Above it was a single set of cabinets.

Under the lone dusty window was a desk with a laptop and a file cabinet.

He sat down on a durable-looking sofa that folded out into a bed.

"Come here, Chicago girl," he said. "Show me how high your standards are."

Drew unfolded the bed and pulled her down into a kiss. He was a bit awkward at first, but they found a rhythm.

He fumbled with her bra strap, but she undid it for him. When he slid the cups from her breasts, he looked a bit awestruck.

Tyesha laughed. "You like?"

"Everything about you is so beautiful, Tyesha," he said.

Almost reverently, he removed her clothes, then his own.

His body was soft, muscles lacking in definition and angle. But she liked it. She liked him.

She grinned. "Lie down," she said and rolled a condom on. Then she lowered herself down onto him.

He gasped and let her ride for a few minutes, both of them grinning with the pleasure of it. Then he pulled her leg forward and turned them over. She enjoyed the warm press of his soft belly against hers. His stroke was unhurried, almost leisurely in his pleasure of their every touch.

He tried to turn them back over so she was on top, but they got tangled halfway there. He continued thrusting while they were on their sides, and he hit a spot of pleasure.

Tyesha let out an unexpected moan.

"You like that?" he asked. It seemed to bring out the investigative journalist in him. He explored every angle until he found the one that made her moan hardest. And he stroked and stroked until she was gripping his neck and coming hard and delicious.

Then he rolled her onto her back and in a few strokes he was climaxing in an ecstatic shudder.

After he finished and removed the condom, they grinned at each other and laughed.

"I really was not expecting my night to end like this," Tyesha said.

Drew shrugged. "As a journalist, I never know where a story will take me. I just have to be prepared for anything. For example, some journalists might quit at this point in the investigation, but I think there's more to this story. What do you think?"

"No comment," Tyesha said, and kissed him, pressing her body against him and feeling him respond.

In the morning, there was a haze of diffuse light from the window. It looked out onto a brick building several yards away.

She got up to pee. The bathroom had been built out of some sort of pantry. It had only a commode and no sink. The acoustics were so loud, she was sure she would wake Drew up.

But when she walked across to the kitchen sink to wash her hands, he didn't move. She began to gather her clothes. Her bra strap was tucked under his arm. She tugged it gently and his eyes slowly opened.

"Good morning, beautiful," he said.

"Good morning," she said. "I've gotta get to work."

"Okay," he said. "Then we'll have to do a quick exit interview."

She laughed.

"So, first the obvious question," he said. "Were you pleased with the experience and would you be interested in a return visit?"

She pursed her lips and looked up as if concentrating. "I'd have to say . . . yes and yes."

"Excellent," he said. "Ah, it turns out that was the only question . . . Oh, wait! Here's the last one. Will you be my date to Nashonna's album release party?"

A slow smile spread over her face. "I'd love to."

Chapter 15

That night, Jody went back to the mobster's house to see Ivan. Kim and Serena were outside the perimeter in the medical van, monitoring the equipment. Tyesha was dressed as the chauffeur again, with Marisol also in the limo just outside the house.

By Jody's request, she and Ivan were alone again in the office.

"I don't know what kind of vodka you had the other night, but I think I blacked out," he said.

"It's a special brand of extreme vodka I get distilled just for me," she said. "And it turned you into an animal. You broke the condom, and when I left here I could hardly walk, you beast. Sorry I left while you were asleep, but my father practically kidnapped me and made me come home. Daddy keeps us girls on a tight leash."

He laughed. "A beast, huh?"

"So like we agreed, you had your way with me last night, and I'll have my way with you tonight," Jody said.

"Sounds good," he said. "Have your way with me."

"I enjoy a little role play," she said, jiggling the communicator in her ear.

"I like it," he said. "What's the game?"

"Cops and robbers," she said. "This room is perfect. So you be the robber, and I'll be the cop."

She walked around looking behind the paintings.

"Oh my god, a real safe!" she squealed. "Okay." She dug in her oversized purse. "Here, put on this hoodie and ski mask."

As he put them on, she slowly peeled off her coat, revealing a fetish cop outfit. A large badge was pinned to a navy blue, low-cut mini dress. Garter belt straps peeked out from beneath the short skirt. Thigh-high stockings disappeared into stiletto boots. She put a cap on her head.

"I can't wait to get arrested," he said.

"I can't wait to lock you up," she said, licking her lips.

"So do you just come in while I'm trying to crack the safe?" he asked, turning the dial.

"No," she said. "That's too simple. We need a jewel box. So you can try to bribe me."

From her purse, she handed him an L-shaped box inside a Ziploc bag.

"So I'll walk in and say freeze, and you walk away from the safe with the box," she instructed. "Halfway across the room, you pull off your mask. Then you come and lay the jewels at my feet, and you beg me for mercy."

"Are you gonna show me any?" he asked.

She smiled deviously. "Not a shred," she said.

He grinned and lowered the ski mask.

"And . . . action!" Jody said.

He turned from the safe, put the painting back up.

"Hold it right there," Jody said.

He turned and walked toward her.

In her ear, Tyesha's voice crackled. "We can't see the gun. Have him hold it up higher."

"Stop," Jody said. "That's no way to present a bribe. Offer it to me like a tease. Come on, try it again."

He tried a second time, and waved it back and forth.

"That looks ridiculous," Tyesha said in Jody's ear.

"You just don't get it," Jody said. "This is not turning me on at all."

"Just tell me what I should do," he said.

"You need to get into the mood," she insisted. "You've stolen some jewels, and they're priceless. You need to be smug about it. You're gonna get away with it. You're gonna bribe this cop and then fuck her. Jody reached under the tiny skirt of the cop outfit and pulled off the thong.

Ivan's eyes widened, and he grinned.

"Yes!" she said. "Like that. Methodical. Cocky. You're gonna get away with everything."

This time, he took it slowly. He set the bag on the desk as he put the painting back in place.

"Freeze!" she said, pointing the gun at him. "Or I'll shoot."

"You won't shoot me," he said through the mask.

Slowly, he picked up the bag off the desk and walked toward her. Halfway across the floor he pulled off his mask. His face, a picture of confidence.

He walked across to where she stood and opened the jewel box, laying the sparkling necklace and earrings at her feet.

"Great work, Jody," Tyesha said in her ear. "We got the visuals."

"Diamonds?" she asked. "Too predictable. I think I need to interrogate you."

She took off his clothes, pulled up a chair, and handcuffed him to it. Out of her purse, she pulled a towel and a packet of lube and started to give him a hand job.

"Where's the rest of the loot hidden?" she asked.

"I don't know," he said.

"You better tell me," she said. "Or you'll be locked up for life."

"Are you the jailer?" he asked.

"Don't get cute with me," she said.

She squeezed him tighter and he moaned.

"Say 'I take what I feel like,'" she instructed.

"I take what I feel like," he panted.

"Louder."

"I take what I feel like!"

"Now I'm gonna make you say uncle."

"Uncle," he croaked.

"Louder!"

She pumped furiously.

"Uncle! Uncle!"

As the spasm of his orgasm began to subside, she discreetly pulled the Taser from her boot. She turned it down to the lowest setting and tased him, turning it up at the end.

"Oh my god," he said. "I've never come that hard."

"Now it's time for you to do me," she said, unzipping her dress.

"Sure, baby," he said. "Just let me . . . God, I can hardly move."

"Come on," she said. "I'm ready."

"No, seriously," he said. "I can't really . . . I might need a doctor."

"That's the lamest excuse I've ever heard," Jody said. "You rich boys are so lazy."

She gathered up her things, including the handcuffs. "I knew I shouldn't slum at the kids' table."

She walked out, leaving him spent and liquid on the chair.

She slipped into the hallway and zipped up her dress.

"Okay," Jody said into her communicator. "He's incapacitated and out of view of the camera."

"Got it," Tyesha said.

The plan was for Tyesha and Marisol to pull out the box they had used to hack the video feed. When they had finished, Jody would stagger out, like she was blackout drunk, and nearly pass out in the front hallway. Tyesha would bang on the front door and Jody would have to be carried out by the guards. This would create the needed distraction while Marisol reconnected the live video feed.

Tyesha and Marisol had just slipped out of the limo when all three women heard Kim in their ears.

"Heads up! Looks like the uncle is back early."

Marisol scurried back into the limo. "Jody, get out of there fast," she said.

"His car just sped past us," Serena said.

Jody put on her bored-rich-girl face and breezed out past security. They were watching sports and barely noticed. Tyesha, dressed as the chauffeur, came out to open the limo door.

"Serena!" Tyesha said, as she made a show of guiding Jody into the limo. "How do we get out of here?"

"Hold on," Serena said. "I think I'll be able to jam the gate lock. That ought to slow them down."

"Good," Tyesha said. "I'll move the car to a more secure location, and we can sneak out later."

"Plus, you still need to get the hack box," Serena added.

Tyesha maneuvered the long car down the driveway and around a bend, out of sight of the guards, then she turned off the road and hid the car in a clump of trees.

"This is a huge fucking car," Jody said. "Can they see us here?"

"I hope not," Tyesha said. "Let them in, Serena. We're as hidden as we're gonna get."

Tyesha, Marisol, and Jody hunkered down to wait. A moment later, a large Hummer sped past them up to the house.

"I don't think they noticed us," Marisol said.

The three women sat in the limo, ears straining for sounds. But once the motor of the Hummer was shut off, the whole property was quiet.

"So here's what I think we need to do," Tyesha said. "Serena, you can open the gate, right?"

"Sure," she said. "But once you take out the hacker box, the system won't let the car back out."

"It won't let the car out," Tyesha said. "But what about a person on foot?"

"Once it locks, it won't open back up," Serena said.

"We could jam it," Kim said. "We used to jam the gate at our high school with a trash can."

"We don't have a trash can," Jody said.

"We have the limo's spare tire," Tyesha said. "We can do this. Jody's the fastest runner. Can you talk her through getting the hacker box out?"

"Sure," Serena said.

"Perfect," Tyesha said. "She can get the hacker box while Marisol and I drive the limo out."

"I can't pick a lock for shit," Jody said.

"Fine," Tyesha said. "Jody and I can get the hacker box while Marisol drives the limo out."

"I can't drive," Marisol said.

"Fucking New Yorkers," Tyesha complained. "Jody, you drive. Marisol, you and I get the box."

Jody moved into the front of the limo. She dropped Tyesha and Marisol on the road on the way out.

The two women crept up along the dark gravel drive. The trees on either side towered over them in dark, hulking silhouettes.

When they rounded the curve, they could see the bright windows of the mansion in the distance. There were three cars parked in front, all dark and quiet.

The walk would have taken only a few minutes at full speed, but the two women moved silently along the soft earth beside the gravel drive. It took about ten minutes. As they walked, Tyesha reached into the small tool case that hung from her waist. She pulled out two pairs of latex gloves, and they both put them on.

226 / Aya de León

"But we still need to create a distraction for when the live video feed goes back online," Marisol said.

"I don't know if this'll help," Jody said, "but the guards were watching sports."

"What sport were they watching in July?"

"Let me look it up," Serena said.

"It wasn't in English," Jody said. "So it wasn't baseball. And the World Cup is over."

"Cricket!" Serena said. "Ukraine is playing against New Zealand."

"Pull up the game," Marisol said. "That'll have to be our best distraction."

When they approached the box, Tyesha handed Marisol the lock picks and she got to work opening it.

With one hand, Tyesha shone a tiny penlight so Marisol could work. With her other hand, she turned on the camera function of her phone so Serena could access the video remotely.

"Got it," Serena said. "The feed is clear."

A moment later, Marisol's tool clicked and the box was open.

A loud cheer erupted from the guards inside the house. Marisol dropped the lock picks. Tyesha nearly dropped the toolbox.

The two women caught their breath, and Marisol held the flashlight and the phone, while Tyesha followed Serena's directions.

"First snip the blue wires, but do it above the splice," she instructed.

Tyesha carefully made the cut with the pair of clippers. Serena directed her to make a few more snips and they pulled the hack box free.

"Now this is the delicate part," Serena said. "Reconnecting the real feed."

"What are the exciting moments in cricket?" Marisol asked.

"I wish Lily was here," Tyesha said. "She's West Indian. She'd know."

The two of them stood still for what seemed to be half an hour. Both of them breathed shallowly, alert for any sign that they needed to run for it.

They heard another explosion of yelling from the guard room.

"Looks like Ukraine is about to score," Serena said. "Get ready!"

Tyesha and Marisol prepared to reconnect the feed wires.

"Now!" Serena said.

They reconnected the wires just as a whoop of triumph rang out from the house.

Marisol locked the box back up, and the two women began running down the driveway toward the entry gate.

Their descent was much louder than their climb up. The air rang with the slapping footfalls of their soft-soled shoes on the moist ground.

For a moment, that was the only sound, punctuated by the occasional distant sound of a car engine. But then they heard another sound—distant at first—the bark of a dog.

"Are you fucking kidding me?" Tyesha asked.

First one bark and then several.

"Dogs!" Marisol yelled into her communicator.

"Where?" Jody asked.

The two women ran faster, the rhythm of their thudding footsteps hitting double-time.

"Don't . . . know . . ." Tyesha panted.

"We're on it!" Kim said.

They came around the bend in the road and could see the front entrance. Off to the far right, they could also hear the distant sounds of the dogs, the deep, resonant barks of canines with thick bodies and locking jaws.

Then the medical van drove up, its headlights swinging in a wide arc to shine on the oncoming dogs. There were three of them, Rottweilers, coming at a dead run. The van turned its brightest headlights shining toward the dogs, temporarily blinding them, and they slowed a bit.

Kim ran up to the chain-link fence and began to rattle it to get the dogs' attention. The pack turned on her and threw themselves against the fence, barking and snarling.

Meanwhile, Tyesha and Marisol came down toward the gate. As they had planned, the limo's spare tire was jammed into the gate.

Just outside, Jody stood by the limo, the rear door open.

Marisol and Tyesha leaped over the tire and began trying to pull it free.

"It's stuck!" Tyesha yelled, and Jody ran to help.

The commotion had gotten the attention of the dogs, and they turned from Kim to the three women at the gate.

The three of them tugged on the tire, but it was awkward. The force of the gate had pressed into the tire and wedged it deep.

As the dogs began running toward them, Tyesha reached into the tool belt.

"Step back!" she yelled. "I'm gonna slash it."

The dogs were nearly to the gate.

Jody and Marisol jumped clear, and Tyesha put one arm around the tire and pulled. With the other arm, she jammed the utility knife into the tire. It burst and she fell to the ground. The gate slammed shut, and all three dogs crashed against the metal, snarling and barking.

Marisol helped Tyesha up, while Jody grabbed the deflated tire, and the three of them leaped into the limo, Tyesha and Marisol gasping for air in the backseat.

"I—fucking—hate—dogs," Tyesha said.

"Speaking of," Jody said. "Your phone has been blowing up with calls from Woof."

"Like I said," Tyesha wheezed. "I fucking. Hate. Dogs."

The following night, Tyesha was sitting on the couch, reading over the latest press release from the strippers' union. She had been working in her room and had noticed the orchid out in her window box. She closed the curtain, but could still feel it out there, like it was watching her. If she left it out there long enough, it would just die of natural causes.

She had just relocated to the living room when the phone rang. It was Woof. Again. She planned to ignore it, but Deza saw his name and picked it up.

"Tyesha Couvillier's phone," she said in a secretary voice. "Deza speaking. Yes, she's right here."

For the first time, Tyesha regretted not telling Deza about the breakup, but she took the phone.

"What's up?" she asked, walking into the bedroom.

"Still trying to apologize," he said. "Like I said in my fifteen messages. I thought about what you said, and I called my agent to see if I could get out of the Car Willis contract. I even contacted my attorney. I realize now that I was wrong, but they already announced it and started the PR machinery."

"So break the contract," Tyesha said. "Artists do it all the time."

"And then get sued," he said. "I'm sorry I did it, but I can't undo it. I just wanted you to know that I really tried, but I was too late."

"Is that why you called?" Tyesha asked. "To tell me why you can't get out of your contract?"

"Not just that," he said. "I called about Nashonna's album release party. I know how much you love her, and I thought you still might wanna go. I can't even make it, but I can keep you on the list as my plus-one. You should go see your girl. It's the least I could do."

"Looks like you're too late on this one, too," Tyesha said. "I'm going with someone else."

"What?" he said.

"Sorry, Woof," Tyesha said. "I have to go. I'll see you around."

She hung up and stepped back out of the bedroom.

"That didn't sound good," Deza said.

"We broke up, okay?" Tyesha said. "It happened the other day, but I didn't want to tell you, because I knew you'd react like this."

"Was it the Car Willis thing?" Deza said. "They just announced it. I shoulda known."

"Yeah," Tyesha said. "That was the thing."

"Well, did he say anything about my demo before you dumped him?"

"I'm sorry, Deza," Tyesha said.

"Did you even ask?"

"Wait a minute," Tyesha said. "I promised one date and to give him the demo. Which I did. I didn't promise to keep dating him til he discovered you, or to do follow-up."

"But this is my big chance, Auntie Ty," Deza said, on the verge of tears.

"Girl," Tyesha said. "Don't be like your mama here. Looking to some man to make your life happen. Just like your DJ ex did all the booking and had all the contacts. Now you want to be Woof's protégée? You need to get your own hustle. Fame isn't gonna show up in the form of a man sweeping you off your feet. What happened with that hip-hop open mic?"

"Not much," Deza said. "The guy said I had potential. That I should come back next week."

"Then go back," Tyesha said. "You want it? You gotta put in the work. I haven't heard you rhyme once since you been here. You used to freestyle all the time when you were in high school. You even had me rapping into a kitchen spoon. Now you're just hovering over my phone. You need to get on your grind. When is the next open mic?"

"Tonight," she said, sucking her teeth.

"Then what are you doing here?" Tyesha asked.

Deza rolled her eyes, but put on fresh lipstick, grabbed her notebook, her purse, a stack of demo CDs, and walked out of the apartment.

A couple days later, Tyesha called the team into the office. Tyesha sat on the desk, with Marisol, Jody, and Kim on the couch facing her. Serena sat next to the desk with a laptop in her lap.

"Unfortunately," Tyesha said, "this cinematic masterpiece can't be submitted for any awards. So this is a private showing, and an homage to the genius of Serena Kostopoulos."

"Oh, this old thing?" Serena said with a wry smile, and flipped open her laptop.

After a moment of static, the camera showed the mobster's office. Then a male figure entered the frame, wearing a ski mask and a hoodie."

"Is that the nephew?" Kim asked.

"Nope," Tyesha said. "That's Marisol in the man suit."

In the video, Marisol crossed to the desk. She removed the painting and cracked the mob safe. After she took out the gun and set it on the desk, she closed the safe door. Then there was a quick glitch in the film, but it resumed, with the figure in the ski mask putting the picture back up.

"That's the cut, right?" Kim said. "That's where it cuts to the nephew!"

"Wait for it," Tyesha said.

The masked man took the gun off the desk and walked toward the camera. Several steps away from the desk, he removed his ski mask, and it was clearly Ivan, the mobster's nephew. As he stepped out of the frame, he yelled, "Uncle! I take what I want." Then the screen went black.

"Damn," Kim said. "That's incredibly convincing."

"It wouldn't stand up in a court of law," Serena said. "But it only needs to convince his uncle Viktor."

"And it'll probably be Ivan's death sentence," Tyesha said soberly.

"I had Raul look up this guy's rap sheet," Marisol said. Her boyfriend was an ex-cop. "He's a serial predator. Over a dozen rape cases settled out of court."

Jody nodded. "I saw the look in his eye when he came after me in that bathroom. He wasn't gonna take no for an answer."

"If anybody has a problem with it, now's the time to speak up," Tyesha said.

For a moment, nobody said anything.

"I say send Viktor the video," Kim said.

Serena closed the laptop. "It'll be my pleasure."

Chapter 16

Nashonna's album release party was located at the Paperclip Records headquarters in midtown.

Tyesha had been to the Oscars with Woof at the beginning of the year, so the Paperclip party seemed less glamorous. But it was trendier, with artists wearing more edgy fashion instead of formal wear.

Drew had on an understated black jacket and dark jeans, with black snakeskin boots. She wore a curve-hugging dress in bright hues of red and gold.

One of the oversized posters on the wall in the foyer was the cover of Thug Woofer's first album, *$kranky $outh*. The image featured a rural field with rows and rows of plants that had hundred-dollar bills where cotton bolls should be. Thug Woofer wore a straw hat and had a wheat stalk sticking out of his mouth. He was pictured driving a solid gold tractor with loaders on the front and back, each filled with women wearing bikini tops, thongs, and booty shorts, with their rumps in the air. Tyesha rolled her eyes as she walked past the poster.

The place was packed. There were no chairs, but Drew managed to find them a tiny standing table at the far end of the room where she could set down her purse.

"Now let me go get us some drinks," he yelled over the music.

She nodded. The opening act sounded great. A trio of young Latina rappers. Nashonna was always good about putting other women on.

As she nodded her head to the music, she felt a tap on her shoulder.

She turned to see Thug Woofer.

"I thought you weren't coming tonight," she said.

"I had planned to surprise you," he said. "Til you said you had another date. You can't possibly be with that bourgie fool. He doesn't know you."

"Is that your surprise? Telling me who to date?"

"No," Woof said. "I wanted to tell you in person that I broke my contract to work with Car Willis. You were right. I read more about it and . . . that shit is sick. I don't wanna be associated with it in any way."

"Good for you," Tyesha said.

"Look," Woof said, "I know you're here with that other guy, but it's only been what? Less than a week? I cleaned up the Car Willis mess. Is there any way we can get past it? Tyesha, I'm really falling for you. You can't tell me you don't feel the same way."

"I don't," she said. "Whatever I felt before is over."

"I told you I broke the contract," he said. "I fixed what was wrong. What more do you want from me?"

"Nothing," Tyesha said. "I don't want nothing from you, Woof. You need to go. I'm with someone else tonight."

"Nah," Woof said. "Niggas like him talk a good game, but they don't know."

"Don't know what?" Tyesha asked.

"Don't know reality," he said. "What they know they learned from a book in school. Some fucking college boy."

"I'm a college girl," Tyesha said.

"You ain't just one thing," Woof said. "You college and you hood. That bourgie nigga know what you used to do?"

"You don't even know him," she said. "He's very pro–sex worker."

"Bullshit," Woof said. "He don't know nothing about getting your hands dirty. How sometimes you gotta do shit you can't write about on your college applications."

"Look, Woof," Tyesha said. "You had your shot. Then two second chances. Don't come up here talking shit about a man who can show respect where you fell short. Drew not only knows me, but he respects me, because he respects women."

"You haven't told him, have you?" Woof said.

Tyesha opened her mouth, but Woof put up a hand. "You right. Not my business. But you heard it here first. Enjoy the show."

Tyesha stood at her table, seething. How was he gonna tell her who to date? How did he know what Drew was really like?

Drew appeared with a pair of champagne flutes. "Sorry that took forever," he said. "Those girls were pretty good, huh?"

"Yeah," Tyesha said, and pulled him into a kiss.

"Wow," he said. "And that was before the champagne."

"Take me home with you tonight," Tyesha whispered in his ear.

Drew laughed. "As much as I love Nashonna," he said, "now I'm gonna be hoping she does the world's shortest set. One number, thank you and good night."

Tyesha laughed and kissed him again.

Two hours later, they were in his cramped apartment drinking wine out of hand-blown goblets. Tyesha sat on one of two tiny stools at a mini table that folded down. She was afraid to move normally or she might knock over her glass.

"So now we move into the second entertainment portion

of our evening," Drew said. He stood up and hung onto a tall pipe next to his fridge.

"I was gonna give you a striptease," he said. "Got any professional pointers?"

"What?" Tyesha asked.

"You know," he said. "From a stripper perspective?"

One voice in her head said to leave it. He thought she'd been a stripper, and that was close enough, especially for a second date.

But she kept hearing Thug Woofer's voice in her head. She wouldn't feel at ease until she had proven him wrong.

"Sorry, no tips," she said. "I didn't really used to strip."

"But I thought—" Drew said. "You said—"

"I waitressed in a strip club," Tyesha said. Then she took a deep breath. "And I occasionally did exotic dancing as part of the package when I was an escort."

Drew blinked. She resisted the urge to sugarcoat it.

"I was a full-service sex worker," she said.

"Full—?"

"Sex for money," she said.

"Oh," he said, with a bouncy little shrug. "That's cool."

But she could hear by his hesitation that it wasn't. The moment felt awkward, stilted.

Then he poured them a couple of drinks and got her laughing again. She thought maybe she had imagined the awkwardness.

As they chatted and laughed, she kept waiting for him to make the move on her. To lean in and kiss her. He had been so eager the first time they had sex. So excited to get her home tonight. But now, since she'd said the words "escort," "full service," and "sex for money," he seemed to be stalling.

She thought about making a move on him herself, but she needed to ask him point-blank.

"Drew," she said, interrupting a funny anecdote about interviewing a Scandinavian pop star. "I know you said it's cool that I used to be an escort, but are you sure?"

"Oh yeah . . . no," he said. "Totally cool. I'm just really . . . you know I'm way more tired than I thought. I've been up since five and that latte I had after dinner is wearing off. Can we maybe take a raincheck?"

She tilted her head to one side and smiled. "Of course." She had used that same face and posture with clients. When regulars were vague about setting another date. Not willing to man up and just say . . . whatever the fuck it was: *I've tried a black girl and it was nice, but now I want to try a Latina.* Or *my wife is getting suspicious.* Or *I lost my job, so I can't afford to see you again.* Whatever it was. Part of what they paid for was the privilege of not having to say anything.

Drew hadn't paid, but he'd certainly treated her like a hooker. All condescension and distance.

"You're right," she said. "I've got an early day myself."

"Let me walk you out," he said.

"No, no," she said. "I'm a big girl and I can take care of myself."

Some part of her was waiting for the sexy joke, or the *Wait, Tyesha . . . stay . . .* But it never came.

As she stood on the street, hand up, trying to hail a cab to Brooklyn, it did feel like a walk of shame. Not for the sex that never happened, but for the humiliation of having gotten her hopes up and been rejected.

The tears began to fall.

Worst of all, Thug Woofer had been right. Him and his smug mansplaining attitude.

Finally, a cab cut across two lanes of traffic to stop for her.

She wiped her eyes and climbed in, giving the driver her address.

In the back of the taxi, she deleted both men's numbers from her phone. She couldn't deal with thugs. She couldn't deal with college boys or stockbrokers, either. Fuck all men.

* * *

She slept poorly and was up before dawn. She decided to go in early and get a head start on all the work she'd been neglecting, between the heist and her love life drama.

Things were quiet in the early morning, and she walked down into the subway with a cup of coffee in her hand and an umbrella under her arm.

Suddenly, she felt a tug on her other hand.

A young man was trying to steal her briefcase. He had on a sweat suit and a lock of dark hair fell in his eyes and obscured his face.

She spun around and threw her coffee on him. He screamed and stumbled back against the steps.

The next thing she knew, she was beating the shit out of him with the umbrella.

"You gonna take my briefcase?" she asked. "My fucking briefcase? Do you have any idea everything I've gone through to get this fucking briefcase, and you're just gonna fucking snatch it?"

He threw his arms up over his head to protect himself. It was a cheap umbrella she'd gotten on the street for five dollars, and it broke quickly. He scrambled up and ran out above ground.

She stood on the steps, panting. She could hear the train coming. She fumbled in her purse for her Metrocard, but her hands were shaking too much. She missed the train.

That day at work was nonstop. They had back-to-back strategy meetings for the union, as well as several grant proposals that needed her attention, not to mention closing out the fiscal year.

It wasn't until nearly eight p.m. that Tyesha had a chance to look through that day's mail.

On the bottom of the pile was an envelope from the DNA test lab.

She opened the express mail envelope, and the business-size envelope within.

They explained that the majority of the hairs were synthetic, or could not be tested because they didn't have the bulb roots. The testing did, however, show conclusively that two of the samples are full siblings and are the children of the father's sample. It also showed that there was another half-sibling who was the child of the father's sample.

Tyesha blinked. Who the hell had Deza been bringing into her house?

She called her niece.

"Deza," she demanded, "have you been doing other people's hair at the house while I'm at work? Are you starting up some cottage industry behind my back?"

"No, Auntie," Deza said.

"Stop lying, girl," Tyesha said. "I have evidence that you've brought somebody up in my house. Did you bring one of Zeus's other kids into my house?"

"Seriously, Auntie," Deza said, "I ain't brought nobody up in here. And all his other kids are in Chicago."

"How you gonna disrespect my house like that, after I took you in?" she raged. "It's scientifically impossible for you to be telling the truth right now. Because you and Amaru been using my hairbrush and it just had—" She broke off, remembering that the brush also had her own hair.

"Please, Auntie." Deza began to cry. "I promise. Please don't put us out. Seriously, I never—"

"I—I'm sorry," Tyesha said, her body feeling light, dazed. "Don't cry, baby. I made a mistake. No, no, hush, sugar. Of course I'm not gonna put you out. My house is your house now." She felt her throat tighten. "We're family."

Shock, Tyesha thought. *This is shock.* She couldn't quite feel the touch of the leather on her fingertips when she picked up her purse. She felt disconnected from the pulling sensation in her arm muscles as she struggled to yank her phone charger out of the sticky wall socket in her office. She couldn't feel the steps under her feet as she walked downstairs and out of the building.

She had been standing on the street for a few minutes before she noticed that it was raining. The drops pelted her face, her hair, her raised hand as she tried to hail a cab. Rain splashed against the soft brown leather of her briefcase, soaking it to an even darker brown. She stood for another ten minutes, getting drenched, as yellow cab after yellow cab passed her by.

Zeus is my father?

She couldn't quite picture his face, but he did look so much like Deza and Amaru, and they did look like her. *Zeus is my* father?

The rain ran down her wrist into the sleeve of her blouse. She couldn't quite feel the dampness seep through her summer-weight suit jacket, her silk blouse, the padding of her push-up bra. The rain thudded against her thighs, soaking through the skirt, the polyester slip, the oversize underwear, because she wasn't going to be meeting Woof or Drew or anyone who might see them. Droplets slid down her legs into her shoes, turning the bright orange color sodden and dull.

A taxi pulled up and dropped two clients in front of the clinic. One of the girls recognized her.

"Tyesha," she said. "Take our taxi!"

If the girl hadn't said anything, she might have stood there for ages.

Still numb, she wandered into the cab, her body smearing rainwater across the vinyl of the backseat.

"Where to, miss?" the driver asked.

Blinking, she came back to herself a bit. "La Guardia," she said.

She sat back in the cab and got an alert on her phone. The clinic was trending online.

She looked and there it was, Drew's article. "Sex Work Is Work: Manhattan Strippers Fight to Unionize."

The article was incredible. Everything she could have hoped for. It was funny, compelling, an underdog story. She was quoted correctly, and he picked all the right snippets of what she said. Under any other circumstances, she'd be celebrating. It was a PR dream. #GoStripperUnion was trending on Twitter, and according to Serena, they were getting a ton of online donations.

When she arrived at La Guardia, she went directly to the airline with which she had all her frequent flyer miles.

"Can I help you?" the petite woman in the navy-and-pink uniform asked.

Tyesha blinked at the woman. Everything felt surreal, almost hazy. "I need," Tyesha began. "I need the next flight to Chicago."

Book 4

Chapter 17

For the first couple of months after her aunt died, Tyesha was totally bereft. Every night, she cried as she lay in her twin bed.

But then her mother began to admonish her: "Girl, you can't be up here crying every day. Your aunt Lu is in a better place. She's with the Lord. That's not a reason for crying, but for rejoicing, like the pastor said at the funeral. We cry for ourselves. So stop being selfish, get up and get ready for school."

That day, she was sitting in English class after the last bell rang, and an older girl she knew from church asked if she wanted to come smoke some weed with them in her cousin's car. Friends had asked before but Tyesha had always said no.

This particular day, Tyesha said yes. She would love to.

The weed was like magic. It got her mind off her aunt. It got her laughing for the first time in months. The cousin was cute. He was a year older and had a broken-down pickup truck he drove to school.

They started hanging out consistently. One day, she stayed late with the cousin and they started kissing. It was much more vague and surreal than the time with Kyle. After they fooled around a few times, they had sex. Tyesha was almost sixteen by then. It didn't hurt, but maybe that was just because she was high. She lay back against the upholstery of the truck's long seat. She felt the cousin pumping inside her. She felt her calf pressing against the steering wheel. It felt good, but also sort of blurry.

The next day, she told her friend, who scoffed at her.

"My cousin?" she said. "You fucking with my cousin? Girl, you can do so much better. Come on."

For Tyesha, the marijuana soon became secondary to the excitement of boys. In particular, she liked older boys.

Her friend took her to some parties and gave her specific instructions.

"Don't drink anything or smoke with these boys," she said. "They'll get you messed up. And if you wanna fuck somebody, don't do it tonight. Just give him your number and do it later. Then he'll have to take you to a movie or buy you a meal first. And don't ever fall for one of these guys. You'll just end up getting your feelings hurt. Enjoy them for the sex and see what you can get them to buy for you."

Soon, Tyesha learned to turn meals and movies into clothes and shoes, and getting her hair and nails done. Some of the young drug dealers were interested, but she didn't want to be like her sister, Jenisse. So she just stuck with boys who had a little cash, like football and basketball players.

And this was how she discovered college athletes. They had money like drug dealers, but they were on the right side of the law.

She had just turned sixteen, when her friend took her to a party at one university. Their basketball team had just won, and the students were jubilant.

The party took place in the apartment of one of the ballplayers. It had a huge living room that had been turned into a dance floor. It was the first time since her middle school dance that Tyesha had been somewhere with a live DJ. He was playing one of the top rap songs of the era, "I Need a Hella Grown Man."

One of the team's point guards didn't so much ask her to

dance as he took her hand and led her to the dance floor, assuming that she would want to.

Tyesha did. He was tall and long-limbed, with a smooth baby face and a tight fade, a little curly on top. On the dance floor, many of his teammates really just stood there and let their partners do all the work. They looked down at the shaking asses and swiveling torsos of the girls and treated the dance like a show, waving their hands in the air while they did a perfunctory two-step.

But Tyesha's partner danced. She figured he must have been a good ballplayer, because his moves were well coordinated. His narrow hips moved in counterpoint to his broad shoulders. They circled each other and fed off of each other's energy. When the dance was done, she smiled and expected him to thank and release her, but he pulled her close for the slower number, and she didn't complain, enjoying the feel of his body against hers, even with the moisture of the perspiration and the menthol smell of his antiperspirant.

They danced together for the whole party. Only after the last dance did he ask her name. "Well, Tyesha," he said, "wanna come over to my dorm and keep the party going?"

She did. The sex was better than with any of the high school guys. They had sex twice. In between rounds of intercourse, he went down on her. She had never had a partner do that before, and it was delicious.

They fell asleep in his double bed, under the oversized Dr. J poster. She woke up the next morning before he did. For a half hour, she gazed at the big room he didn't have to share, the bright tile bathroom, and the shelf full of books. She remembered that she used to like reading. She and her aunt would go to the library every week. Since Aunt Lu's death, Tyesha hadn't gone once.

After the ballplayer woke up, he took her to breakfast at his dorm. Tyesha had never seen so much food outside of a supermarket. He paid for her as a guest, and she was invited to eat whatever she wanted. Workers were ready to make her fried eggs, omelets, or waffles. There were ten kinds of bread for toast. Twenty cereals. Donuts. Pastries.

She sat down at his table with a pile of eggs and a waffle smothered in marshmallow sauce with chocolate chips on top.

As she ate, she realized that the ballplayer was sitting with teammates, and several of them were showing off the girls they'd bedded the night before. They openly compared them. Apparently the Asian girl was prettier in the face, but Tyesha had a better body. The light-skinned girl was cutest overall, but she had acne, which kept her from being a perfect ten.

Maybe on a different day, the competition would have stung or felt demeaning, but today she only cared about one thing: college. She was going to college, so she could live someplace like this.

From the time her aunt had died, Tyesha had wanted to feel connected to her. She had prayed at night, talked to her, tried to hear if her aunt was talking back some kind of way. But Tyesha's own voice seemed to be talking alone into the empty night. For the first time, she felt sure that her aunt Lu was on board for this plan. Tyesha could almost hear her voice. "Yes, baby. College. That's what I'm talking about."

As Tyesha headed out of the dorm, she walked by the residence hall office. She was looking for the campus map so she could find the nearest subway stop. She hadn't expected to find a young black woman sitting at the desk.

"Can I help you?"

"No," Tyesha said shyly. "I'm not a student. I'm just a guest."

"That's okay," the staffer said. "Do you need something?"

"How do people go here?" Tyesha said. "I mean, is it just good grades to get in or what?"

The girl gave her a stack of pamphlets, including a minority pre-freshman flyer.

On Monday, Tyesha took them to the guidance counselor at her high school. They started working on a plan to get her into college.

After that, she gave up on high school boys completely. She only dated university boys who could help her reach that one goal.

She joined a bunch of different extracurricular activities, which got her mama to shut up and stop nagging her about where she was and what she was doing.

When her friend came up pregnant, she was careful to get another birth control shot. Although it wouldn't protect her from chlamydia or gonorrhea. She started using condoms.

Then she started using them for birth control, as well. When one of them broke, she used emergency contraception. She continued to date college boys and leveraged her nights in their dorm rooms into informal tours.

By the time she was admitted to all the schools where she'd applied, she already knew which dorms had the remodeled bathrooms and the good barbecued chicken.

The day she graduated with a full scholarship to Northwestern, her mama was proud, and she knew her aunt would have been, too. Looking back, Tyesha tried to recall if she'd even wondered about her father at that time. Seeing some of the other kids in her graduating class with a mom and dad cheering for them, would she have wondered about him? Or would she only have stayed focused on the absence of her aunt, the flesh-and-blood loved one who was missing, not the ghost that never was?

The morning after Tyesha got the results of the DNA test, she landed at O'Hare. Her clothes had dried in the canned air of the plane, and her hair had curled up from the rain, then matted down where she had slept on it. Her head nestled between the window and the seat back for three hours of dreamless sleep in the same position. The flight attendant had to wake her.

Her eyes had fluttered open to see a middle-aged Asian woman smiling and nudging her shoulder.

"We've landed in Chicago," the woman was saying.

Tyesha's first thought was *I'm from Chicago. My mama still lives there.* And then she recalled why she had taken the trip. Her mother and Zeus. She had to confront Jenisse.

She wiped her face and stood up. In spite of having no luggage in the overhead compartment or beneath the seat in front of her, she was still the last passenger to leave the plane. She walked down the jetway in a haze of disorientation.

Even through her daze, she could tell that something was wrong with her appearance by the frowning faces around her and the way people gave her a wide berth. In the bathroom, she saw that her hair needed to be dealt with. She rummaged through her purse but couldn't find a hairbrush. Instead, she found a navy cotton handkerchief wadded up in the bottom of the side compartment. She smoothed it out the best she could and tied it over her hair.

It had been nearly four years since she had been home. She took a cab directly to her sister's house. Chicago on an early summer morning looked like something out of a half-forgotten dream. But the old neighborhood looked the same. When the cab pulled up to Jenisse's house, she felt her heart start to beat fast.

Her sister and Zeus lived in a house in Avalon Park. It was mostly black, but more middle-class than South Shore, where their mother still lived. Tyesha paid the driver and banged on her sister's door. After a few minutes, she began to lean on the doorbell. Finally, she heard a muffled shout from within the house.

"What the fuck?" Jenisse's voice rang louder. "Zeus, how you gonna come back from New York early and forget your fucking keys again?"

But then Tyesha saw a brown shadow move over the peephole.

"Tyesha?" Jenisse said. "What the hell you doing in Chicago?"

She opened the door.

Tyesha strode in. "You in New York. Me in Chicago. Our family is just full of surprises."

The living room was done in shades of beige and tan, with a creamy leather sofa set. There were vintage jazz photographs on the walls. Sepia images of Billie Holliday and Thelonious Monk adorned the wall facing Tyesha. Below them was a bar for entertaining and a largely open passage to the next room, through which Tyesha could see the lacquered wood dining room set. All the surfaces were spotless. As Tyesha recalled, the family really lived in the kitchen and family room, which were in the back of the house.

"What went wrong with the girls?" Jenisse asked. "They too much for you? You come begging me to take them home?" She leaned around Tyesha. "Or better yet, they both in the cab? You came to drop those heifers off?"

"What?" Tyesha said. "No, they're in New York at my apartment. I came to see you."

"Why on earth—"

"You stole Mama's man," Tyesha said. "I always wondered why he was so fucking much older than you. But you took him. With your fast teenage ass, you took your own mama's man."

Jenisse began to laugh. She laughed so hard, she fell back on the couch, and her kimono fell open, exposing a length of toned leg and a short expanse of her belly with a sprinkling of silvery stretch marks. Jenisse was liquid with the laughter. She began to almost howl with it, tears falling down her face.

"You think it's funny?" Tyesha said. "You think it's so fucking funny that you took her man. That Zeus is my father, not some shadowy guy whose description kept changing."

"No, I—" Jenisse tried to speak, but the laughter prevented her. When she could get enough breath, she said. "No, I think it's funny that you think so." And then she was seized with another fit of laughter in an even higher key.

"This is bullshit," Tyesha said, and she turned to walk out.

"Wait," Jenisse rasped, gripping her side.

She reached for a bottle of water, and took a swig. She began to cough a bit, titters still shaking her body like tiny aftershocks.

"You wanna tell me the joke?" Tyesha demanded, arms at her sides, clenching and unclenching her fists.

"You got it all backward," Jenisse said. "Every single bit, college girl. You see the numbers but you can't do the math."

Tyesha could tell Jenisse was savoring the moment. Finally, she had something and was teasing Tyesha with it. The sister who dropped out of high school taunting the one with the master's degree.

"What then?" Tyesha asked. "Tell me how I got it wrong."

"It's the opposite of what you think," Jenisse said. "I had him first. Mama fucked *my* man."

And there it was again. The dazed feeling. Like when she looked at the DNA results and couldn't make sense of it. Mama? Their mama?

"That's right," Jenisse said. "So, if there's a lying, thieving bitch you need to call out, that would be our mama. So put that on your next fucking Mother's Day card."

Chapter 18

If the ride from the airport was like a half-forgotten dream, the ride to her old apartment was more like a too-real flashback. She couldn't get a cab from Jenisse's house, so she just started walking. After half a mile, her feet began to hurt in the pumps from her previous day at the office. She stopped and waited for a bus. She got on with a cluster of kids headed to school and adults headed to work.

The kids talked loud and joked, their bursts of laughter erupting at intervals. She remembered that feeling. Back in elementary school, when the front and sides of her body were straight lines, she ran with a crew of kids from her neighborhood. Every moment that wasn't school or church was playing. Kickball, jump rope, tag in warm weather. Snowball fights in winter. Anything could be a toy. If you didn't have anything, you would laugh, tell jokes, do imitations of teachers and ministers. As long as she was with her friends, it was fun. Everything was funny. She didn't have a daddy, but that wasn't anything special. It didn't steal her joy.

Back then she felt light inside. Now she felt empty, felt nothing. Like her chest was full of air. Or maybe she was a stuffed doll, filled with cotton balls or a fluffy polyester fiberfill.

The blocks of public housing looked exactly the same. She knew just where to get off for her old apartment. Just before the playground, with the top of the climbing structure jutting up over the parked cars. Just past the KFC.

As she rode down the familiar street, the revelations made everything seem surreal. *Every time I rode up and down this street, Zeus was my father. Every time I walked up to my apartment, I was the daughter of a woman who cheated with her own daughter's man.*

The buzzer was broken, as usual, but a group of kids exited just as she stepped up.

"See?" one of them said. "We missed the bus cause yo slow ass."

The large metal door slammed behind her, and she proceeded to walk up the dingy staircase. As always at this time of year, it smelled of urine, bleach, and summer funk.

Three floors up, she banged on her mama's door.

"Just a minute," she heard the familiar contralto voice.

Her mother opened up with her eyes wide.

Tyesha just couldn't reconcile Jenisse's revelation with this aging woman in a headrag, bathrobe, and fuzzy slippers. For a moment, she just gaped at her mother. For the first time, she noticed the smoothness of her mother's barely lined skin, the classic black beauty in the planes of her face, the thick bust and hips half-smothered under the robe. For the first time, she saw her mother, not as the dowdy Jesus-loving church mother she had turned herself into, but the voluptuous woman she had been before she got saved.

"Tyesha?" she said, startled. "Is everything okay, baby? How come you ain't in New York? You got Deza and Amaru with you?"

The apartment was exactly the same. The large color television—a flat-screen now—was showing the news. And Mama's worn chair facing it. Her walker next to it for the days it got really bad, especially in winter.

The coffee table with old copies of *Ebony* and *Essence* and a bowl of candies.

The walls covered with photographs. Tyesha's graduation photos: high school, college, and grad school. And the bible on the table right next to the chair.

Her mother shuffled forward to hug her, but Tyesha leaned easily out of the way, and crossed to pace in front of the couch.

"What's wrong?" her mother asked.

Tyesha didn't know where to begin. She looked up to see the meteorologist standing beside an illustration of sun and clouds over Chicago. She picked up the remote and muted the TV.

"Is Zeus my daddy?" she blurted out.

Her mother knelt down, closed her eyes and began to pray.

"No, Mama." Tyesha walked over and pried her mother's hands apart. "You've had almost thirty years to talk to Jesus about this. Especially if you count the time you were pregnant. So now it's time to talk to me. Is Zeus my father?"

"Yes," her mother said in a voice barely above a whisper.

"And he was with Jenisse before he was with you?" Tyesha asked, towering over her mother.

"Yes."

"Are you kidding me?" Tyesha asked, her forehead puckered, her eyes blinking in disbelief. "Are you fucking kidding me?"

"Of all the things I ever did, I don't think there's anything I'm more ashamed of," her mother said. "I wasn't even thirty. Here comes my fifteen-year-old daughter with a grown man. I thought I was gonna show her he was bad news. Not right for her. I was gonna break them up. Gonna save her."

"By fucking her man?" Tyesha asked, incredulous.

"I remember going to her and telling her what had happened, what the fool she called 'her man' had done. A man who would be with her own mama. But it didn't work that

way. She took it in stride. 'He has other women. So what?'
Jenisse said to me." Her mother looked out the window. "He
told her it didn't mean anything. He would have other ladies,
but she was the queen."

Tyesha collapsed onto the sofa, but her mother didn't seem
to notice. She was still on her knees. The monologue became
almost a prayer of its own. "I was so young when I had her.
Not done being cute and silly. I competed with her when she
was young. Mostly I won. This time she was determined to
win."

Behind her mother, Tyesha saw the image of a doctor's office on the TV, which cut to a newscaster with the headline
"MEDICAL MALPRACTICE."

Her mother went on: "Was a couple of trifling niggas I
was seeing at the time." Tyesha blinked. She couldn't ever recall hearing her mother use the n-word. "I just said you must
be one of theirs. When they found out I was pregnant, they
stopped coming around. Didn't none of them come forward
trying to claim nothing. I don't think Jenisse knew until Deza
was born and she looked so much like you had looked as a
baby."

"I was nine," Tyesha said, a sudden, sharp recollection.

Her mother nodded. "Still a few baby pictures I don't
know which is which."

"She started being so mean to me," Tyesha said. "I was always trying to figure out what I had done wrong. I could
never understand it. We had been close and then . . ."

Years later, when Tyesha had learned about post-partum
depression, she had clung to that as an explanation.

"I apologized to her so many times," her mother said. "I
insisted you weren't Zeus's, and I begged her not to take it
out on you. At one point, she threatened to get a DNA test.
But I think she didn't tell him, because she was trying to keep
him focused on her own kids. Lord knows there were always
plenty of other baby mamas coming around in tight dresses

with they hands out." She shook her head. "I certainly didn't wanna be one of them, so when I found out I was pregnant, I just started going to church. I asked Jesus to forgive me."

"Why didn't you ever tell me?" She couldn't look at her mother. Instead, she looked at a silent TV segment with elementary school children doing jumping jacks.

"Like I told you, I was just plain shamed," her mother said.

"I had a right to know," Tyesha said.

"I never knew who my own daddy was," her mother said. "It don't kill you not to know. Though I always told myself I wouldn't do that to my kids. Jenisse's dad was locked up, so she didn't have him, but she knew where to find him. But you having a daddy I couldn't claim? I wasn't no teenager. I was older than you are now. I sowed spite, and I reaped shame."

"But I was gonna find out eventually," Tyesha said.

"I kept waiting for Jenisse to tell you in a moment of evil," her mother said. "But she never did. I just figured if it didn't come out when you were a teenager, it never would."

"Jenisse wanted a DNA test for Amaru," Tyesha said. "So Zeus would pay for her athletic boarding school."

Her mother pursed her lips. "Around the time Jenisse got pregnant with Amaru, they were kinda broken up. I know she was seeing other men. He was never sure if Amaru was his. And then, when she grew up to be gay, well, he wasn't sure he wanted her to be his."

"Well, that's fucked up," Tyesha said. "And she's definitely his. We all are."

Her mother began to cry. "All these years I begged Jesus to forgive me. And I seen how good your life was going, and I assumed He did. But now I know it's you I need to forgive me. You and Jenisse."

Tyesha looked at the screen. A slender white homemaker was smiling and wiping the counter with some miraculous cleaner.

Tyesha shook her head. Her mother was fourteen when she had Jenisse? Amaru was fourteen. She imagined Amaru with a baby, suddenly responsible for another person's life. Amaru could barely remember to put the lid back on the toothpaste. Her mother, competing with her own daughter, setting out to spite her and getting caught in her own trap.

She wasn't sure she felt it, but she couldn't deny her mother the clemency.

"I forgive you, Mama," she said, and embraced her. Tyesha held on, as her mother shook with sobs.

Tyesha felt lost. She couldn't get a flight out until midnight, and it was only afternoon. She had borrowed a pair of her mother's old sneakers and found herself wandering around the neighborhood with her ruined fancy New York shoes in her hand.

And then, without realizing it, she found herself at the burned-out remains of the Urban Peace Accord youth center. Almost fifteen years later, it still hadn't been repaired. Except the basketball courts, which had only been minimally damaged. They had gotten new nets later that same year, but by now they had frayed into ragged strings. A Boys' and Girls' Club had popped up next door.

Tyesha stood by the edge of the court. The memories flooded in from the night she had stood there with her aunt.

"Hey, girl," a throaty woman's voice said from behind her. "Tyesha, right?"

She turned around to see Sheena Davenport, Amaru's mentor from the WNBA, grinning at her out of the driver's side of a white luxury car.

"I thought I told you to look me up if you ever came to Chicago," she said, taking off her shades and looking Tyesha up and down.

"It was an unexpected trip," Tyesha said, returning her smile.

"Well, how long are you here?" Sheena asked. "I'm waiting on this girl, a great player, but I don't think she's gonna show. At one thirty, I'm outta here. Wanna come have a drink with me? I know a place near here with a great lunchtime cocktail menu."

"Sure," Tyesha said, and walked around to the passenger side. Her mouth smiled, but she still felt numb inside. The car's interior was the color of chocolate. She slid into the plush leather seats.

"Your niece has definitely got talent," Sheena said. "I'm just sorry she wasn't able to go to that athletic academy."

"There still may be hope," Tyesha said.

"So what brings you home to Chicago?" Sheena asked.

"Some . . . family business," Tyesha said.

"Are you staying long?" Sheena asked. "Can I invite you out on a proper date?"

"I leave at midnight," she said.

"Maybe an improper date then," Sheena said and grinned, putting a hand on Tyesha's knee.

For the first time since getting the DNA test, Tyesha felt something familiar. Being turned on. She breathed it in. Sex. If nothing else made sense, sex always did.

She leaned in and kissed Sheena.

"Hold up," Sheena said. "I'm still on the clock waiting for this girl for the next fifteen minutes. I can't have her come here and see me kissing somebody while I'm supposed to be waiting for her."

"You said she's probably a no-show," Tyesha said. "Let it go. Let's get out of here."

She pulled Sheena into an intense kiss. Sheena kissed back, and Tyesha's scarf slipped off.

Sheena peered more closely at Tyesha, then took her hand off her thigh.

"Are you okay?" Sheena asked.

"I'm fine," Tyesha insisted, and slid closer on the long bench seat.

"Uh-uh," Sheena said. "This ain't gonna work."

"What do you mean?" Tyesha asked.

"I mean, you got something going on that a little lesbian moment isn't gonna fix," Sheena said.

"I've been with women before," Tyesha said.

"This isn't about—" Sheena broke off. "What's up with your hair?"

"My hair?" Tyesha said. "You don't want to get down because of my hair?"

"I don't want to get down because something ain't right with you, girl. You don't look sexy, you look upset."

"I'm not upset," Tyesha said.

Sheena's mouth slowly opened. "Oh, that's right," she said. "You a Couvillier." She gave Tyesha a quizzical look. "How you gonna be standing on the spot your auntie died and not be upset?"

"What do you know about it?" Tyesha asked.

"I know there were flowers and candles at the base of that telephone pole for nearly a decade," Sheena said. "I know your mama was the one bringing the flowers for years, til she got too sick."

"My mama?" Tyesha said.

"This ain't New York," Sheena said. "This part of South Shore is like a small town. I don't just know Amaru, I know all your people. And I knew your aunt."

"Well, you don't know me," Tyesha said, and stormed out of the car on the traffic side. A driver swerved and honked at her.

She took off walking fast down the street in the opposite direction of the traffic, so Sheena couldn't follow in the car.

She remembered that night. She had stood beside her aunt as she spoke to the crowd assembled on the basketball court.

She was nearly as tall as her aunt by then. Tyesha held the megaphone aloft, while her aunt held the microphone in one hand, and her carefully prepared speech in the other.

They stood on the court because the center had been burned to the ground. Their auditorium, their chairs, their sound system, all reduced to rubble and char. The stench of gasoline and flames was still so strong that they stood with their backs to the street, against the chain-link fence at the far end, because the smell was just a little better.

Her aunt had rescued the sign: URBAN PEACE AC-CORD, spray-painted on a piece of plywood. On the very bottoms of the letters the wood and paint were singed. This was likely because they had balanced the sign on a plastic ledge above the door frame and glued it in place. Her aunt had always meant to secure it better, but had never gotten around to it. When the building burned, both the plastic ledge and the glue melted. The sign fell down just beyond the reach of the fire.

Her aunt held up the sign during her speech. She held it up as a talisman that they shouldn't lose hope.

"You can't burn down an idea," her aunt had bellowed. "You can't burn down the desire for a better life, a better community."

The assembly offered yeses and amens.

"People wanna come and tell me that some gang members did this," she said. "I don't know any gang members. I know young men with names. Young men I've known for decades. These are our young people. Some police gang task force is not the solution. The police are part of the problem. Sometimes I think the police are the biggest gang. We are the solution. This center is part of the solution and I will rebuild it as many times as I have to!"

Later, Tyesha would hear stories about high-level gang leaders who had been won over by her aunt. They wanted to leave the life, they insisted, but they had too many ties to the police department. Even if they could convince the drug king-pins that they wouldn't snitch, the cops weren't about to let them walk away.

But that came later. All that Tyesha knew from that night on the Peace Center's basketball courts was the smell of burned building and that giving a speech makes you a target.

Tyesha recalled the screech of tires as the car came around the corner. The quick whip of dreadlocks brushing against her face as her aunt looked over her shoulder. And then her aunt had pushed her down, pushed her away. And Tyesha had been down on the concrete when the bullets sprayed from the car window.

She had screamed. Kept her head covered. And then had stood to find her aunt lying in a pool of blood. "Auntie!" Tyesha had shrieked and run to her. Had gathered her in her arms, the best she could. The blood had soaked her clothes.

Around them all were screaming and scattering. Several other people appeared to have been shot, as well.

"You okay, baby?" her aunt had asked. Even dying, she was worried about someone else. "Did they hit you?"

"I'm okay," Tyesha had assured her aunt through her tears. "You gonna be okay, too."

By then, her mother was running up to them. Someone had called and told her.

"Please, Jesus, oh please, Lord Jesus," her mother begged, her body rigid, clenched in prayer.

But her aunt was dead by the time the ambulance came wailing to where she lay, only a few minutes later.

Tyesha screamed as her mother pried her hands from the ambulance gurney.

They sobbed together as the ambulance took her aunt quietly away.

A week later, Tyesha stood in the church for the memorial. She had her carefully written speech in her hand. She had on a blue dress, stockings, and low-heeled black pumps. She had white gloves and even a small blue hat. Her mother didn't insist she go to church anymore, but when she did choose to go, she needed to dress up.

She stood beside the pulpit, waiting for her turn. And then the pastor introduced her. He ran down her list of accomplishments: valedictorian of her class, on the track team, tutoring younger kids in math. "We expect great things from her, just like from her aunt Lucille. Please give a warm godly welcome to Tyesha Couvillier."

The applause thundered, but she felt frozen, her feet planted in place as if they'd grown roots.

"Go on." One of the boys gave her a little push, and Tyesha could move again. But instead of going up onto the platform and reading her speech, she turned back toward him, pushed past all the kids, and ran out of the building. Later, she would overhear her mother talking to some of the other church women: "It was just too soon."

Tyesha had never spoken in public since that day. It wasn't just the memory of her dying aunt, but also the terror of speaking up. It made you a target. Not just for gang violence. Once, when she googled Aunt Lu in college, she came across a blog post by an anonymous investigative journalist who claimed he had a mountain of circumstantial evidence that the cops were behind her aunt's murder. And the arson, too. Nothing could ever be proven, so the story had been killed by the journalist's editor. But there was a PDF file with evidence. Tyesha's heart beat hard as she considered clicking on it. But instead, she closed the window on her browser. She didn't need some anonymous journalist's evidence to corroborate what she knew for sure: Her aunt was dead, the center was burned to the ground, and she would forever connect speaking in front of crowds with that terrible day.

* * *

Tyesha couldn't recall where her aunt was buried, but she did know where she could find another shrine, this one more durable than the one that had been on the street next to the basketball court.

Two blocks down, she came to her mother's church. Since she had left Chicago, it had expanded from a single storefront to take up half the block, and they had redone the façade with stained-glass windows and a large golden cross.

But in the front hallway she knew they had a low glass cabinet with a small shelf dedicated to her aunt. She had been a deaconess in the church. There she was, smiling, surrounded with artificial flowers. All her awards and plaques. Her deaconess gloves folded in front of the picture.

Tyesha pressed her hand against the glass.

One of the women of the church came out from the office. She was sixtyish, light-skinned, and thickly built. "Are you here for choir rehearsal?" she asked. "It doesn't start until—"

Tyesha opened her mouth, but all that came out was a howl of grief.

She sank down onto the goldenrod carpeting, keening and weeping. The woman managed to lower herself down onto one hip and squeeze in next to Tyesha. She patted the younger woman's back as she wailed and wailed.

Tyesha wanted to shriek with rage for losing her aunt, with terror from the shooting and the burning and the bone-chilling knowledge that the killers weren't local teens, but men in uniforms who killed with the full blessing and protection of the state. She wanted to shriek for her mother who had been a teenage mom, stealing her teenage daughter's man, and twenty-nine years of lies, with two sisters who had been at each other's throats for twenty of those years. She wanted to rail for her own broken heart, and Thug Woofer, whom she could never trust again, but somehow he kept haunting her, even beyond his number-one rapper status, she was unable to get over him; unable to have him; unable to move on.

So Tyesha just crumpled in this stranger's arms and sobbed. Her face puckered with inarticulate wailing, her face coated with tears and snot, smearing into the flowered print of the woman's dress.

"He'll fix it for you," the woman promised, unconcerned about her clothes. "Oh, won't He fix it."

Two hours later, Tyesha stood in front of Jenisse's door for a second time that day. It was evening now, still light, but with long shadows. Tyesha still had her designer pumps in her hand. Her makeup was cried off, and she had left her scarf in Sheena's car. The mess that was her hair was revealed for all to see. She had been wearing the same clothes for more than thirty-six hours. She smelled like she needed a shower.

"What you want?" Jenisse asked when she came to the door. She was dressed in a camel-colored dress with nude pumps and dark lipstick. "And what the hell happened to you? You got a homeless makeover?"

"You were right," Tyesha said. "I can't believe Mama did that to you. That's one of the most fucked-up things a mother could do to a daughter."

Suddenly, Jenisse's face puckered, and she looked like she might cry. Tyesha went to hug her, but Jenisse waved her away and took a deep breath.

"I need a cigarette," Jenisse said, and walked Tyesha through the house to the back porch. The older sister sat down on a wicker loveseat and motioned for Tyesha to sit across from her on a matching chair. The railed wooden deck stretched the length of the house and led out to a grassy yard. On the rail beside Jenisse was an ashtray, matches, and a pack of cigarettes. She pulled one out and lit it.

She took a deep drag into her lungs and spoke. "Yeah, that shit was fucked up," she said, exhaling smoke. "I'm just sorry I took it out on you. Every time I saw you, I thought about what she did."

"Well, it's good to know why you were such a bitch to me all these years," Tyesha said. "Now that the truth is out, do you think maybe you could stop?"

Jenisse laughed. "I'll think about it," she said, and took another drag. "Being a bitch is one of the few things I'm good at."

"You're good at advocating for your kids," Tyesha said. "You think Zeus will pay for Amaru's school now that the paternity test came back positive?"

"He better," Jenisse said. "But in the meantime, I'm glad they're staying with you in New York. I was never the mama they deserved."

"They love you," Tyesha said.

"That's just cause I'm they mama," Jenisse said. "But I know I didn't really wanna raise babies; I was just trying to keep Zeus. But look at you. You stayed out the trap. You got a good job. No kids. You got that rapper chasin' you."

"Not anymore," Tyesha said.

"So fix that," Jenisse said tapping ash into the ashtray. "Deza told me how it is wit y'all. A million chicks wanna fuck with that nigga and you like, he ain't good enough."

"He was gonna do an album with Car Willis," Tyesha said.

That stopped her sister. "He doing an album with Car Willis?"

"No, but he was gonna," Tyesha said.

"Girl," Jenisse said. "People who ain't from Chicago don't know how it was. He canceled the album?"

Tyesha nodded.

"Then get over it," Jenisse said. "Wait, is he a good fuck?"

Tyesha laughed. "Yeah."

"Then call his ass. Fuck him. Enjoy it."

"If I could do it like that, I would," Tyesha said. "But I like him too much."

"So?" Jenisse asked. "Let him know you want him to put a ring on it."

"It's not that simple," Tyesha said. "He doesn't exactly see me as the wifey type. I used to be an escort. That's actually how we met."

Jenisse grinned and stubbed out her cigarette. "An escort? I thought you were the big college girl."

Tyesha sucked her teeth. "How do you think I *paid* for college?"

"I was, too," Jenisse said. "That's how I met Zeus. I was always afraid he didn't wife up with me because I had been a ho."

Tyesha shrugged. "He's as wifed up with you as he'll ever be with anybody."

Jenisse sighed. "Here's the big mistake I made. We talked about getting married at one point, but he had this big prenup. I refused to sign it because I thought it meant he thought of me as a ho, that he didn't trust me. But I learned my lesson. A nigga like him needs me to prove I'm loyal and not after the money. If you love your rapper, put him on a marriage track. Let him know you want him to put a ring on it. After a year, if he don't propose, drop his ass. Thug Woofer will probably want a prenup, and you'll think that it means he doesn't trust you. It means he wanna trust you. He needs to know you ain't after his money to believe you really want him. Besides, with all you got going, the prenup might end up protecting you. You should write a book about the stripper strike, going from being a ho to running that clinic. You might end up being the one with the money in twenty years. Wait and see."

"Maybe so," Tyesha said. "What about you and Zeus? You ever gonna get married?"

"You trying to make me your stepmama?" Jenisse asked.

Tyesha cringed. "I still can't wrap my head around it."

"We ain't never getting married," Jenisse said. "He put some money away for me. When he dies, I'll be better off not being associated with his estate. Meanwhile, we know how to make it work. I let him fuck other women from time to time, and he lets me buy what the fuck I want."

Tyesha laughed. "Now that everything's out in the open, will you talk to Mama? She wants to make it right with you."

"I'll think about it," Jenisse said. The two of them looked out into the gathering dusk in the yard.

"Mama's an old church lady now," Tyesha said. "Forgive her. She's gonna be your only family here, now that the boys are locked up and Amaru's going to school, and Deza's working on her music in New York."

"Like I told you," Jenisse said. "I'll think about it. Now let's get you cleaned up. You can't go back to New York City like this."

Jenisse walked Tyesha back to the house, into the part that they actually used.

Tyesha arrived back at JFK in an old pair of Jenisse's jeans and a Chicago T-shirt. But before she went home or to the office, Tyesha went to see Zeus. Outside his room, the hotel corridor was empty. She hoped that meant that Reagan had returned to Chicago or crawled back under his rock.

As a kid, she had fantasized about one day meeting her dad. In the younger years, he was a dashing, powerful man, not unlike Zeus. But he would sweep her away in a montage of father-daughter activities that she saw white kids do on TV like ice-skating and berry picking.

She knocked on the door.

Unfortunately, after a few minutes, Reagan answered.

"Umph," he grunted. "To what do we owe the pleasure?"

"You got no pleasure coming from me, Reagan," she said. "Where's Zeus?"

"Tyesha." Zeus stepped out of the bedroom dressed in a dark suit. "Good morning."

"Good morning," she said, almost shyly. How had she not noticed it before? His big eyes. He had the thick eyebrows she was so careful to pluck. The goatee sort of muted the shape of his lips but they were so like hers. His lighter brown skin mixed with her mama's dark brown would perfectly blend to her coloring.

He cleared his throat. "I wanna thank you for keeping the girls," he said. "I shoulda did something sooner. Please let me give you a little something for them."

Tyesha shook her head. "No, Zeus," she insisted. "It's fine. I got a good job and they been helping out around the apartment," she said. "Actually, I came to talk to you about something else."

"Go ahead," he said.

She cut her eyes at Reagan. "Can we speak privately?" she asked. "It's a family matter."

"This is family," Zeus said. "Reagan is like a son to me and is in on everything, as he's gonna inherit the business one day."

"Yeah," Reagan said. "I knew your aunt Lucille, and was part of her program."

She fixed a hard stare on him. "Please don't speak her name to me," she said. "I just came back from visiting the place where she was shot."

Reagan dropped his eyes.

"Anyway," she said, "as you know, Jenisse asked me to get DNA samples from the girls, and here are the results. They're yours," she said handing him the envelope. "Both of them."

"You came all the way here to tell me that in person?" Zeus asked.

"No." Her voice dropped slightly in volume. "There was a—well, I couldn't get a saliva sample from Amaru. She refused to cooperate. So I used the hairbrush, and they tested me by mistake. Apparently, I'm your biological child, as well."

"Oh, shit," Reagan murmured.

Zeus's eyes widened. "I had no idea," he said.

"I just wanted to come by and explain what it says on the results paper," Tyesha said. "Doesn't seem to me that anything needs to change. I mean, I don't want anything from you. But I'd like to be the one to tell Deza and Amaru . . . in my own time, if you don't mind. My mama kept the secret all these years, but it's out now."

He looked at her more closely. "I can't believe I never saw it before. You and Deza favor so much."

Tyesha shrugged. "I just hope you'll consider sending Amaru to that school. She's got so much talent. Anyway, I gotta get to work. I'll see you around."

As the door clicked behind her, she let out a small shudder. The experience of telling Zeus had been nearly as surreal as finding out he was her biological father. But looking him in the face and telling him was refreshingly real. As she walked back to the elevator, she felt like she could breathe easier.

Chapter 19

The impromptu trip to Chicago hadn't been her first time leaving and returning to New York since she'd moved there. Yet, unexpectedly, it reminded her of the first time she'd arrived.

Tyesha had always told everyone she'd moved to New York to get away from the craziness of her family, but it wasn't the whole truth. There was also a basketball player named Tariq. He was six foot three and headed for the NBA.

They had started as a casual hookup after a party in the spring of her freshman year. But then the following fall they had an introduction to African American studies class together. Nearly all the young black women in the class began to dress more provocatively after they saw that Tariq, one of the school's star players, was sitting in the front row. But Tyesha did the opposite, and dressed down. He had already seen what was under her clothes. No need to have it hanging out like the girls in the cleavage sweaters and short skirts. If he was interested in getting another shot, he would need to step up.

And he did. Three weeks into the class, he showed up at her dorm room, asking if she had the homework info. It was an obvious ploy—the information was on the class website—but she played along. She left him standing at the door, while she went and looked through her notes. Then she gave him the info, nothing more.

The following week in class, she found it hard to pay attention, with Tariq sitting in front of her, his ripped shoulders sticking out of the Chicago Bulls jersey. The professor was giving a lecture on sharecropping: the former slave owners used a credit system to lend the seeds, tools, and other goods to the formerly enslaved. And of course, they owned the land. The formerly enslaved only had their bodies and the work they could perform. The former slave owners set the price—of both the supplies and the cash for the crops—but also did the counting and kept all the records. At the end of the season, the formerly enslaved owed whatever the bosses said they owed, and had produced whatever the bosses said they had produced. And they had no rights the law would uphold. So after every season of arduous labor, where black folks worked as hard as they had under slavery, they were further in debt to the owners. By law, sharecroppers couldn't leave if they were in debt, but had to stay and work the land until the debt was paid. Which, by virtue of the system's structure, would be never.

Tyesha was outraged.

One of the students in the classroom shrugged. "That was a long time ago. People need to get over it."

"Was it?" the teacher asked. "Some of you may have had grandparents or great grandparents who worked under this system. That's quite a disadvantage if some of you had grandparents accumulating wealth while others had it systematically stolen. Some labor is compensated, other labor is not."

"Like the NCAA," Tariq said. "They got us out here hustling for no money with the hope of getting to the NBA. Meanwhile, we're making a mint for these colleges while we get a substandard education, and if we get injured we get nothing."

In that moment, Tyesha began to see Tariq in a new light. Maybe he was more than a pretty face and a nice ass. Tyesha still didn't dress up for class, but she started going to basket-ball games.

A week later, he dropped by again, explaining that he didn't really understand Toni Cade Bambara's introduction to *The Black Woman*, and could she help him?

Sure, she could.

Later, he would say it was one of the most awkward times in his dating life since middle school. He wasn't used to hav-ing to do anything more than show the least bit of interest, and girls would throw themselves at him. Tyesha was careful to avoid setting up a dynamic where he thought he just needed to drop by and get laid. After a few weeks of studying, he worked his way up to putting an arm around her. She lifted it up and put it back in his lap.

"Tariq, I know we hooked up once," she said. "And it was nice. But if you'd like to get at me again, you'll need to take me out on a proper date. No offense if that's not what you're into. Plenty of girls around here would be glad to hook up with you whenever you come calling. I'm just not one of them."

He would like to take her out, he told her. He would like that very much.

They started dating, and by the middle of the semester, they were in love. She spent every night in his single room, which was much larger than the double she shared with a pre-med white girl who was never there except to sleep.

She sat in the front row at all his games and didn't even worry about female competition because he had picked her over all the sexy girls throwing themselves at him. "I'm done with groupies," he had explained to her, more like vowed, when he wanted to lock it down and make their relationship exclusive.

She had never felt like this before. Every love song. Every romantic movie. He called her "my girl," talked about being all "wifed up" with her. The sex was bliss. He wanted to be with her every night. He never said "I love you," but he texted her lines of love songs. Even years later, there were slow jams she couldn't hear without thinking of him. In love. For the first time.

And it wasn't just about the love that was between them, it was also being the one chosen by a baller like him. It was special to be chosen by somebody, but all the more delicious to be chosen by a man that so many young women wanted. She teased him about it, but he scoffed. Those girls don't have a damn thing that I want.

She loved going to the games, so it was with resignation that she had to pass on an away game in November. She had to study—her grades had been slipping with all the late-night sex. Therefore, it was with enthusiasm, not suspicion, that Tyesha looked on the team's Facebook page to see photos of one of their away games in November. And it was only because she knew every inch of his tawny brown skin, including the scar on his forearm, that she could identify the arm slung over the hips of the grinning light-skinned girl as belonging to her man. He was cropped out of the picture, but that telltale forearm scar was connected to the fingers that held an ample handful of the girl's hip. He palmed the roundness of it like a basketball. The wrist bone's connected to the arm bone.

She felt sick to her stomach. And stupid. What had her friend told her? Her friend that couldn't keep from getting pregnant had warned her never ever to let herself fall for one of these boys. Her friend hadn't even been in love with the baby daddy. But she had let herself fall for Tariq. She felt so smug thinking he only wanted her. But if he was fucking around with girls at away games, was he fucking with other girls on campus, too? Were some of them laughing behind her back? How could she have been such a fool? She didn't cry. Didn't tell anyone. Just felt a cold, hard spot in her chest, like a block of ice.

The next several days were a string of texts she didn't respond to, calls she didn't pick up, and eventually visits she ducked, joining the pre-med roommate in the science library. She finished studying for the exam that kept her from joining him at the away game and got an A.

Finally, in class on the following Tuesday, she walked in as if nothing had happened. But this time, she was dressed for a nightclub, in spite of the freezing winter weather. On the way into the room, she took off her coat, as if unveiling a priceless piece of art. Then she sat across the room and completely ignored him.

He cornered her after class was over. "What the fuck, Tyesha?" he asked in a hiss.

"I saw those photos of you with your hand on that girl's ass," she said. "Funny thing, you said you weren't coming back because you were tired."

"I asked you to come with me," he said. "It was our toughest game yet. The pressure was crazy. If you'd of come, nothing woulda happened."

Her carefully plucked eyebrows rose. "So it's my fault you couldn't keep your dick in your pants?" she said. "To hell with you, Tariq. You go fuck whoever you want, because I'm through with you."

"Forget you then!" he said, as she strutted away, winter coat over her arm, so he could watch her walk away, hips switching in the ass-hugging skirt and the badass stiletto boots.

But later that night, he appeared at her door, drunk and apologetic. He said he loved her. Something he'd never said before, only hinted at. He needed her. She was the best thing that ever happened to him.

They had sex, but the next day, she found herself calling to check on him. Dropping by practice to see if he was getting too cozy with the cheerleaders. She had him back, supposedly had his love now, but it didn't feel the same.

"I can't focus on my classes," she told her mentor. "All I can think about is what he's doing."

"I've seen it so many times," her mentor said. She was a middle-aged black woman with a salt-and-pepper Afro. "Girls get caught up in these athletes and don't focus on their own education."

"Should I break up with him?" Tyesha asked.

"I can't answer that," her mentor said. "But ask yourself this: did you come to college to try to be somebody's NBA wife? Is that your dream? Because these athletes have big careers that are very high maintenance."

Tyesha shook her head. She hadn't come for that. She wasn't ready to break up with him, but finals were coming up, and she needed to keep up her GPA. She began to duck him with the excuse that she needed to prepare for her exams. She continued to hide out with her roommate in the science library and studied her ass off.

The day after her last final, she slept for twelve hours, then woke and packed up all her stuff. Mostly just clothes, books, papers, and some linens—the dorms provided all the furniture. She shipped nearly all of it to her mother's house in Chicago, just kept an overnight bag and a couple of cute outfits.

She texted Tariq that she'd meet him at the game that night. They could celebrate the end of the semester afterward. Just as she was walking across campus to meet him, she got a text:

you here yet? I really need a kiss before the game. I swear, girl, you're my good luck charm.

As she did an about face and headed to the subway, she realized she would never be able to explain it to him. He had called her that before she'd caught him with a hand on the hip of the girl in the photo. Back then, it had been cute, endearing, intimate. But now, it was just . . . belittling. She wasn't a rabbit's foot. She wasn't a horseshoe or a leprechaun.

Her mentor's words came back to her. She hadn't come to college to be some ballplayer's girlfriend and certainly not his personal talisman. Her aunt Lu would never approve of this foolishness. But if she saw him again, with those lips, those long, hard limbs, that charisma, she knew she would succumb. The pull of the NBA wifey would lure her off her own path. She couldn't risk it. She walked to the subway and headed home to Chicago. Inside her chest, the ice melted.

On the train, she leaned against the window, as the elevated tracks took her back to South Shore. The fur-trimmed hood of her parka was pulled low over her face to hide her crying.

She never saw Tariq again—not even on TV, as he didn't make it to the NBA. She dropped out of Northwestern and applied to transfer to Columbia.

The first time Tyesha arrived in New York, it was at Port Authority, on a Greyhound bus. She had struggled to take her rolling suitcase and her oversize backpack to the subway and gotten on the wrong train. By the end of the day, she had hauled all of her possessions up and down six flights of subway stairs before she arrived at her Columbia dorm.

But she had arrived in New York with a firm sense of who she was. Tyesha Couvillier, daughter of Monique Couvillier, niece of Lucille Couvillier. No known father.

This time, she arrived from Chicago in Manhattan on a plane. But with the revelations in her life, it was as if she never quite landed. Neither the car service she took from the airport nor the familiarity of the city landscape could keep her from feeling that she was even more lost than that girl on the wrong subway train to Columbia.

She came in late and wandered past Deza and Amaru sleeping on the couch. By the time she woke up mid-morning, the apartment was empty. Still dazed, Tyesha made her way to work on the subway without even paying attention.

Everything felt strange and different, even as everything was familiar and mundane.

When she got to the clinic, Lily was waiting for her.

"Oh, my god, is everybody okay?" Lily asked. "Serena said you had a family emergency."

"They're fine," Tyesha said. "What's been going on?"

"Teddy threw that mobster's nephew outta the club," Lily said. "And now he turned up dead in the river."

"What?" Tyesha said. "When?"

"Yesterday morning," Lily said. "I can't believe you haven't heard. It's been all over the local news."

Tyesha realized she had passed dozens of newspapers on the subway with "River Murder," "Stripper Harasser," and "Mob Connections" headlines, but they hadn't even registered.

Lily spent ten more minutes explaining all about her union plans. But Tyesha couldn't take any of it in.

That afternoon, Tyesha had a visitor who wasn't on the schedule. Serena usually called on the intercom, but this time she knocked on the door.

"A pair of gentlemen to see you. The older man calls himself Zeus," she said. "Should I show them in?"

Tyesha's mouth contracted into a tight circle. "Show Zeus in. Tell his associate to wait outside. And keep an eye on him."

Zeus walked into her office and took it in. The leather and dark wood furniture, the expensive carpet, the upscale décor.

"You done good for yourself, baby girl," he said.

Tyesha wasn't sure if she liked the intimate nickname or not. "What can I do for you?" she asked.

"You heard about that murder?" he asked. "Ukrainian mob?"

"Yeah," she said.

"I hear they got some beef with you, or with your clinic," he said. "I got separate beef with them, but I wanna make sure you're protected, I mean, now that I know you're my daughter."

"That's really kind of you to offer, but—"

"I'm headed back to Chicago after I wrap up my business here," he said. "But Reagan could stay behind as a bodyguard. Just temporarily, of course. Til everything calms down."

"I don't particularly care for Reagan. I would feel safer with him at a good distance," she said.

Zeus chuckled. "I know the womenfolk don't like him," he said. "He's a little rough around the edges, but he's loyal. And he would do anything for me."

"Thanks, but no thanks," Tyesha said.

"Maybe Reagan isn't the one for the job," Zeus said. "But I have my ways. Now that we're family, your safety is my business."

Tyesha shrugged. "If you say so."

He stood. For a moment, she wondered if they were supposed to hug now. But he just nodded a good-bye and walked into the outer office.

Watching him walk out, she saw another reason she had never caught on to their resemblance. His tall, slender stature had thrown her off. He was well over six feet, while she was short like her mother. But then, so was Deza. Amaru and her brothers had gotten his height.

A moment later, she walked out to ask Serena a question, and Reagan was still lurking behind. He was staring at the door of her office, his face screwed into a grimace of hostility, almost rage.

The moment he saw her, his face transformed into a leer. "What a shame," he said. "I'd be glad to guard your body anytime."

"Serena," Tyesha said. "Please call security."

"Don't bother," he said. "I'm leaving with Zeus."

He had on his creepy smile, but she couldn't shake the

memory of that hateful look. She had seen that look once before, flying out of a client's apartment, running for her life.

He wasn't really her client. He was a guy Lily knew. They
didn't use the word "client" then. Lily would say, "I fuck him
for money when I get really broke."

Tyesha had met Lily met when they were waitresses at a
bar near Columbia. After about three months, Lily said she
could make much better tips at a club downtown. Skimpier
outfits, and strippers in some of the rooms, but everyone got
paid more. After a while at the strip club, Lily mentioned
that she sometimes had sex with guys for money—discreetly,
guys she knew. Tyesha thought it seemed kind of exciting—
something you see on TV or in a movie.

One night Lily brought her regular client and his cousin
into the club. Lily's guy was a little rough, but the cousin
seemed okay. Lily said the cousin would pay a hundred dollars
to have sex with Tyesha. Other than getting paid, it didn't
seem that different from a regular hookup.

A couple months later, Lily's mother got sick, and she had
to go back to Trinidad. When Lily's regular client came
around looking for her, Tyesha told him she was gone.

"Well, what about you?" he asked.

"I don't think so," she said.

"What?" he asked. "You'll fuck my cousin but not me?"

"I liked your cousin," she said.

"You like two hundred dollars?" he asked.

She did, but she needed more to make it worth her while,
especially with the term starting. Unlike his cousin, he was
certainly not someone she would have fucked for free.

"I like three hundred dollars," she said.

"Okay."

Tyesha would get off work in about half an hour. He sat
at the bar and drank and watched her work. She felt a little
bit like prey.

On the way to his apartment, she stopped by the drug-store for condoms and lube. First they argued about condoms in the cab.

"For three hundred, I expect to go raw," he said.

"Look," Tyesha said, "I don't know what arrangement you had with Lily, but you need to wear a condom if we're gonna do this."

Grudgingly, he assented, as they made their way up to his shabby apartment.

The moment he closed the door, he started stripping off his clothes. No conversation, no eye contact.

She went into the grimy bathroom and disrobed, putting in some lube. Nothing was going to turn her on about this. When she came out, he didn't even take any time to look at her body when she stretched out on the bed. He just thrust his way in and commenced pounding away.

"Women in the sex industry." The term floated into her mind from some of her public health reading. As she lay there, bored and uncomfortable, she realized that she had definitely crossed some kind of line.

They tried several different positions; none of them seemed to do much for him. He lost his erection a few times, and she was quick to make sure the condom didn't slip. He got his hard-on back with a lot of manual stimulation, but couldn't seem to get off. She tried moaning a bunch, like all this mindless banging was actually doing something for her, but that didn't help any.

Tyesha tuned back out. She thought about how she wanted to set up her schedule this semester, weighed the pros and cons of two different classes that met at the same time.

On their third switch from doggie style to missionary, she looked at the clock.

"Hey," she said. "We been at this over an hour. I gotta get to school."

"It's this goddamn condom," he said.

Tyesha was an urban studies major. She planned to get her master's in public health, and she knew all the stats on HIV among black women. She was not about to let a strange man fuck her without a condom.

"Look," she said, pulling back so he slid out of her, "you need to just bust a nut in the next five minutes, or you can give me my money right now."

"Fuck that," he said. "I ain't giving you no three hundred dollars if I don't get off."

Tyesha stood up and started putting on her clothes. She realized that she'd been stupid not to get the money up front. Even if he did finish, he still might not pay her.

"You need to give me my money," she insisted. "At least the original two hundred."

"Bitch, I ain't giving you shit," he said.

She grabbed her purse and walked out the door, slamming it behind her.

"You limp dick nigga," she yelled at his closed door.

She was storming down the staircase when he flew out of his apartment door in a rage.

She had looked up to see that same undiluted look of hate that Reagan had worn.

She fled down the stairs, but was slowed up having to struggle with the lock on the downstairs door.

He grabbed her arm and spun her around. His thick fist connected with the side of her face. Tyesha literally saw stars as her jaw broke. The impact knocked her through the open apartment door into a pair of people coming in. Tyesha shrank back against the woman who had unwittingly caught her.

The pair stared at the client, who wore only a white T-shirt. Tyesha turned and ran away, hoping the client's lack of clothes would keep him from pursuing her. That look of hate seemed capable of anything.

Tyesha had to quit waitressing in the strip club for the

next three months, while her jaw healed. The bruising was gone after a week, but her jaw was wired shut. It did not provide the glamorous image that the strip club wanted. She went back to working at her old job, where they didn't mind if the waitresses talked through clenched teeth, as long as they were fast with the drinks and got the order right.

Two months later, her face healed, but she wasn't interested in going back to the strip club. She was afraid the guy would come looking to hassle her.

It had comforted her immensely to know that she could avoid the client by changing jobs. Reagan, on the other hand, knew the address of her job, her home, and everyone she loved.

Tyesha blinked and watched Reagan walk away, the gray trench coat billowing a bit behind him. He looked like a cartoon villain. Father or no father, she couldn't wait til Zeus and his shadow went back to Chicago.

Chapter 20

That evening, the community room at the clinic was filled with women in skimpy summer clothes, with high heels and brightly colored hair. The union was having its first big meeting to plan strategy.

Just as Lily was about to call the meeting to order, Hibiscus strolled in.

"Look like all crab fine dey hole," Lily said, sucking her teeth.

Hibiscus shrugged.

"Whatever it was that changed your mind, we're glad you made it," said Giselle, the brown-skinned Latina.

Lily walked to the front of the room. "I'm calling this meeting to order," she said from the podium. "We just have two pieces of business. First of all the demands. Are we agreed on the following? We want a raise. We want health benefits if we work over twenty-five hours a week. We want sick days and vacation. Overtime pay for holidays. Worker's comp, unemployment, and health insurance. No fees for dancing. Bring back the second dressing room. Plus a retirement fund. All those in favor say aye."

"Aye!" came the loud chorus from the room.

"All those opposed say nay."

There wasn't a sound.

"Any abstentions?"

After a moment of quiet, one woman said, "I'm not big on abstinence."

The room filled with laughter, but then Lily called for them to quiet down.

"So those demands passed unanimously," she said. "But this next issue is more controversial. The question is whether or not we want to be a union shop or an open shop. That is to say, does everyone who works there need to be part of the union? So we'll have a discussion and then put it to a vote. Raise your hand if you have a comment or a question."

"I don't like anyone telling me what to do or what to join," said a girl with blue hair and several lip piercings. "That's why I do this type of work. I say everybody should be able to choose."

"Hear hear," said Hibiscus.

"I disagree," said Tara, the white union organizer with the lotus tattoo on her chest. "The whole point of the union is unity. We need to be representing everybody."

"I agree with the idea," a young woman in a jumpsuit and combat boots said. "But it's a huge move to just get a union. The owners aren't gonna like any of this. Can we go for our unanimous demands this year and negotiate for union shop next year?"

"But if we're not a union shop, they can hire a bunch of other dancers this year who would undermine the process for next year," said Giselle. "Just like they hired a bunch of part-timers after they fired all the activists."

"Then that's part of the work," said the girl with the blue hair. "If we get guys to put twenties in our thongs by looking irresistible, then we can also get new girls to join the union by making it irresistible. But I got guys in my family in union shops that are lazy. They don't even have to hustle for their workers' loyalty because they have a monopoly."

The arguments continued, and by the end, there was a decision by a slight majority to put union shop in the original demands, but be willing to take it out if there was push-back. The rest of the demands were non-negotiable. They vowed that if the owners wouldn't meet them, they would strike.

A few days later, things had almost returned to normal. Tyesha hadn't told Deza and Amaru about the DNA news or that she had been to Chicago. She needed time to digest it herself. Zeus, her father? Her mama moving in on Jenisse's man? Jenisse's hatefulness motivated by jealousy all these years? Deza and Amaru her nieces but also her sisters?

But several nights of pizza and bad reality TV with the girls had her feeling normal again. Things were moving forward with the dancers' union. She had even taken the number of a hot guy on the subway. Not that she was gonna call him, but it felt good to know she had options.

And then, a week after her return from Chicago, Serena said she had a visitor.

"Who is it?" Tyesha asked.

"He didn't give a name," Serena said. "But he looks like that rapper Thug Woofer. Except dressed casually."

Tyesha felt a clutch in her solar plexus.

"Okay," Tyesha said. "Send him in."

Woof walked in, and Tyesha grudgingly admitted to herself, he looked good. He had on workout clothes and they fit him nicely.

"Didn't this used to be Marisol's office?" he asked, looking around at all the mahogany and black leather décor. "I distinctly remember—"

"Woof, you shouldn't have come," Tyesha said. "I asked you not to call me. That didn't mean to just show up at my job instead."

He shook his head. "I'm not here to see you," he said. "Well, not directly. I'm here to talk about Deza. I listened to the demo and it's—she's amazing. I want to talk business with her. But there's no contact info."

Tyesha nodded. "At the time, I guess she assumed the contact would go through me."

"It's just as well," Woof said. "She's really young, so I want you to chaperone the meeting. I read about all that Car Willis stuff, and if I'm gonna have a female protégée, it needs to be completely clear to everyone in the world that I'm mentoring her and not some other crazy predator shit."

"Protégée?" Tyesha said. "Wow, that's—that's great. She's gonna be over the moon."

"I have a flight out at midnight," he said. "Is there any way we can meet this evening?"

"I think it's fair to say that Deza would never forgive me if I said no," she said. "Why don't you come by my apartment?"

"Okay," he said. "See you tonight."

Tyesha called Deza, and after ten minutes of shrieking, she calmed down enough for Tyesha to get a word in.

"So we'll be meeting with him at the house," Tyesha said. "I just need to text Woof that I'm running a little late."

"Oh my god oh my god oh my god!" Deza squealed.

"Uh-oh," Tyesha said. "I can't text Woof. I deleted his number from my phone. Maybe Marisol still has his number."

"Why would your old boss have his number?" Deza asked.

"Long story," Tyesha said. "Lemme jump off and call her."

"No need," Deza said. "I have his number."

"What?" Tyesha said. "How'd you get Woof's number?"

"I stole it from your phone," Deza said. "Duh."

"Are you fucking kidding me?" Tyesha said. "That's a violation of my privacy."

"I thought I might need it someday," Deza said. "And now here we are. You're welcome."

Tyesha laughed. "Shut up."

"Oh, Auntie Ty," Deza said, "I can't believe you did this for me."

"Now that you're nineteen, you can just start calling me Tyesha."

"Aww," Deza said. "But I'll always think of you as my auntie."

"Of course," Tyesha said. "But we're gonna be peers soon—agewise, I mean. Anyway, I'm gonna text him now."

That evening, Tyesha sat with Woof and Deza in her tiny kitchen. The orchid sat in the middle of the table, which was covered with music industry paperwork.

"So I was thinking we could start the tour off in Chicago," Woof was saying. "Young talent is at their best with the home court advantage. It'll be a big reunion for your fans. They'll have missed you since you've been in New York. And for this first tour, you'll need a family member as a chaperone."

Deza turned to Tyesha. "Auntie?"

"Sorry, baby, I already have a job," Tyesha said. "But you know who might be available? Your mama."

"Are you kidding me?" Deza said. "In what universe?"

"I'm just saying." Tyesha put a hand under Deza's chin. "She's gonna be your mama your whole life. I think she's learned some lessons now that you and Amaru stood up to her. Not to mention that you'd be the one in the power position for the first time. Promise me you'll think about it?"

"A chaperone isn't optional," Woof added.

"Fine," Deza said. "What's the next step?"

"We need to meet with some executives at Paperclip," Woof said. "Again, you should have someone there to represent you. An attorney or a family member. Tyesha, I know you're busy, but I'm glad to work with your schedule. How's Friday?"

"Friday's fine," Tyesha said. "I want to check with Eva Feldman, as well. She's an attorney."

"Great," said Woof. "I'll be back in town by then and can join in."

The next day, Tyesha and Marisol met with Teddy and Etta Hughes in advance of their meeting with the union. This time the couple came to the clinic, and the four of them met in Tyesha's office.

"So we just want to give you a heads-up on the demands," Tyesha said.

The husband and wife were seated on the couch, and Tyesha had offered them all drinks to celebrate. Marisol poured herself and Tyesha glasses of rum as Tyesha made a vodka with cranberry juice for Etta and a scotch for Teddy.

The four of them raised glasses and drank.

"Just to clarify," Tyesha said, "the union wants a raise, vacation and sick leave, health insurance for full-time workers, and a 401(k) account."

"Actually," Teddy said, licking a little scotch off his lips, "I changed my mind. I don't really want a union in my club."

"What are you talking about?" Tyesha said. "We gave you the gun last week."

"What gun?" he said. "I don't have any gun."

Marisol turned to Etta. "I thought you said we could trust him. That you would make sure he kept his word."

"Teddy, what are you doing?" Etta asked. "When you threw that gun in the river, you said you'd keep your promise."

"I finally got my club back from the mob," he said. "I'm not about to turn it over to a bunch of chicks. I didn't get into this business to be pussy-whipped. Not by you and not by my employees."

Tyesha smiled. "So that's your plan, Teddy? Backstab the women who rescued your ass?"

He shrugged. "It's not backstabbing. It's just business."

"What a shame for you," Tyesha said. "It's really too bad that I never trusted your ass, and I gave you a duplicate gun. And the original gun is in a bank security vault somewhere in Manhattan. Feel free to look for it."

"You're bluffing," he said.

"Am I?" Tyesha asked. She pulled a glossy photograph out of her briefcase of a safety deposit box with a gun in a Ziploc bag inside.

"And you know what else?" Marisol said. "If we were to turn in the gun to the cops, I can't imagine what Uncle Viktor would do if he figured out you manipulated him into killing Ivan, his own flesh and blood."

Tyesha shrugged. "So while we were prepared to let you negotiate with our union, now we're just gonna own you outright. So I think you'll be agreeing to those demands. Plus, for the 401(k), we'd like you to contribute matching funds from your profits, as well."

"I fucking told you to play it straight with these girls," Etta said. "But no. You can't fucking listen. You're just always trying to take advantage. You keep trying to fuck people over, and you just keep fucking up."

That night, Tyesha brought home a bottle of champagne.

"Do I get some, too?" Amaru asked.

"Just enough to toast," Tyesha said. "We're celebrating Deza's big break in hip-hop and the union victory on my job."

The three of them toasted and then ate dinner.

"I gotta go out to my friend's game," Amaru said and headed out.

As Tyesha and Deza cleared the table, Deza asked, "So Woof broke his contract with Car Willis, and he's obviously still into you. Why is it you're not fucking with him?"

"He's a rap star," Tyesha said. "He's not relationship material."

"Why not?" Deza asked. "Because he's on stage? Because he's famous. It's just as easy to get cheated on by some trifling nigga down the block as a superstar."

"Yeah, but with the trifling nigga, you don't have your whole life on blast."

"You know who you sound like?" Deza asked. "My ex."

"What?"

"You're just like him," Deza said. "Attracted to the performer, but then resentful of the spotlight. That's how DJs are. They want to be the invisible hand that controls everything. Move the crowd from a little booth with a bunch of toys. Head down, barely even acknowledging that they're outside they mama's basement. Passive aggressive motherfuckers."

"Excuse me?"

"I mean we emcees have issues, but at least we're up front about it," Deza said. "We want attention. We ask for it. We earn it. We get it. DJs want attention but they also don't want attention. He picked me because he thought he could control me. That I would be the cute girl who made his set hot. But I started to fill up that limelight. Then he had to find another little cute girl. Fuck him. I'm through with DJs. Never again."

"What the hell are you trying to say about me?" Tyesha asked.

"Can I speak my mind?" Deza asked. "Now that we're heading for being peers or whatever?"

"Please do."

"No. For real," Deza said. "You ain't gonna kick me out if I say something you don't like, right?"

"No. I might be pissed for a minute, but we're family."

Deza took a deep breath. "When you were in high school, and me and Amaru were living with you and Grandma in Chicago, you used to rhyme just as hard as me. But when it was time to get up in front of people, you always pushed me forward. Just like nowadays. The other night, I was rapping into a wooden spoon, and you straight grabbed it from me and started some crazy rhyme about strippers needing health insurance. And I never would have tried to rhyme 'insurance' with 'prurience,' particularly because I never even heard of that shit before, but that's what I mean. You feel that passion for the spotlight, and you're attracted to that passion for the spotlight, but then you turn around and hold it against Thug Woofer. Why don't you ever get up and do your own thing in front of people, instead of trying to be the chaperone for my career?"

"Deza," Tyesha said, "everybody in the world can't be an emcee. Somebody's gotta clean the studio and run the health clinics of the world."

"See, Mama's the same way," Deza said. "I don't want her on the tour with me, because she'll be trying to live out some part of her own dreams through me."

"You're comparing me to Jenisse?"

"I'm saying there's a way you both be trying to live your lives through your men," Deza said. "She wants the money. You want the power. There, I said it."

"You're wrong," Tyesha said. "You're totally wrong about me."

"Fine," Deza said. "Then prove it."

"How?"

"At the hip-hop open mic."

"What?"

"And you're getting on the mic."

"No way."

"Yes," Deza said. "You remember that rap from when I used to stay with you in your college dorm. Your friend used to beatbox."

"What?" Tyesha said. "Absolutely not."

"You rapped that damn song into hairbrushes, broom handles, kitchen spoons, and flashlights," Deza said. "Now you can rap into a fucking microphone. You do this, and I'll perform at your clinic's benefit after I get famous."

"You're gonna do that anyway," Tyesha said.

"I'll make some of my famous friends come along," Deza said. "And hopefully you'll be back with Thug Woofer, and he can spit something, too."

Two hours later, they were standing on stage at a small Brooklyn club. It was located in the basement of a sneaker store and packed wall to wall.

The host doubled as the DJ. He was a young Puerto Rican man in a dashiki and a giant set of earphones pressing down his afro. As he faded down a Latin house remix he introduced them. "Give it up for Deza Starling and Tyesha Couvillier!"

"Wassup, New York?" Deza asked.

Several folks whistled. She was starting to develop some fans in the city.

"I been here a bunch, but this is my girl Tyesha," she said. "She's a little nervous so show her some love."

The audience applauded and cheered.

"I'll show you some love, sexy girl," a guy in the front said.

"So this is a rhyme we wrote a while back, and we're performing it together in public for the first time."

The DJ put the beat on and Deza began:

> *"Black girl Black girl, so much to say*
> *So many obstacles get in the way*
> *But we ain't scared of this big, bad world*
> *We gonna be there for you, badass Black girl."*

Tyesha sort of murmured along in the background. The spotlight was blinding. Deza had warned her about that and suggested she use it to block all the people out. Just pretend they were alone in the apartment.

Deza did her verse, and Tyesha could feel her heart beating faster and faster as it got closer to her turn.

When it was time, she missed her cue, so Deza came in and did the chorus again.

"Black girl Black girl, so much to say—come on, Tyesha."

Tyesha closed her eyes and chanted along with Deza.

Then after the chorus finished, she just kept going, from memory, eyes still closed:

> *"My name is Tyesha but you can call me T*
> *So much of this world that I want to see*
> *They tell me that I'm sexy, they tell me that I'm*
> *   fine*
> *But I want to be respected for the power of*
> *   my mind . . ."*

As she rapped, she blocked out the audience and recalled the girl she'd been, about Deza's age, when they'd written the piece. She was away from home for the first time in college. She hadn't taken any of the boys seriously because she was afraid that falling for some guy would throw her off her game. That she would get distracted and not do her best in school. It was her only shot to get out of the hood, and she couldn't fuck it up. But now she was in New York, and she had the good job. Wasn't her position secure enough that she could take a chance with Woof?

She closed her eyes and nodded her head and the lyrics fell from her mouth, automatically. This had been her subconscious anthem for all these years. Before she knew it, she had looped back to the chorus, and Deza was singing along with her.

Tyesha opened her eyes and saw Deza alternately crouching to reach out to the audience and striding across the front of the stage. She began motioning for the crowd to chant along with them. Finally Deza stuck the mic back on the stand and swung both hands up in wide arcs, clapping above her head and pressing the crowd to yell the final lines. Deza turned to the DJ and drew her finger across her throat, cueing him to cut the music. For the final line, the crowd's voices rang clear throughout the crowded club:

"We gonna be there for you, badass Black girl!"

"Yes!" Deza said snatching the mic back up. "Give it up for my girrrrllll Tyesha!"

The audience roared and Tyesha just stood there for a moment, grinning and blinking back tears.

Chapter 21

On the subway ride home, Tyesha recalled one of her first conversations with Woof. She had asked him, "How do you get up in front of all those people? I swear that would scare the shit out of me."

He had shrugged. "Er'body scared by different things," he said. "Me, I freeze up during tests. That's why I didn't graduate high school. My mind goes blank. I can't say I'm scared, but I don't know what you call that."

Tyesha had always been good at tests. Always good at putting her thoughts down in writing.

Maybe that was also part of her stage fright. She had been letting Marisol write the words. Tyesha needed to speak her own words. She pulled out her notebook and began scribbling furiously.

"You writing rhymes?" Deza asked.

"No," Tyesha said. "I'm writing my speech for a press conference day after tomorrow."

The train pulled up at their stop, and Tyesha and Deza walked above ground. The evening was warm and the foot traffic was light.

"Auntie," Deza said quietly. "Why'd you move to New York?"

Tyesha sighed. "Too much family drama," she said. "I thought I might never finish college."

She opened the door to the apartment, and the two of them walked in to find Amaru already asleep on the couch. Tyesha motioned for Deza to come into her room to talk.

Deza sat down on the bed and took a deep breath. "You didn't need to get two degrees and move to New York to run a health clinic. Auntie Lucille's clinic in Chicago been waiting for you since the day she died. It was supposed to be you there running it. Not some old white lady from Hyde Park who got cultural competency."

"I couldn't—" Tyesha began. She started to straighten one of the pillows that was slumped down. "We hadn't even buried her yet, and already people were standing out in front of the funeral at Gatling's talking about how I was gonna take over the center. I was only fifteen. Besides, it was Auntie Lu's dream, not mine. All those boys. Like I was supposed to be able to be their leader? They were all trying to fuck me. She was the caring mother figure they never had. Not me."

"Mama said you saw her get shot," Deza said.

Tyesha nodded and could feel her eyes filling.

"But I still don't understand why you had to leave," Deza said. "You didn't have to take over the damn center if you didn't want. Buy why'd you have to leave?"

How could Tyesha explain it? She had given up her full-ride scholarship at Northwestern because her grades were slipping by virtue of being too close to home. Deza coming to stay when she "ran away"; last-minute requests from Jenisse to babysit Amaru; late-night calls from her nephews—who were nearly her age—to help them out of scrapes when they had gotten on Jenisse and Zeus's bad sides.

Even moving to New York wasn't enough. At the end of her junior year in college, she lent the younger nephew her tuition money for bail. He promised to have it back to her within the month, but skipped out on his court appearance, and she lost everything. She was forced to drop out of school for a semester. And when she lost her Columbia housing, she learned firsthand how expensive New York really was. It ended up taking her nearly five years of hustling in the city to save up enough to go back and finish her degree.

"Our family is fucked up," Tyesha said. "Your mama. My mama. Your brothers. I couldn't—I just had to get out of Chicago."

"Stop talking about leaving Chicago," Deza said. "You didn't leave Chicago, you left *us*. One day you were there and the next day, you called to say you were moving." Deza began to cry.

Tyesha wanted to protest, but she had learned at the clinic to just let people cry. And to comfort them. She sat down next to Deza and put an arm around her, but Deza pushed it away roughly.

"You fucking left us," Deza spat, furious. "You knew Mama was crazy and Grandma was no help and Zeus was useless and his 'like-a-son-to-me' bodyguard was around all the time, and Auntie Lucille was dead and you *left* us. How could you leave us? You were the only one. The only one left we could trust." She threw herself down on the bed and began to sob in earnest.

Tyesha didn't know what to do. She just sat there for a moment. Did Deza want privacy? Had the crying woken up Amaru? She crept toward the door.

"What?" Deza said. "You bout to leave again?"

"No," Tyesha said, and sat down on the bed. "I'm sorry I left. I—I'm sorry I didn't think about how it would affect you. I'm sorry it was so rough."

Deza curled into Tyesha's lap and sobbed hard. Tyesha kept expecting Amaru to come knocking on the door, but apparently she slept through all of it: the howling sobs, the hiccupping as Deza caught her breath.

When Tyesha went to get some tissue for Deza to wipe her face, she heard Amaru's heavy, even breathing from the couch.

"I was nineteen when I left," Tyesha said. "Your age."

Deza turned sharply. "No, you weren't," she said.

Tyesha nodded. "I had just voted for the first time, but I couldn't drink legally."

"You were really just nineteen?" Deza asked, incredulous.

Tyesha nodded. "Do the math."

For a moment, she could see her niece actually doing the arithmetic in her head.

"Somehow I thought you were older," Deza said, and blew her nose. "I guess that's what you mean about us becoming more like peers. Our ages are almost like sisters, even more so than auntie and niece. I mean, there's less difference between our ages than between you and Mama."

"Yep," Tyesha said, stroking Deza's hair. "Almost like sisters."

Two days later, Tyesha stood at the podium in the multipurpose room for another press conference. Marisol, Lily, Kim, Jody, and Eva and the other union reps stood behind her.

The press was assembled in their seats, including Drew. She avoided his eyes. He'd called and left a message congratulating her on the article, but no talk of them going out again. He acted like she was just any other journalism subject. Didn't even ask her to call back.

Tyesha could feel her whole body shaking, but she planted her feet, gripped the edges of the podium and began.

"My name is Tyesha Couvillier, and I'm the executive director of the Maria de la Vega clinic here. I want to honor my predecessor, Marisol Rivera, who grew up in this very neighborhood and founded this clinic along with Eva Feldman."

Her throat began to feel tight, so she cleared it and went on. "Our mission is to provide services to sex workers. Mostly that means sexual and emotional health and life skills and career planning. But I wanted to make sure the clinic was the headquarters for this union fight, because this fight is personal to me. Not because I was a stripper, but because I'm an African American woman."

She looked out past the crowd and pictured her aunt Lucille. "See, I'm not from New York. I'm from Chicago. My grandparents were from Mississippi, and their ancestors were brought from Africa in slavery. They picked cotton on a large plantation. And one day, slavery was over, and they were free. Or were they? They didn't own land, have any tools, couldn't read or write—because it had been illegal to teach literacy to any enslaved African people. Plus, if they tried to build businesses, they were lynched. So my family did what so many black folks did, they became sharecroppers. All they had were their bodies and the work they could produce."

She opened up her briefcase, the lovely leather one Marisol had given her, and pulled out a branch with three bolls of cotton. She set it on the podium and continued. "And the way the Southern sharecropping system worked, my ancestors rented the land and the tools and the landowners set the prices for everything. And they loaned them everything they needed to live—for a price, a price that the landowners set. They set the price of the tools and the seeds, and the little bit of food and letting them live on the land. And at the end of every year, most black families were further in debt to the landowners than the year before. And the only way out was to run away to a big city in the North, which is what my grandparents did. They snuck out in the middle of the night, and they came to Chicago."

Tyesha reached into her briefcase and pulled out a silver thong and set it on the other side of the podium. "Now if you're a woman working at a strip club in New York, there is no city to run away to. Did you know that most strip clubs charge the dancers a fee to dance? When the owners own the stage and the lights and the pole and the seats and the bar and they jack up the fees so high, and all you got is your body and the work it can produce. And sex work is work, so sometimes dancers end up doing oral sex or vaginal sex or anal sex . . . I hope I'm not offending anyone, but I'm just reporting the facts. We believe in decriminalization of selling sex between consenting adults, but coercion of any kind, be it trafficking, threats of violence, or predatory working conditions in strip clubs are coercion and they undermine consent.

"To be honest about it, poverty undermines consent. But these clubs are profitable, so there's no reason that working dancers should be broke. We've looked over the finances at the One-Eyed King, and there's plenty of money for the dancers and the other workers and the managers and the owners, and even the investors. But profit is not enough for the owners, they want sky-high profits, and that can only come at the expense of the dancers, by having them working below living wages or coercing them into full-service sex work if that's not what they want to do. And we say no. We demand labor conditions that will allow dancers to make a living dancing, in clean and reasonable conditions, with sick leave and vacation. The managers and owners have shown— over and over again—that they are unwilling to provide those conditions, so our workers formed a union. We are only demanding a right to democracy. Journalists and cartoonists want to laugh at us and parody us, and individuals want to send memes around on the Internet? We don't care about that. We care about thugs threatening us. We care about cops stopping us and threatening to arrest us for 'soliciting for the purposes of prostitution,' stopping any brown woman in certain neighborhoods of New York who 'fits the profile.' If you wear tight clothes in Manhattan, you're sexy. If you wear tight clothes in these over-policed brown neighborhoods, you might end up in court with a case for prostitution. This is our whole agenda: that women *not* be coerced into selling sex if they don't want to.

"So for all these reasons, and more, our union met with the owners of the One-Eyed King, and I'm glad to announce that they agreed to all of our demands, including a 401(k) program."

"That's right!" Lily yelled from the front row, and the audience erupted in laughter.

When the ruckus died down, Tyesha went on. "As a black woman, I'm still waiting for my forty acres and a mule," she said. "But I'm glad to know that the exotic dancers of this city have a union shop where they can work, and know that they have this clinic behind them a hundred percent."

She picked up the twig of cotton and the thong and slid them into the briefcase. On the inside flap, she had put a picture of her aunt Lucille. Tyesha touched the smooth photo paper for a moment before she lifted her face to the audience.

"So on behalf of all the union members and all my African American ancestors, I thank you for coming, and for caring about justice for all."

As she looked up from the podium, the applause was thunderous. The dancers in the back whistled and some blew noisemakers.

Marisol leaned forward and whispered in her ear.

"*Nena,* you were fucking fabulous," she said. "I knew you were the one to take over the clinic. You do us proud."

Tyesha smiled and turned to the audience. "Any questions?"

That evening, Tyesha was headed out of the clinic when a homeless black woman asked her for some spare change.

"Yeah, sis," she said, and dug in her briefcase. She gave the woman five dollars and walked farther up the street.

Just as she was about to turn the corner, a thickset white guy grabbed her and attempted to pull her into a van.

Tyesha screamed and began to struggle against his grip. He had her arms pinned to her sides, but she clawed and kicked at him.

A nearby woman shrieked "Oh my God!" and a man in a suit pulled out his phone to call 911.

Tyesha's shoe fell off, and she craned her neck to bite the man's arm.

But before she could sink her teeth in, the homeless woman came around the corner and began shooting. The van screeched away. The man let Tyesha go and took off running.

Bystanders dove out of the way. Tyesha dropped her brief-case and ducked behind a bus shelter, as the woman shot at the thug. He hadn't gotten far down the block before she hit him in the left leg. He went down, and she ran up to him.

"This is a message to your boss from Zeus," she said, and reloaded the gun. With each of the next five words, she put another bullet in his leg: "Don't. Fuck. With. My. Family." With each shot, the man screamed in pain. Onlookers shrieked and ducked for cover.

Tyesha's own legs were so weak, she sank to the ground.

A town car pulled up and the woman half lifted Tyesha into it. She retrieved the shoe and briefcase, then gave the driver Tyesha's address.

"Watch yourself, girl," she said, and handed Tyesha her five dollars back.

Chapter 22

By the time the town car dropped Tyesha off, she had gone from shaking violently to a persistent low-grade tremor.

The driver turned to her over the back of the front seat. "I have orders from Zeus to stay outside your house," he said. "Call this number if you need a ride or there's any trouble, okay?"

Tyesha couldn't speak. She just nodded, took the card, and gathered her purse.

She stepped out of the car to see Thug Woofer waiting at her front door.

"I'm sorry to just drop by," he said. "I have Deza's contract for her to look over. I tried calling but your phone was off all day."

As Tyesha stepped into the apartment's exterior light, he could finally see her face.

"Tyesha, are you okay?"

She shook her head as she lifted the keys to the lock. Her hand was shaking so hard, she could barely open the door.

"Let me get that for you," he said, and unlocked the door.

"Somebody tried to—" she began, but then she started to cry. "He tried to grab me. But then this woman shot him and I got away."

"What?" Woof asked.

They stepped into the living room, and she collapsed onto the couch.

"It's this—I've made some enemies at work," she said. "The Ukrainian mob. One of their guys. They tried to kidnap me."

"And somebody shot the guy?" Woof asked, sitting beside her on the couch.

"It was—I guess"—she couldn't quite find the words—"I think I told you there's a big drug dealer from Chicago in my family. I guess one of his people shot the guy to protect me. I don't know. My whole fucking life is turned upside down."

"Tyesha," he said, "I know we're not together anymore, but I really care about you. What can I do? Are you safe here? Do you want to come over to my place?"

"Just stay with me til the girls get home," she said.

"I can do that," he said.

She lay on his lap and cried until her body stopped shaking and she fell asleep.

When she woke up, it was pitch black outside. She was under a blanket with her head in Woof's lap, and he was reading a paperback novel.

"What time is it?" she asked, sitting up.

"A little after midnight," he said.

"Where are the girls?" Tyesha asked, suddenly panicked.

"In your bed," Woof said. "We didn't want to wake you."

"You didn't have to stay," she said.

"You looked like you needed the sleep," he said.

"You been right here this whole time?" she asked.

"Yes, and I really need to pay the water bill," he said, dashing for the bathroom.

"I can't thank you enough," she said when he came back, but he waved it away.

"By the way, you were right," she said. "About Drew—the reporter."

"I'm sorry," he said. "I mean, guys like him—bourgie types—they don't know what it is to struggle. To have to use everything you got. They get things handed to them. You scrap for everything you have. I admire you for being ambitious and doing what you had to do. I know it seemed like I judged you for your past, but I was just threatened. You're an independent woman, and a guy like me is used to always having the upper hand. Always getting his way. And I had feelings for you, so I tried to take you down a notch by taking a jab at what I thought was your weak spot. But it's actually where you're strong. I mean, I been following you in the news, 'sex worker advocate Tyesha Couvillier.' You been fighting for justice for your folks."

"Thank you," she said. "I didn't know you were keeping up with me like that."

"I been following you on Twitter," he said. "With my secret identity account."

She laughed. "What's your secret identity?"

"If I told you it wouldn't be a secret," he said. "So, on a different subject, now that I'm about to be mentoring Deza, we're gonna cross paths. I know I'm lucky to get as many chances with you as I already got. But if there's any way you can forgive me—"

"Woof—"

"Let me just finish," he said. "You walked away from me the morning after I met you because I was an ass. Then you walked away again because I was a dick. And with the Car Willis thing, you walked away because I was just—totally insensitive. And guess what. I'm not gonna promise you that I'm perfect now. Because I'm not, and I'm gonna fuck up sometimes. But with you I keep getting better. And I keep striving to be better. And I just want to get serious with you, Tyesha."

"Serious like what?" she asked.

"Like exclusive girlfriend and monogamy and all that," he said.

Tyesha took a deep breath. "In your first album, you vowed never to get married. Is that still how you feel?"

"You want me to propose?" he asked. "Cuz I dunno if I'm ready for—"

"No," she said. "I'm not ready, either. I just want to know that something as serious as marriage is on the table. I eventually want a husband and a family. I don't just want to be your self-improvement plan, where I help you become a better person, then we both move on. We gotta be building something. Do you wanna build something with me?"

"Oh, hell yeah, Tyesha," he said. "Just draw me the blueprints."

This time when they made love, it was different. There was no sign of Woof the showman. He just kept his eyes on hers, as they each took off their clothes.

Before he touched any particular part of her body, he just pulled her close, pressing their skin together from neck to ankle.

The kisses started with a tenderness that reminded her a bit of their first kiss. Nothing to prove. Nothing to accomplish. No rush. No pressure.

They lay there and kissed for nearly half an hour. His hands in her hair, fingers tracing soft lines down her back.

And then, at some point, things heated up. His hands were on her ass, her breasts, sliding down between her legs.

He rolled on the condom, but didn't enter her yet. He kissed her pubic mound, then slid down further, using his tongue.

She moaned and then caught herself.

Woof put a finger to his lips. "Shhhh!" he said. "We don't want to wake the children."

Tyesha blinked. Like a flash forward. This might actually be them someday, making love in a stolen moment, with kids to keep from waking.

She pulled him into her, almost regretting the condom. She wanted so much with this man. But there would be time for that later. Now, there was only pleasure and feeling him inside her and against her and kissing her and whimpering into his mouth, trying to muffle the noise of her orgasm from the girls in the next room.

"Do you think they heard anything?" she asked.

"No, I thought we were pretty quiet," Woof said.

In the morning, she asked how the girls had slept.

"Great," they said.

But later, after Amaru and Woof had both left, Tyesha smiled to herself as she caught Deza stripping the sheets off the couch to wash them.

That night, after work, Zeus's driver dropped Tyesha off at the house.

"No need for you to stay," she told him. She expected Thug Woofer to come over for dinner with her and the girls. He would either stay the night or take her to his place.

She was setting up the kitchen for the four of them. She pulled the small table out from the wall and was taking a frozen pizza out of the oven when she heard a knock at the door. She was expecting Woof, but through the peephole she saw Reagan, Zeus's bodyguard.

"What do you want?" she asked.

"I got a message from Zeus," he said. He had on the gray trench coat and wore a dark cap.

"What is it?"

"I don't know," he said. "He wouldn't let me read it." He held a thick envelope up to the peephole. "Can I come in?"

"Slip it under the door," she said.

He leaned down, and she heard the scrape of paper against wood. "It won't fit," he said.

She wished she had gotten that chain. "Okay, fine," she said and opened the door a crack.

He reached the envelope in. It was plain white paper with her name on it. As she reached for it, he grabbed her wrist and swung the door open.

For a second, time slowed down. There he was, with that hateful look on his face.

With a jolt of adrenaline, she kicked him and tore her arm free, running toward the back of the apartment, hoping to lock herself in the bathroom or bedroom. But he was too fast: he cut her off, cornering her in the kitchen behind the small kitchen table.

"You uppity little bitch," he said. "Think you too good for a nigga like me. I'ma fuck you then wring yo princess neck."

"Zeus will kill you if you lay a single finger on me," she said, unsure if it was true but trying to bluff.

"Are you kidding me?" he said. "Zeus will think it's the Ukrainian mob and start a war with those white boys. He'll probably get his ass killed and then I can take over the business. Being 'like a son to him' and everything."

"Reagan," she said. "You're right, we're like family. So don't do this. My boyfriend is coming over any minute. Just back off and we'll act like this never happened."

"Boyfriend, huh?" he said. "Then you probably wore some lingerie for him. I guess I'll have to work fast."

Their eyes locked. He had her trapped behind the table, but if he didn't move quickly enough, she could get away. She stood, coiling internally to spring left or right, depending on which way he lunged. As she stood there, she noticed a warm feeling next to her left hip. It took a second to realize that Deza had left the flatiron on. Again.

She glanced down for a split second to see which end was hot. The handles were facing her. She kept her eyes locked on him and her ears open for any sound of Woof.

Outside, she heard horns, a siren, a truck rolling by, but no sound of footsteps approaching her door.

Slowly, she reached for the flatiron. Finally, she had it in her hand.

"Reagan," she said, all the pleading out of her voice, "seriously. Don't do this."

"Quit stalling, bitch," he said, and tossed the entire table to the side.

She kept her hand gripped tightly on the handle of the iron, and when he came at her, she pressed it to his face. He screamed and jumped back, covering his burned cheek with his hands.

"You gotdamn bitch," he screamed and ran toward her, half-blind.

With the flatiron in one hand, she looked around wildly for another weapon. Off the stove, she grabbed the cast-iron skillet and swung it at him, connecting with the side of his head.

He went down in a heap, and she backed into the living room. The skillet and the flatiron lay on the kitchen floor near him, as well as the overturned table, and the orchid, which lay upside down and crushed, the blood from his temple oozing toward the spilled dirt.

Tyesha turned from the sight in the kitchen when she heard a noise. When the half-open front door swung wide, she expected Thug Woofer, but it was Zeus standing there. He nearly filled up the doorway.

"Baby girl?" he said. "Is everything all right? Did another one of those mobsters try to fuck with you?"

"It was Reagan," Tyesha said.

"That's crazy," Zeus said. "Reagan left for Chicago this morning. I was on my way to the airport, but I just came to say good-bye."

"He's knocked out on the floor of my kitchen," Tyesha said.

In three long-legged strides, Zeus had crossed the living room and saw his right-hand man, his face burned, and the side of his head bloodied.

"What the fuck?" Zeus stepped back out of the kitchen.

"He said he was gonna fuck me and wring my princess neck," Tyesha said, her voice flat with shock. She slumped down onto the couch.

Zeus pulled out his cell phone and made a call.

"I'm over there now," he said. "Get me on a later plane and come by here. Bring supplies. I have a mess to clean up. Okay, I'll see you in fifteen."

As they waited, Tyesha and Zeus sat across from each other in silence.

Tyesha felt rattled beyond words.

"He was like a son to me," Zeus said.

"No Zeus," Tyesha said, her body shaking with both residual terror and swelling rage. "No, he wasn't. He wanted to kill me so you would go to war with the Ukrainians, then get yourself killed and he could take over."

"But I been knowing him since he was a boy," Zeus said.

"You don't need any more sons," Tyesha said. "You have two kids. Two daughters." The word caught in her throat as she added in a whisper, "Three."

She began to cry. Not sobbing, not making a sound. The tears just flowed from both eyes, down her face. They pooled under her chin and dripped down her neck into the collar of her T-shirt.

"I don't understand daughters," Zeus said quietly, all his gangster affect dissolved. And in that moment, she looked more like him than she had ever looked like anyone. It was his unguarded face that looked almost identical to hers. A face he rarely showed. "I told Jenisse I didn't understand daughters," he said. "I was in a group home, then the military. That's what I understand." He banged his hand on the couch. "I understand lieutenants and soldiers and generals and loyalty. I understand sons."

Tyesha was still shaking, but the rage made her bold. "It's not like it's gone so well with your two actual sons."

"Of course it has," Zeus said. "They'll be out in a few years. Meantime, they're safe. I take care of them. I put money on their concessions. No one fucks with them. I even got them married with conjugal visits."

"That's your plan?" Tyesha said. "Either they're on the streets selling with you or they're in jail?"

"That's the business I run," Zeus said. "That's what I got to offer. Other boys was begging to get in with me."

"Like Reagan?" Tyesha said.

Zeus shook his head. "I don't know what to do with daughters," he said. "Only with sons. I know how to reward loyalty and punish traitors."

"What about Jenisse?" Tyesha asked. "How you gonna reward her loyalty?"

"I don't know," Zeus said. "I give her everything she wants. She don't wanna get married."

"Like hell she don't," Tyesha said.

"She told me she didn't," Zeus said.

"What?" Tyesha said. "Fifteen years ago? Try asking again."

"You think she'd say yes?"

There was a knock at the door. Zeus put a hand up and stood to answer it.

"Who's there?" he asked.

"It's Woof," a man's voice said. "Who the fuck are you?"

"It's okay," Tyesha said, and went to open the door.

Woof walked in with an expression that was equal parts quizzical and pissed.

"What's going on, Tyesha?"

"Woof," she said. "Meet Zeus, my father."

"Oh," Woof said, putting out a hand. "Melvyn Johnson. Pleased to meet you, sir."

They shook hands.

"He's also Deza and Amaru's father," Tyesha explained. "They don't know. I didn't know til last week."

"Right," Woof said. "I won't mention it."

There was another knock at the door.

"Who is it?" Tyesha called.

"Zeus here?" a woman's voice asked.

Zeus rose to open the door.

Tyesha saw the same woman who had shot the Ukrainian thug in the leg. She walked in quickly, followed by the driver who'd picked her up. He had an oversize suitcase.

"What's going on?" Woof asked, as Zeus and his two employees walked into the kitchen.

"You don't want to know," Tyesha said. "Come on outside. I need some air."

Five minutes later, the two employees came out and carried the suitcase out to the street.

As they loaded it into a dark sedan, Zeus came out of the apartment.

"I'm sorry," Zeus said. "I wish I could stay longer."

She leaned toward him awkwardly, and they hugged.

Really, he reached around and patted her back, as she hung onto his neck.

As they pulled apart from the mismatched embrace, they heard a shout.

"Daddy!" Deza yelled from down the street. She and Amaru ran toward them.

In the moment before they arrived, Woof turned to Zeus. "Sir, I want you to know that my intentions toward your daughter are very serious."

"Thank you for letting me know, son," Zeus said, and then he had the two young women hugging him.

"You came to say good-bye to us?" Amaru asked.

"And to give you the good news," Zeus said. "Your mama convinced me to send you to that athletic school."

"Are you serious?" Amaru asked. "Are you serious right now?"

"Yes," he said. "And to congratulate your sister on her record contract."

The double-parked sedan honked. "I got business to take care of," Zeus said. "I'll see my girls soon."

He hugged the two young women, and then he was gone.

The girls bounded into the house, elated. "Do I smell pizza?" Amaru asked. "Is it almost ready?"

"Any minute now," Tyesha said. "But let's eat in the living room, okay?"

Later that night, Tyesha and Woof went over to his house. The moment they were inside, he asked, "Is everything okay? What the hell was that?"

"That was—" Tyesha searched for the words. "That was my family."

"Do you want to tell me what's going on?" he asked.

Tyesha looked him in the face. "No," she said. "I just

want you to hold me. Just let me have a moment where I can relax and there's nothing I need to do."

"I can do that," he said.

He unzipped her jacket. He took off her shirt, her bra, and her jeans. He left on her underwear and undressed himself. Then he laid her on the bed and slid behind her, curling his body around her like a shield.

Chapter 23

The next day, Teddy Hughes formally signed the contract between the strippers union and the One-Eyed King. Tyesha used their leverage to get Teddy to close down the Brooklyn club for a private party. All the dancers plus all the clinic's employees and their guests came to celebrate.

To kick off the entertainment, Deza performed one of her songs and promised she'd be back on stage later with some of her rapper friends. But meanwhile, one of the dancers also worked as a DJ, and she was spinning deep house music and Afrobeat.

For party favors, Tyesha had shredded all the sign-in sheets into confetti. She also had stacks of Monopoly money all over the club.

Tara and Giselle had tied ribbons to the center pole and several of the girls were skipping around it like a maypole, tossing the confetti. Kim and Jody were dancing together on one of the stages, barefoot and in their underwear. Kim was putting Monopoly singles in Jody's boy shorts, as Jody made it rain rainbow-colored cash over Kim's head. Both of them were laughing hysterically.

On one of the tables was a giant red velvet cake that said "VICTORY!" with a sexy lady justice holding up a scale, and two strippers hanging off each side.

Lily was cutting the cake, but when the DJ mixed into a Calypso song, Lily shrieked and leaped up to dance. She snatched up the T-shirt Jody had taken off and was whipping it in circles over her head, like the blade of a helicopter.

When the song faded out, Deza took the microphone.

"Give it up for the DJ," she bellowed as she strode back onto the stage.

When the applause died down, she spoke into the mic more quietly, almost conspiratorially: "Next up, I want a round of applause for the woman behind the union, representing for Brooklyn by way of Chicago, my auntie, Tyesha Couvillier!"

The girls stood and cheered. Lily blew a police whistle. The DJ scratched on the record.

"So we promised to bring some of my rapper friends, and here they are," she said. "First off, fresh off his *Melvyn: The Real Me* tour, Thug Woofer!"

The cheering was nearly as loud as it had been for Tyesha, but the screams of surprise were certainly louder.

"What's up Brook-LYNN?!" he boomed, strutting onto the stage, and the crowd roared back.

"So this is a ladies' night," Woof said. "And I don't think I have anything to add to this incredible evening. But the young lady behind it all is someone very, very special to me. And recently, due to some technical difficulties, I was unable to be with her for a very special show. So I asked a friend of mine to join us tonight, because I thought you all might wanna be part of it, too. So without further ado, please welcome . . . Nashonna!"

Before Tyesha could stop herself, she was out of her seat and shrieking.

Nashonna strutted onto the stage in a buzz hairstyle and cutoff army fatigues.

"This union is a victory for all of us!" she shouted. "I couldn't wait to come celebrate with y'all. Get my beat, DJ!"

318 / Aya de León

When the opening beats of the song came on, the ladies went crazy, all their voices singing along with the star:

You didn't care what the stripper had to say
You let the pole get in the way
You had some kind of jones
to see me dance to some weak hip hop with fake-ass moans.

Nashonna began a moan, and halfway through stopped abruptly and cackled with laughter.

Into the mic, she said: *"You paid to see me make it clap."*

And then she pointed the mic into the audience and all the women yelled back:

"WELL, MOTHERFUCKER, NOW YOU GONNA HEAR ME RAP . . ."

The dancers went crazy. Nashonna leaned back and trust-fell off the stage and crowd surfed.

Tyesha made her way through the melee to find Woof. He was leaning up against the wall near the DJ booth.

She ran over and threw her arms around him.

"I can't believe you got Nashonna to come," she said.

"Are you kidding me?" he said, laughing. "My stock went up with her once she found out that I'm your man."

She leaned into an openmouthed kiss.

"But seriously," he said. "We were supposed to go to that show together. It was my fault for fucking up with the Car Willis situation."

"I shouldn't have gone with Drew," Tyesha said. "That was just petty of me." She kissed him again.

Woof bit his lip. "That straining sound is me breathing mindfully and not saying amen."

"So I guess we're both petty," Tyesha said, laughing.

"No, baby," Woof said. "We're just in love. I love you, Tyesha."

He wrapped his arms tightly around her and pulled her close. She could feel his heart beating hard.

"I love you, too . . . Melvyn," she said.

He laughed and pulled her into an intense kiss, so deep that they didn't notice when Deza and Amaru began to shower them with sign-in sheet confetti, like rice at a wedding.

Except it was at a strip club, with a stripper's union. And an ex-stripper-turned-rapper rapping about being a stripper. So really it was more like a Vegas wedding.

THE BOSS

Aya de León

ABOUT THIS GUIDE

The suggested questions are included
to enhance your group's reading of
Aya de León's *The Boss*.

DISCUSSION QUESTIONS

1. Tyesha and her sister have a contentious relationship. What are some of the factors that have pitted them against each other? Do you have female peers in your life with whom there is significant conflict? What might be factors outside of the relationship that contribute to the conflict?

2. Tyesha had to step in repeatedly to rescue her nieces, Deza and Amaru, when their parents were unable to function in a healthy way. Was that a good choice for her? For them? Do you have people in your life who call you to come rescue them? How do you handle that?

3. Thug Woofer is the number one rap artist in the U.S. How does that impact the relationship dynamic between him and Tyesha?

4. What were some of the warning signs that Thug Woofer had difficulty respecting women? What were some of the positive signposts that he had changed? Is that type of change realistic? What are some of the risks when a woman trusts a man with a history of anger issues?

5. In the book, the mob was a major obstacle to allowing the strippers to unionize. In the real world, however, the owners and managers of strip clubs often mistreat the workers, even if organized crime is not involved. Are there ways that you or other workers are mistreated in your industry or workplace? What can you do about it?

324   /   Discussion Questions

6. The dancers in the union were divided. Some favored greater security and protection, but some favored greater independence. As a worker, do you favor more security and protection or independence? Can you have both?

7. The sex industry is the only industry in which women workers are consistently paid more than men. And yet there are many men who mistreat their workers in an attempt to make as much money off their labor as possible. How do you see women workers being mistreated in your workplace, industry, or doing domestic labor (housework/childcare)?

8. The mob boss's nephew was a sexual predator. He had a history of paying hush money to women he'd assaulted, and we saw him attempt to assault Jody. Was it justified to frame him for the robbery, even if it got him killed?

9. Car Willis is an artist who has a history of sexually predatory behavior, as well. In the real world, should artists be judged by their behavior offstage, or simply based on their art?

10. Tyesha is afraid to speak up publicly. Where does this fear come from? Were her fears justified in the present or based in experiences from the past? What are some areas in your own life where you are afraid to speak? Do you think your fears are about present danger or rooted in the past? What can you do about it?

Connect with Us

Visit us online at
KensingtonBooks.com
to read more from your favorite authors, see books
by series, view reading group guides, and more.

Join us on social media

for sneak peeks, chances to win books and prize packs,
and to share your thoughts with other readers.

facebook.com/kensingtonpublishing
twitter.com/kensingtonbooks

Tell us what you think!

To share your thoughts, submit a review,
or sign up for our eNewsletters, please visit:
KensingtonBooks.com/TellUs.